the
SWEETEST
AGONY

the SWEETEST AGONY

VICTORIA LUM

To all the girls who feel less than for
whatever reason, you're perfect, just the way you are.

I have voices in my mind, monsters in my head.

It's not the "I'm hearing voices" of the psychological thriller variety, but more of an incessant chatter of nonstop opinions on every action I take, a seatbelt tethered to my waist keeping me from reaching out and taking risks. It's like the annoying malware running in the background of your computer and no matter how hard you try to purge it from the system, it sticks to you like slime. In my case, I get daily reminders of how people will all leave me at some point because, despite outward appearances, I'm flawed inside. Marybeth Connors, my therapist back in college, used to tell me this is, in clinical terms, my general anxiety disorder talking. Logically, her diagnosis makes sense, but emotionally, it's still a horrible place to be in most of the time.

But today? Those voices can all be quiet because *nothing* will shake my good mood.

Absolutely nothing.

Why?

Because James, my best friend, is moving back from London.

I think a smile is permanently plastered on my face.

"Whoa, look at you! What's going on, Jess? It's Monday morning. The smile on your face should be illegal." Rebecca Winslow, known to all her friends as Becca, smirks at me as I set down my bag and laptop in the cubicle next to hers.

We both work at Anderson and Little, one of the largest accounting firms in the world where she and I are both senior audit managers. We're on the partner track, attempting to be two of the youngest female partners at the firm. Instead of the expected passive aggressiveness one might expect with a fellow competitor, we bond over being two of the small female pool of candidates up for promotion at the firm. If we women lift each other up and celebrate our successes instead of tearing each other down, will we make more strides in pay equity and promotion opportunities?

I like to think so.

"James called me last night. He's moving back to LA for good! I'm so excited. It's been years since I've seen him." I set a cup of coffee and a chocolate croissant in front of her. "For you, your usual triple-shot latte with coconut milk and a bonus pastry just because. But seriously, cut back on the caffeine. You'll give yourself a heart attack one of these days."

"You're so awesome! What would I ever do without you?" Becca takes a sip of her coffee and groans in pleasure.

"Luckily, I don't think you'll ever have to find out." I grin at her expression. Seeing the joy I put on the faces of my friends is better than receiving presents for myself.

"Is this the James Chapman who is your 'just friends only' best guy friend who lives in London? And he's moving all the way across the world? Conveniently to where you are, even though his family is based on the East Coast?" She has always doubted our friendship status. As if James and I can be anything else other than best friends.

Ridiculous.

I raise my right eyebrow and deadpan, "Yes, my *best friend* is moving here, where his sister also lives."

"Hmmm...all right, all right. I'll stop talking since this conversation clearly won't go anywhere." She mimes zipping up her lips.

I turn on my laptop, bracing myself for the influx of emails to greet me when my mailbox loads. "Yep. I haven't seen him since..."

I crinkle my forehead in concentration. "When Nana passed, so, almost eight years now. We talk around once a month or so, but it's just not the same as having him here in person. I'm so excited!"

"Wow! You haven't seen him for that long?"

"Yeah. For half of the time, we were poor students with no money to fly internationally and I refuse to use my parents' funds. Hence, I drive the trusty, reliable compact car costing less than Mother's outfit of the day."

I hear the clicking of her keyboard as she types away. "What about the last few years?"

"Both of us have crazy work schedules and I wanted to go visit him, but we just can't get our schedules lined up. I told him come hell or high water, I'm flying out there this year and camping outside his flat no matter what, even if he spends all his time at work and I only see him for half an hour a day. But now he is coming back and this is even better!"

"That's great, Jess. So happy for you. I can't wait to meet him." She pops her head above the cubicle wall, her pale-green eyes glinting with humor. "You *are* going to introduce us, right? I'm your work partner-in-crime."

I roll my eyes. "Duh." The constant pinging from my laptop draws my attention back to the screen. I sigh, looking at the hundreds of emails sitting in my inbox waiting for me to address. Another long day ahead.

"How was your weekend?" Becca murmurs from her side of the wall.

"Uneventful. Worked a lot as usual. I was at Ben's for a dinner on Saturday. He had a party, and they went to a few bars afterward, but I bowed out. Not really my scene these days. I feel like I'm outwardly young, but my soul is tired. What I want more than anything is to sleep and spend my days bookstore hopping instead of bar hopping. Now that sounds like fun times for me." Ben has been my boyfriend since college. Lately, things have been a bit strained.

"I hear you. I think I pulled in sixteen hours of work this weekend. The staff complains we give them so much work to do, but I don't think they realize we work much more than they do. At least they are unabashedly logging off for the weekend when they send us files to review at five p.m. on Fridays."

"Exactly. We are stuck in the middle, not good enough to be at the top, but not hip enough to be part of the younger crowd." I roll my tense shoulders and hit reply on one of the more pressing emails. "I'm so not looking forward to the partnership panel later this year. All the preparation that goes into it. And what if I don't get the promotion? All the work out the window."

The list of worries is a mile long. *Nope, Jess. None of the negativity today. It's a good day.* Thinking back to James, I smile, the usual tightness in my shoulders loosening a bit as I come up with a list of things to do to prepare for his arrival in a few days. "So, how are things going with you and Craig?"

The tapping of fingers on her keyboard halts at my question. "We're fine—just too busy and not enough time to see each other. We just need to work some things out."

Craig is Becca's boyfriend of many years and good friends before that. He works in the tax department at our company. Lately, their relationship has been going through some rough moments as well. Sisterhood in solidarity, I suppose. Perhaps one of the perils of our busy careers.

"I hope you guys get through this. It'd be a shame if you break up. You guys have known each other for years. I'm rooting for you." I roll my chair to her cube and give her a big hug.

The day passes by in a blur as I busy myself with team calls, client meetings, and reviewing audit files. I stare at the laptop screen, my eyes glazing over, a tension headache starting to form.

"Hey, Jess. Your food is at the receptionist's desk," an intern informs me and taps me on my shoulder.

I look up in confusion but thank him nonetheless. *Huh? I didn't order anything. Shit, it's two already. Probably should get something to eat.*

Ding. Text message alert from my phone.

James: Your favorite In-N-Out cheeseburger, well-done fries, with a chocolate milkshake should show up around now. Someone owes me a favor. I know you're probably going to skip lunch today and work yourself to death. Don't do that. You got this Jess. You got this.

My heart warms at the text.

Jess: Thanks for the meal. You know me too well. Miss you and can't wait for you to be back.

James, this is why you are my best friend.

A ping from my laptop draws my focus back to the screen. The audit files need a lot of re-work, and the deadline looms closer. My pulse kicks up and my head hurts, thinking about the work I've temporarily forgotten, which is quite uncharacteristic of me. I need to go check in on the team before lunch.

Sigh. Deep breath in. Deep breath out. I got this. As Marybeth used to say, "You have to move forward to move through." I repeat the mantra as I walk to the conference room.

Taking a fortifying breath, I open the door to the room my team is cloistered in. The chatter comes to an abrupt stop at my entrance.

"Hey, guys, how's the work coming along?"

Ten pairs of eyes peer up from their laptops and stare at me. The two senior associates and the manager trade glances, communicating in a secret code.

"It's coming along. I don't think it will get done in time though. We are still working through your review comments and there are a few sections we haven't finished yet," Tony, the manager, answers.

The collective team freezes in their chairs, and the temperature of the room feels like it drops ten degrees.

"Look, I get this is hard work, but the deadline is what it is. We have to make this work. Think of this as a good learning experience, right?" We can't afford to miss the deadline on this audit engagement. It's a high-profile, new client to the firm and is a make or break engagement for everyone in the room, not to mention a test case as to whether or not I'm partnership material.

Janet, the senior associate, rolls her eyes at my statement, earning her a quick elbow nudge from Tony, who is sitting next to her.

"It's really not that bad, right, guys? I'll be working alongside you all this week, and this is a moment to show the partners your commitment to the job." So what if none of us had a full weekend off for the last three months? Work-life balance? That's the mythical unicorn that is useless office jargon people throw around, but no one has seen in reality.

"Look, team, think about how good you'll feel when we file this thing." I attempt to placate them. Someone has to be the voice of optimism, right? Optimism I don't feel, but complaining won't help our situation at all.

The air in the room is dense with awkwardness. *God, they hate me.* Unease crawls up my body as my face heats up. *Nope, none of that today.* I snap the bracelet against my wrist, relishing in the sharp bite of pain that served as self-punishment for not being someone who doesn't give a crap about what other people think.

"Do you know, I once read a study up to seventy-five percent of executive women experience imposter syndrome?" James chuckles as he listens to me complain about work, his ocean-blue eyes fuzzy on the phone.

I narrow my eyes at the screen. "How do you know what I'm thinking as always?"

His full lips tilt up to the right in a smirk. "I've known you for how many years now? Twenty years? Plus, you're gnawing on your bottom lip again. You do that when you're stressed."

"Nineteen. Not that I'm counting," I retort, releasing my lip from the savagery of my teeth.

The clicking of the keyboard brings me back into the room as the memory of an earlier conversation with James fades away. The team has resumed working. I sigh. Imposter syndrome, that must be what this feeling is.

"**E**xcuse me, coming through." I navigate the crowd of people that has gathered by the arrival area at the Tom Bradley International Terminal of the Los Angeles International Airport. It's a surprisingly sizeable crowd, given it's almost seven p.m. on a Wednesday night. The atmosphere sizzles with excitement and impatience as people stand around waiting for their loved ones to arrive. "Sorry, I'm just going to stand...over here."

I settle in the front of the crowd with my handmade sign which says, "Welcome Back, James, the Best Friend Ever!" My hands grow clammier by the second. *I can't believe he's going to be here! What does he look like now, in person? Is he still the cute, lanky nerd who watched* Harry Potter *marathons with me from years past?* Even though we occasionally video call each other, the resolution is fuzzy sometimes, and it's still different than seeing someone *in person* and feeling their entire presence. I adjust the bag of pastries from the famous Cuban bakery, Portolitos, that's hanging on my arm to make sure the box is still upright. *Any minute now. I hope he still likes pastries. What if he doesn't anymore? Maybe I should have gotten him something else.* My mind whirls a thousand thoughts a minute as I contemplate what I should have or shouldn't have done, my eyes still focused on the now-offending bag on my arm.

"Jess." A deep husky voice, unfiltered by the phone, familiar and unfamiliar at the same time, reaches my ears.

Time slows as my heart thuds loudly in my chest. You know the moment they show in movies when everything is moving around you, but you're at a standstill?

Well, this is it for me.

I slowly look up, cataloguing the large feet in flip-flops, finely muscular calves, cargo shorts, an impressively broad chest stretching out a gray cotton T-shirt which shows a hint of the dips and valleys of muscles clearly familiar with the gym, strong biceps, and a veiny forearm which has me itching to trace it with my hands.

James grabs the bag and sign from my hands, sets them on the ground next to his carryon suitcase, and pulls me into his embrace. His warm, muscular chest. Sandalwood and an unidentified spice that smells like safety—if there is such a smell—hits my nostrils. I freeze, suddenly at a loss for words. My pulse races as his large palm cradles my head against his chest and I hear the thundering heartbeats which seem to mirror my own.

I pull away, looking up at him for the first time. A man, not the boy I remember, stares back at me, his angular jaw covered in a five o'clock shadow, his piercing blue eyes gazing into mine. His luscious, deep-mahogany locks are effortlessly tousled, as if he spent minimal time on his appearance. There is a shocking dichotomy between this man standing in front of me and the "guy" I interact with over the phone. I'm having trouble reconciling between these two individuals, who have apparently been the same person all along. Perhaps over the phone, you can't see the entire figure, feel the heated presence, smell the masculine muskiness, and get the full experience.

His full lips tip up into a grin. "Long time no see, Jessica Kingsley."

I blink.

One...

Two...

Three times.

I'm rendered speechless by my emotions and bodily reactions. Finally noticing his piercing gaze, I quickly shake my head and ramble, "I brought you some cheese rolls, those potato balls you loved...if you still like them...the guava strudels are to die for, but now I'm seriously doubting my selection since I'm not sure if you even eat this stuff anymore given you look like that."

He barks out a loud laugh. "What are you talking about?"

I wave my arms up and down toward his torso. "You're clearly fit. Maybe I should have brought something healthier instead. Maybe I should have gotten you a protein shake or a steak. No, takeout steaks taste horrible. What am I talking about? Maybe a yogurt. Yes, that's a healthy snack with a good amount of protein." I blather on and internally cringe at my word vomit. *What's wrong with me? This is James, your best friend.*

"What's gotten into you?" He chuckles. "Stop overthinking. I'm definitely craving Portolitos. I haven't had those amazing pastries in ages. You know me too well."

I fiddle with my bracelet, feeling a little more settled. I forgive myself for my temporary moment of insanity.

His eyes drop to my hands. "Still wearing the bracelet, huh?"

"Of course, this is my lucky bracelet, which you know since you gave it to me." I tuck my hands behind my back, feeling a little self-conscious. "Why are we having this conversation here? Let's go to my car and get you situated. By the way, I made you some food for the next few days since you'll be jetlagged. Remind me to take it out of my trunk when we get to your place."

He chuckles, his deep voice sending shivers down my spine. "Thanks. You're the best, Jess." He places his hands lightly on my waist, sending involuntary tremors through my body. James sweeps his arm out. "Lead the way, Ms. Auditor."

The drive back to Manhattan Beach is relatively quick at this late hour, and I can't help but sneak glances at this familiar stranger as he calls his sister, then his parents, to report on his arrival here.

"Don't worry, Mom, the company already set everything up. It's mostly furnished too." He glances sideways at me, his eyes glinting from the streetlights. "Yeah, ten minutes from Jess's place. We're almost there."

I glance away, not wanting to be caught staring as unusual nervousness thrums through my veins. *What's going on with me?*

We soon arrive at his condo, a mere few blocks from my apartment. He glances back at me. "Come on in. I think you'll like this place. My assistant already furnished it to my requirements, and they sent some people over to start unpacking last night." He unlocks the door and carries his luggage along with my pastries and freshly made meals inside.

"Your assistant, huh? And you call this 'some unpacking'?" I holler at his retreating backside. There are maybe ten boxes stacked neatly in the corner of the living room. The large room has a lovely floor-to-ceiling window facing the street outside, which is empty of the usual beachgoers because of the late hour. "Your inner OCD is showing."

"You call it whatever you want, but I always feel unsettled whenever I arrive at a new place until I unpack...or in this case, when someone helps me unpack." He meanders over with two plates of potato balls and guava strudels and sets the plates on the coffee table next to the plushiest sectional I've ever seen.

I plop down on the daybed section of the sofa. "Ahh...this is so comfortable." I close my eyes and sigh in contentment. "How did they set up the condo so quickly?"

He sits down next to me. "I see my sofa choice was the correct one. I knew you would love this. It's called the cloud sofa. I just picked out the pieces I wanted, and my assistant set it up for me earlier this week so I didn't have to deal with moving in chores when I arrived." He starts on his second potato ball. "This stuff is so delicious; they should be illegal."

I grin, the earlier temporarily lapse in sanity behind me as we fall back into an easy rhythm. "Look at you, moving up in the world. Chief Director of Data Science at Brighton Capital, the biggest capital firm on the West Coast, huh? Who knew the geeky kid from elementary school would now be one of the most important men in West Coast finance?"

"Please. Flattery will get you nowhere. It's just hard work and the right opportunity." He dismisses me with a wave.

James has always been one of the hardest workers I know.

"Well, I think if anyone deserves this opportunity, it's you. If only Chad the bully could see you now. Sucker!"

"Chad was an insecure kid who probably had a bully at home. I haven't thought about him in forever." James washes down his second potato ball with a few gulps of water. Chad used to torment him in elementary school. It was ironically because of Chad, James and I met. Sometimes, the best things happen out of the worst situations.

"So, when are you starting work?" I ask, changing the subject.

"Friday. The sooner the better. Meetings are piling up and I need to catch up on a lot of things to bring myself up to speed with everything."

"That soon? I'm glad I caught you today then. Once you start work, I may not see you, Mr. Workaholic."

"Pot calling the kettle black, Jess." He crosses his arms, drawing my attention back to his muscular forearms which could be part of the stock photos for "alpha male" on Instagram.

"How's Liz doing? I haven't met up with her in ages."

He smiles, no doubt thinking about his sister. "She's doing well. The kindergarteners at school are keeping her busy. She sent me some photos of them. They're a cute bunch. I'm probably going to host a housewarming gathering next week, so you guys can catch up then too."

"Great! I'll look forward to catching up with her. I really should be better at keeping in touch, but work tends to get in the way."

"Don't worry about it, she totally understands. She told me she was going to call you in two weeks if you don't contact her before then." He rises from the couch and disappears down the hallway into one of the rooms. "I got you something. Give me a second." His voice echoes from the back of the house.

I take the opportunity to admire at the minimalistic furnishings in the room. The large windows let in a cool, salty draft. Thick gray curtains flutter in the breeze. A soft wool carpet the color of the turquoise Caribbean waters is centered in the living room area.

A few well-worn books are placed on top of a three-tiered coffee table. The room is still missing some personal touches, which may be in one of those ten boxes stacked in the corner.

Our living quarters couldn't be any more different. My apartment a few blocks over is filled to the brim with bright artwork, fuzzy blankets, and personal knickknacks, but despite the different decor here, there is a wonderful sense of calm, quiet, and inner peace in his condo. I feel *at home.*

James returns with a slim, rectangular box that is elegantly wrapped in a silk bow and a smaller, nondescript square box. He sits down close next to me. Sandalwood wafts through the air. I inhale deeply. This may be my new favorite scent.

"Here you go. This is the first time I'm giving you souvenirs in person as opposed to in the mail." His lightly calloused fingers gently take my hand and place the presents on it. His touch lingers, inciting me to involuntarily shudder.

"You cold? I can close the windows." He appears concerned.

I flush and quickly assuage him. "No, I'm good." I stare at the present and change the subject. "Ooooh, I know what the small box is, but what is this large one?" I gently shake the package, giddy with excitement. Who doesn't love presents?

I carefully open the package and therein lies the most exquisite assortment of chocolates I've ever seen. Each piece is fashioned after chess pieces and appears to be hand painted with vibrant colors and gold leaf.

"Wow. This is amazing. I don't think I'll ever be able to eat these. They are like artwork."

"I found these in a hole-in-the-wall chocolatier called Bertrand's near my flat in London. They still hand make their chocolates weekly and every piece is meticulously hand-printed by an old granny named Gertrude. She's such a character. Apparently, she took over the shop after her husband of fifty years passed five years ago. She said they met back in the war when she was a nurse and he was an injured soldier and they had dreams of opening a chocolatier because he loved chocolates and thought they symbolized eternal devotion and hope. She said when she works on the chocolates, she feels her husband's presence as if he's still there with her."

He continues, "Gertrude said her chocolates are magic and bring good luck and love to those who buy them. Now the last bit I'm skeptical of, but she seemed so steadfast in her opinion and I knew you have a big chocolate addiction and love all things lucky, so I bought one of their limited editions for you to binge on." His voice is soothing and smooth, like the finest aged whiskey. There's definitely a different quality to a voice when you're hearing it in person than over the phone.

I bring my palm to my chest. "That's amazing. I love how these chocolates represent her love with her husband and how the love continues even after he is gone. What a touching story. Now, I don't know how I'll ever eat them."

I stare at the chocolates wistfully. To many people, a gift of chocolates is the most unoriginal souvenir to give to someone. But James knows I'm a hopeless romantic at heart and a chocoholic to boot, so this present, with its touching backstory, is perfect in every way. How lucky Gertrude must be to have experienced a deep, once-in-a-lifetime love.

He grins. "I know you were going to say that. Gertrude told me to tell you the good luck only transfers to the consumer if they eat the chocolates. To quote her, 'Love is to be experienced and savored, not to be held at arm's length, and stared at. You may taste the initial heady taste of sweetness, followed by some bitter undertones, and finished with a lasting, rich aftertaste.' But that is life, right? Gives more meaning to the saying 'Life is like a box of chocolates.'" His gaze is suddenly intense and pierces my soul as he stares into my eyes. The room suddenly feels warm.

James blinks and shifts away. "Anyway, the point is, eat the damn chocolates or I won't be buying you any more souvenirs when I travel."

Tension broken, I playfully poke him. "In all seriousness, thank you. You don't need to buy me all these gifts when you travel."

"Nah, I like buying presents for you because I know you'll enjoy them. Got to keep the friendship alive, right?"

I put the chocolates on the table and proceed to open the small box. I have a good prediction about what this one is. James knows I have been collecting snow globes since childhood. When my family moved from place to place, I never felt like I truly had my roots planted anywhere, and somehow, I left a piece of myself behind each time. To keep a piece of my temporary homes with me, I would buy a snow globe at each location. James has kept up with my tradition, sending me snow globes from abroad when he travels.

There it is, a pristine, limited-edition snow globe of the queen's jubilee celebration. "This is beautiful, James." I gently shake the crystal, admiring the small bits of glittery snow swirl around, settling on the golden miniature of Big Ben. "Someday, I'd like to visit London, to meet Gertrude, and to see your home for the last few years."

"I'll take you when you have time," he promises.

I smile, knowing he truly means it. The problem is me since I don't take time off from work. At twenty-eight, I feel like I should have my life together by now. When I was in high school, I would dream about settling in one place, having a true permanent home, meeting the right man, getting married by twenty-five, and having two kids by the time I turn thirty. Now I'm approaching the milestone birthday, and I feel inadequate. I have my job; I have Ben, but somehow, I feel neither of those things are truly mine. And if I don't continue to work very hard, they'll both slip through my fingers.

"Thanks. I know you will." I set the snow globe on the table. "So, how are you and Claire doing?"

James's normally clear, blue eyes shutter down. "We broke up."

"Whoa. What happened? When? You didn't tell me!"

"It's nothing warranting discussion. It's probably a long time coming." He grunts out the bare minimum to answer my question.

"See? This is what other people are talking about. James Chapman, a private man of few words. If I, as your oldest friend, can only get two sentences from you regarding such a big event, I can only imagine what strangers or coworkers get out of you."

"I don't see a need to air out my business. There's nothing much to say. People break up all the time," he grumbles as I venture into the nagging territory.

Sensing I will not get much more out of him, I give him a soft nudge and grab the remote. "Do you want to watch the game from yesterday? I missed it and you were busy. The replay is on demand. ULA vs UCSC? Western finals! We'll beat your precious Trojans this year."

"College ball—how I've missed you. European football is just not the same. I wait forever for them to score a goal. They say the anticipation is part of the experience, but I'm always half-asleep midway through a game and by the time I jolt awake from the sudden cheering, they've already scored the goal." He sighs contently as I turn on the new Samsung flatscreen hanging above his fireplace.

"Seriously, how do you already have a flatscreen and cable fully installed and ready to use the second you arrive?" I mutter.

"It's all part of the package, Jess, all part of the package. Don't look at me like that. Green is not a good color on you." James stands. "We need a game snack. I'll go make some popcorn. My assistant stocked my pantry and kitchen already."

"Of course he did." I roll my eyes at his A-lister lifestyle.

"Ha. Jealousy does not become you, Jess. But get used to this feeling when UCSC whoops your team's ass today." James and I have never agreed on a sports team, from football to basketball, we always root for opposing teams.

"We'll see about that!" The screen comes to life, showing the beginning of the third quarter. "You'll eat your words, Chapman. We're two touchdowns ahead of you," I holler at him.

"No way. Shit!" He comes running back with the cheesy popcorn goodness mixed with a side of M&Ms, just the way I like it.

Then, the unthinkable happens, one missed interception later, the UCSC running back is making a fifty-yard dash down the field.

"Yesss... See, Jess? This is what happens when you gloat too early," he taunts gleefully. "I think—"

My phone rings, and the caller ID shows it's Ben. "Hey, sorry, Ben is calling. I got to take this."

James's lips flatten. "Of course you have to. Give Ben my regards."

I walk over to the kitchen and answer the call. "Hey, how are you doing?"

"Hey, babe, took you a while to answer the call. Were you on the phone?" Ben says in way of greeting. He's been busy for the last two weeks, so we haven't had a chance to speak for more than five minutes until today.

"Oh sorry, I was chatting with James. He just arrived, and I dropped him off at his new place." An apology slips out automatically, even though sometimes I wonder why I'm apologizing in the first place.

"Huh. James again. I don't understand your friendship, really. I'm sure you're a different person now than you were in high school. Seems like you talk an awful lot for a relationship based mainly on your childhood experiences." They have only met each other one time when my grandmother passed away, so he doesn't understand the scope of our friendship.

"Honey, why are we doing this again?" I sigh and rub my temple with my free hand and stare out the kitchen window into the darkness beyond. "I told you this before. We've always kept in touch, so yes, even when we were apart, he's still my best friend. It's just the way it is." If I could get one dollar for every time we've had the same conversation regarding how odd my friendship is, I would probably be a millionaire by now.

"Yeah whatever," he mumbles as he changes the topic, "Call me when you get home? And...miss you, babe."

"Miss you too." I disconnect the call, feeling a bit unsettled, the familiar restlessness circling my gut. Rolling my shoulders back, I shake my head, trying to dispel my thoughts. *He just cares about you. That's where his complaints are coming from.* I walk back to the living room and plop down on the couch next to James.

"I still think ULA has the best team ever. And if they lose this one, it's just a one-off." I grab a handful of popcorn and M&Ms and toss it at him, trying to break the odd tension in the room.

He blocks it with a cushion, the harsh lines of his face relaxing into an easy smile. "Don't be a sore loser, Kingsley. You should have listened to me. What do I do for a living? I *analyze* data. You should know better than to go against a data man. UCSC has totally got this."

I snort, a bit peeved at the current state of the game. "It's only third quarter, Chapman, don't count your eggs too early."

"Chickens, Jess. The saying is 'don't count your chickens too early'," he gloats. "If you are going to trash-talk me, at least get the saying right."

"Whatever. You'll see. The night is still young."

"Whatever. What are we, back in fifth grade? That's the best you got?" He gives me a slap on the back. "Man, this is great. I miss this. I miss this a lot."

Me too, James. Me too. "It's good to have you here. Here's to more in-person hangouts in the future." I hold out the bucket as a peace offering. "I'll clean up the mess." I gesture at the results of my adult tantrum, the scattered popcorn and M&Ms on the couch and carpet.

"Don't worry about it. I like my best friend to be the inner feisty badass I know is inside her all along." He grabs a few pieces of the couch popcorn and pops them into his mouth.

I don't worry about it because this is James. He always accepts me for who I am, flaws and all. He's always been here for me and always will be.

We settle on the couch and take turns jeering at the screen, and the evening passes by in a blur. We finish the game (UCSC won, damn him), order takeout at a favorite Thai place of mine down the street, and we argue if Pad See Ew or Pad Thai is better (team Pad See Ew here. I still don't understand why anyone wants peanuts in their cooked food). I help him finish unpacking the remaining ten boxes. Even though we aren't doing anything special or going anywhere unique, I feel content. My best friend is by my side again. Nineteen years of friendship, of which we have spent over a decade living apart, we are finally together at the same place, same time again.

Life is good.

CHAPTER 3

James

I dust my hands off as I finish cleaning my apartment and putting away my belongings in their proper locations. Almost done. Just need to hang up a few pieces of artwork and photos later on. I tug off my shirt, wipe off the sweat on my forehead, and toss the shirt into the hamper. I shrug out of the rest of my clothes and turn on the shower. Staring into the mirror, I notice the scruff on my face and the muscles I've worked hard to build. I'm a far cry from the short, helpless boy in elementary school, the one who was bullied constantly on the playground.

"Get off of me! Don't butt into business that isn't yours, new girl!" Chad screams.

I open my eyes and make out a blurry shape of a girl my size clawing at Chad's back, yelling, "Stop it! Give him back the glasses, you stupid pig! And it's Jess, you big bully!"

With a temporary new target in sight, Chad drops me to the ground and faces the newcomer. "Don't think just because you are a girl, I won't hit you! You pissed off the wrong person. I'll make your life here miserable!"

The little girl, who I'm sure is younger than me since she is my size, replies defiantly, "I wouldn't do that if I were you! My dad is the biggest lawyer in town. He'll make your life miserable aa...aaand not just at school! He'll make you miserable every-where you go!"

I freeze on the ground, shocked as I behold this reenactment of David and Goliath from Sunday's bible class.

The steam fogs up the mirror, distracting me from my thoughts of that fateful day when Jess and I met, when she saved me from Chad when he and his minions stole my glasses on the playground. A day that changed my life forever. Jess was the girl who saw past the tiny, insecure boy on the playground, who befriended me, and gave me all her love and joy when I wasn't worthy of it, before I made something of myself. It's easy to love someone who is successful like I am now, but it takes a special soul to love someone at their lowest when they have nothing to offer and to remain loyal all these years. Chuckling at the memories, I step into the shower, the hot water providing much-needed relief to my sore muscles.

God, she's even more beautiful in person than I could ever imagine. The love I've tried to shove away to the deepest crevices of my heart came tumbling out the moment I saw her. Memories and computer screens don't do her justice. I close my eyes and remember the hug I gave her at the airport earlier today; how her soft body molded to mine, the luscious curves begging me to touch, to caress, to worship. Her unique scent of strawberries and cream, the wide, hazel eyes and light smatter of freckles on her pale skin... all designed to tantalize me.

I didn't miss the way her pupils dilated when she first saw me, the way her breath caught in her throat when I pulled her in for a hug, the way she stared at me on the drive here when she thought I wasn't looking. Perhaps she's finally seeing me as more than her best friend, as a man of flesh and blood. I had to use every ounce of energy in me to hold back, to not scare her away, to do this the right way.

In time, James. All good things take time. I grip my throbbing hard-on which has made its appearance at the thought of Jess. Fuck. Hasn't it been a long time already? Decades. The longest fucking foreplay of my life. I stroke myself a few times, easing the tension that's been building in my body for what feels like forever, and it doesn't take long before I come all over the tiles with her name on my lips.

Shuddering deeply, my body temporarily sated but emotionally still on edge, I quickly rinse off and exit the shower. Wrapping a large towel around my waist, I saunter over to my dresser and throw on a faded MIT sweatshirt and a pair of boxer briefs and flannel pants. I grab a book from the bookshelf and make myself comfortable on the bed. It's past midnight, but I'm still wide awake from jetlag. Might as well read to pass the time.

Just before I settle into the historical world of world wars and heroes, my phone chimes with a text.

Jess: Can't sleep. I'm so excited you're finally back. So happy.

My chest warms at her message. The plan is on and is headed in the right direction. I'll finally be able to win her over.

James: I'm happy too. It's been long overdue.

Jess: The Double Js back together.

I smirk, thinking about her reference to our nickname back in middle school and high school.

James: Get some rest, sweetheart. I have the day off, but you have work tomorrow.

Jess: XOXO *shriek!* You're back! G'night!

I set my phone back on the nightstand and pick up my wallet, taking out the shiny penny that has never left my side after all these years. Jess gave it to me the day she rescued me from Chad...the brave little third-grader who stood up to a gang of fifth-grade bullies to rescue the helpless, little runt of the fifth-grade class.

She rummages through the pocket of her jeans, grabs my hand, and deposits something small onto my palm.

"We are friends now. Here is my present to you, my lucky penny. I found it a week ago on the ground and the year is when I was born. It must be lucky because I met you today. Friends forever!" She scoots closer to me and closes my palm around the penny. A breeze flutters by and the air smells like strawberries and cream. Goosebumps prickle my skin.

"Friends forever," I promise.

I smile at the fond memory. *Be patient. She's still with Ben right now, don't scare her away.* But knowing how their relationship has been going based on what she tells me on our calls and my impressions of the prick when I met him all those years ago, what they have is coming to an end soon. I just need to be patient, be by her side and show her this mature version of me, and be ready for her when she moves on from him. Perhaps this time around, she'll finally open her eyes and see what has been there all this time, how we should have been together all along.

I rub the coin in my fingers. *Heads, you'll be able to convince Jess to love you back. Tails, she'll see we're not "just friends" and we'll get together finally.* I toss the penny into the air, unafraid of the result.

I'm not here to lose. I'm here to fight to my last breath.

"**H**ey, sis! Over here." Emily, my younger sister, waves from the corner table on the outdoor patio of the swanky new "it" restaurant, Le Cirque. They designed the restaurant to be on social media, with green foliage hanging from the ceilings or from rafters of the outdoor patio for the perfect photo opportunity. Exotic flowers of every color intertwining with thick strands of ivy separate most tables from each other, giving the patrons an illusion of dining in the middle of a rain forest. I can't imagine the amount of upkeep to ensure all this greenery stays alive.

"I'm so glad we can do brunch." I give her a hug before I take a seat across from her. "How did you manage to swing this? I hear it's nearly impossible to get in unless you know someone."

"Exactly. And I do know someone. I know many someones." She smiles smugly. Emily appears completely at home at the restaurant. Her shoulder-length, dark-brown hair is tied up in a ponytail, and she has on a bright, neon-pink statement sweater which completely blends in with the trendy aesthetics. "The owner is one of our clients and I worked on the launch. I also met Antoine, the executive chef, who is absolutely delicious."

Emily works as an image consultant for one of the top public relations firms in Los Angeles. There is no shortage of clients here in the capital of entertainment and her clients not only include celebrities, but also prominent executives, politicians, and popular influencers. With her bubbly, passionate, extroverted personality, she's perfect for the job. She lives in downtown LA to be closer to her work and clients.

"Are you two a thing?" I ask as servers bring up an assortment of small pastries, from miniature eclairs decorated with flowers to flaky croissants dipped in chocolate.

Emily shrugs. "For now...maybe for a few months. He's charming and cooks really well. You know me, I don't do serious relationships."

At twenty-five, Emily, or Ems to her girlfriends and family, is three years younger than me, and our personalities couldn't be any more polar opposite. She never takes my parents' criticisms to heart and couldn't care less about the opinions of other people. She marches to the beat of her drum and is proud of it. I admire and envy her for her attitude. I wish I had it in me to put everyone else's opinions aside and live my life fearlessly.

Not only are our personalities very different, but our love lives are polar opposites as well. I dream of being with my soulmate and having a permanent home. Emily subscribes to a "dump them before the relationship fizzles out" theory. Our youngest brother, Steven, well, he's perpetually single and not from a lack of opportunity, as I've seen girls throw themselves at him when we visited him in New York last year. He just appears to be uninterested.

"By the way, you aren't checking your messages. Just a warning, Mother is on a roll today, so pick up when she calls or you'll get it later."

"Argh, what did I do this time?" I take a sip of water as I brace myself for what's coming.

"I've no clue. I think it has something to do with Cindy getting engaged to her old-money boyfriend. You know how she gets." She shrugs and grimaces.

"Ugh, a case of keeping up with the Joneses." I sigh, knowing I'll get an earful later on.

"Yuuup, sorry, sis, you're the oldest, so you'll get the brunt of it. You've always been the poster child to the perfection they want from us. God knows I'll never reach their standards. Ha. And Steven is a guy, so of course their standards for him are different."

Steven, at twenty-two, lives in New York and is busy as an entry-level banker at an investment bank. I'll argue he's the smartest one among us because he up and moved halfway across the country to get away from our parents.

My phone buzzes loudly on the table.

"Ugh, it's Mother. I better pick up. Wish me luck." Emily scrunches up her nose and crosses her fingers for good luck. We all know it's better to pick up Mother's call than to let it go to voicemail and suffer the repercussions later. Taking a deep breath, I gird my loins and answer, "Hi, Mother."

"Jessica, how are you doing these days? I haven't heard from you this past week." A saccharine voice filters across the line.

"I'm doing fine. Nothing new to report about my life. Just busy with work. Deadlines coming up." I brace myself for the inevitable, my stomach plummeting to the floor.

"Well, I hate to remind you that you're twenty-eight. Do you know Cindy Vaughn got engaged to Daniel this week? She's two years younger than you. He's the heir to his family's real estate empire. You aren't getting any younger, you know. Your father and I didn't send you to a private school so you can become a workaholic spinster," she admonishes me, clearly getting warmed up for a familiar tirade.

Audrey Lee Kingsley is the traditional Stepford wife, except she's Chinese, and she doesn't live on the East Coast. In her opinion, a woman's value in life is to marry a rich, powerful man, procreate, and raise picture-perfect children, who'll then repeat the cycle. Pursuing your dreams? What is that? Wanting financial independence and making something out of your career? Rubbish. She married my father, whom she met at Yale, and followed him around the States in our many moves during my childhood as he rose up in the ranks of his company. Now, he's the general counsel of Transamerica Corporation, an international conglomerate that has business interests from e-commerce to transportation.

Unfortunately, while my parents achieved career and personal successes, my siblings and I were shuffled from place to place, the moves affecting us in different ways. I, for one, have always felt adrift, never belonging to one place, and friends I've met throughout the years have faded into strangers or acquaintances either because of the natural passage of time or because of my mother's vicious vetting of our friendships throughout childhood. Only James and, by association, his sister, Liz, have remained a constant in my life, somehow passing muster and deemed as acceptable by my parents. My hunch is Mother doesn't think the Chapmans, with their white-picket-fence, middle-class background, will impact our family's standing in any way. They're considered neutral.

"... You need to take care of your skin. There are too many freckles on your nose. You're already so fair, and with your age, I won't be surprised if you start getting age spots. Who'll want you then?" she rambles on in her usual criticism of everything from my work to the lack of a diamond on my ring finger. I know I should be used to her by now but I can't help tensing up, my pulse quickening, as the beginnings of nausea churn in my gut. She stresses me out.

"Mother, I got it, I've been completing my ten-step skin routine each day." I haven't, but what she doesn't know won't kill her.

"Don't you sass me," she berates. "By the way, how is Ben? I haven't seen him in weeks."

You and me both. "He's busy working. We're meeting up tonight."

"Make time for him. Wear the new Chanel dress I got you last time. You need to make an effort. How else will you keep his interest? No one wants a wilted cabbage for a wife. Also, I sent you the contact for the Hollywood personal trainer. I heard he helps Hollywood starlets get into shape. You're getting fat. Don't let yourself go," she criticizes, her previous saccharine tone dissolving into the acerbic vat of acid which is her true nature. Ben is her ideal son-in-law: successful, good-looking in the Eddie Bauer catalogue type of way, from a family of good stock—otherwise known as old money.

"Got it, Mother. Oh look, incoming call, I have to go."

"Don't you hang up on me, young lady! Don't—"

"Sorry, Mother. Goodbye! Talk soon!" I quickly hang up, my

fluttering pulse giving way to a brief flash of guilt. *Stop it, Jess. You have nothing to be guilty for. It's not like you were rude to her.*

Emily slow claps dramatically. "I *almost* believed you had an incoming call. That was some amazing performance right there."

I groan, "Ugh. Don't make fun of me." I squeeze the flab of my tummy fat, feeling self-conscious. "Mother says I'm getting fat. Do I look fat to you?"

Emily rolls her eyes. "You always look great. Don't listen to her. No one can ever measure up to her definition of perfection."

My knees jiggle in a nervous tic. "She says Ben isn't going to want me if I let myself go. I'm not letting myself go, right?"

"Sis, are you okay these days? You seem to be more tense and anxious every time I see you." Emily clasps her hands on top of mine. "I don't want you to regress."

I snatch my hands away. "What are you talking about? I'm fine." I bite my lips and still my knees.

She smiles sadly at me. "I don't think you should've stopped therapy all those years ago. You shouldn't go at this alone. There's no shame in having anxiety."

I let out a nervous chuckle. "I'm fine, Ems. You're overthinking things." *I can handle this myself. I don't need help. I am normal...just like everyone else.*

I sigh but perk up at the news I'm about to disclose. "Enough about this stuff and Mother. She gives me a headache. By the way, James is back!"

"Oh, he is? For good?"

"Yes, he has a condo two streets from my place. It's already immaculately decorated. Such an overachiever." I take a sip of a sparkling drink which seems to be a mimosa of sorts, but with exotic fruit juice in it.

"That's great! I know you guys have been close all these years. Must be nice to have him back in the same time zone. Send me his address. I need to send him a welcome-back gift." Ever the PR networking specialist, Emily pulls out her phone and starts to order a gift for my friend.

I shake my head. "No need. I already got something from both of us. Speaking of which, sorry for the last-minute notice, it totally slipped my mind, but he has a housewarming at his new place tonight. You free? He told me to invite you. Liz will be there too."

Emily's eyes light up, excited at a prospect of another party. "You're in luck today. My calendar is clear. I'll be at your place later and we can go together?"

"Sure, Ben is coming as well. He keeps complaining about how he won't know anyone there, but now you'll be there. Plus, he and James technically met a few times, of which one time was in person."

"Yeah...I don't think they like each other that much," Emily comments nonchalantly while cutting up an elevated croque madame with specialty cold cuts added instead of the usual ham. "Hmm...this is different. I don't know what seasoning and sauce this is, but it's really delicious. Well done, Antoine."

"You really think so?"

"The dish? Totally, I think I want the recipe for this."

"No, I mean, you think Ben doesn't like James?" I frown, concerned. Sure, they didn't seem to be overly exuberant when they saw each other in the past, but then again, they don't know each other very well.

Emily stares at me. "You don't know that? I can't confirm it since neither of them told me anything, but it's pretty obvious to me. There's always a weird vibe."

I dig into the truffle three-cheese omelet. "I hope that's not the case. I really want my boyfriend and best friend to get along."

"Don't worry, sis, I'll be there to act as a buffer this time and will analyze the situation and report back. I got this. It's in my wheelhouse," she replies with a determined glint in her eyes.

"Okay, but I think you may be wrong. I guess we'll see." My stomach clenches, unease filtering through me. I hate for people I love to be unhappy. It's probably too idealistic, but I wish for everyone around me to just get along.

"Look, I may be wrong, which is known to happen sometimes, and I know I'm not the biggest Ben fan, but you clearly like him, so I'm going to figure this one out for you. From my experience, impressions can always change, despite what others think," Emily reassures me. "Speaking of Ben, how is he doing lately? You told me you haven't seen him in a bit, but he had a party last weekend?"

"Yeah, he told me he was pretty busy with work the last few weeks. We were supposed to have a dinner date back at his place last week, but when I got there, he had a party going. I think he forgot about our dinner." I debrief her on the events of last week.

"Did you confront him about the missed dinner?"

"I didn't outright confront him, but he knew I was upset about the dinner. I just don't want to cause any more friction over trivial matters."

"Jess, you have to stop subscribing to Mother's theory of pleasing the man to keep him. I mean, I don't think Mother is truly a happy person. Who can be happy uprooting their lives every few years way back then and not really having genuine friends? Her and Father are so formal to each other; I've never seen them argue before. I don't think that's healthy. How do you really know someone if you don't work through any disagreements?"

I sigh. This is an argument I've had with myself many times in my head, but just thinking about rocking the boat makes me break out in hives.

The server comes by to set the desserts down. It's a beautiful assortment of petite desserts and cakes that are very much social media worthy.

True to form, Emily whips out her phone. "Let's take a selfie for Steven. He's missing out on a lot of good food."

She sends the photo to our group chat.

Emily: Wish you were here, little bro. The French food is divine, and this place is the cutest.

Minutes later, he responds.

Steven: I think I'll take a steak or a burger over anything that is cute and girly. It does seem like a place you two will enjoy.

A few minutes pass and another beep sounds from the phone.

Steven: If you come visit me, I'll take you to a fantastic omakase place I went to last week. It's a hole-in-the-wall with none of the extra stuff, but the food is excellent. The fish is so fresh; it tastes like they literally just caught it from the ocean.

I think my brother has missed his calling to be a Michelin restaurant reviewer. He takes his food very seriously and has a very sensitive palate. What to me is just "delicious," he can discern most ingredients with a simple taste.

Jess: Will be at James's later on for housewarming, will send you pics. XOXO

I press send as Emily and I head out to prepare for the evening ahead, nerves gathering in my stomach for inexplicable reasons.

I stare at my reflection in the mirror and spray a small spritz of perfume as the doorbell rings.

"Coming! One sec," I holler.

James did not tell me the dress code of his shindig tonight, but I presume it's probably dressy casual since it's a housewarming. I choose an open-shoulder cream knit dress hitting at mid-thigh and pair it with a brown calfskin belt (no Chanel dress for me, sorry-not-sorry, Mother). The dress hides the extra few pounds I've gained on my waist but highlights my lean legs. Then I finish the look with a messy French braid to bring a casual flair to the ensemble. I keep my makeup simple with a nude gloss and a winged cat-eye.

Satisfied my appearance is the best it'll ever be, I open the door to greet Ben and Emily, who apparently have arrived at the same time.

"We bumped into each other in the lobby!" Emily exclaims. "Looking good, Jess, love the dress on you."

"Hey, babe, traffic sucked. I wish you'd move closer to the westside; it takes forever to get down here," Ben protests.

"Don't be such a downer, Ben." Emily rolls her eyes. "Doesn't Jess look great?"

Ben gives me a cursory glance. "Jess is beautiful, as always. If you're all ready, let's get going. The sooner we make an appearance, the sooner we can head out."

My heart sinks. I wish he didn't feel like going to see my friends is such a chore. It seems like lately, or perhaps it has been going on for longer than I'll care to admit, Ben and I have been on separate tracks despite being on the same train, if that's at all possible.

The drive over, with its many stop signs and traffic, is filled with idle chitchat about traffic patterns and the weather. I observe Ben's profile, his dirty-blond hair carefully arranged into a *Mad Men*-esque hairstyle, his honey-colored eyes, and his clean-shaven face. He still resembles the boy I fell in love with from college, but sometimes I feel as if he is really a stranger in disguise.

"Ben, are we okay? You seem a bit distracted lately."

As much as I don't want to rock the boat, it seems like we need to have this discussion, but it's been difficult finding alone time with him these days and our former daily phone calls have dwindled to two or three short calls each week, with either one of us usually needing to hang up because of work or other obligations.

He grimaces. "You want to have this chat now?" He takes in my expression and sighs. Ben reaches over and links his hand with mine. "Sorry, I was a bit short with you. I just have a lot on my mind. I know you're trying."

A heaviness settles in my stomach; his response does not bode well. It's not the usual "everything is fine babe, just busy these days" response.

"We don't have to talk about this now, of course. We seem to miss each other a lot these days, and I want to see if there is anything I can do to reconnect us."

In the past, I used to stay over at his place for the weekends, but with his work schedule and my deadlines, we barely have time to meet up, let alone stay over. The last time we were intimate must have been at least three weeks ago, and the whole act was quick and unremarkable. I remembered feeling like I was only going through the motions. At the time, I told myself we had been together for almost a decade, and it made sense for things to settle down and not be like the passionate affair of the honeymoon phase.

Ben lets go of me and drags his hand through his hair. "Look, I don't think it's any one event or problem, really. But…"

"Hey, Jess, I forgot to ask you, what did you get for James? How much do I owe you?" Emily wraps up a phone call and inserts herself into our conversation, seemingly unaware of the charged atmosphere between us.

"Oh, I got him a limited collector's edition of the World War II documentaries from the *History and Nature Channel* and a bottle of bourbon from this French brand he loves. He had his eyes on the documentaries for a while now. Don't worry about paying me back. Technically, I dragged you guys to this party."

"I know you have this handled. You know him the best!" Emily chirps. Ben's frown deepens as we pull into a parking spot next to James's condo.

I grab our wrapped gifts and we head up the steps. Soft jazz and faint laughter drifts through the open window. Emily rings the doorbell, seemingly excited to see James and Liz as well.

"James! Long time no see. So happy you are back," Emily gushes as James opens the door to greet us. She throws her arms around his waist for a brief hug.

He grins, his smile reminiscent of the actors they use in toothpaste commercials. "Great to see you too, Emily. I'm glad to be back."

His gaze trails over to me and for a split second, his expression freezes and his eyes darkens into a smolder that disappears as fast as it appears, leading me to wonder if I've imagined it all.

"Hey, Jess," he says softly.

Tucking a loose strand of hair behind my ears, I smile. "Got you something I think you'll like. You can thank me later." I hand him our presents and add, "Technically, it's from all of us." I motion to Emily and Ben standing behind me.

Ben extends his hand, his face stern and aloof. "James. So, you're back for good, huh?"

The men stare at each other in a strange standoff. Golden eyes meet with sapphire ones, an unknown message passes between them.

James grasps his hand in a tight handshake. "Ben, haven't seen you in a while. Yes," he replies, glancing over at me. "I believe I'm back for good."

Emily nudges me as the men continue their staring contest. She whispers, "See? Weird vibes!"

I give her a glare just as James smooths his expression into a polite smile and gestures with his hand. "Make yourself at home, guys. Most of these folks are my new coworkers and Liz is in the kitchen setting up the buffet station."

Ben grabs my hand and leads me inside with James trailing behind us. Moments later, I hear an exuberant screech.

"Ems! Oh my gosh, I'm so glad you could come. I haven't seen you in the longest time," Liz exclaims from the kitchen, her golden-brown hair swaying as she dashes toward us.

Emily goes in for another one of her koala hugs. We used to joke her hugs are better named as koala hugs instead of bear hugs because she's so petite.

"I've missed you, Liz. This is it. I'm creating a group chat for you, me, and Jess. We need to have regular girls' nights since we all live in the same county. LA traffic is no excuse. Work is no excuse." Emily narrows her eyes and points her finger at me.

I snort. "I agree. My bad. I'm all in favor of a regular girls' night." I turn to Ben. "Honey, I'm going to catch up with the girls. Do you want to network with some of the folks here? James is one of the execs at Brighton Capital, so you guys are technically in the same industry. Some guys here may be interesting to talk to."

Ben nods and heads to the living room, seemingly more enthusiastic at the prospect of networking with potential power makers of the west coast finance scene.

"Liz, how's the school year going for you? Are the kindergarteners treating you well?" I inquire while the three of us lay out the platters of food from Luciano's. The heady aroma of freshly baked bread, vine-ripened tomato pasta, and creamy seafood alfredo fills the air. My stomach growls at the sight of the comfort but not waistline-friendly food.

"The kids are great. Kindergartners are one of my favorite age groups to teach. For a lot of them, it's their first foray into the public school system and so many things are new to them. They're so readily amused at the smallest things and easily pleased for the most part. The kids forgive and forget all the time too. One day they're not friends with each other and the next day, they make up and are the best of friends. Sometimes I think us adults have something to learn from them." She laughs as she no doubt is remembering the antics of her students. "Jess, by the way, thanks for the snacks and care package you sent over when I stressed about work last week. So sweet of you."

"Aww. Glad you liked them. No need to thank me. That's what friends are for." I smile back at her.

Emily glances over from her side of the kitchen counter and pouts. "What about my care package?" At my eye roll, she continues, "I'm sure the little kids are cute, but I don't know how you do it, wrangling them all. It must take a lot of patience. I like children as much as the next person, but I can only take them in small doses."

Liz chuckles. "You do the same thing, Ems. Instead of kids, you're wrangling full-grown adults with your job. I think you may have the short end of the stick."

"I'm with Liz on this one. Ems, I can barely keep my team, my boss, and my clients happy, and we're all working toward the same goal. You have to force people to do things they either don't want to do or things that don't come easily to them." I shudder, thinking about the horror stories Emily has told me over the years from individuals she has worked with before.

"It's not too bad, you just have to find the proper leverage," Emily says wryly. "But there are some good stories for sure. Do you remember the he-who-shall-not-be-named actor who complained he was getting type-casted into playboy and action hero roles who we finagled into volunteering at senior retirement homes for an entire year to show his 'serious' and 'mature' side? He wasn't a fan in the beginning, but I think he ultimately came around at the end. Plus, the grandpas and grandmas loved him." Due to non-disclosure agreements, Emily can never share with us who her clients are.

"Is he a Donnelly? Tell me it's one of the Donnelly brothers. They're so hot in the movies," Liz prods. Liz is a big fan of the Donnelly brothers, reigning action stars in a series of blockbuster films.

"Nope. My lips are sealed." Emily smirks.

"Liz, you may as well give up. I've been trying to get this out of her forever. Steven and I went through the IMDB website for American actors, but she always says 'nope.'"

"I'm not giving up yet! Ooohhh, maybe it's one of those Korean actors from those Netflix shows. Maybe you guys got the wrong country."

Emily just shakes her head in amusement. "On another note, Jess, did you get back to my friend about the audition?"

"Whoa. What audition?" Liz's eyes widen in surprise.

"Yes, I got back to her. I'm passing on it. Too busy with work... and I just...can't."

Emily sighs. "Are you sure, sis? You always loved to sing. It's a great opportunity to do something you like on the side." She turns to Liz and explains, "A friend of mine is searching for a backup singer for her small play and you know Jess, she's a great singer and it's something she has dreamed about in the past."

Liz glances at me as I fidget under their scrutiny. "It's okay, there's always next time, right?" At my grateful smile, she continues, "I'm going to start rounding up folks for dinner. Ems, want to help me get the guests hanging out in the backyard? I'll get everyone inside the house."

Liz and Emily walk toward the living room and the adjoining French doors leading out to the backyard. Liz keeps throwing out names of famous actors and Emily mimes one of the "hear-no-evil, speak-no-evil" monkeys and mimes zipping her lips.

I snicker at their banter as I throw away the platter covers and set up the serving utensils. Surveying the counter, I realize we don't have enough paper napkins. I rummage around the kitchen, opening the pristine white drawers and European-styled cabinets.

"Yes!" Finally finding a large pack of napkins hidden in the back of the top shelf, I press my hands on the counter for leverage as I reach up to retrieve them. My fingers skim the package but only succeed in pushing the napkins farther into the cabinet. *Argh.* I'm not short by any means at five feet six inches, but apparently, I still have height challenges. I try again and my fingers brush against the package.

Almost...there...

"Let me get that for you," a warm baritone says from behind me, still so unfamiliar without the filter through a phone, as I feel a large presence at my back. Sandalwood and a hint of mint invade my senses this time.

I jump at the sudden interruption, my hands slipping on the counter as I volley back, and a muscular arm slithers across my waist to stop my descent.

"Easy there," James whispers.

"James! You scared me." I inhale sharply, my heart pounding, and I'm suddenly breathless.

He chuckles, his voice deep and smooth like whiskey, as he effortlessly retrieves the napkins from the shelf. He takes a step back, his arm falling from my waist, leaving tingles in its wake.

"So easily startled these days," James teases, his eyes twinkling.

"Am not!" I resort to responding like a five-year-old.

"Am too!" He waggles his brows, responding in kind.

I struggle to keep a straight face. "Nice turnout you have here."

"Yeah, not bad. We have a few folks out there eager to mingle with the head data guy because they hope I can prioritize their projects first. But yeah, a pretty good turnout overall," he replies with a satisfied smile on his face.

James is underselling himself. His mind is brilliant, and I bet people truly find him interesting to talk to.

"How's the new job going? Adjusting well?" I ask.

"It's going pretty well. There are a few top priority projects the firm has in flight and I was able to introduce a new project management system for the team, which everyone was excited about. The team is smart, works hard. I can't complain right now."

I nod. "Oh good, I'm glad it's going well. I know you'll do well; you always do." I glance up at him. "I know I told you this last time, but I want to say it again. I'm so glad you're back. I miss having my best friend with me. Calls and video chats are just not the same."

James wraps an arm around my shoulder and nestles me against him. I lean briefly against his solid chest, relishing the weight of his arm around me, and close my eyes in a moment of contentment.

Home.

Is this what home feels like?

"I'm thrilled to be back too, Jess," he murmurs into my hair.

"This seems cozy. I hope I'm not interrupting anything."

I jump, startled, and disentangle myself from James's embrace.

"Ben! Don't be silly. I was just telling James how glad I am to have my best friend back by my side." A feeling of guilt and nervousness washes over me. *Why am I nervous? It's not like we are doing anything wrong.*

"Just seemed really chummy from my end," Ben grunts, staring at James.

James holds Ben's gaze with a mask of indifference, not betraying his thoughts.

"You know James is like the older brother I never had." I laugh nervously and glance up at James, hoping for reassurance, but he stays silent. He appears calm, only betrayed by a muscle twitch in his jaw as if he's holding himself back from speaking.

"Hmm...whatever you say. Babe, are you ready to leave in five minutes? I got a few numbers from the guys and made some good connections. The traffic will be bad if we stay longer."

The traffic won't be bad for me since I live two streets over, but it's clear Ben doesn't want to stick around.

"Ben, we only got here twenty minutes ago. We haven't even had dinner yet. Why don't we stay for dinner and by then, traffic should be much better?"

Ben glances at his phone. "Babe, don't you remember you're trying to cut out carbs from your diet? This dinner is Italian. Not good for the waistline. Keep your mind on the goal, right? Also, we have that date you apparently forgot." There is no date. I scrunch my brows as I stare at him, confused, but he glares at me defiantly, as if daring me to challenge him.

James balls up a napkin and tosses it in the trash. He strides out of the kitchen without a backward glance.

Ben smiles at me. "Come on, let me take you out on a date. You have been saying we haven't spent time together in a while, right? Let's go out tonight. Just like old times."

He winks at me and for a moment, I see the college boy I fell in love with. Being in a relationship is also about compromise. Ben doesn't want to go to this housewarming, but he has made an effort to attend and now I should attempt to meet him halfway.

"Fine. Let me say goodbye to the ladies and James first." I leave the kitchen and find Liz and Emily by a corner, chatting as they finish rounding up the guests for dinner.

"I'm leaving early, ladies. Ben wants to head out."

Liz and Emily glance at each other.

"Already? We just got here," Emily says.

"Yeah, I forgot I have a date with Ben tonight. But you stay. I'll come by later and pick you up when you're ready to go." I twiddle with the jade stone on my bracelet, unwilling to meet Emily's eyes, which I know will be full of questions.

"Don't worry about it, Jess. I can drop off Ems when we are done over here." Liz's kind voice draws me away from my guilt. She gives me a sympathetic smile. "Enjoy your date." She holds up her phone. "Girls' night, remember!"

I smile genuinely this time. "Of course!" I search around the living room. "Have you seen James? I want to say bye to him."

"I think I saw him head to his bedroom." Emily gives me her best *this-is-not-over* quirk of an eyebrow and points toward the hallway.

The hallway is dark except for a dim light emanating from a door that's cracked open. Guilt and heaviness weigh me down as I slowly open the door and walk inside.

James's room is a statement of masculinity. Dark wood and calming gray. Sharp edges and clean surfaces. A large king-size bed immaculately made with a thick white comforter lies in the middle of the room.

James stands on the other side of the room away from the door, looking out the floor-to-ceiling windows. His hand holds a small object he keeps twirling around his fingers. I knock on the door, but he doesn't stir, appearing to be deep in thought. I'm suddenly overcome with an urge to wrap my arms around him, to somehow offer comfort to him, to chase away the loneliness surrounding him.

I clear my throat. "James?"

His fingers pause and he slides the small object back into his pocket. "You're leaving?" he quietly asks, still staring out the window. He slips both of his hands in his pockets, the motion flexing his corded muscles as the shirt molds to his body.

"Yes, I am. I forgot about a date with Ben." I tiptoe cautiously up to him. "Are you mad? If you are, I'm so sorry."

Still staring outside at the view of the back gardens, he chuckles humorlessly. "Why are you sorry? You haven't done anything wrong. Don't apologize when you have nothing to apologize for." He turns toward me, his sapphire eyes piercing mine and my breath catches at the sudden intensity. "You can do so much better, Jess, so much better." He doesn't need to let me know what he is talking about.

"Ben isn't always like this. We've been together for so long, you know? Some of the initial politeness can fall away over time when you're comfortable with someone. He's just a bit stressed with work these days. In time you'll see. He's usually not this grumpy." I make excuses for Ben, but deep down inside, I wonder if there is a kernel of truth to what James is saying.

James shakes his head. "You don't need to convince me. I just want you to be happy. I want you to be free to be who you are, who I know you truly are, a beautiful person inside and out. You and I are okay. We'll always be okay."

His lips tip up in a tight smile, as if sensing my discomfort. "Best friends forever, right? Oh yeah...and apparently an older brother you always wish you had. Go home. I'm sure we'll text each other to hang out later on."

My heart warms at his sentiment, and I give him a quick hug. "See you later, Chapman." I wave my wrist in the air and point to the bracelet there. "I've never taken this off...still on me since the day you gave it to me on Valentine's Day back in middle school. We'll always be okay. You and me."

I stare at the starless sky outside the window, my hands clenching around the penny in my pocket.

Older brother, my ass.

My forehead rests on the glass, the coolness doing little to calm the heated swirl of emotions inside of me. There's a fine line for me to tread right now. I won't be the third party in any relationship. That's just against my moral code. But how can I let her see I'm anything but her friend or a brotherly figure? Her mind may not have caught up yet, but I know her body is responding to me. The catch in her throat when I helped her with the napkins, the subtle glint in her eyes when she realized it was me.

Fuck.

The longer I stay in the friend zone, the harder it is to get out of it. And I've been swimming in the deep end for over a decade. Is it still possible to climb out of the water and find my land legs?

I close my eyes. *Snap out of it. This shit has gotten you nowhere in the past. Break the cycle, James. Break the damn cycle.*

My mind wanders back to the red bracelet she still wears reverently each day.

Your relationship with her is deeper than any friendship, she just doesn't realize it yet.

• • •

Sixteen Years Ago

I'm glad Jess is here to stay. I won't admit it to anyone, but I've been dreading the day when her family moves away. My social standing has improved slightly in the last few years. I have a few friends I hang out with, but Jess is still my best friend. Even though she's in the middle school building and I'm on the high school side, I walk with her to school each day where she'll tell me about school gossip and what her worry of the day is.

She worries about the most random things:

"What should I wear to the school dance?"

Anything, what do I know about girls' fashion?

"Do I look stupid in braces?"

"No, Jess, you don't look stupid. If you do, then everyone does because so many people have braces." You look cute.

"Why does Billy always make fun of me?"

Because we are all immature. I'll bet ten dollars he has a crush on you. The only reason I'm not mean to you is because I have an older sister who has trained me on the proper ways of treating girls... aka don't make them cry.

I've finally grown a few inches and have caught up to the class average height. I'm still no jock, but at least I'm average and don't stand out now. The bullies seem to have moved on to other targets.

"Jess, I got you something for Valentine's Day." I take out the small purple velvet pouch from my pocket, my hands cold and clammy suddenly. I discreetly wipe my hands on my jeans and hand her the pouch. We're hanging out in her house after school today. Her nana is over watching her little siblings and we get to spend some time watching her favorite Harry Potter movies.

"It's something small. If you don't like it, you can throw it away or give it away." I nervously drum my fingers on my lap as I wait for her to open the pouch.

Jess's face is full of excitement, and she gently takes out the contents of the pouch. "This is so pretty, James. A red bracelet!

What is this stone?" She slides her small fingers over the pale-green, heart-shaped stone.

"It's jade. I did some research and I read in your mother's culture, this stone brings health and good fortune and, of course, the red symbolizes luck. I know you love your good-luck charms."

Jess stares at the bracelet in wonder and tries to clasp it onto her slender wrist. "This is the best present ever. Is this very expensive? Mother said I shouldn't accept expensive presents from others."

"Here, let me help you." My uncoordinated fingers fumble around for a minute or two and finally close the clasp of the bracelet on her wrist. The moment feels significant for reasons I can't identify.

"It's not too expensive. I saved up some money from chores and just happened to see this at the mall the other day and thought it would be perfect for you. It can't be returned, so you better keep it," I lie.

She lovingly caresses the bracelet. "I'll never take this off. This is so beautiful." She leans over and gives me a quick peck on the cheek. "Thank you."

I freeze. She gives me pecks and hugs all the time, but somehow this one feels different, at least to me.

"Finish the food before it gets cold," I remind her, suddenly eager to change the subject to get rid of these weird feelings.

"Ha. You sounded like Mother just now." Jess gives me a sly glance.

"Ugh. Please don't." I pretend to be angry and fail miserably. We burst out laughing a few seconds later.

"Best friends forever, James. Best friends forever." She sighs contently as we resume our movie night.

Somehow, that's when things started shifting for me but by the time I realized, it was too late.

• • •

"James?"

I lift my head from the window and turn toward the soft voice from the doorway. The penny feels heavy in my pocket.

"Emily." I soften my face into a smile. "You enjoying yourself?"

Emily slowly approaches me and give me an impish grin. "Of course, parties are my jam. I just want to tell you dinner is set up already. Don't want you to go hungry at your own housewarming."

I laugh, the sound foreign to me. "Thanks." I flex my hands and take them out of my pockets. *Breathe, James. You can't dismantle Rome in one day. You knew this would happen. Two steps forward, one step back is still progress.* Squaring my shoulders, I walk past Emily toward the living room.

"Give her time."

My footsteps falter and I slowly turn back. Emily may be a firecracker, but she's observant. It seems like everyone knows of my feelings for Jess, except for Jess herself. The fucking irony.

"Don't you think I've already given her enough time?" I don't even bother pretending to not understand what she's referring to.

She smiles sadly in sympathy. "Jess is...complicated. Our mother has done a number on her over the years. You didn't see it because you were away for so long. She's with Ben because he's familiar. He's comfortable. She'd rather be with him than risk being alone because deep down inside, her anxiety tells her she's not good enough and everyone will leave her."

I suspected as much but didn't realize how bad things have gotten for her. I swallow the lump in my throat, wishing I got my head out of my ass sooner and came back for her earlier.

Emily continues, "But...despite her so-called perceived issues, she has a fire inside her. And I think all of us can see the relationship isn't working out or they would've gotten married long before now."

My teeth clench at the thought of Jess getting married to the asshole. My breath falters as I fight an impulse to chase after Jess and tell her to break things off with Ben.

She glances up, her warm brown eyes staring intently at me. "Now that you're back, as long as you continue to push her boundaries...she'll wake up and see. I know she will."

"I hope so. God, I hope you're right."
There are some things you don't survive.
For me, losing Jess would be it.

Thump. Thump. Thump.

Buzz. Buzz. Buuuzzzzzz.

Disoriented, I rub the cobwebs of sleep from my eyes and glance at my cell phone charging on my nightstand. Eight thirty a.m.

2 Missed Calls from Ben

Yawning, I clamber out of bed as I prepare to call Ben back. Work has finally slowed down, giving me a quiet few weeks to prepare for the next audit. Waking up so early in the morning on a Saturday isn't part of my plan.

Thump. Thump. Thump.

Buzz. Buzz. Buzz.

I jump up, startled. So, I didn't imagine the knocking at my door or the ringing of my doorbell. I slip on my favorite terry-cloth robe. The mornings by the beach are especially cold and humid with the marine layer invading the air.

"Coming! One minute!" I call out as I hastily throw my hair into a bun and scramble to get to the door. I peek through the peephole. Ben stands there, pacing back and forth. *This is so weird. Why is he here so early in the morning?* I look at my attire and cringe. *Crap, I'm completely unpresentable.* My mother's words ring in my ears. *Always keep up with your appearances with your man. No one likes a sloth or someone who "gives up on themselves." There are so many younger, more beautiful women out there, just waiting to take your man. You need to keep him interested.* She practices what she preaches. I've never seen a hair out of place on her. Even on the rare days when she was at home, she dressed like a housewife from the fifties with makeup carefully applied.

You're so much more than your appearance. I repeat to myself, but years of conditioning is hard to get rid of.

I throw open the door. "Ben! What are you doing here so early? I'm sorry. I didn't know you were coming over, so I'm not prepared yet." I hastily brush the loose strands of my messy bun.

Ben grimaces and purses his lips. "It doesn't matter. Look, can I come in? I want to talk."

Bewildered at the sudden turn of events, I gesture him in. A million scenarios run through my brain, none of them good, the circumstances perfect fodder for my anxiety.

Ben walks to my well-worn, blue-velvet armchair by the window where I do most of my reading and sits down, his hands clasp over his knees.

"Do you want anything to drink or eat? It's early. Did you have breakfast yet?" My hands fiddle with my bracelet as I attempt to play my usual role as the perfect girlfriend, but the entire rhythm is off. I distinctly feel this is a situation I can't control, even though I'm on my home turf.

Ben shakes his head and remains silent, his gaze fixes upon his hands.

Dread coats my stomach as I gingerly approach him and take a seat on the edge of the sofa next to him, my muscles tense, as if preparing to fight or flee.

"Is everything okay, Ben? You're making me nervous." I tug the jade heart on my wrist and fight the urge to bite my lips.

"Look, I don't mean to do this so early, but I don't want to put this off anymore. I've given this a lot of thought over the last few months. I don't know how you feel but..." He pauses, finally looking at me, his eyes full of guilt. "I don't think this is working anymore."

The silence is loud.

When biology textbooks say an animal has a flight or fight response, they forgot to say there is also a freeze response. I stare at him, shocked and also speechless. I can only hear the blood rushing in my ears. Did I hear what I think I just heard? No, it can't be. I'm the perfect girlfriend. There must be a misunderstanding.

I feign ignorance, finally recovering my vocal abilities. "What do you mean? I know we have both been very busy with work. Do you want to realign our schedules so we can see more of each other? I just finished a large audit so my time is freeing up for the next few weeks—" I stand and start pacing in front of him.

"Stop it, Jess, you know what I mean. We..." he points at us, his finger a knife to my heart, slicing me open, "aren't working out. I think you know deep down it hasn't been working out for a long time. Tell me you don't feel the same thing."

"No, no, no. That's not true. We've been together for a very long time, and every relationship has its trials and tribulations. It's not always exciting." I nod to myself, the denial easier to swallow than the truth which has absolutely lain dormant in the depths of my mind for a long time. I work my lips into something I hope resembles a convincing smile. "Yes, that's it. We are just in a lull. I think we both got carried away with work and forgot to put each other as a priority. We're too complacent. I'm glad you brought this up. Now we can prioritize each other and work on us." I nod again, needing to convince myself.

Ben holds up his hand. "Jess. No. No, no, no!" He stands abruptly and stomps to the window, his hands messing up his usually pristine hair. "This is *exactly* our problem. How are you being so nice even now? How can you even *smile* and pretend to be so understanding when I'm saying we should break up? I don't know you. I don't think I ever truly knew who you are."

He turns around, his eyes flashing a thousand accusations. "I know I'm going to sound like an ass, but you're always so...perfect. Perfectly dressed, the perfect smile, very accommodating and understanding all the time. This is probably the first time in months I've seen you in anything other than perfect hair and makeup. No one can be like that twenty-four seven. And I know you aren't like that. Yes, you have anxiety issues, which I'll never understand. I don't know if this is related, but I think you're so worried about what other people think you put all this pressure on yourself to act a certain way, but this is a problem, you do this to me too. I'm supposed to be one of the closest people in your life. I don't know who you truly are, and I wonder if you know who you are either."

No, this must be a mistake.

I twist my hands behind my back, out of sight, struggling in vain to control my emotions. I tried *so hard*. I don't usually let my inner chaos show because I don't want to stress other people out. Who wants to be with someone so high-strung all the time? I have my emotions reined in because I want to avoid this.

"Ben, is something else going on? This is so sudden. Let's not say anything we can't take back." I let out a halfhearted chuckle, hoping to diffuse the tension in the room.

"Jess, my mind is made up. I just thought you deserved to know in person, considering we've been together for so long. I at least owe you that." He grabs his keys from the kitchen counter and turns back to face me. "I wish you the best. You and me, we're missing some pieces and I think it's best we part ways." He turns from me and closes the door behind him with a click.

Just like that, my future walked out of my life.

I sit down in shock, my hands shaking uncontrollably as I slide to the ground. Millions of thoughts race through my mind as I try to make sense of the situation, but the turmoil inside me is threatening to break loose with every breath I take. I pull out my phone from my pocket. My breaths are short, my heart is racing, and I pant for air which doesn't seem to land in my lungs. I count internally.

Five counts in, eight counts out.

Drops of liquid splash onto the screen and I realize I'm crying. Bile rises in my throat, and I fight to keep down the contents of my stomach. My fingers are cold and clammy as I swipe to my contacts and hover above James's name. Something unknown holds me back from dialing his number and instead, I type a message to the newly created girls' night group with Emily and Liz.

Jess: SOS. I'm sorry to be a bother but I'm wondering if we can have a girls' night tonight?

My phone dings immediately.

Liz: Of course! Is everything okay, Jess?

I swipe the wetness on my face, but the tears are now pouring down in earnest.

Jess: Ben dumped me.

Liz: Will be there. I'm in Irvine, but am heading back up anyway. What time do you want me to be there? I'll bring dinner.

Emily: That asshole. I never liked him. I'm an hour away and will bring wine and chocolates.

Jess: I'll be here. Any time is fine.

I slowly rise, drag myself back to bed, and curl into a fetal position under my comforter. I'm so tired, so exhausted, my eyes heavy from crying. I close my eyes, hoping I can just disappear from reality.

• • •

Thump. Thump. Thump. I jolt awake, disoriented by the sound coming from my door. A sense of déjà vu hits me as I try to make sense of my surroundings. Sunlight streams in from the windows, indicating it's at least midday. My eyes are swollen and tired, my mind frazzled. The memories of this morning come rushing back like a tidal wave.

Ben left me.

"Jess! If you don't open your damn door, I'll break it down," a muffled masculine voice yells from the other side of the door.

James. James. James. I recite to myself as I desperately run toward the door, as if the solution to all my problems is standing right outside.

I throw open the door and leap into the welcoming arms of my best friend, not caring I'm still in my sleepwear.

Sandalwood. Warmth. Comfort.

I sob loudly, suddenly unable to hold back my tears. This time, instead of sadness, the dominant emotion coursing through my veins is anger. "How dare him!" I pant in between breaths as James gently rubs my back.

"I got you. I got you." He tightens his hold, his arms locking me into his chest. "Let it all out. Don't hold it in."

My lungs burn as if I can't get enough oxygen in, my tears creating a large, wet spot on his sweater, and my nose is runny and so very disgusting, but James appears to not care.

"How *dare* him. He dumped *me* because I was too nice or too 'perfect,' How dare him!" I jab my fingers on his chest with each sentence as I grind my teeth in fury.

The vein on his neck pulses. His jaw tightens as he remains silent and continues his soothing ministrations to my back. I can't see the rest of him as I bury my face in his sweater, not caring I'm probably ruining an expensive piece of clothing. He drops one hand, sweeps me up from the ground, and closes the door with his foot in one fluid motion. He shushes me and gently lays me down on the sofa, my head on his lap. He blots my eyes and nose with a tissue he procured out of nowhere.

"He was supposed to be it, James. He was part of the plan. I'm already behind on the plan. I was supposed to be married with kids by now." I know I'm making no sense, but I continue rambling. "How do you just throw away a decade-long relationship over something so...so...so..." I struggle to find the word. "Pathetic!"

Words continue to tumble out of me. "He said he knows I have anxiety, but I hide from him. What the heck does that even mean? I share with him things I'm anxious about...my work and stuff like that. He always said I was overthinking and doing this to myself. I try to be understanding when he does things I don't like because I *know* I overthink and I'm afraid if I tell him what I really feel, he'll think I'm crazy, and leave me. I don't want him to leave me!" I pour my heart out, fresh tears falling, my face a swollen mess.

"So, if I show him how anxious I am, how crazy I feel sometimes, then he'll love me? If I walk around wearing sweats with no makeup on, he'll think I'm genuine? What counterintuitive logic is this? I want to protect him from my brand of internal crazy and see what I get in return. He thinks this is fun? I suck it up all the time. I swallow my emotions and pride to make him happy, to make his life easier and this is the result?" Multiple stages of grief show up simultaneously: sadness, resignation, anger.

Deep down, I've questioned myself time and time again whether or not I should've stopped therapy all those years ago. Maybe this is a sign the monster can't be contained by sheer willpower alone. *But anxiety is a sign you're weak. It's a disease for the privileged.* Mother's words echo inside me, adding chaos to the madness within.

James brushes his hands over the messy strands which have escaped my bun, his fingers gently massage my scalp. I close my eyes, feeling exhausted again after my tirade.

"Jessica Kingsley. You aren't crazy. Your anxiety is *not* a flaw. The right person will love you, all of you, the happy parts, the anxious parts, the sad parts, because those parts of you are what makes you...*you*. The right person will love your kind heart, your intelligent brain, your thoughtful self. The right man will feel like the luckiest guy alive to have a girlfriend who thinks of his needs, who is so perfect, so-called 'flaws' and all. He'll be the luckiest person on earth because he has the love of an angel."

His hands cradle my face, tipping it up so my eyes meet his. Dark-blue eyes simmer with an intensity that threatens to vanquish the monsters in my mind. "And don't you *ever* doubt any of what I've said. You're perfect just the way you are. Ben is an idiot for not appreciating you."

My breath catches in my throat for a different reason this time, my train of thought temporarily suspended as I get lost in the turbulent pool of his stare.

His voice turns raspy as he whispers, "Any. Man. Who. Does. Not. Appreciate. You. Is. A. Fool. The biggest fool for not realizing who he has." He holds my stare, his thumb gently tracing my bottom lip. The voices in my head silence and the only sounds I can hear are the blood rushing through my veins and our heavy breaths comingling in the small space between us.

Buzz. Buzz. Buzzzzz. The sudden doorbell jolts us from our trance. His fingers drop from my lips as I jerk up into a sitting position.

"The doorbell...someone is here...the bell...I need to get it," I mutter incoherently.

"Let me get it. Just relax." James stands, his eyes now the usual color of a tranquil lake, the familiar gaze of my best friend, leading me to think, *Did the moment really happen? Or was that a figment of my imagination?*

James opens the door, revealing both Liz and Emily with bags of takeout and drinks.

"James! How are you here?" Emily asks, surprised.

Liz bites on her lips and smiles apologetically at me from the doorway. "I called him. I knew we were both far away, and I thought you'd want to see James. He can get to you sooner since he's so close by. Hope you don't mind."

"Of course not. Thank you," I reassure her with a small smile.

The ladies put down the food on the kitchen counter and gingerly approach me. Emily reaches me first and envelops me in her signature koala hug. Liz wraps her arms around us in a group hug. James lingers behind in the kitchen, giving us some privacy.

Fresh tears appear in my eyes. What did I do to deserve these wonderful women in my life? I'm not even a good friend. I don't make enough time for them, but here they are, dropping everything they were doing because I simply texted them.

"Thank you for coming. I know you girls probably have other stuff going on and I must have disrupted your plans..." I begin as they detach themselves from me.

"Don't be silly!" Liz admonishes, her blue eyes eerily similar to James's from a few moments ago. "This is a girlfriend emergency. *Of course* we need to be here. You'd do the same for us." Emily nods vehemently in agreement.

James carries over a large tray with a few plates of Italian food—my comfort food of choice—and three glasses of red wine. "Ladies, your food and refreshments." He sets down the tray with a flair and a wink. "I'm going to head out so you can talk about how horrible men are." His playful expression turns solemn as he stares at me. "Jess, I'll check on you later, okay?"

"Okay. Thank you for coming." I nod, a small grin reappearing on my face.

"No need to thank me. I did what any best friend would do." He walks to the door, his hands gripping the doorknob and pauses for a moment, the muscles on his back bunching in tension. Just as I stand to ask him if everything is okay, he strides back with determination and pulls me into a tight embrace. His breath grazes my ears as he whispers, "Remember what I told you earlier. You are perfect the way you are." Then he releases me, the burning intensity in his gaze searing my soul as he backs toward the door and promptly exits from my apartment, leaving me bewildered and breathless at the same time.

"So, what happened?" Emily asks, as I chug down my first glass of petite syrah, my favorite red, which I usually savor on a normal day, but today, the wine might as well be water; tasteless, a vehicle to numb my pain.

I pour myself another glass of wine and proceed to guzzle the drink, not wanting to relive yet another failure in my life.

"Whoa. Slow down and pace yourself." Liz swaps my glass with a cup of water and pushes the plate of food in front of me.

I take a sip of water and stare at the seafood spaghetti, stomach churning from the alcohol I consumed. Tears prickle my eyes as I recount the events of my morning with Ben to the girls. I know I should eat something to settle my stomach, but the thought of food makes me nauseated.

"...and that was it. He just left." I sniffle, finishing my third glass of wine. "Then James showed up, and he stayed until you guys came over." Somehow, I didn't want to tell them what James said to me earlier. His words felt sacred and private, even in my current state.

I feel a little tipsy, the wine finally kicking in and numbing the edge off my pain. Silence fills the room as the girls are rendered speechless. I stare at my empty wineglass as my internal naysayer lets loose in my brain. *They must think I'm pathetic. Who gets dumped for being a good girlfriend? Here I am, twenty-eight, oh God, what will happen when Mother finds out? What if this is it? What if it's all downhill from now?* An incessant chatter of negative thoughts clouds my brain, thoughts I normally attack with the methods I learned back in the day from therapy, but I'm just too tired to fight them today. I take a deep breath, gather my courage, and finally look up at my sister and friend, expecting to see judgment in their eyes.

Emily's lips flatten; her eyes narrow and are full of anger. Liz's mouth gapes in shock, as if she just heard the most ludicrous thing ever.

"I know. I know. I'm very lame. I can't even get the girlfriend thing down," I grumble to myself.

"What on earth are you talking about, Jessica Kingsley?" Emily pounds her fist on the coffee table. "The asshole!"

She throws her hands in the air. "I know this doesn't help you right now, but this is exactly the type of shit the self-centered bastard would pull. I never, *ever* liked him, but you always seemed to enjoy being with him, so I didn't say anything."

Liz nods in agreement. "You guys were together for so long. I didn't want to say anything either. But I never liked the way he treated you. He didn't seem to appreciate you enough. None of this is your fault, Jess. Don't beat yourself up. You didn't do anything wrong."

"But if I didn't do anything wrong, why did he break up with me? This makes no sense. And he couldn't tell me anything other than I was too put together for him and he didn't know me," I wail, face heating up and fresh tears pool in my eyes. "We were together since I was a sophomore in college. If he didn't know me, who actually does? I don't know what to do anymore."

I normally pride myself on being prepared for all outcomes, being ten steps ahead so I can control the outcome of a situation. I have a Plan D if Plans A, B, and C don't pan out. It keeps my worry monster under control. If I make a mistake, I make sure I learn from it and never make the same mistake twice. I'm at a loss with Ben. I still don't know what I've done wrong. Why has he fallen out of love with me? What can I do to not experience this heartbreak again?

"Look, I don't think you did anything wrong other than maybe putting his needs above yours. And even that to me is not something you did wrong, per se. Your heart was in the right place. But maybe it's okay to disagree and be a little truer to yourself so others can get to know the real you. I think if you meet the right person, you shouldn't need to try so hard to mold yourself in his image," Liz suggests gently.

"I just want to be loved. If I try harder, maybe he'll stay."

"No, no, no, no, Jess. This is exactly why I don't have long-term boyfriends," Emily disagrees. "Men can be such jackasses. They want you to be independent and have your opinions, but once you are completely true to yourself, they'll have an issue with you being too self-sufficient and not caring about them enough."

She takes a sip of her drink and continues, "I know you're different than me, Jess, and you want to have someone with you long-term, but even so, I don't think you guys were really a good fit. I always thought you loved harder than he did. And I think in the right relationship, the guy should love you more so he'll hang around when the mundane starts to kick in after the initial passion fades."

Liz chimes in, "I actually agree with Emily for once." Liz is searching for her soulmate. She used to tell me she wants what her parents have, and the Chapmans are a hard act to follow. I've witnessed impromptu slow dancing at night when they thought we were in another room.

"I don't mean the part about the guy having to love the girl more, but the part where you guys were not a good fit to begin with. I think the integration will be both ways if you meet the right person. You'll both compromise for each other when you run into disagreements. It shouldn't be so one-sided."

Liz grabs my hand and gives me a hopeful smile. "Jess, you're a real catch. You have such a big heart. You'll meet the right man who'll be the yang to your yin." She pauses and arches her brow, sharing a pointed look with Emily. "Maybe you've already met him and you just didn't realize."

"And in the meantime, I think you should try a page from my book. Have fun dating, enjoy the honeymoon phase, and then end things before things get more serious and it becomes not as much fun. You'll see, guys will line up around the block for you. Ben is missing out," Emily suggests as I sip the last of my wine, losing track of how much I've drank today already.

My vision blurs at the edges and I bob my head, feeling warm and buzzed. "Before then, I'm going to call Ben." I nod to myself. *Yes, I'm Jessica Kingsley. I'm not taking this shit lying down. Relationships need to be protected, and I'm going to fight for us.*

"What?" Emily gasps. "That's not what I had in mind at all."

"Ten years of a relationship can't be over with a stupid conversation," I slur. "He's probably regretting this."

I pick up my phone and quick dial Ben. It rings five times and goes to voicemail. I press redial.

Straight to voicemail.

The same thing happens the next two times.

I tap open my Instagram app and scroll to his profile page. His last post is dated one hour ago. Ben has his arms around a smiling blonde with Santa Monica Pier as a backdrop. He writes, "The Cali life. Sunshine, babes, beaches. Can't complain."

Anger churns in my chest as heat rises to my face. I grip my phone tightly.

"Jess? You okay there?" Liz asks, concern in her voice.

I wordlessly hand over my phone. Liz stares at the post and growls, "Bastard."

Emily peeks over her shoulder. "The motherfucker. Already has a new girl lined up."

I grit my teeth and clench my fists until my nails dig into the tender flesh of my palms. "Yes, Ems, you're right." I attempt to stand, but the floor feels unsteady, and I plop back onto the sofa. "I'm going to date around. I'll find someone better." *I'll find my home, somewhere or someone who'll be my safe haven.*

"That's the spirit, sis! Don't worry, we'll help you along the way. The dating scene has changed a lot since you were in college, but we'll get you set up," Emily enthuses.

Liz glances at the two of us, skepticism shining from her eyes. "Um...don't want to be a Debbie Downer but Ems, are we in the best position to help Jess? I mean, of course we'll be there along the way, but look at me, I'm still single, searching for Mr. Right and you... Well, no offense, you don't do relationships. You hook up and dump."

"Heeeyy...just because we aren't walking examples of success as defined by the patriarchy and my mother doesn't mean we don't know men! I know what men like and you do too. You have a lot of admirers; you just reject them," Emily counters, sounding just as buzzed as I am.

"I think we need to enlist the help from someone who knows men better...maybe an actual man." Liz still appears dubious at being appointed as my co-dating coach.

I nod, the alcohol in my bloodstream flooding me with a courage and positivity I didn't have before. "That sounds like a plan. Yes, I need a dating coach. A guy who will train me on how men think and what they want. Screw Ben!"

"Yes, screw Ben! You'll find a better fish in the sea." Emily pumps her hand in the air as a sign of unity.

"Um...who'll be the guy to help you?" Liz questions.

Only one face comes to mind. There is only one person I trust to not lead me astray. "James." The idea sounding better as time passes. "Yes, James will be perfect for this. He'll help me, right?"

Something unidentifiable flashes in Liz's eyes, gone as quickly as it appears. She slowly nods, her caramel hair shines with her movements, and a small, secret smile graces her lips, as if she knows something I don't know. "Yes...he'll be perfect for the role."

"It's decided. The three of us will help you navigate the new dating world and help find the right guy for you," Emily says, determined. "Go call him, Jess. Get him on the plan."

I take out my phone and put it on speaker as I dial James's number.

"Jess, you okay? Did talking to the girls make you feel better?" His calming voice is a balm to my anxious soul.

"Actually, they're still here and you're on speaker. We have something to ask you, and we need to ask you right now. This is important to my happiness, and we know you want me to be happy, right, James?" I press, my mind still a bit numb from the wine. The words come tumbling out of my mouth with no filter.

James's familiar deep chuckle sends a burst of endorphins through me. I always love his voice. Soothing. Safe. Comforting. "Oookay? What do you need me to do?"

"*Ineedyoutobemydatingcoach,*" I mumble quickly in one breath, both excited and embarrassed at the same time. My skin prickles from mortification.

"What? I totally didn't understand what you just said."

Taking a deep breath, I enunciate slowly, "I. Need. You. To. Be. My. Dating. Coach."

One second.

Two seconds.

Three seconds.

Silence on the other end. James rendered speechless?

The girls and I glance at each other, confused. Liz clarifies, "Um. James, you still there? We've decided Jess needs to go back to the dating scene and meet someone else who'll appreciate her. But we also think neither of us really knows what men think and thought maybe... Maybe she can use the advice from an actual guy, someone she can trust. It won't be a lot of your time, maybe one practice date and someone she can go to for advice."

"And naturally, the person is you, James. You guys are best friends forever," Emily chimes in.

James clears his throat, indicating he is still listening. "Is this what you really want, Jess?" His words are slow and filled with a surprising intensity.

I picture him furrowing his brow. "Yes, but it's okay if you don't want to do it. It'll probably be an inconvenience...and annoying, I'm sure. And you're busy with work being the chief data guy and all, and this'll probably be embarrassing for you. You know what? I don't know what I was thinking. It's the alcohol talking—" I ramble on, backtracking, the earlier excitement quickly turning into embarrassment. *Why did this seem like a great idea a moment ago?*

"I'll do it," James replies resolutely. "This is obviously important to you. And if you need to get advice on men from a man...I'd... rather the man be me."

Relief floods my body. "Are you sure? I don't want to make things weird or uncomfortable for you."

"I'm sure." He pauses, as if he wants to say something else, but decides against it. "I'll do it. Look, I need to go. Call me once you ladies decide on the details."

"Thank you, James. I owe you big time," I gratefully exclaim as I disconnect the call.

The ladies grin and Emily waggles her finger in the air in the form of a checkmark. "Dating coach is confirmed. Let the planning commence." Emily pours more wine into our glasses.

"Cheers! To better and greener pastures." Liz raises her glass in a toast. We clink our glasses together to celebrate new beginnings, the storm clouds in my heart dissipating, letting in a few rays of sunlight.

Game on. Ben, screw you.

CHAPTER 9

James

Thanks for the help. It's getting late on a Saturday night. Go home and call it a day. Can you give this file to Liam on your way out?" I hand a folder with the newest data analyses for the Board of Directors to my assistant as I stare at the laptop in front me. He closes the door behind him with a soft click. The charts and graphs start to blur together after a few straight hours of working overtime, which comes with the territory in a high intensity industry.

I close my eyes and rub my temples, thinking back to the events earlier in the day. They finally broke up. I got what I wanted without having to lift a finger, and yet, seeing the anguish on Jess's face really makes me want to strangle Ben and tell him to wake up and see what he's giving up, to give him a piece of my mind for hurting her that way.

Emily: Jess is fine, don't worry. We'll take good care of her.

Liz: I never liked the damn bastard anyway. He already has a new girlfriend lined up. Bro, rooting for you. I've got a good feeling about this. Don't waste the opportunity we've created for you.

Fucking bastard. He never deserved her.

I laugh mirthlessly at the texts on my phone. Of all the things I was planning to do to win Jess over, I never imagined being her dating "advisor" is one of them. My initial reaction was to say no, I'm not going to help prepare her to date other men because I'm right here, but the more I think about it, the more I realize this may be the in I've been searching for. Perhaps I can use this opportunity to let her see me in a different light, as a man taking a woman he's interested in on a date instead of being the best friend.

I'm hoping this will end better than it did all those years ago in high school.

• • •

Fourteen Years Ago

I'm a ball of jittery nerves. I'm going to ask her out tonight, take the brave step forward to move our relationship from best friends to something more. My mind whirls with a thousand different scenarios, pinning me in an undercurrent of emotional whiplash.

Jess saying yes to going out with me and staring at me with those adoring hazel eyes rimmed with the palest green as she says, *I've been waiting for you to ask me.*

Jess saying no and making fun of me for asking her. This one causes my pulse to race and makes my palms clammy.

Jess telling me she already likes someone else. A dagger to the heart, a fatal wound I'll never heal from.

Jess leaping into my arms and pulling me in for a kiss when I ask her. Okay, the last one is a bit of a stretch, but a guy can dream, right?

I fiddle around with the crimson tie Liz picked out for me for the Homecoming dance. Staring at the reflection in the mirror, something I rarely do, I attempt to smooth out the stubborn cowlick which insists on sticking out like a sore thumb. Liz also helped me pick out a tux for the evening. I feel like a kid dressed up in my dad's clothes. The tux hangs a little too loosely on my frame, but was the only size the store had for my height. I lament my lack of foresight. I should've tried some of the workouts the jocks at school swear by to build some muscles.

"Late bloomer," I mutter under my breath, frustrated at myself. How can the nerd get the girl when his competition resemble like the high schoolers you see on TV shows?

"Aww...my little bro is all grown up." Liz comes down the stairs in her midnight-blue gown with her hair up in a twist. She feigns wiping a tear from her eyes and snickers.

"Shut up, Liz. I feel so weird in this outfit."

Liz pats my shoulders. "You look great, bro. Trust me, I picked the right tux for you. It's a bit big on you, but then again, all the guys your age look more or less the same, so you'll be fine."

I shrug, still staring at my reflection in the mirror. I probably spent more time in front of this mirror tonight than I did the entire year.

"So...are you finally going to get your head out of your ass and ask her out?"

My hands pause at my lapels. "What?"

"Come on, James, no use denying it. I know you better than anyone. You like Jess, right?"

"Of course I like her. She's my best friend," I deny. *Am I that obvious?*

Liz cocks her brow. "You know I don't mean that. You like *like* her right? I know you. You two have always been attached at the hip, but for the last few years, I see those blushes when you think no one notices. How she doesn't know is beyond me."

I remain silent, not wanting to lie to her but not quite ready to admit it out loud yet. Whatever she sees on my face betrays my thoughts.

"You know, you should just ask her out. Don't drag it out. Take it from me, the longer a guy stays in the friend zone, the harder it is to get out of it. Just be brave and ask her. What's the worst that can happen? If she says no, you'll feel bad, but at least you tried, no regrets." She gently encourages me.

That's not true. The "no" doesn't necessarily scare me. The thought this could make us lose what we currently have does. What if my declaration makes things so weird and awkward she doesn't want to be friends anymore? What if she pulls away and doesn't want to hang out with me again? The idea of losing Jess makes my gut churn, and I suddenly feel sick to my stomach.

I pull out the lucky penny Jess gave me in elementary school from my pocket. It has been in my wallet all these years. I give it a quick rub, hoping the luck will be on my side today.

"We'll see," I reply noncommittally.

After Liz's date drops by to pick her up for the dance, our parents insist on driving me to Jess's place.

"Honey, doesn't James look all grown up?" my mom gushes from the front of the car.

"He sure does. This takes me back to the day when I took you to prom. I knew you were it for me then." Dad reminisces and gives mom a quick peck. They're so in love with each other even after all these years, and while their public displays of affection are nausea inducing most days, they do make me want what they have...with Jess, the not so little anymore girl who stole my heart a long time ago.

Soon, I arrive at Jess's palatial home. Holding on to the box that contains the red rose corsage and boutonniere, I rock back on my heels and ring the bell.

The door whips open and I behold the goddess in front of me, my breath knocked out of my lungs. Nothing can prepare me for the sight of Jess in a red chiffon dress that skims her slim curves. I don't know where to look first. Her heart-shaped face, the familiar prairie-colored eyes framed by lush, dark lashes. The smattering of freckles on her nose she laments about, but to me, is just another sign of fairies sprinkling their magic dust on her. Her full lips painted in bombshell red, begging me to taste them. I'm not sure I'll survive the encounter. One strap slides off her shoulder and my fingers itch to trail my hands on the smooth skin. She looks like a young blossom in spring, on the verge of flowering into full bloom, and I'm the bee, posturing at her feet, begging for a taste of her sweetness.

"Earth to James. Hello? Jaaames?" She waves her hand in front of my face.

I quickly close my mouth, which apparently has been gaping this entire time, and quickly give myself a shake.

"Hey, Jess. You clean up nicely." *What the heck, Chapman? What is "clean up nicely?" That's the best you got?* I give myself an internal slap in the face.

Jess beams, and the cutest blush crawls up her face. "Thank you. Mother picked this dress for me. She said it goes well with my complexion and hair and apparently will make me seem more curvaceous than I actually am," she whispers the last part.

My eyes involuntarily drop to her chest, to the gentle swells hinted by the modest neckline of the gown. A nice handful. Perfect. "You look fine." I nod mutely as blood rushes south.

Jess pulls me in for her usual quick hug, and I gingerly wrap my hands around her. I close my eyes, reveling in the warmth of her lithe body, my favorite smell of strawberries emanating from her hair.

After we pull away, I take out the corsage from the box and gently slide it up her wrist.

She giggles. "This is going to be so much fun! I love dressing up."

At this moment, Mrs. Kingsley comes to the doorway and gives me one of her famous intense stares that'll wither any living thing. We let out a collective sigh of relief when she finally shuts the door after reminding us about curfew.

"Sorry, Jess, but your mother is a really scary person," I whisper.

She shrugs, staring down at her feet. Whatever I just witnessed must be a tiny sliver of what she goes through every day. I wish I could take her away from it all. I see glimpses of her mother's criticism in Jess daily. Jess is one of the most self-critical people I know, and it seems no matter what she does, the bar set for her by her parents seems to get higher and higher.

She had her first anxiety attack last month and called me in the middle of the night, gasping for air. I was so terrified but managed to talk her through it. Apparently, she got a B- on her biology test and woke up from the nightmares of telling her parents about it. The brave little girl I met all those years ago has been slowly shrinking into a husk of her former self, and I'm helpless to do anything about it, other than to be there for her, to support her, and to encourage her. It frustrates me to no end.

My parents, sensing the sudden change in atmosphere, quickly step out of the car and usher us inside. They joked the entire way to the school and the earlier tense atmosphere quickly lifts.

We park a block from the school to avoid the traffic up ahead.

"Wait." I pat Jess's hand as I quickly unbuckle my seatbelt and race around the car to open her door, like one of the heroes from her favorite romance novels.

"Awww...James, thank you." Jess blushes prettily as she takes my outstretched hand and slowly steps out of the car. The lucky penny weighs heavily in my pocket. It seems like it's working its powers.

"You're welcome." I hook her arm through mine as we walk toward the auditorium. The balmy night breeze kicks up the smattering of brown leaves from the ground, the beginnings of the short fall season, if you can call it that, between the sweltering heat of summer and the cooler temperatures of winter in Los Angeles. Stars twinkle in the clear evening sky; the moonlight casting shadows from the tree branches above us. The air fills with promises and hope, the atmosphere magical.

The night passes by too quickly. We dance to a few pop hits Jess loves from the Backstreet Boys. She puts some of her dance background to use, moving her svelte body to the beat of the music, rolling her hips as well as Britney Spears's backup dancers. I sway by her, mesmerized by her hypnotic movements and the joy radiating from her face.

"This is so much fun! I never thought I'd thank Mother for putting me through ballet and jazz dance classes. High school dances are so awesome!" Jess hollers, throwing her hands up as the last notes of the song fill the air.

Her joy is contagious, and I laugh. "Glad you're having fun! I never thought I was a school dance type of guy, but this is pretty cool."

Or maybe, it's fun because I'm here with you.

She nods. "I need to go on a bathroom break."

"Okay, me too. I'll come with you."

We walk toward the bathroom where Jess is indicted into the head-scratching ritual that is girls going to the bathroom in groups. I quickly go into the boys' bathroom and complete my business. Then I wait for Jess around the bathrooms. I roll the lucky penny between my fingers. *Please let her say yes. Please let her say yes. Please let her say yes,* I chant under my breath. I'm going to do it. I'm going to ask her out.

Giggles emerge from the girls' bathroom. "So, Jess, what's up with you and James?" one of the girls asks.

My hands still as I crane my head toward the doors to listen to her response.

"What do you mean?" Jess asks, seemingly confused.

"Oh come on, you're at Homecoming with a junior. All of us are talking about it. You're living the dream. And you guys hang out so much."

"He's just James, my best friend. You guys know that," she responds. My heart pounds so loudly, I can barely hear her.

A different girl chimes in, "That's what you keep telling us. He's cute in a nerdy way. Do you like him that way? Even a little bit? If you don't, I won't mind you introducing us later on."

A few seconds of eerie silence passes by as I await her answer with bated breath, my hand tightly clutching the lucky penny. The world stills around me as if we're all waiting for her response.

"Ha. That's funny...and ridiculous. James is my best friend. In fact, he's like an older brother I never had, but always wanted." She chuckles, as if the possibility of being with me is absolutely absurd. "Christine, if you like him, I can introduce you guys later. He's really nice and is good boyfriend material. You pass my faux-sister bestie seal of approval."

The girls laugh, their happiness a scalpel to my heart. "Speaking of guys, did you see Billy admiring you earlier, Jess? He couldn't take his eyes off you. Didn't he used to pick on you?"

"No way!" Jess exclaims. "He was staring at me? Yeah, he used to be a bit annoying when we were younger, but I think he grew out of the phase. He's actually pretty nice these days." More laughter sounds from the bathroom.

I stumble away from the building, a painful tightness in my throat, my heart bleeding out as my chest spasms in pain. I've heard about the mythical heartbreak from movies and books, but I've always thought the descriptor was overly dramatic.

Until now.

The wind picks up, and what felt like a hopeful, warm breeze a moment ago now feels cold, as if the wind is mocking me too. The trees rustle as if ridiculing, *who do you think you are, why do you even think Jess will like you that way?* I fight the thousand emotions whirling inside me, trying to calm the madness, the heaviness, the sadness.

"James? James? Where are you?" the melodic voice I've come to love calls from behind me.

I open my palm, wanting to hurl the defective lucky penny as far away from me as possible, but I can't seem to part with it, this piece of Jess I physically carry with me always.

I step out of the shadow and walk back to her. "Hey, took you long enough. Where are the other girls?" I attempt to say light-heartedly, thankful the darkness obscures my face.

Jess looks at me, her eyes reflecting the stars from the sky. "You look a little flustered. You okay? Oh, the other girls went back to their dates."

I rub the back of my neck, forcing myself to appear nonchalant. "I'm fine. Let's go back in. I think we can squeeze in a few more dances before we need to head home."

"Okay!" Jess chirps. "I hope they play some nice slow songs next. I'm all danced out from earlier and could use a break."

Inside the auditorium, Elvis Presley's "Can't Help Falling in Love" blares on the speakers. One of the teachers must have picked this classic gem. Jess grabs my hand and pulls me to the dance floor. "I love this song. A classic, but a goodie."

She twines her hands around my neck as I lightly place mine on her hips, leaving enough space between us to fit the chasm that is what remains of my heart.

"Silly, you have never slow danced before? Come closer, I'm not going to bite." She pulls me flush against her body and places her head on my chest.

The scent of strawberries wafts in the air, a smell I used to love but currently want to run away from, my body and mind warring against each other.

Elvis croons about the fools who can't help themselves and fall in love, hoping the other person will return their affections.

What irony.

I close my eyes, enjoying the feel of her warmth, her small curves pressed up against mine, and pretend the last fifteen minutes did not happen. My mind dreams of a world where she loves me back. I envision my girlfriend in my arms, twirling away to the sound of the music. My hands tighten around her waist as I transport myself from the bleakness of reality to the beauty of my dream.

"You need to move, silly! Don't just stand there. We need to get you some dance lessons later. You won't have any game with moves like that when you go to college," Jess teases, tearing me away from my trance.

I force a halfhearted chuckle. "Sorry, this is my first dance too." I start swaying slowly. "Is this better?"

She beams. "Much better. I'm so glad you are here, James. Thank you for being such a good friend." She snuggles closer.

"Me too, Jess," I whisper back, cradling her head on my chest. There's an indescribable, exquisite pain that comes from being so close to the person you love and yet so out of reach at the same time. The thorns of unrequited love bloody my hands, and yet, I can't seem to let go. It's only a matter of time when the rose will wither, and I'll be the one left with scars. I vow to myself I'll never dance with her again unless she feels the same about me. My heart can't take it. I can't bear it. Our friendship won't survive it.

"May I cut in?" a voice sounds from over my shoulder.

"Hey, Billy," Jess says shyly, tucking a stray lock behind her ear. She glances up at me. "You don't mind, right?"

My jaw clenches, but I reluctantly release her. I grimace in the way of faking a smile. "Of course. I see a few friends outside, so I'm going to chat with them. Have fun, Jess. Meet me in fifteen?"

Jess nods, skepticism in her eyes. I smile back in reassurance, letting her go. She beams at Billy in his Abercrombie and Fitch model glory. He takes her hand and leads her into the heart of the dance floor, disappearing from view.

I step back into the darkness outside.

Friendship.

Perhaps the lucky penny did work after all, revealing Jess's answer before I ask her; before I do irrevocable damage to our friendship. My soul splinters at the thought of not having Jess in my life. Yes, better to have her in my life as friends than to lose her completely.

Friends. That's all we are and all we'll ever be.

• • •

Even though the dance was a long time ago, the pain I thought was gone is now back with a vengeance. It's like coming back to LA has reopened the wound for me.

This time, things will be different. The ending will be different. I'm no longer the helpless boy with nothing to offer. I'm worthy of someone like her now.

I pick up the phone and make a call.

"Hey, it's James. Yes, I'm back." I grin at the greeting from a long-time client from the other end of the line.

"Look, I have a favor to ask. I want to get in at The Beach." I type away at my laptop, sending a few more emails before shutting down the laptop for the night. "Yes, I know it's the hottest restaurant in town and there's a waitlist five miles long. But you owe me one. I saved your ass from buying that stock two years ago."

I pack my bags and head out of the office, waving at a few team members who are still hard at work. "Yes, there's someone I'm wining and dining who deserves the extra fanfare. Save me the best table, okay?" I roll my eyes at his response. "You can grill me about her later...and yes, we're even...for now."

The elevator doors ding open as I disconnect from the call. I'm going to be the best damn dating coach she'll ever have.

So much she'll not want to go on a date with anyone else.

"So, you're sure you still want to make partner? You know, it's a lot of hours and stress. Not really conducive to a young lady's lifestyle." Richard Prescott, aptly nicknamed "Dick" officially and "Dickhead" unofficially in the office, is one of the senior partners on the partnership panel this year. "You know, if you get married and have kids, it'll be very hard to juggle between work and family," he whispers to me as if doing me a favor by unveiling the hardships that go with being a partner at the firm. *Something I've worked years for. So no thank you, I don't need your unsolicited advice.*

My thumb smooths over the jade heart on my wrist and I take a deep breath, rearranging my face into one of gratefulness. "Thank you for looking out for me, Dick. I'm definitely sure I want to be a partner. I believe I'm very capable and have previously considered the issues you pointed out. I'm confident I'll be able to handle any situations that come up." *Stop being such a sexist. Men take care of family nowadays too. I'll only be with someone who can hold his own in the household, not that it's any of your business.*

"All right, dear. Just want to make sure you have thought this through." He arches one brow, appearing unconvinced. I have the highest billable hours at the firm and more importantly, am able to bill any overrun hours I incur on my jobs, yet I still have to put up with this sexist crap. There's a reason why there aren't a lot of women at the top. Who wants to put up with this? *I'll make it up there. I'll help change the tides for the women after me.*

A sudden flash of uncertainty grips me. *Can I do it? If Dick doesn't seem convinced, is he seeing something I don't see?* I clutch the jade, and James's past encouragements filter through the haze of my thoughts. *Yes, this is just another instance of imposter syndrome. I got this.*

I square my shoulders, staring out into the sea of suits and sheath dresses. I spy some hors d'oeuvres and cocktails. "Excuse me, Dick, I see the CFO of a public company I've been courting for a few months. I'm going to say hello." I smile politely at him as I make my way to the other side of the room to continue networking at the firm-hosted finance and accounting professional event.

"I see you've escaped the slimy encounter unscathed." Becca sidles up next to me. "He's such a dick."

I snort. "What else is new. I'm used to it."

"I don't know how you smile and put up with it. I always give him a piece of my mind. He doesn't bother giving me 'unsolicited advice' anymore."

I shrug. "What am I going to do? Tell him how I truly feel? I doubt that'll go over very well."

"You never know. He told me he likes my 'mettle.' Don't put up with that shit." Becca gulps down the rest of her champagne.

"I admire your guts, Becca, I always do. I wish I could be more like you. You need to fight for a spot for me when you make it." Even though we're both going for the same promotion, we're going about it in completely different ways. I'm the poised, graceful candidate and Becca is the firecracker and bulldozer. I marvel at the way she speaks her mind and just goes after what she wants with no qualms about anything.

"Oh shut up. You'll probably make it before I do. I may be a tad too outspoken." She rolls her eyes as if making fun of herself.

"I wouldn't be so sure of that." My breathing becomes quicker as my pulse flutters wildly in my veins. I'm unsure if this is the mythical gut feeling people keep talking about or if it's my usual cycle of intrusive thoughts. "I don't have a good feeling about this."

Becca's eyes turn serious. "Don't think too much about it, okay? Just do it. Everything will fall into place later. You got this." Everyone around me seems to believe I got this but I can't help but wonder if I'm going about this completely wrong.

Just then, Tony, another senior partner at the event, joins our conversation. He is one of the partners I actually enjoy working with at the firm, the antithesis of Dick.

"My favorite ladies. How are you two doing? Got any good networking done here?"

"Can't complain, Tony. Just wrapping up my engagements and I have a few proposals with prospects in the pipeline. I was able to reconnect with a few of them earlier today. Fingers crossed for some good news this week," Becca responds with ease as I ponder how to best answer his question. You want to appear confident but not oversell and fail to deliver later.

"Wonderful, Becca. No pushback on the proposed fees?" Tony inquires. This feels like a test.

Becca passes with ease. "Come on, Tony, who are you looking at?" She chuckles confidently. "Of course they fought on the fees, but I went in at a thirty-percent markup, showed them the audit fees other companies their size were incurring, gave them a ten-percent discount, and convinced them it was a great deal."

Tony nods, pleased at her response. "Good. Good. Did they seem favorable with our position?"

"I'm ninety percent sure they're going to sign with us. After all, one of them is already asking me for accounting advice this past week. I threw in a freebie here and there. Another one is taking me golfing this weekend. I'll get to work on my swing." She winks.

Tony grins. "That's what I like to hear. Go easy on them. I still have nightmares after we went golfing last month."

"Nah, you liked it, Tony. It's not every day you get pummeled by an excellent golfer. Someone has to keep things interesting around here. But you never know, maybe it was an off day for you. I'm always here for a rematch."

Tony guffaws, his loud laughter drawing a few pairs of eyes on us. "I'm definitely taking you up on it. Don't be so sure of yourself yet."

He turns to me and sobers. "What about you, Jess? How are things going with you?"

I flash the high-society smile my mother has trained me on since I was a toddler. "It's going well, Tony. Finished an IPO earlier with a staffing shortage but was still able to collect on all the overrun charges. Prospect-wise, I also have a few in the pipeline. One is close to completion this week. It's a public company and the fees should be lucrative."

Tony dips his head in affirmation. "You're feeling good about this one?"

"I believe so. We had a few lunches, and they already asked for a few revisions. I think they'll get back to me by next week."

"Okay, sounds good." He smiles softly. "Let me know if you need any help. Always here to offer it."

"Thank you, Tony. Definitely appreciate it." Tony winks at both of us and saunters off to join another group of professionals.

I groan internally. That could have gone better. If Becca is Picasso, I'm a toddler's pale version of Picasso. I replay the last few minutes in my mind. Sweat gathers on my forehead as the exchange loops repeatedly in my head. Blood rushes to my face as I dissect every second of the conversation, searching for any flaws or gaffes. I don't think I said anything incorrectly, but it felt...off. Maybe I should have stuck with therapy. Things seemed to be better when I was meeting with Marybeth back in college to help deal with the frequent anxiety and panic attacks after Nana's passing. *No, you don't need help. You are doing just fine. Who doesn't worry about things from time to time? You just worry about them a little more than the average person. You have it handled. You are normal.*

"Tony totally loves you." I smack my hand on my forehead.

Becca laughs. "He's one of the few good ones. I always like making fun of him. He likes you too."

"You think?"

"Yes, I think. He seems happy about your proposal progress and everyone in the firm knows you have the highest utilization rate. You and I are completely different people, so people will respond to us differently. Don't overthink it," Becca reassures. "Okay, girlfriend, I'm going to mingle. Let's get them." She flashes me a smile and disappears into the crowd.

I take out my phone and text James.

Jess: Currently stuck at this networking event. My brain is fried. I don't know how everyone else makes this look so easy.

A response quickly comes back from him.

James: I hate it too. If it helps, fake it 'til you make it. Treat it like any other social event instead of assigning so much weight to it.

Then he followed up with an Oprah meme on networking.

James: You get my business card, you get my business card, and you get my business card... everyone gets my business card!

I snicker under my breath, the tension loosens slightly in my chest, and I read the rest of his text.

James: Just saying, if I'm a prospect, I'll bend over backwards to get the business card from you.

Jess: By the way, are we still on for tonight?

Tonight is the first official "dating coaching" meeting. Even knowing it's James, I can't help but feel very nervous, like a fish out of water. I haven't casually dated in such a long time and even before Ben, I didn't really date around. He pursued me and I got together with him. That was the end of that. My experience is extremely limited. What if I totally suck?

James: Yes, we are. I'll be at your place at eight, is that all right? I have a late meeting in the office.

Jess: Sure, no problem. I'll take care of dinner. Thanks for doing this.

I slip my phone back into my purse and observe the sea of black-and-gray attire with dread. Have to jump back into the shark-infested waters and hope I make it out alive.

• • •

I set the table with two plates of fresh tomato and shrimp pasta in a light garlic cream sauce I whipped up earlier this evening. I rather enjoy cooking when I have time. It feels very similar to meditation—my body moving automatically to chop, dice, sauté, as my mind works through the recipes I've planned for the evening. Then, the dish will be ready, an evident fruit of my efforts. It's extremely satisfying. I pull out a bottle of chardonnay and place it on the table with two wineglasses. Should I set out some candles? No. That'll be too much like a date. But am I supposed to pretend this is a real date so he can assess me? I waffle back and forth between decisions, wondering what I should expect from this evening. *This is James, your best friend. Even if you royally mess this up, it won't matter.* The thought does little to calm the jitteriness pervading my body.

Staring at the mirror in the bedroom, I scrutinize my appearance for the evening. I take out my top bun and let my hair down, soft waves cascading down my shoulders. I debate changing my cashmere sweater and leggings into something more formal but decide against it. This isn't a real date, I remind myself. This is only James.

The doorbell rings and I scramble to open the door. James stands there, looking very much the powerful executive he is and less like the best friend I grew up with. His slim, dove-gray suit clings to his imposing figure. The starched white shirt is opened at the neck, revealing a slither of skin and muscles. A royal-blue checkered tie which brings out his eyes hangs open loosely around his neck, as if he is coming home to his family after a long day of work. I swallow the lump in my throat as my body involuntarily heats up. *Not the boy I used to know.* Warmth rushes to my face and I finally look into his eyes, as if I'm a kid caught stealing from the candy jar.

He stares at me with a wry grin and flashes his pearly whites, thankfully not commenting on my obvious perusal of him just now.

"Hey, you. Ready for some lessons on how to date in the modern world?"

I scrunch up my face in dread. "Ugh. I guess I'm as ready as I'll ever be." I usher him in. "Hope you're in the mood for some pasta."

"Smells wonderful. Thank you." He wraps one muscular arm around my waist and pulls me flush to his side. He gives me a quick squeeze as he sets his briefcase by the door and shrugs off his suit jacket. I automatically take his jacket from him to hang it up. The entire scene feels surreal, like I'm in another alternate universe where James is coming home to *me*.

James rolls up his sleeves, revealing the veiny forearms that are akin to catnip for me, and rummages through the kitchen drawer to find a wine opener. He proceeds to pour two full glasses of wine and sets them back on the table.

"So, did you do what I asked earlier this week?" We sit down and begin eating our meal, the entire scene feeling strangely, yet wonderfully, domestic.

"I did." I retrieve the sheet of paper from my chair and hand it to him. James asked me to draft a sample online profile for him to review. Apparently, online dating is one of the main avenues for meeting people nowadays.

I hold my breath as his eyes move down the page. I can recite what he is looking at.

Name: Jessica "Jess" Kingsley
Age: 28
Height: 5'6"
Eye color: Brown
Hair color: Black
Occupation: Auditor

Brief Bio: I'm a hardworking professional who is currently a senior manager at an accounting firm with career aspirations of becoming a partner soon. I'm a pro at balancing different priorities and can speak two languages fluently. I graduated summa cum laude from college (go ULA!) with a degree in accounting. I enjoy reading, cooking when I have time, and chocolates. I'm the eldest of my siblings with one younger sister and brother. I'm looking for a guy who is interested in a long-term relationship, is family-oriented, and also has a professional career he is passionate about. If you fit the bill, I hope we can meet to see if we are a good fit for each other.

The bio is a bit vague. I wasn't sure what to put in there and didn't want to be overly exclusionary. What if I exclude suitable candidates who don't necessarily fit the bill?

James blinks once.

And he blinks a few more times.

Then, he does the worst thing he can possibly do to my already fragile ego. He bursts out laughing. One hand clutching his stomach, the other hand gripping the paper, his entire body shakes. Mirth dances in his eyes as he tries poorly to contain his amusement.

"Oh God." He groans between chuckles, finally setting down the paper. Both of his hands cover his face as if he doesn't want to look at the offending document any longer.

"What?" I demand, my face hot to the touch. I know it'll need modifications, but I don't expect this reaction. "I read bios should be short and sweet because no one wants to read an essay when they are swiping."

He rubs his face and pinches his nose as he wills his body to calm down. "Yes, yes, that's very true, but man...are you applying for a job...with this?" He bowls over in laughter again.

"James Chapman. If you're just going to sit there and make fun of me, then you can consider yourself fired as my dating coach. I *knew* this was a bad idea. Damn you, Liz and Ems."

Still shaking from laughter, James slowly sobers up. "Sorry, sorry, sorry. Ahem, I shouldn't be making fun of you. But this is pretty hilarious stuff."

I give him a hard glare and he sheepishly continues, "Okay, obviously this needs some work. You want to be short and sweet, which it is, so kudos for that, but you want to sound interesting, to hook the reader in. Give some fun details but no need to lay out a cliff notes of your history or resume."

I nod, grabbing a notebook from the counter and start taking some notes.

"And these photos you picked, they are great for LinkedIn or professional organizations. I mean, they are gorgeous and very polished, but men aren't really looking for professional photos. They're hoping to get a glimpse of the girl in her real-life environment. I'll choose some more natural photos of you in action, doing something you like.

"This is a start, but we definitely have some work to do to improve your bio. It's like an advertisement for yourself. In the sea of bios, you want yours to stand out for the right reason. You want the guy to be able to quickly scan it and be curious enough about you to swipe right," he concludes, pausing to gauge my response.

I groan, rubbing my temples, my body tense from discomfort at the idea of advertising myself to the world. You'd think I'm a middle-aged divorcée looking to get back out in the dating world with my apparent ineptitude with these online dating apps. Why can't things be simple like they were in college? Boy meets girl at a bar or event, boy asks for her number, boy calls girl, dates ensue, they get together. Done. This online advertisement for myself makes my skin crawl. I poke at the remaining spaghetti on my plate.

"You going to finish that?" He eyes my plate as he polishes off his own.

"Ugh, I just lost my appetite. Have at it." I hand him my leftovers.

He moans obscenely as he finishes the last few bites of the meal. "See, this is the stuff you should highlight. What any guy will do for a home-cooked meal like this? It's so good."

"I don't want to be Miss Fifties Housewife, James."

"No one says you need to be a stay-at-home wife if you advertise your cooking skills. Here, don't sweat it. I'll help you with your bio. Do you have your laptop?"

"Yes."

I retrieve my laptop from my bedroom. Staring at the Word document on the screen, I ponder where to start.

The hairs on my neck stand up as an imposing presence warms my back. Sandalwood wafts in the air. James slowly leans over me and cradles me in his arms to set his hands on the keyboard. I freeze, butterflies fluttering in my stomach as my nerves wake and stand to attention.

"So, here I'll make this change...and this." He slowly types away, each keystroke flexing his long fingers and showcasing the corded muscles on his forearms.

"And I'll talk about your passion for life, which isn't only in your professional life but also in your personal life," he whispers, his voice ghosting over my ears, setting my skin on fire.

My hands clutch my sweater in a white-knuckled death grip, inadvertently tugging the wide collar off one of my shoulders. I shiver, even though the air is getting warmer. My breathing quickens as anticipation fills the air.

James pauses as silence permeates the room, leaving only the sounds of our heavy breathing in the air. He shifts closer, every centimeter feeling like a caress. "If I'm on this app," he continues, his gravelly voice dropping an octave, "I'll want to see your best features... Where will I start..." He nuzzles my hair and inhales deeply. "Yes, this hair, every man's dreams."

I gasp, my body locks in tension as heat shoots to my core and I shiver at this rough and husky voice. Wetness seeps through my panties as my mouth parts, my body and mind not getting the message this is our best friend, James. I slowly wiggle around my chair, trying to relieve the ache building in between my thighs, praying he won't notice.

His nose skims my bare shoulder, eliciting goosebumps all over my arms. My nipples peak into hard buds under my sweater and I thank God I'm wearing a thicker bra today. My eyes fall shut, as if hypnotized. The clattering of the keyboard stops. He groans softly behind me as if he is feeling every sensation coursing through my body.

"Strawberries, you smell so good," he rasps, his voice rusty.

He wraps his hands around my silky locks and gives them a tug, eliciting a sharp gasp from me as I tip my head up, baring the quivering pulse in my neck to him. My eyes flutter open, unfocused, as I remain hypnotized by the sensations in my body and the tension in the air.

"It's my sha-aampoo," I stutter.

I want to turn my face to stare into his eyes but am also afraid of what I'll find there. I feel like I'm standing at the edge of a precipice, facing something completely unknown and scary, yet exhilarating.

Riiiiiing. Riiiiiiing. Riiiiiing.

James's cell phone blares to life, pulling me back from the edge. The warmth behind me quickly dissipates as he steps back. He strides over to the kitchen counter to answer the call, his back toward me, his hands clenching.

"Chapman," he answers, his normal baritone voice confident, and his posture slowly relaxes.

"Got it. I'll be there in an hour, need to wrap up some things here first. Thanks." He concludes his call. He rolls his shoulders as he turns around, his face devoid of the previous emotions I sensed in his voice, leading me to wonder if it's all in my head.

"Sorry, Jess, I need to run. An emergency came up at work. All hands on deck. Email me the document and I'll send you back my edits."

I stand, my hands still shaking from moments ago, and I nod. "No worries. I'm no stranger to work emergencies. Thanks for doing this." I point to the laptop on the table.

He cocks his head to the side, his piercing blue eyes smoldering with intensity, his familiar smile now full of secrets I can't decipher.

"Anything for you, Jess."

I came *this close* to kissing her. Her sexy lips were inches away from mine, just begging me for a taste. One little taste. Thank God the office called at that moment because I know it's way too early for us to kiss or for me to dramatically shift the landscape of our relationship. With Jess's anxiety, she'll overthink the smallest actions and she'll spiral.

I groan as I walk toward my car for another late night in the office again. I'm so hard I can burst.

Think data models. Market analyses. Numbers.

Lately it's harder and harder for me to control myself around her. Just simply being in her presence makes me hard. Smelling her scent makes me hard. Wrapping those luscious, shiny locks around my hands make me...hard.

Damn, I need to change this erotic slideshow in my head if I have any hope of getting work done and going home to sleep tonight.

As part of my job, I analyze data sets, risk models, and figure out how to enter the market at the opportune moment to achieve the goals of the company. I just need to do the same with Jess.

Knowing Jess, we're headed toward the right direction. Slow and steady will win the race. Things are already shifting. I can feel it every time we're together. I grit my teeth and start the car, gunning the accelerator as an alternative means to let out my frustration.

Patience, James. Patience. There's the long-awaited date coming up soon. This is an opportunity for you to show her how good things can be between us.

Victory is yours ahead, not another heartbreak.

. . .

Thirteen Years Ago

"Hey! Sorry to keep you waiting." Jess jogs down the steps, her thick hair swishing behind her in a high ponytail.

My heart skips a beat as I glance up from my phone and behold the Siren running toward me. I learned in my advanced placement biology class that love is just a series of bodily chemicals and functions, creating a sense of happiness and attachment. I'm not sure I believe that. Surely, the way my heart automatically beats and flutters every time I see her must be more than a dosage of dopamine and oxytocin, right? The way the world seems to pale against her, the way I'll miss her when we aren't together, that must be more than just a chemical reaction, right? My body apparently hasn't received the memo this girl isn't mine and will never be mine in all the ways that matter.

"No worries. I'm not comfortable driving to and from school yet, anyway. I still have my permit even though I'm finally taking my driving test next week. So, a walk sounds good." I wrap her in what she has recently deemed as the big-brother hug, even though the feelings I have for her are anything but brotherly. I savor the softness of her body against mine, her head tucks under my chin now that I've finally grown a few more inches and am at the six-foot mark.

Jess sighs contently. "You give the best hugs. Always makes me feel better instantly."

I laugh softly and gently squeeze her shoulder. "Did you have a bad day?"

We start walking home in the unforgiving summer heat, the blistering sun merciless to those who aren't indoors or in their cars. *Like you, idiot, who actually chose to be out in the open when you have a car at your disposal.*

"Just stressed about my PSAT scores and diet again. I've already cut down on the fast food and have started an exercise program, but Mother said my physique is still not up to par and I won't have many years until I go to college where I'm expected to look good and attract the right type of men." Her head hangs low, defeated, her face paling as she reflects on her earlier conversation.

"She knows the primary purpose of college is to get a good education, right? Not to find a husband?" I utter sardonically.

Jess nods absentmindedly, as if still reflecting on her mother's words. "Yeah, she says she's aware of that. But she also said the prime dating pool is at college and it's harder to meet the right person once you are out in the workforce. She said a woman is like a car. They're beautiful on the lot when they are brand spankin' new, and then once you drive it off the lot, they immediately depreciate at a rapid speed."

She starts playing with the red bracelet I bought her. A spark of hope flashes through me. If she's still wearing the bracelet every day, do I still have a chance?

"So, in her example, I guess college is the new car lot and the real world is when we get driven off the lot and start getting old?" She grimaces, as if not looking forward to her bleak future. Sweat beads her forehead, her breathing quickens as she hunches over, and her hands grip her knees as she tries to catch her breath.

"Hey, hey, hey." I snap my fingers in front of her face, knocking her out of her despondence and what I've come to recognize as the beginning of her anxiety spiral.

"That is pure bullshit. Don't buy into that crap. You're not a car; you'll never be a car. It's not even the right comparison. If anything, I think women are like art. The first few strokes on the canvas may be simplistic, and then after the entire work is done, the more you look at it and see it in different times of the year, in different lighting, the more you fall in love with it." I pause on the side of the road, tilting her chin up to look at me. The rays of sunlight reflect in her irises, the golden-brown hues rimming with flecks of emeralds.

"Wow. I like your analogy much better. Thank you." Her full lips pull up into a small smile. The color returns to her face and her breathing slows down. The tip of her tongue darts out to wet the corners of her tempting mouth. My eyes automatically track the movement as images of me softly kissing the same corners flash through my mind. My breathing quickens as I will my body not to respond.

We resumed our saunter toward home. "Don't live your life to please others. Live for yourself," I reply.

"Easy for you to say. Your parents are so awesome." She gives me a playful shove. "You know, this is the longest I've ever stayed in one place. We would move every two to three years when we were kids. I didn't ever really have any roots or friends until you. My family was all I had. I don't want to disappoint her."

I smile, thinking about my happy childhood. As chaotic as my household is, my parents were so warm and affectionate, the complete opposite of the Kingsleys. Perhaps I shouldn't judge unless I've lived a day in her shoes.

"Sorry to overstep. Hope you aren't mad. I just want you to be happy. Screw what other people want from you."

"No, don't be sorry! I know you're saying this out of love. Like I said before, I'm glad you're my best friend." *Best friend. Brother.* Words I absolutely loathe coming out of her mouth. "You do wonders for a girl's ego," she teases.

"It's not flattery, but reality. If only you could see how other people see you." I gently place my arms around her shoulders. "You are perfect. Just the way you are."

She softens against me as she wraps her arm around my back. It's so easy to imagine this is a date, and my girlfriend is by my side. I take a deep breath and pull myself out of my beautiful daydream. *Dreams, that's what they are*, I remind myself.

Her large house looms ahead, still as imposing as it was when we were younger. She disentangles from me and exclaims, "I forgot to tell you something important. I can't believe I didn't tell you earlier."

Raising my right eyebrow in question, I wait for her as her eyes dart around surreptitiously. She leaned in and whispers, "Billy kissed me at lunch today. My first kiss! I think we're a couple now." Her face flushes a pretty pink, as if she's embarrassed and happy at the same time.

I've always wondered how the word heartbreak came to be. A heart can't break. After all, it's just a muscle pumping blood to our body. But now I realize how aptly named the word is because nothing else can describe the sharp pain in my chest that takes my breath away. I clench my hands into a tight fist as I struggle to show happiness for her when I want to do nothing more than to punch a wall, to shake her and ask her why, or to kiss the luscious lips I've been dreaming of for years in order to show her everything I've been bottling inside.

"R-really? You and Billy, huh?" That's all I can manage as I fight to even out my breathing, the invisible noose choking my neck.

"Yep." She twirls a strand of her hair around her fingers, her face dreamy as she recalls the events. "He was so sweet to me. He asked me if he could kiss me and then if I could be his girlfriend."

I tear my gaze from her, a turmoil of emotions roiling inside me. I chuckle humorlessly. "I guess I was right those years ago. He was into you."

Jess pauses and gasps, as if recalling what I said a few years ago. "You totally called it!" She giggles again. "Jess and Billy, it has a nice ring to it, don't you think?"

She spins around and waves her hands in the air, her long locks cascading around her, very much like a fairy dancing under the sun. She's mesmerizing.

I clench my jaw so hard the muscles start to ache. Deep down, I knew this would happen eventually. Someone would capture her heart. But nothing has prepared me for this moment. I just want to crawl into bed and sleep, forgetting today, and perhaps dreaming about a world where she is mine...and mine alone.

A few weeks pass by and a sudden chill settles over the city. Los Angeles rarely rains, but when it does, it's usually a welcome respite to the blistering heat. I sit on my living room couch, staring at pouring rain hammering against the windows, the streets devoid of people as folks hide in their houses due to this unusual weather. No one wants to be caught in traffic during the rain. The sky is gray, the wind is howling, the clouds are blotting out the cheery sunshine we're used to seeing. Befitting my mood, I think, as I reflect on the conversation Jess and I had a few weeks ago, when she sliced my heart open with her news regarding Billy.

I haven't seen her much this week. Naturally, she wants to spend time with her boyfriend. I scoff at the word, angry at myself for caring, angry at her for not knowing, angry at him for taking her away.

Lightning flashes across the sky, followed by the roar of thunder as Mother Nature throws a tantrum, punishing us all. Even the sky feels my pain. For once, things are working in my favor.

"Wow, it's really pouring out there huh?" Dad comes up behind me, staring out the window.

"Yep," I grunt, keeping my eyes on the fantastical elements outside, the storm mirroring the tempest in my soul.

More sounds rumble in the background as I continue to drown in my misery. A second pair of footfalls come up behind me. Mom whispers something to Dad.

"Son. We have something to tell you."

I turn away from the window, temporarily distracted by Mom's serious tone, which is very uncharacteristic of her usually energetic self. Mom and Dad are sitting down in the armchairs next to me, their faces somber.

"What's going on? Your faces are scaring me. Did something bad happen?" I ask, my heart thundering for a different reason.

Lightning flashes across the sky and another rumble of thunder reverberates around the house. A harbinger of doom. Temporary silence fills the room. The grandfather clock quietly ticks away, as if counting down to the moment when everything changes. Unease prickles my skin, my sixth sense coming alive. I have a feeling something will happen that'll change the course of my life forever.

My parents glance at each other. Dad gives an imperceptible nod to Mom.

"Honey, we're moving to Boston," she says softly.

"W-what? When? Why?" I demand. My life is over here. My friends are over here. *Jess is over here*, my soul whispers to me.

"You know Grams is getting old, and she needs family to be around her. Your sister is already out there for college. Your dad also got a really wonderful job offer to work for a prominent engineering firm there. It seems like the right time for a move," Mom explains, oblivious to my inner turmoil.

"You *can't* just move because this is all 'convenient' for you! My life is here. Why did no one ask me?" I stand up and my body shakes with shock and anger. "I don't want to leave. I want to stay *here*!"

Mom gets up and slowly approaches me. "Honey, I know this is hard for you. We weren't really sure about this until the job opportunity came through this week. We didn't want to tell you if we weren't sure about it. And, you'll be off to college soon anyway, so we just thought..."

I yell, "What *did* you think? That I'd be happy about this? That it doesn't matter anyway because I'll be off to college? My friends are here. *I* want to be here." My chest heaves, fingers clenching. "Jess is here!" The words finally explode out of me.

"James... Oh honey." Mom wraps her arms around me as I feel the prickle of tears in my eyes. I halfheartedly struggle as my mom hugs me even tighter. I can't imagine living in a city without Jess. Who'll she go to when she has issues? Who'll take care of her when she is sad or anxious?

"Honey, I just thought...didn't you tell me Jess has a boyfriend now? I know you loved her for a long time, but it pains us to see you like this, so despondent. Won't it be a good thing to get away from this? To have a fresh start?"

Oh yes, Jess has Billy now. The reminder sobers me. My hands fall to my sides, hanging loosely as the bleeding in my heart slowly extinguishes the anguish and inferno within. Unshed tears cling to my eyelashes.

Sensing my change, Mom reassures, "Honey, you can still keep in touch with her. We can come back and visit. You can call her. Maybe later on, you may end up in the same college. If it's meant to be, you'll find your way back to each other."

"Son, I remember my first heartbreak. It was very painful." Dad clasps my shoulder. "You're not truly a man until you experience the pain and then you'll grow from it. And you'll find the right someone who deserves the new you. This will become the past and you'll come out stronger than before."

I disentangle myself from my parents and nod in defeat. "I get it. I just need some time to process this. When are we leaving?"

"In three weeks. We'll complete a home school curriculum for the rest of the quarter, and you'll start at your new school next quarter," Mom replies.

I bow my head and study the lucky penny I pulled from my wallet. "Just give me some time, then I'll prepare my things," I whisper, staring at the shiny copper that still appears to be as new as the day I received it.

My parents lightly pat my shoulder and exit the room, leaving me to my thoughts. I stare at the weeping clouds, the world that once was in technicolor now a muted gray. I take out my phone and hover above Jess's number. Taking a deep breath, I dial.

"Hello?" Her sweet voice comes across the line. Raucous laughter fills the background.

"Jess." My mouth dries.

"James? Is everything okay?" she inquires. I can picture the little frown marring her perfect face.

"I...I have something to tell you." I take another fortifying breath, my heart clenching in pain, as if being stabbed by multiple daggers.

"Okay... Sorry for the noise in the background. I'm at a party at Billy's place."

Billy. Yes, she has Billy. This is probably just harder on me. *She won't be alone, so you don't need to worry about her, James.*

"No problem. This will be quick." My breathing grows ragged, my fingers rub the smooth penny, the defective penny that has never brought me the luck I wished for.

"I'm moving to Boston."

And so, this begins the end of us.

"**W**hat about this guy?" I show the profile on my screen to Liz, who is sitting next to me on the sofa in my apartment. The guy is easy on the eyes. Blond hair, blue eyes, a lawyer by trade with muscles like one of the superheroes on TV.

"Hmmm..." Liz scrutinizes the profile on my *InstaConnect* app. She quirks her mouth to one side. "Nope. Too many red flags."

Emily grabs the phone with the enthusiasm of a toddler. "Let me see!"

We decide to have our girls' night earlier in the afternoon since James is picking me up tonight for our simulation "date." Now that he has fixed my profile, he tells me he needs to see me in action to gauge how I behave around potential male interests. My stomach churns at the thought of going on a first date again, even though it's with James. Will it be weird and awkward? I quickly push the thought aside. Of course not, it's James. *He won't judge you.*

"Oh yeah, totally too many red flags. He's 'not looking for any drama.' What does that even mean? He doesn't want to argue? He wants you to acquiesce to all of his opinions?" Emily frowns, swiping through the photos. "Ugh. Half-naked men in the bedroom. I don't know why they do this. Is this supposed to show how hot he is and indicate his prowess in bed? It's so cliché."

Liz nods along as if commiserating in the mutual pain of wading through a swamp infested with leeches coming in the form of horrible *InstaConnect* profiles. "I've seen so many half-naked selfie photos too. I don't know why they do that either...and look at this gem, he says he 'works hard, plays hard.' From my experience, that usually means he's a party animal. I don't peg you for that lifestyle, Jess."

"Nope. Definitely not me. Drop me in a bookstore or a poetry slam instead, please." I sigh. "This online dating thing feels so unnatural. We're judging people based on a paragraph or two and a few photos? And the men are doing the same to us? How do you possibly know if there is any chemistry or other qualities about the other person? Surely, we're much more than a handful of superficial words on the screen?"

Liz clinks her glass of rose with mine and takes a big gulp. "Hear, hear. I totally agree with you, but that's the world these days. I guess it's more efficient than going out and trying to meet someone, but seriously, it's so exhausting. I sometimes wonder if I unintentionally swipe left on guys that are right for me because they don't know how to write a good profile. And because there are so many choices now, no one really sticks around to find out if there are more layers of someone to discover. Everyone defaults to quickly cutting their losses and moving on."

Liz has been dating on and off the past few years, not quite settling down with anyone because she claims she hasn't met the one yet. She's a hopeless romantic, and understandably so, since she has witnessed her parents' loving relationship growing up. I'd want the same too if I were in her shoes.

"Well, I tell you, that's why it's easier just to date around and have fun." Emily smirks. "Use them and dump them. Go in with no expectations. That way, if you like a guy because of his profile photos, go out with him, maybe spend a few weekends holed up in a hotel and then move on. If he's cool, then hang out longer. No pressure." This is very on brand for Emily, who never has a shortage of men to cater to her needs. Perhaps it's her devil-may-care attitude that attracts men to her like bees to honey.

I pick up the phone and swipe left on the bedroom guy. A few more profiles of half-naked men appear on my screen.

"Ewww...this one says he's ten inches long. TMI." I shake my head and swipe left.

"Guy holding a baby... Oh look, he says it's not his. I assume this is the same as a guy holding a fish?" I look up at the girls and they nod vigorously in unison. "All right then, swiping left. The baby is really cute though," I say wistfully. I do love children. My plan is to have them soon, but alas, life doesn't often work out the way you want it to.

A new profile pops up on the screen. Golden-brown hair in a tousled but put together hairstyle. Emerald eyes and a smile that can double for a toothpaste commercial. Dimples. A strong Roman nose and a jaw that can cut glass. I can't help but smile at the photo; this guy's smile is infectious. Parker Wellington. Thirty-four years old. Architect. I swipe through a few photos, him with friends at a bar, him at a book fair (Huzzah! He reads!), an artsy one of him holding a baby in silhouette so the baby's face isn't clear.

"What about this one?" I show the screen to the ladies, who crowd in to stare at the profile with the attention of a trader analyzing stock performance on the floor of the New York Stock Exchange.

"Ooo very cute. From appearances alone, I'll say ten out of ten." Emily whistles in appreciation.

"It says he's 'looking for a long-term partner, someone to share life's adventures with and someone to ride with him on the ups and downs that come with the territory.' Seems like he's looking for something serious and long-term, which aligns with what you're searching for," Liz concludes, her eyes glued to the screen. "And he's really hot."

"What about the baby pic? Isn't that a no go?" I ask, directing them to the last photo.

"You're right! There's a baby pic." Emily scrolls down farther on the profile. "Oh, here it is. Unlike the other guy whose baby is just a prop, Parker actually notes 'you must love kids because he's a widower and a proud father of the cutest four-year-old on the planet.'"

Liz's eyes tear up. "Aw...he lost his wife. Poor little girl, losing her mom at such a young age."

"I think he's a good candidate if you don't mind kids, Jess. He seems sincere and not likely to jerk you around. He should be a good first date for you since you haven't been out in the world for so long." Emily hands the phone back to me and finishes the rest of her drink.

I drink a sip of water and stare at Parker's smiling face. Do I mind kids? No, I actually don't. I want children for myself, so if he's the one for me and he happens to have a kid, I won't mind that at all. Mind made up, my fingers tremble as I complete my first "right swipe" on the app. I let out a huge breath. Suddenly, I feel a little lighter than before. For better or worse, I'm moving forward, and that's a win for today.

"Done. Swiped right."

"Hurray! Cheers. To Jess, moving on and finding the right guy." Liz dabs her eyes with a tissue paper. She's one of the sweetest souls I know. How she's still single, I'll never understand.

We clink our glasses together and laugh. It's good to have the girls around.

"So, what are your plans with James tonight?" Emily asks.

I bite my lower lip. "So, after the disaster that was my dating profile..." I begin. The girls snicker since I previously shared the PG version of the night with them. "James thinks it'll be a good idea to take me on a fake date to see how I 'behave' when I go on dates. I don't know what he's so worried about. Ben and I went out on dates all the time," I mutter, a bit offended at the notion I don't know how to date.

"Sorry, girl, I'm with James on this one. I know this is still a sore spot for you, but you and Ben didn't exactly end up in a good place, right? It doesn't hurt to get another man's perspective on you 'in date mode,'" Emily says, as pragmatic as ever.

I believe her. This is her strong suit, her ability to analyze a problem and to provide solutions or paths forward, something she does daily as an image consultant.

I reluctantly concur. "He's coming over at six to take me to The Beach," I answer, referring to a popular restaurant by the pier.

The establishment sits on stilts above the ocean and the views are known to be spectacular.

"That place is so hard to get into," Liz exclaims, as if amazed by her brother's efforts.

"I know. He told me the restaurant owner is one of their clients, so he was able to get a last-minute reservation."

"How convenient." Emily cocks her brows, skepticism on her face.

"You did the same with brunch at Le Cirque," I deadpan, daring her to contradict me.

"Hmmm...whatever."

"Okay, regardless of his *intentions*, I just have *one* rule for all of this practice-dating thing you guys have going on," Liz announces.

Emily and I stare at her quizzically.

"I absolutely don't want details of any hookups between the two of you," Liz declares, appearing a little green at the thought of her brother's sex life. Emily busts out in laughter as I stare at Liz, the idea never occurring to me before.

My face turns burning hot as I recall his raspy voice in my ear the other night and my body's involuntary reaction. *No, Jess, this is just basic biology. You had a moment of attraction that sometimes happens between a man and a woman. Nothing more, nothing personal. A fluke.*

"Oooo you're so red, sis! Did something already happen?" Emily waggles her brows, grinning gleefully.

"Nope. Nope. Nope. Not listening." Liz sticks her fingers in her ears and starts humming, resembling the kindergarteners she teaches at school.

"Oh, stop it! Nothing happened. It's James, you people. We're best friends, nothing more. He's like the older brother I never had," I proclaim, hoping my voice sounds confident, even though there is a nagging kernel of unease inside me.

"Uh huh...whatever you say, sis." Emily's grin mocks me.

Liz exhales. "One more thing on this topic then we're moving on." She pauses for maximum effect. "Use protection kids, always use protection."

Emily's raucous laughter fills the room as Liz's cackling joins hers. I grab the nearest pillow and toss it at them. I shake my head at their amusement.

Me and James. What nonsense.
Or is it?

CHAPTER 13

Jess

Nervously fiddling with the red beads of my bracelet, I glance at the clock on the living room wall. Five forty-five p.m. I stride to the full-length mirror by the door and check my appearance. Loose waves set in a light-hold hairspray. Check. Makeup artfully applied—a smoky eye with winged liner and nude lip gloss. Check. Tags removed from clothing. Check. I bought a new dress for this occasion, a black satin piece with a sweetheart neckline in the front, a deep V-cut back, and a hem hitting at mid-thigh. Crystal-studded Louboutins sit by the door.

I take a deep breath. *This is just for practice, Jess. Nothing serious. You're just going out with your best friend. You can do this.* I breathe out, timing my exhales longer than my inhales in an effort to calm the butterflies in my stomach. I pace around the foyer, jittery for no apparent reason, my body locks in a fight-or-flight dance as I wait for James's arrival.

I can do this. I can do this. I repeat to myself. *This is just for practice. This is Jam—*

Buzz. Buuuuzzzzzz.

I jump, my heart in my throat, pulse racing as I clasp my hand on my chest. I shakily smooth out my dress one last time and take one last fortifying breath before I open the door.

"Hey, gorgeous."

James's eyes travel down my body in a quick sweep, his eyes flashing in appreciation. James decked out in date wear is a sight to behold. His normally tousled hair is carefully combed, and my fingers twitch with an impulse to run through the thick strands. He wears a slim-fitted black suit with a crisp, pale-blue shirt that drapes over his muscles like a second skin. The attire brings out the brilliant blue of his eyes, which are currently fixed to my face in a smoldering stare.

I gape at the Adonis before me, rendered speechless. My breath hitches. At my expression, he slowly smiles, his expression suave and confident, and reaches out from behind him with a bouquet I didn't see before as I was too distracted by this familiar, handsome stranger that's apparently James.

"I got these for you. They are gardenias and gladiolus. The florist said they mean loveliness, integrity, and strength. Just like you."

I gather the gorgeous bouquet and slowly caress the delicate petals. The sweet smell of gardenias permeates the air.

"They are lovely, thank you. You didn't have to do this. This is a practice date, after all." I glance up at him from under my lashes.

"If we're going to do this, we should do it right. And you should always expect to be wooed on a first date. You deserve nothing less," he says gently, his voice smoky as he pins me with his gaze.

I smile shyly at him, my voice catching in my throat. "Come in. L-let me set these inside and we can get going."

He follows me inside the apartment and lingers in the foyer. I quickly close the door behind us and set the flowers on the kitchen counter. My hands touch my warm face, my pulse pounds in my ears. Even though I know this is not a real date, my body apparently doesn't care. I lightly rub my hands over my heart to soothe the pounding beats and remind myself while the man outside may not resemble the boy who left for Boston all those years ago, he's still the same person inside.

This is James. This is just practice. This isn't real. I chant softly to myself. Three deep belly breaths later, I smooth my expression into a polite smile, one I'll give to a new man on a first date and meet him in the foyer.

"Ready?" He extends his elbow to me, his muscles flexing under the fitted suit jacket. He should give his tailor a nice tip for doing such a great job.

I gingerly hook my arms around his. "Let's go." I stare at the ground, feeling uncharacteristically shy.

The drive to the restaurant is quiet. An unspoken tension fills the air, throwing me off-balance. It's as if we can't decide whether to behave normally or to behave like this is an actual real date. We engage in small talk about the weather—I can't believe we're talking about the weather—and he tells me about some projects he is involved in at work. I fiddle with the hem of my dress and sneak glances at him. This familiar stranger, with his sapphire eyes focused on the road, one hand on the steering wheel, the other hand resting on the gearshift, he looks like he has stepped right out of a luxury car commercial. The synapses of my brain are misfiring, having problems connecting this male specimen next to me to my best friend of many years.

He glances sideways at me, his beautiful lips—something I should not be noticing—tip up in a secret smile, and he reaches over to cover my hand, which apparently has moved from fiddling with the hem of my dress to toying with my bracelet. Warmth envelops me, tingles traveling up my body as his calloused hand squeezes mine, his thumb lightly circling the sensitive skin of my wrist. Goosebumps prickle my skin as I draw in a shaky breath, unable to control the sensations in my body.

"Okay. I have some rules for you." His deep baritone voice echoes in the car.

I tear my gaze from our hands and peer up at him in confusion. "Rules?"

"This dating advising thing, I don't want it to affect our friendship." He stares ahead as the restaurant comes into view. "You're my best friend and you'll forever be my best friend, no matter what you do or say. I want you to get out of your head and don't be afraid of offending me or doing something I don't like while we're 'practicing.' This is just a dinner between us. Jess and James. Take the pressure off." He gives my hand a soft squeeze in reassurance, as if sensing my inner turmoil.

"Just a dinner..." I echo.

"Yes, just a dinner between us. No stress."

My nerves still as we sit in the quiet car. Apparently, we've already arrived, but I was so lost in my thoughts I didn't notice.

"Ready?" Another glance, another warm smile.

I nod. *This is just a dinner between Jess and James.* I repeat the mantra in my head as James opens the car door and escorts me to the restaurant.

The Beach opened five years ago and since its opening, its popularity hasn't waned. Now that I'm physically here, even without tasting the food, I can see why. Doormen hold open the doors for us as we enter an impressive white-marble foyer. The crystal chandeliers hanging low actually use real candles, the warm light flickering off the high ceilings and white walls, giving an intimate glow to the room.

"Chapman for two." James laces his fingers with mine, sending a fissure of awareness through me. I flush as goosebumps reappear on my skin from such a simple gesture. Thank goodness the lighting is low in here.

I engage my five senses, a tip Marybeth gave me in the past to use whenever I felt anxious or out of sorts. This occasion definitely calls for some tricks.

Sights. I glance at the dining area beyond the foyer. White tablecloths, three candle votives of different sizes decorate each table. Each table spaced far apart from each other, with potted plants inter-spacing the room, creating privacy for each party. Floor-to-ceiling windows showcase the Pacific Ocean in its full glory. The sunset on the horizon, the sky in brilliant flames of red and yellow trailing off to the deepest purple and blue. The million-dollar view.

Sounds. The quiet chatter of the patrons. The clinking of silverware against plates. Soft laughter. Beautiful melodies of the harp and violin as musicians become one with their instruments.

Smells. Lavender and sea salt, an interesting combination that works well together. Fragrant aroma of butter and seafood. I take another deep breath. Sandalwood, reminding me of the man standing next to me.

Touch. Long fingers caress mine in an intimate dance, shivers dance up my skin, heat shoots—

I snap myself out of the meditative state. I should have stopped at the smells.

The waitress leads us to a corner table, which I presume is high in demand given the two walls of windows on both sides. James pulls out my chair as I sit down and stare at the views, completely awestruck. I feel like we are dining on water.

"Wow. This is beautiful," I exclaim in wonder, mesmerized by the waves washing up to the windows and the vivid watercolor painting the sky.

"I know in those romantic movies you watch I'm supposed to stare at you and agree with you," James begins sardonically as I switch my attention to him.

"But I agree, the view is definitely very beautiful. And as for you..." he continues, reaching over the table to clasp my hand in his, lifting it up to his lips, "you always dazzle me, more than any ocean views, more than the warm sunset in front of us. You're absolutely breathtaking." He holds my eyes in a piercing stare as he softly kisses the back of my hand.

My breath catches. Time slows. Heart skips a beat or two. I'm held captive by his stare and his softly spoken words. I wrench my gaze away from his and force a light chuckle.

"Wow, James. You're good. Really good at this. Definitely not the nerd I remember back in high school."

His eyes shutter as he pulls back. "Rule number one, when a man compliments you, accept it. You're worth all the compliments."

Right. This is just practice. "Okay. Got it. I just feel weird sitting there and 'accepting' praises. God knows I have a lot of flaws. I mean, who doesn't? I definitely stress eat during my busy season and I haven't been to the gym so I have a belly pooch I need to lose, and—" Words tumble out and I'm helpless to stop the tirade.

"Jess. Jess. Look at me." He squeezes my hand and I realize

his fingers are still intertwined with mine. I start to pull away, but he holds on tight, forcing me to look up at him.

"Just say thank you." He smiles. "Women are very hard on themselves. Us men are simple creatures. We don't notice the details, only the big picture. I only see a gorgeous woman, in a dress that should be illegal, willing to share a meal with me. Your perceived flaws are all in your head and aren't a reflection of reality. If you don't believe you're worth the compliments and praise, why will others see you as such?"

I swallow the lump in my throat. "T-thank you."

"Good girl." He nods as he lets go of my hand to peruse the menu, his unfamiliar dominance throwing me off. His praise is an arrow to my core. Unbidden images of him whispering the words to me in bed as our limbs tangle together shock me. Do I have some sort of praise kink I don't know about?

I quickly glance away and stare at the menu, hoping he doesn't notice my fluttering pulse. The menu has no prices, temporarily confusing me and thankfully drawing my attention away from my wayward thoughts.

"I know it's a bit chauvinistic, but a lot of high-end restaurants have two sets of menus for guests. One set for men with prices and another set for women without prices." He quirks one brow at me.

"You have an uncanny ability to read my mind," I mutter, hoping he didn't read my thoughts a minute ago.

He barks out a laugh. "No, you just have a very expressive face." He sets his menu down and continues, "Don't worry about the prices. Let me treat you. We've been apart for so many years, I haven't had a chance to take you out for your eighteenth or twenty-first birthdays, or to celebrate your promotions at work. This is long overdue."

"Well, if you put it that way. I'll take it." I hum happily, the earlier tension temporarily dissipating.

We order a dozen fresh oysters on the half shell as an appetizer, a pan-seared salmon with truffle cream for him, and jumbo scallops with garlic aioli for me. The server melts into the background after taking our orders, leaving us to enjoy the intimate environment.

James pours wine into my glass, a sauvignon blanc recommended by the restaurant's sommelier.

"Thank you for fixing my online profile." I swirl the glass before taking a small sip, the crisp notes refreshing to my senses.

He chuckles. "You're welcome. You definitely need the help, no offense." His eyes sparkle with mirth.

"Hey, it was my first time. How was I supposed to know what to write?" I defend myself. "Anyway, you must have done a good job because I got a lot of candidates on the app."

James studies the wine intently, unwilling to look into my eyes. He mutters something under his breath which sounds like *not surprised*?

"What did you say? Sorry I didn't hear you."

He glances up and shrugs, his voice flat. "Nothing. Glad I could help. That's what I'm here for."

I nod, a bit unsettled by his change in tone. "Anyway, how's work going?"

Work. Always a safe topic for any first date. Not that this is a first date. Or a real date.

James warms up immediately and proceeds to tell me about the current projects he is heading up. Both he and I live in the world of numbers, but our roles can't be any more different. Whereas I make sure the numbers being reported by companies are accurate, a "numbers police" of sorts, his world involves analyzing massive quantities of data to predict behaviors.

"I really believe with our increasing reliance on technology these days, there's a treasure trove of data for us to comb through. The behavior patterns are lying out there, waiting for us to review, and I think this platform I'm working on will be in the forefront of predicting consumer behavior before it actually happens. Can you imagine what'll happen if companies can predict what you want to purchase tomorrow, how you want to spend your money before you spend it? The applications are endless and not only for capital investments, which my firm naturally is focused on." He gestures with his hands animatedly as he describes the initiatives he is part of. I've never seen this passionate side of him before, as our overseas video or phone calls mainly consist of checking in with each other and filling each other in on our personal lives.

"Enjoy your meal and let me know if you have any needs." The server appears from the background to place the plates of food on the table.

James thanks him and proceeds to distribute oysters to my plate. I drizzle a dash of lemon juice onto an oyster and slowly bring it up to my lips, carefully sliding it into my mouth in order to not spill on the table or on my dress. It's rather difficult to elegantly eat oysters in public.

The oysters melt in my mouth, a fresh taste of the ocean fills my tastebuds. "Mmmm...this is so fresh and delicious," I moan as I swipe my tongue quickly across my lips to lick off the juices.

The soft melody of the harp fills the moment of silence. I peer up to find James's dark gaze snared to my lips, a look of hunger in his eyes disappearing as quickly as it comes, leading me to wonder if it's all in my head.

"So, if your platform is a success, do you think you'll stay at the firm long-term, or are you going to be searching for your next project?" I follow up, genuinely interested in his work.

James clears his throat and finishes his food. Dabbing his lips with his napkin, he takes a large gulp of water, his Adam's apple bobbing in the strong column of his neck with each swallow, something else I haven't noticed before.

"The firm gives me a lot of resources to work on these projects because they stand to have a high return on investment. It's nice to have such a big budget and it'll be a good way to jumpstart my research. But my plan is to eventually go into academia, publish some papers, and continue the research. I'm hoping one day I'll be able to give back to society and leave my mark in the data science field."

I quietly savor the scallops, cooked to perfection, and contemplate his answer. He seems to have his future figured out, a target he is marching toward, one he is passionate about. What about me? What do I really want? Is it really to make partner at the firm? Or is it something I want because it's the next rung on the ladder, the next checkmark on my list?

"That's impressive, James. I really think if anyone can achieve that, it'll be you." I look him in the eyes, hoping he can see my sincerity.

A soft smile graces his face, his eyes crinkle at the corners. "What about you? Partnership?"

I frown, staring into the dimming sunset, the golden hues melting away to a clear night sky. "That'll be the next logical choice. Panel interviews are at the end of next month. We'll see... The competition is tough and I'm not sure I have too much to bring to the table that others can't do better. My friend Becca is also up for interviews this year and she's such a rockstar. If she gets it and I don't, I'll truly be happy for her." And I honestly will. While I doubt my abilities, I have an unwavering belief in her capabilities. She'll make a brilliant partner and set a good example for all the women trying to follow in her footsteps in the firm.

"Ye of little faith. Take it one step at a time. A path will reveal itself." He sits back, staring out into the starry sky. "I believe in you. Your heart is in the right place, but your mind is in overdrive, preventing you from moving forward. I think deep down, you know what you want, but you just need to take the thinking out of it."

I sigh, exasperated at myself. "That's the problem. I overthink a lot. It's like the constant chatter in my brain sounds a lot like Mother, reminding me of the perils of every decision, scrutinizing my every move, questioning if I'm ever good enough."

"Or, perhaps, you're more prepared for any outcome that's thrown at you than other people. And when you finally make a decision, you have made one that you'll not regret because you have put in a lot of effort into analyzing it at every angle. Your anxiety can be called vigilance, right?" James counters. "Double-edged sword, your self-perceived weaknesses are also your strengths." He glances at me. "And I'd like to think that your strengths make you who you are, someone who cares a lot, even too much, about everything and everyone."

"Well, if you put it that way..." I return his smile.

"Now, tell me why you're on the app."

"What? James, you know—" He stops me with a quelling look. Right, this is a fake date. He's not supposed to know my history.

"Well, I just got out of a long relationship, and I want to see what's out there. What about you?"

"Same here. I'm searching for that special someone to spend the rest of my life with." His smoldering eyes glitter in the candlelight as he holds my gaze.

I swallow, taken aback. The conversation has taken a turn in a direction I had not anticipated. The lines of fake and reality begin to blur.

"So, what are you looking for in a partner?" I inquire, attempting to steer the discussion back to familiar waters.

His eyes bore into mine, the royal blues darkening into a deep blue-black. He leans forward and unbuttons his blazer. "Someone who has a good heart, someone who's loyal to a fault, someone who'll stop injustices when she encounters them in the world. Someone without artifice." The silence crackles between us as I'm ensnared by his stare.

He blinks, glancing away, and resumes our game. "What about you?"

"I—just like what you said," I agree, not knowing how to respond to his question. They say agreeing with someone's opinion endears you to them, right?

"Rule two, don't answer what you think I'll want to hear. Tell me how you truly feel. Variety is the spice of life, right? The right man will truly be interested in what you have to say, even if your opinion differs from his."

I purse my lips and try again. "I guess I'm looking for someone who'll accept me for who I truly am. Someone who loves bookstores more than bars, who prefers quiet evenings at home rather than going out. Someone who doesn't mind I may think too much, speak too little. Someone I'm comfortable with, who'll cherish me for who I am." *Someone who will stay for me. Someone who will be my home,* I finish in my mind, already revealing far too much and leaving me feeling too exposed. I'm not sure if it's the alcohol releasing my inhibitions or if it's the company, but the words flow out automatically. *Now he'll probably think you are too needy,* the nagging voice in my mind says.

James dips his head in acknowledgement. "Who wants noisy bars when you can have the company of books and coffee? Traveling far yet not going anywhere at the same time. Sometimes, you don't have to go very far to find what you're searching for." His eyes indecipherable as he holds my gaze.

"Would you like any dessert for tonight?" the waitress materializes next to the table as I find dessert menus in front of me, the dishes apparently cleared off the table during our conversation.

I look wistfully at the menu. They have an array of sorbets, cakes, and a molten chocolate souffle with coconut cream and homemade French vanilla ice cream. *You probably shouldn't eat desserts. Metabolism slows down as you age. You don't want to let yourself go.*

I push the menu away and smile at the waitress. "No thank you, I'm good. The meal was delicious."

"What about you, sir?" the waitress directs her question at James, whose eyes are on me.

"I'll have the molten chocolate souffle. Thank you." The waitress nods and takes the menus away.

I quickly glance at him, surprised. I thought he hated chocolate. "Have I finally converted you into a chocolate lover?" I tease.

He taps his long fingers on the table.

"Ha. No, you haven't. The dessert is for you. Rule number three: men like women to eat what they want to eat. Contrary to popular belief, we don't enjoy eating with someone who's picking salads or forgoing dessert because she thinks it'll make her more lady-like. I always appreciate a woman who has no qualms with ordering the steak or the dessert because she wants to." His eyes flicker to my face. "And I know you wanted the souffle. If this wasn't a practice date, you'd have ordered it, waistline be damned."

"You're right." I smile, shaking my head at myself. "This evening is throwing me off. Half of me wants to behave like I'm on a date, and half of me wants to behave like I'm having dinner with my best friend. I think I'm just very confused."

"Who says it can't be both?" he questions. "Why can't you behave like your normal self while going on a date?" I'm distracted by his fingers now drawing circles on the base of his wineglass. "I happen to think your normal self would be fun to take on a date."

I peer up at him, not making out his eyes, as his profile is half in the dark because of the flickering candlelight and the moonlight streaming in from the windows. "T-thank you," I hedge, this is a compliment.

Rich laughter fills the air. "Good girl. You're learning fast."

The rest of the meal passes by uneventfully. The souffle is heavenly. My mouth salivates at the thought of the warm, decadent chocolate melting on my tongue. The check materializes itself in front of James when I wasn't looking. I offer to pay for my portion of the dinner as this restaurant most likely charges an arm and a leg for the meal we just had. As I reach across the table to grab the check, James stops me with a quelling look.

"Call me old-fashioned, but as a gentleman, I like to pay for dates, even if this is a fake one and you already agreed before, so don't fight me on this one."

"Oh, well, thank you."

I haven't met this side of James before. But then again, I haven't really spent any time with him in person for almost a decade. The boy with the heart of gold who was working jobs after school is now this imposing man in front of me. Even though we have kept in touch with each other frequently throughout the years with phone calls and video chats, it's as if I'm finally waking up to see the boy on the screen transforming into a man. Or perhaps, most likely so, this transformation has occurred long ago, and I just haven't noticed.

I smile at the waitress on the way out. "Thank you for such a wonderful meal and for this table with the view. I'll be sure to pass along compliments to the manager."

James places his hand on my back, warm against the bare skin there, awakening the nerve endings of my entire body. He leans down and whispers into my ear, "That's a nice thing you did. It's hard being a waitstaff. Very underappreciated job."

"I just want to treat others how I want to be treated. Nothing special."

James shakes his head. "I've been on some dinners where my date is rude or arrogant to the waitstaff. That's usually a red flag for me. Just because you are paying for a service doesn't mean you are inherently better than the person performing the service. You, Jess, have a kind heart."

I blush from his compliment. Somehow when I'm with him, I never feel like I'm lacking. It's a freeing feeling.

"The weather is wonderful tonight. Do you want to take a walk on the beach?" He takes off his jacket and drapes it over my shoulders, anticipating the ocean breeze.

"That sounds good. I don't want this evening to end yet."

He leads me down a private entrance to the beach where we take off our shoes and leave them in a dark corner to retrieve later.

James's hand trails down my arm, eliciting shivers that have nothing to do with the chill from the ocean. He slowly intertwines his right hand with my left, his much larger hand fully envelops mine. The entire process feels much more intimate than it actually is. I glance up at him in surprise.

"We're still on a date," he reminds me, his brow raised as if challenging me to contradict him.

I smile. Fine. Fake date it is.

We walk along the water in companionable silence. The clear night sky is filled with thousands of twinkling stars, providing a beautiful backdrop to the full moon. There's no one else on the beach except for the two of us, strolling on the quiet shores. The waves wash up softly onto the sand, caressing the pebbles and leaving behind souvenirs from the sea. The occasional call of a seagull punctuates the intimate silence. There's a light breeze, sending a small chill down my body. I burrow myself deeper in his jacket, surrounding myself with the familiar scent of sandalwood as he tucks me closer to his side, his body a furnace, warming me from within.

"So, how did I do?" I stare at the glittering lights of the pier in the distance, nervousness churning inside me.

"The date?" He stops in his tracks and looks into my eyes.

I nod, anxiously waiting for his verdict.

"Despite everything I said earlier about all those rules, this was the best date I've ever been on, fake or not." The blacks of his pupils overtake the stormy blue in the moonlight. His hand slowly cups my face in reverence, his thumb caressing my cheeks that were cold a moment ago but are now burning hot. "If this was real, I'd definitely ask you on a second date again, and I wouldn't follow the ridiculous three-day rule."

I close my eyes and lean into his caress, hypnotized by his raspy voice and his warmth surrounding me. I'm mesmerized by this feeling he gives me, the feeling I'm enough, just the way I am.

"Let me tell you what I see," he continues, his thumb grazing my lower lip as if testing the texture. "I see a woman who has a big heart and cares so much about what other people feel or think, she prioritizes her needs last. I see someone who roots for her competition instead of looking at them in envy. I see someone who wants to make her parents happy, even though they have never put her needs first. I see a woman who's lost, looking for her home and place in the world." My eyes remain closed. I don't want to wake up from this moment of deep intimacy, this moment of clarity, this moment that feels so normal and yet significant.

His breath catches and he snatches his fingers away from my face, as if burned. I slowly blink open my eyes, his face coming into focus, and I stop my impulse to reach back for him.

"What if I can't find my home?"

I think deep down, that's my biggest fear. Perhaps the constant moves from my childhood traumatized me somehow. Nothing is ever permanent. No one ever stays, no matter how hard I try to hold on to them.

He steps back from me, letting go of my fingers as if slowly waking himself up from this mutual trance we are in.

"We'll make one." He motions for me to follow him as I ponder his words.

What does he mean?

I feel strangely at peace. No noise in my head. No to-do lists in the background. There's a rare tranquility in my soul. In this moment, there's only me, this man beside me, the moon, and the stars, reminding us how insignificant we are. The waves crash slowly on the shore in a soothing rhythm, the grains of sand solid beneath my feet, each salty breeze lightening my steps.

We walk quietly along the water, both of us lost in our own thoughts. James glances at me and gives me a reassuring smile, his eyes holding many unspoken promises. Comfort. Peace. I smile back. Somehow, I know at the end of my journey, wherever it may be, this man will be there by my side.

want this evening to go on forever, but all dates must come to an end. But for most people, good dates end with a promise of a next one. For me, I'm not sure this is in the cards *yet*. This "fake date" has felt more real than any dates I've been on in the past. A twinge of guilt reminds me how, despite my best intentions and actions, I haven't really been truly living before. With Claire. With anyone else.

I want to keep strolling on this beach with Jess, even if we're doing nothing, as long as she's by my side. Ever since college, I've pursued my goals with grit and determination. Some may say my experience with bullying in childhood has given me an unquenchable thirst to prove myself. This has served me well academically and professionally as I climb my way to the top of the food chain. But I know this strategy won't work with Jess.

Patience, James, don't frighten her. She just got out of her longest relationship.

"Come on, it's getting late. Let me take you back home." I reach for her hand again, relishing the softness of her skin as she slides her dainty fingers across mine.

I give her a squeeze as we stroll back to retrieve our shoes and return to my car.

The drive back feels much shorter than the drive to the restaurant, even though I do my best to drive well within the speed limit, hoping to prolong the ride as long as I can. I steal glances at her as I grip the steering wheel, my fingers desperate to caress the smooth skin where her dress meets her thighs. Jess appears to be in deep thought, her beautiful lips slightly pursed as she twiddles her bracelet on her wrist. *My bracelet.* Soon, we arrive at her apartment, and I park the car in the front and walk her to the door. Adrenaline pulses through my veins as I contemplate my next move. Move too fast and she'll be spooked. Move too slow then...well, we'll be exactly the same, languishing in the despairing pool of "friendship."

"Thank you for a great night." She stares up at me through her thick lashes. Uncertainty laces her demeanor as her fingers clench and unclench by her sides. Jess unlocks her door and turns around. She softly bites her lip as she waits for me. I step closer, slowly, when I want nothing to more than to run up the steps, haul her against me, and kiss her senseless.

"No, thank *you*," I whisper on an exhale, our breaths mingling in the narrow space between us.

Gently clasping my hands on her shoulders, I lean in slowly. *One taste, James. You know you want to.* Jess's breath hitches. Her eyes flutter shut. Time slows as she stands there, her head tilting up, and I reach for her hand again, each slide of my fingers against hers an intimate embrace. She shivers.

No.

I want our first kiss to be real, not under pretense. As much as I want nothing more than to give her the kiss I can feel her body is asking for, I don't want her to explain this away as a by-product of our fake date. When I kiss her, she'll know it's because I want to. Not because of any fake exercise. I settle for the consolation prize.

"This has been more than anything I've ever wished for." I brush the softest of kisses on her cheek, my breath ghosting over her ears. She trembles ever so slightly.

So close and yet so far away.

She opens her eyes and looks up. Her eyes are molten amber as her pupils overtake the irises. Her mouth parts, seducing and inviting me like a Siren's call. I clench my hands into a tight fist and back away, each step a test of my willpower. The increasing distance and the cold air rushing in are akin to the curtains falling after the conclusion of an epic play in the theater.

Backing up a few paces, I force myself to give her an easy grin, a smile she's familiar with. The practice date is over. I feel bereft, as if I've lost something I never had in the first place. Jess blinks at me and rubs her hands on her forearms, even though there's no chill in the air. She smiles tentatively at me, raising her hand in a wave.

Flashing my keys in the air, I call out, "Sleep tight, Jess. You'll do just fine in the modern dating world, despite what you're worried about. As I always say, you got this." I motion for her to enter her apartment.

Laughing softly, she shakes her head as if my confidence in her is ridiculous. If she only saw what I see.

"'Night, James. Glad I got a passing grade from you, ol' wise one," she calls out before closing the door softly behind her.

I exhale fully as I stand there for a few minutes, staring at her closed door. I want to stride up there and bang on her door until she opens it, and when she does, I'll pull her into my arms and never let go. I want to tell her everything I said on the date is real. That nothing is remotely fake about it. That it's been *years* for me, standing in the shadows by the sidelines, watching her with other people while I desperately try to move on, but failing, time and time again. I want to tell her how much I love her. How my world has been in multi-tonal gray all those years apart despite my best efforts and technicolor vision has only recently returned, now that I'm by her side again.

In time. Knowing Jess and her worries, the decision has to be hers and hers alone.

In time. I've waited for years. What's a little more?

• • •

Eleven Years Ago

Sweat drips down my brows as I lean against the punching bag at the gym. Boxing is definitely harder than it looks. Now that I've finally grown to my full height, true to my parents' late-bloomer predictions, I've decided it's time I start working out to build some muscles to balance out my tall, lanky frame. There aren't too many people at the gym in the morning. Then again, I'm at MIT, a college known for its academic prowess, not athletic teams. The quiet suits me. I get to burn off some restlessness and think at the same time. Ever since I left LA, there has been a sense of discontentment following me everywhere. I haven't been able to exactly pinpoint the reason.

My phone vibrates on the padded ground. I contemplate whether to go another round at the punching bag but decide against it.

"Hello?" I wipe the sweat from my face with my towel.

"James? It's Jess."

I grin, happy to hear her voice so early in the morning. "Hey. It's not time for our scheduled phone call yet. You miss me?"

"Yeah, yeah, yeah. Whatever you say. I have a dilemma and I want to get your thoughts on it. And since I'm up at the crack of dawn and no one I know is awake yet, I thought I'll call you." A barrage of weird sounds filters through from the background.

I pack up my gear and head toward the locker room. "Ha. So, you are calling me just because I'm the only person you know in an earlier time zone. I'm *so* honored," I reply sarcastically. "Anyway, what are you doing over there? Packing?"

"I have a date tonight. This guy's name is Ben. He goes to ULA. I'm trying to find the right outfit. I got this new dress I stashed away somewhere...if only I could find it. It's a beautiful cream color. Apparently, the color washes me out, so I shouldn't wear it. But it's so pretty, I can't help myself. I want to see if I can make it work."

My chest briefly constricts at the mention of her date. I don't know if the heart ever heals from a heartbreak, or in my case, *the* heartbreak. Or if it's like an ACL injury, once you recover, you never regain full use of the ligaments and you just have to make do with the new range in motion and the resulting scar. The pain has gotten better over time now that I'm across the country, but it has never quite disappeared.

"Let me guess, that's another commandment from your mother? Just wear what you like. I'm sure you'll look fine." *I've never seen you look anything less than gorgeous in any color you wear.* "Please don't tell me you're calling me for fashion advice." I whip off my shirt and stare at the full-body mirror by the lockers. I think my muscles have gotten a little bigger. I flex my biceps and squint my eyes. Maybe…just marginally bigger. Progress.

More rummaging in the background. "Why are you whispering anyways?"

I towel off the sweat from my body. "Well, as you know, it's a perfectly respectable hour here in Cambridge; there are people around. I was working out when you called and now, I'm in the locker room. Apparently, a lot of people haven't completely woken up yet and don't appreciate loud noises at this hour."

"Wow, you working out? I don't think I've seen that before."

"Oh, I tell you, I'm going to be a new James the next time you see me." I envision myself with the sculpted body of superheroes.

"Uh huh, I'll believe it when I see it," she replies noncommittally.

"I can smell the skepticism from here…if that's a thing. I'll prove you wrong."

I wrap myself in a towel, grab the usual toiletries, and head over to one of the open showers. I pop in these underwater earbuds a classmate designed and lent to me for testing.

I warn Jess, "Hey, FYI, I'm testing underwater earbuds right now and I'll be hopping into a shower. Try not to imagine me naked."

"Ewww…that's too much info. I need to cleanse my mind. I'll pretend I didn't hear that." She groans dramatically.

"Haha." I laugh, turning on the shower, savoring the steaming-hot water on my sore muscles. "So, what are you calling me for?"

Jess sighs. "I need to finalize my major declarations for college applications. My parents want me to do something practical, like accounting or law. I don't know how I feel about that."

These earbuds work quite well, surprisingly so. "Well, what do you want to do if money isn't an issue and if your parents are…not your parents?"

"If I'm not so worried about being judged or being in the spotlight, I may want to go into the arts, or something involving music, like the theater. But I guess that's not really practical or suited for my personality."

"And secretly declaring a vocal performing major isn't going to work, right?" I finish slopping on shampoo and body wash and prepare to rinse off.

"Nope, they're paying for my education, so I have to abide by their rules. Maybe a minor will be enough to scratch the itch...argh, shit."

Thump. Ziiiiiiip. Thump.

"What's going on there? You doing jiu-jitsu or something?"

She mumbles, her voice obstructed by something. "I just tried on the dress." *More heavy breathing.* "Whew, that's better, uh... but I'm not so sure."

"Huh?"

"Oh, I just tried on the dress, but it's a tad tight. I do need to watch what I eat. Anyway, it's too tight. I don't think I can wear underwear underneath it, so I took it off to see how that'll look. But yeah, not a wise choice...looks kind of obscene, can't go outside looking like this. I need another dress."

I picture her standing before me in the skintight cream dress sans underwear, every dip and curve showing. Are her nipples poking through? Can I see a shadow between her thighs? Lurid thoughts fill my head, creating a vivid, tantalizing image. Blood rushes through my veins and makes its way down south.

Crap, I'm hard.

I grit my teeth and breathe in the soap scented steam. I grip my erection with my hand and quickly turn the temperature to icy cold. It seems rude to secretly fantasize about her without her consent while she's on the line.

"Uh...yeah, that sounds like a good idea," I rasp, willing my raging hard-on to go away.

"Hmm...I think so too." She sighs, then pauses. "You sound winded. What are you doing, running a marathon in the shower?"

I bite the inside of my cheek, distracting myself with the pain. "Just practicing the Norwegian art of ice bathing. Supposedly good for your health."

"You men are so weird. Anyway, yeah, I want to get your thoughts about college."

I turn off the shower, my emotions hanging by a thread. Jess has this effect on me, and it appears the distance hasn't improved the situation. "If you need to appease your parents, choose one of those practical majors you're most interested in, and then continue practicing your hobby on the side. You never know where life will take you. Maybe someday the side gig can become the main gig."

"You have a point... I'm leaning toward accounting. The classes seem all right, and this sounds kind of nerdy, but I think it's pretty interesting dissecting all those numbers. Law gives me nightmares. Being buried in a mountain pile of legal books doesn't seem like a good way to pass my time. And I don't think I'm cut out to argue for a living."

I'm inclined to agree with her assessment. Despite her moment of bravery when we were kids, Jess is more of a people pleaser; confronting people for a living will kill her.

"And ULA has a great accounting program. It's close to home, so I can be there for Ems and Steven. I don't feel right leaving them behind. I don't really want my parents to focus on them if I move away."

Disappointment slices through me, effectively dousing the inferno burning inside me. I guess after all this time, I've still been holding out hope she'll come to the East Coast for college.

"I think I just need to go over this out loud with someone. Someone who I know won't judge me. This has been very helpful. Thanks, James." More sounds come from her side. "Aha! Found another dress. I'll wear this on the date tonight. So, what about you, James? I don't hear you talking about girls. There must be really hot girls at MIT," she sniggers, teasing me.

I finish changing into a simple pair of jeans and a blue, button-down shirt. "There are some options out here," I reply vaguely, thinking about Claire, a girl in my economics class who seems to be interested in me.

Perhaps that's what I need to cure myself of the unacceptable thoughts toward Jess. Maybe I just need a new target for my sexual frustration. The sudden moment of clarity gives me hope. Maybe

I'm not destined to have a malfunctioning heart forever and I just need to put myself out there. *Heck, Jess is out there dating, and she considers you to be her brother.* Her words still haunt me to this day.

"I'm considering asking a girl out from class."

Jess squeals so loudly I have to pull the earbuds out. I need to tell my classmate the earbuds definitely work under water. Now, how will anyone actually talk on the phone *under* the water is beyond me. Not sure if they have really thought out the usefulness of the design, but hey, in the shower, the device works.

"I've been waiting for this moment, James. I'm here to help," she exclaims, excited about the prospect of me dating. "I have tips to give you!"

"Really?" I reply mockingly.

"Okay. You know I'm a feminist, but I *do* think there are some golden old-school rules to abide by. First of all, always pay for a girl on the first date. It shows you're sincere and interested. Second of all, pay attention to the details. If she's cold, give her your jacket. If she's warm, turn on the AC. Ask her about herself. The little details show you're attentive. Third of all, don't try to get in her pants on the first date. That's just plain rude. No girl wants to be a quick lay unless they say so otherwise."

"Uh huh. Sounds pretty simple."

"You'd think so. But I can't tell you how many times one of these rules was broken during my dates in the past. You start with these three easy rules, and you'll already be going in with a second date in the pocket, *if* that's what you want."

I sit down on one of the benches inside the gym as I observe couples walking by, hand in hand. My heart clenches, wishing she's here with me. Turning my attention back to the phone call, I reply, "Thank you for the advice. I'll remember to do these three things on my future dates. Hey, I have to run to class."

"Sounds good. Tell me all about your upcoming date, whenever that happens!" she chirps, then hangs up. I stare at the black screen on the phone, already missing her voice.

A few minutes later, I step out of the doors into the crisp New England air. Fall in Cambridge is utterly beautiful. Foliage of warm reds, golds, and yellows dots the campus like a scene in a postcard. Fallen leaves flutter in the breeze, creating a kaleidoscope of colors any artist will want to capture. I take a deep breath, inhaling the possibilities in the air. I wish Jess were here to see this. This will definitely feed her romantic soul.

There's a reason I'm drawn to big data and analytics. I'm logical. Solution-oriented. Perhaps the best way for me to get over Jess is to start dating. Rationally, there has to be someone else in this world who can fill the Jess-shaped void in my heart. It's only hormones and biology after all, neurotransmitters and biochemistry really. Maybe moving on will help me become the platonic friend Jess needs me to be. Maybe my rational side can override the rollercoaster of emotions and what feels like the longest-lasting hangover in my life. Maybe then, I can finally stop yearning for something I'll never have.

Fall is my favorite time of the year. Well, technically, it's winter according to the calendar, but that's really a misnomer since winter doesn't exist in Los Angeles. The weather finally cools ten to twenty degrees. Instead of the blistering heat in the upper nineties to the hundreds, the temperatures hover between the chilly sixties to the balmy seventies. James used to make fun of me when I complained about how cold I was when the temperature was in the high fifties or sixties. I would be decked out head-to-toe in puffer jackets, cashmere scarfs, and leather boots when he would either be in the middle of an East Coast blizzard or something equally atrocious. *But you guys have earthquakes, Jess. The whole ground literally shakes and falls apart,* he would always kindly remind me.

Now is the time for the temporary lull at work, the calm before the storm of year-end audits, the time of pumpkin spice lattes, even though I'm not a fan of cinnamon, which Ems will call blasphemy, and the holidays galore. There's Halloween, where everyone goes crazy in my neighborhood. There always appears to be an informal competition for which house or condo has the best haunted house set up and if you go to the several theme parks in the area, everywhere is fully decked out in spooky decorations, as if the future of the nation depends on it. As much fun as Halloween is, what I really love about fall is Thanksgiving and Christmas. Something about being with the people I love and chilling at home while pretending it's freezing outside really warms my insides.

This year, however, is especially fantastic, because James is here, and he'll be joining the Kingsley siblings in our Yosemite cabin adventure along with Liz. I can hardly wait. But first things first, got to get the boring stuff done, stuff like...preparation for the upcoming year-end audits.

"Becca, Becca, Becca...fancy seeing you here today." I snicker as I pass by her cubicle.

"Har, har, har...you're chipper today." Becca laughs, then stretches. She has clearly been at it for a lot longer than me.

I set my laptop in my cubicle and power it up. "It's fall! What's not to love? What time did you get in today?"

She yawns. "Six. I wanted to beat traffic and take advantage of the few hours of quiet before the emails start flying in."

I nod. I can commiserate. Once nine a.m. hits, the inbox pretty much goes through a nonstop workout. The sounds of incoming messages ping through the laptop like a broken alarm clock. I usually mute my computer whenever I'm not on a call. I plan to be in and out today, meet with my team to go over pre-audit planning work, call a few prospects, review some schedules, then head out before the rush-hour traffic. Maybe I'll actually get to eat dinner at home at a reasonable hour. I'm expecting this week to be relatively quiet, since it's the week of Thanksgiving. Hopefully, most of the clients are closing shop early and are in a holiday mood, aka, not bothering me.

"I'm so excited. It's Thanksgiving this Thursday and we have a glorious long weekend ahead of us. James and his sister will join us on our annual camping trip." I rub my hands together gleefully, like a kindergartener at the prospect of trick-or-treating.

"Ah. James, huh?" She gives me a sideways glance. "So, now you're single and available, any chance you and your 'best friend' will finally explore this romantic tension between you guys?" She finishes the statement with air quotes.

I blush, heat creeping up my neck. "That again, Becca?"

Most people seem to think a man and a woman can't truly be platonic friends. I used to call that bullshit (internally, of course, because I don't want to start anything), but lately... I'm not so sure anymore.

"Hold on a second. You're actually red and there's no immediate denial." She leans over her cubical wall. "What happened?" she whisper-shouts.

Honestly, I don't know how to answer the question. Did anything truly happen? Nope. Yet, somehow, things feel different in a way I can't describe.

"No, nothing like that. I think I'm just adjusting to him physically being here. It's different talking to someone on the phone and seeing them through a screen than interacting with them in person. It just feels a bit off-kilter. I'm sure this is just an adjustment period. And I'm sure it's mostly on my part, probably making it all weird in my mind." I frown. "I don't even know what I'm talking about."

Becca squeals. "This is better than watching *The Bachelorette*. Mark my words, he's into you and you're finally catching up. Based on everything you told me before, I'm sure that's the case. Call it a gut feeling and I haven't even met the guy."

I roll my eyes. Her and her infamous gut feelings. But...she's usually not wrong with her gut feelings. Can it be? I quickly dismiss the idea and close the pandora's box. Nope, not going there. *He's your best friend. He's just like an older brother you never had.* Yeah, keep telling yourself that. *Lately, nothing between us feels remotely platonic.* Nope. Nope. Nope. Shut the thought down right now. *He is the only person aside from your blood relatives who have stuck by you all these years. Don't complicate things.* The risk-averse auditor in me is clamoring away to keep the can of worms closed. Too much is at stake. Our friendship means far too much for me to even *entertain* the idea of us becoming anything more than friends. My mind whirls with the barrage of thoughts, like a computer with too many windows opened.

"Whatever you say, Becca. You'll meet him, eventually. I'm thinking of asking him to come to the annual gala with me since now I'm—as you kindly pointed out—single." I sit down and attempt to work.

"Yessss. I've been waiting for this moment forever. Trust me, my radar is never wrong, and I'm sure I'll confirm it when I see you guys together in person." She grins ear-to-ear.

"Well, sorry to burst your bubble, but I'm meeting a guy I met on *InstaConnect* for coffee after Thanksgiving."

"Really? So now there may be *two* men in your life?" She grins gleefully as if excited by the news.

"Oh my gosh, you're hopeless!" I laugh, shaking my head. "Enough about me. What about you? How are things going with you and Craig?" I click open my inbox and sure enough, a hundred unread emails sit there, mocking me.

Becca gives me a one-shoulder shrug. "As you know, we talked it out. He insisted there was nothing going on and I caught him grabbing lunch at work with a colleague, nothing more. Maybe it's just my insecurities. We're working on it. I think he's making more of an effort to hang out with me now and at least call me on the nights we're not together. So, that's progress."

I breathe a sigh of relief. "See? Maybe your gut feeling is *wrong*." I've always been rooting for them. They've been together for such a long time with so much history. It would be a shame for them not to work out.

"Never! I'm not convinced yet. But we've been together for so long, I owe it to us to make this work... And at the end of the day, I love him."

"I agree, not that you're asking me for my opinion." I stare at my Outlook calendar and jump up with a jolt. "Crap, meeting with my team in five. I'll be back." I quickly gather my things and speed walk to the conference room. *Have to maintain poise in the office. A partner candidate should not look so harried. Fake it until you make it, Jess.*

The entire team is hard at work when I walk into the conference room. As usual, the hum of conversation quiets once I enter the room, and the temperature drops ten degrees. I hate this. I hate how I can't seem to connect with them.

"Hi, team. Thanks for coming in on a short week."

A few of them grunt in the affirmative and some even manage a grin. I guess that's progress.

"So, let's go over the audit plan."

The senior associate begins walking through the tedious questionnaires that are literally the same at every audit engagement. I stifle a yawn as I stare at my inbox again. An email captures my attention.

Jess,

Roger just called me, and they are proceeding with the acquisition. They want to close the deal out by the end of the month. Just wanted to let you know. Now that the deal is on, there are due diligence procedures we need to complete asap...

My eyes glaze over the rest of the email from the audit partner. Fire drill. Shit. Shit. Shit. Shit to the nth degree. Fuck my life. Fuck this shit. This job absolutely sucks. Fuck!

The room is eerily silent as I glance up from my screen. The senior's mouth gapes as the team stares at me in shock. The manager covers his mouth in a poor attempt to hide his smile.

Shit.

Did I say all that out loud? I glance around at the horrified expressions on their faces.

Yep. Apparently, I did. *How unprofessional, Jess. You know better than this. You're supposed to rein in your emotions and be the voice of management. Instill positivity in times of stress. Lead by example. Smile in the midst of chaos. Poise and grace.* I berate myself, this time, internally.

The manager whistles. "Dang, Jess, I've *never* heard you cuss before. It's pretty hilarious, but I don't think I want to know what made you go off like that."

I groan, covering my face with my hands, my skin heating with embarrassment. "That was utterly unprofessional of me, guys. I'm so, so sorry. You shouldn't have to witness that. Tony just emailed saying the acquisition is on and they're closing the deal before the end of the month. You know what that means."

A collective groan fills the conference room. "Shit, man, that totally sucks." The senior seemingly recovers his voice. "Sorry, but now that I know you feel the same way, well, I don't see a reason to mince words."

I survey the team, everyone muttering curses under their breath. This is uncharted territory for me. They usually clam up whenever I'm in the room, but somehow, they're complaining to me, in my face, right now. I'm suddenly unsure of what to do. Do I join in, because heck, I have a lot of unsavory comments I want to say about this ill timing? Or do I go back to my usual face-of-the-firm behavior?

"Yes, this totally sucks." I hedge my words carefully. "I feel bad, guys. I know the holidays are coming up. Again, it was totally unprofessional of me for going off like that. But...the timing is really awful."

The team nods in unison, everyone bemoaning about their wrecked Thanksgiving plans. I was looking forward to the camping trip as well. The idea of disconnecting for a few days with the people I love, no work, just movies, board games, and hanging out now all up in flames. Screw it, I've given enough of my life to work and I'm sure the team has as well.

"Guys, we aren't canceling Thanksgiving if I can help it." The team pauses amid their grumbling and looks up at me. This is all very uncharacteristic behavior from me, but why not? I'm apparently on a roll today and no one has complained to HR...yet. "I want all of us to disconnect for this long weekend. In fact, I *insist* on it. The work will still be here when we're back and as long as it's done on time, I'll handle the partner."

The manager nods in agreement. "Sounds fair. So, what's the plan?"

I gather the team around and walk them through the plan of attack. The senior and staff break out separately to carve out the details of the timeline and the steps to completion.

I sit back and watch the team work. The manager rolls his chair next to mine and whispers, "I just want to say, Jess, thanks for not canceling the holiday. I'm sure everyone appreciates it. This is refreshing...I guess you're not what I've been hearing about."

"What do you mean? What have you heard?"

He looks at me nervously, afraid he has said too much, but musters up his courage. "Well, the manager and staff groups all know you're very smart and nice, but you're a bit unapproachable, no offense. And you're known to have the whole gung-ho 'we'll get it done come hell or high water' type of commendable attitude. It's nice to see this side of you. I guess you're on our side after all."

"Huh. Of course I am. Geez, I'm sorry I made you guys feel that way." I'm honestly taken aback. I always thought I was doing my job by toeing the company line, but I never realized the team was feeling this way.

"Nah, water under the bridge. Guess you're not a robot after all." He winks at me.

"Ha ha." I laugh softly. This is the first time I feel like they included me as part of the team. Maybe James is right, maybe I should try being myself for a change.

"This is so nice. I'm very excited for this weekend." Liz flops onto one of the leather sofas in the large living room with a sigh. I smirk as I carry our luggage inside from the doorway of the cabin. Jess will be driving up with Emily and Steven after their family Thanksgiving dinner. Knowing her family, I'm sure it's going to be a painful dinner for her.

"You want me to pick a room for you?"

She waves me in as she snuggles deeper into the sofa. "Yes, yes, any room will do. Thanks, bro. I'm going to rest my legs here… such a long ride to Yosemite. I'm tired."

Laughing, I carry the suitcases into two random rooms I picked for us. "You didn't even drive. I should be the one resting," I holler as I start unpacking my things—old habits die hard. Jess would totally make fun of me if she was here.

"Get some water for me, will you?" TV sounds from the living room. I don't think Liz will move from her spot the rest of the evening.

"Get it yourself! I'm unpacking."

Liz groans and moments later, I hear her voice at my doorway.

"So, how are things progressing with you and Jess? How did the fake date go?"

I pause in the middle of hanging my coat in the closet. "It went fine."

"Right, that's not going to fly with me."

I turn to face her, pinning her with a stare. Liz takes a sip of water from a bottle and leans casually against the doorway, completely unfazed.

Seconds pass by and I sigh. "I think we had a moment or two during our date. It sure as hell didn't feel platonic to me. Even if this is all new to her, there's no way she didn't feel anything, unless she was a statue."

Liz grins and winks at me. "That's what I thought. I'm not supposed to break girl code, but I think she's more unsettled these days...in a good way. She blushes when we mention you. So, this weekend provides a golden opportunity for you guys."

"I've got it under control. Don't worry about me. Trust me, I'm done trying to pretend she's not the one for me. Made that mistake before, not doing it again."

. . .

Ten Years Ago

"James, this is so nice. Long overdue. Thanks for organizing this." Claire beams at me as I pull out the chair for her at a nice steakhouse near campus. "So, what's the occasion?" Pulling a chair out for a lady. Check. Jess's tips flash through my mind and I groan, trying to shove her from my thoughts and focus on the girl before me.

"This is me, making an effort."

Claire and I've been seeing each other on and off since last year. It has been relatively casual for this past year since we both are busy with coursework and grad school application preparation. She really is a great girl, very smart, down to earth, a body which belongs in a lingerie catalog, and she cares about her family. She checks all the boxes on my ideal girlfriend checklist. And yet... something always feels missing and not from a lack of effort on my end. It's like reading the most well-written novel and yet not being able to immerse yourself in the story.

Claire brushes her mahogany-red locks away from her face and studies the menu. "Bone-in ribeye, that's what I'll have. If this is a dinner to get me back in your good graces, I'm going to milk it." She winks at me.

"Ouch. My wallet." I dramatically moan, my hand on my chest feigning pain. A girl after my own heart, she's no stick-thin model who picks at her food at mealtime. Another checkmark for her.

"You're the one who chose a steakhouse. Not me! What do you expect me to pick, a salmon filet?" She snickers at my outburst.

I smile softly and shake my head. "Go ahead, knock yourself out. I know I owe you a nice dinner for flaking on you the last few times you called me. These exams are killing me."

"Ugh. Let's not talk about exams. Hanson is a nightmare. You're so right; I don't know why I decided to take his course." She bemoans now that our topic has changed to coursework. Claire is actually a year younger than me, but she took a lot of advanced courses in high school and is able to fast track to advanced courses in college as well.

The server sets down our entrees with a thump fifteen minutes later and tosses the bill on the corner of the table. Okay, fine, this is not the most top-end of steak houses, because, frankly, who can truly wine and dine on a college student's budget? To us, however, the food is still an upgrade from the usual questionable fare on campus. We dig into our meals wholeheartedly, determined to get the most bang out of the buck.

A buzzing vibration in my pocket alerts me to an incoming phone call. I discreetly slide the phone out under the table to see who it is. *Jess.* My immediate impulse is to pick up right away, but then I look at Claire, who is devouring her steak like she hasn't eaten in three days, and I decide to decline the call. I'll call Jess back later.

I quietly slip the phone back into my pocket, Claire none the wiser, and continue with my food. I'm trying to make an attempt to be more present with Claire. She deserves that.

The phone vibrates again, and I sigh inwardly. Maybe I should just turn it off. I take out the phone again and glance at the screen. *Jess.* She doesn't often call me outside of our regularly scheduled phone calls. Usually, we'll trade texts or emails here and there, and when she calls outside of our scheduled calls, if I don't answer, she'll usually send a text reassuring me all is well so I don't have to worry about her. She *never* calls twice in a row. My pulse picks up as a foreboding feeling permeates me. Sweat gathers on my forehead. The phone buzzes again, the sound now a harbinger of misfortune.

"What's wrong?" Claire stares at me mid-bite, noticing I'm staring at my vibrating phone.

"Sorry—I know this is rude, but I need to take this. I'll be back." I excuse myself to walk toward the restrooms and answer the call.

"Jess? Everything okay?"

The silence has never sounded so loud. Usually, she'll answer the call with her peppy voice that usually brings a smile to my face.

"Jess? You there? You're scaring me."

Whimpers and sniffles come through the line.

"J-James...she's...she's..." Jess's voice breaks, her sniffles progressing to all-out sobs.

"Sweetheart, what's wrong? Are you okay? Please tell me you are okay." I pace back and forth by the bathroom entrance, my heart in my throat. I feel nauseated.

"I'm okay, James, but Nana..."

My heart sinks. Jess's grandmother is in the hospital with pneumonia. Things were on the up and up the last time we spoke, but now, I'm not so sure.

"James, Nana is gone."

Her weeping breaks the scars on my heart wide open. I'll do *anything* to take away her pain. *Anything* to be there to dry her tears.

"Oh Jess, I'm so sorry. I know how close you were with her." I lean against the wall, my fingers rubbing my sore eyes, which are starting to prickle with wetness. I feel so helpless being all the way across the country, so far away from her. All I can offer her right now is my presence and my voice.

Jess pants for air in between sobs. "It was so sudden. One moment, we were told things were getting better and she may even check out of the hospital at the end of the week. The next moment, everything took a turn for the worse. Then...then...she was just... gone."

I clench my fists, angry at the world. Yet another person Jess loves leaving her. Life is so unfair.

"The funeral is the day after tomorrow. I—I have to go. Mother is calling me. I need to help with preparations. I just wanted to hear your voice, James. Sorry for bothering you. I know you're probably busy. Don't worry about me. Hearing your voice has helped a lot. I'll talk to you soon," she says hurriedly as I hear some muffled sounds in the background. I'm sure she is frantically wiping her face clean of tears before her mother sees her because, heaven forbid, she looks less than perfect after her grandmother *died*. She disconnects the call with a click.

I slowly lower my phone from my ear and take deep breaths, willing my galloping pulse to calm.

Jess needs me. My head chants.

Jess needs me. My heart repeats.

I pull up the browser on my phone to search for plane tickets from Boston to Los Angeles. A flight leaves in two hours and tickets are still available. Yes, I need to go to her. My pulse thuds in agreement. I quickly purchase the ticket and rush back to the table.

Claire finishes her steak and is scrolling on her phone when I approach. She peers up at me, concern in her expression. "Everything okay? You were gone for a long while."

"Sorry, Claire. I need to head to the airport to fly back to LA. Jess's grandma passed away. She's a mess, and she needs me." I grab my keys, fish out four fifties, and throw it on the table. "I'm so sorry. I'll make it up to you. Stay, have dessert, take my steak with you since I don't have time to eat it anyway. Thank goodness you drove today."

Claire frowns and nods. "Jess, huh?" Her voice flattens as if she knows something I don't. "Don't mind me. Someone died, so I should be the least of your concerns. Don't worry. Go. I'll be okay," she reassures me. I don't deserve her kindness.

I give her a quick hug and dash to my car. I still have time to quickly swing by my apartment and pack a bag.

Hours later, I stand in front of her parents' home at eight in the morning, holding two drinks in a carrier: a triple espresso for me and a hot chocolate for her. I stifle a yawn as I ring the doorbell. I arrived at LAX past midnight last night and by the time I settled down in the hotel, it was past three a.m. The flight was unfortunately delayed due to some inclement weather issue.

The door swings open.

"James? What are you doing here?" Jess stands at the entrance, dressed in a mid-length black dress, looking all too frail. The dark circles under her eyes tell me she did not sleep a wink all night. A sudden breeze blows by, ruffling my hair, fluttering her dress. She shivers.

I set the drinks on the floor and tug her toward me, my warm hands enveloping her clammy ones. She collapses as I wrap my hands around her tightly, wholeheartedly, sturdily, holding her up.

I'm finally here, where I should be all along.

Silence surrounds us, yet a million phrases pass between us where our bodies touch. *I'm here. You'll be okay,* my touch murmurs to her. *I know. I'll be fine now that you're here,* her embrace whispers to me.

Wordlessly, she disentangles from me and leads me to the living room. A small crowd of people in black gather around the sitting area. I pay my respects to Mr. Kingsley, who stands solemnly by the fireplace while Mrs. Kingsley plays the perfect wife, delivering refreshments to the guests who have gathered.

"Mr. Kingsley, I'm sorry for your loss."

He nods and awkwardly pats my shoulder. "Thank you, son," he gruffly replies.

"James, thank you for coming out here. You're at MIT now, right?" Mrs. Kingsley hands me a glass of water and peers up at me, her face somber.

"Yes ma'am. And no need to thank me. I'm exactly where I should be." I wrap my hands around Jess's small waist. Mrs. Kingsley glances at my protective gesture and quickly looks at Jess, who's staring into space, seemingly unaware of her mother's scrutiny.

Mrs. Kingsley dips her head in acknowledgement and shuffles off to attend to the other guests.

"Come on, sweetheart, let's get out of here," I whisper to Jess, who follows me as if in a trance.

I lead her down the hall to her room and sit down on her bed, facing the window. The skies are unusually gloomy today, matching the mood of the household. She sits down next to me, still uncharacteristically quiet. I slowly wrap my arms around her in comfort, knowing there's nothing I can say to take the pain away. The most I can do is to be her shelter from the storm, to be her home, however temporary that may be. Jess rests her head on my shoulder and closes her eyes. Nonsensical thoughts flow through my mind. Is she comfortable on my shoulder? Is it too bony? The boxing has started to pay off, but I'm still far away from my goal of gaining more muscles to match my frame. I shake those thoughts away. *Silly. Jess doesn't care. She just needs you here.*

We haven't said any words since she greeted me at the door. Sometimes, words are just unnecessary. The silence is heavy but comfortable. I softly rub her arms as she cries silent tears onto my shoulder, every shudder from her a stab into my heart. Every tear on my shoulder a wound to my psyche. I've never felt so helpless before.

"Shhh...I got you," I whisper, dropping a featherlight kiss onto her hair. "I'm here. Let it out." I close my eyes and wrap my other arm around her as she quakes in sadness.

Moments go by and her sobs slow, then still. My arms still wrapped around her, she looks up at me, her eyes bloodshot, mascara running down her face, her nose red. She's still the most beautiful creature to grace this earth. I stare into her doe-like hazel eyes and the moment slows to a stop. I can count every tear-tipped eyelash on her eyes. Our breaths intermingle and dance together, filling the silence. I slowly lean in, drawn by her magnetized gaze and rosy lips. Her eyes slowly shut.

"Jess! Sorry, I got here late. Apparently, I got the am/pm mixed up on my alarm," a masculine voice interrupts us.

Jess and I jolt apart, the previous moment broken by the proverbial bucket of ice water. I whip my head around to stare at the intruder. Shaggy dirty-blond hair. All-American smile. Physique like a jock. Recognition flares inside me. Ben.

Ben narrows his eyes and stares at me. "Babe, this is?" He cocks his head at me.

Jess jumps to a standing position, her flushed face a welcoming sight in comparison to her pale appearance from earlier. "Hi, Ben, this is James, my best friend. James, this is Ben. You might recognize him from the photos I sent you."

Ben walks over and holds his hand out. I grasp it in a firm handshake as he pulls me into a jock hug. He slaps his other hand on my shoulder and says loudly, "Thanks for taking care of my girl. I got this." Then, he warns in a low voice, out of range for Jess to hear, "Don't get any ideas. Know your place, *best friend.*"

I give him a tight squeeze, my hands white-knuckled, and force my face into something hopefully resembling a grin. Right, Jess isn't my responsibility. She has a boyfriend. I step back. "No problem. Nice to meet you," I grit out between my teeth.

Ben interlaces his hands with Jess's, and she willingly follows him. I trail behind, staring at their intertwined hands. My heart clenches again, this time for another reason.

The funeral service proceeds as well as can be expected. The pastor gives a sermon about life after death. Mr. Kingsley gives the eulogy for his mom, and in a rare display of emotion, he chokes up at the mention of his mother supporting him through law school as a single parent when he was young. The day passes by in a bit of a blur, and I can barely remember a single word uttered during the ceremony.

I sit a few rows behind the family, staring at Jess hunching over her Nana's casket in tears. My mind and heart tell me to stand next to her, to hold her up, to wrap her in my arms, and to wipe her tears. My fingers clench into a fist, as I redirect my pain into my grip and force myself to sit still as Ben wraps his arms around her in comfort. The breeze kicks up leaves at the ceremony. Jess shivers, exhausted from both the grief and the elements. Ben tightens his arms around her, lightly rubbing her shoulders.

Give her your damn jacket, you idiot. She's cold. My nails dig into my palm, creating half-moon marks that will probably bruise later, but I'm oblivious to the pain. Any physical discomfort is completely eclipsed by the agony of my hemorrhaging heart. Just as I'm about to walk up to give her my coat, politeness be damned, Ben finally untangles his scarf to drape over her shoulders. Jess finishes her goodbyes and softly lays a white rose on Nana's casket. Her eyes unfocused, her hands shaking, she fumbles her way back to the seat with Ben next to her.

I make my way up the aisle to pay my respects to Nana. *Nana, if you're still hanging around, please take care of Jess. Please let her find joy again. Please let her find someone who deserves her, someone who'll love her above all else. Even if the person isn't me, please lead her to the person who'll protect and take care of her as she deserves.* I quickly wipe the tears pooling in my eyes and place my rose on Nana's casket.

As I walk back toward the seats, I see her sitting alone, her hands clasped on top of her lap, her head dipped low, curtains of raven hair covering her face. I scan the area and spot Ben with a group of men in the back, smiling at something that was being said. *The fucking bastard.*

I sit down quietly next to Jess, pull out a packet of tissues from my coat pocket, and set it next to her. I clasp her hand in mine and gently rub her frigid fingers, hoping she can take what's left of my warmth. If I had the power to set myself on fire to keep her warm and take away her pain, I'd do it in a second.

"James." She slowly breathes out.

"I know, Jess. I know." I slowly breathe in.

"I can feel her here. Watching over us." She trembles, her fingers curling around mine.

I tighten my grasp. "They say those who love us never truly leave us behind. We always carry a piece of them in our hearts, keeping their spirits alive. Nana is looking down on us and she won't want to see you like this, Jess. She lived with positivity. We should do the same. Grieve now, but more importantly, celebrate her life, celebrate her. Take care of yourself. That's what she would want."

Jess squeezes my hand. "Who knew the nerdy kid back then would be so good at comforting people?" She musters a chuckle, the fire briefly returning in her eyes.

I laugh softly, looking at her small hand in mine. "I'm a man of many skills. You just never noticed." *You never did notice me the way I noticed you. But it's okay. You've given me more joy than I've ever expected.* I snort in self-derision.

"Hey, babe, the service is ending. Let's go, I'll drive you back." Ben reappears in front of us.

Ignoring him, I release her hands and stand. I rub my temples, weariness from the traveling and the emotions of the last two days catching up to me.

I say softly to her, "I need to head back to the airport now. If it wasn't for the exam in two days, I'd totally have stayed longer. I'm so sorry for your loss, Jess."

"Thanks for being here, James. I can't tell you how much this means to me." She peers up at me with a shaky smile.

"Always. Anything for you."

It takes all my remaining willpower to turn away from her and leave her behind yet again. This time, in the arms of another man.

My cell phone buzzes on my ride to the airport.

Claire: James, I think we should take a pause on our relationship, if you can call it that. I don't think you're ready to take this a step further. And I don't know if I'm okay with you being half there. We can talk when you get back.

Shit. I groan, putting my hands to my face. What a clusterfuck. What should I do? My head wants to move on, but my heart refuses to let go. I stare at the raindrops pelting the car window, wishing the storm could cleanse me from within.

CHAPTER 17

Jess

I gently shake Steven, who is sleeping like the dead in the passenger seat. "Hey, wake up. We're here. Go inside and find an available room to sleep. You've had a long day today." He took the red-eye from New York City last night and has been up and about since the crack of dawn.

Steven stirs and grumbles, "What about the bags and groceries?"

"Don't worry, I'll take care of them. Hey, get Ems while you're at it, okay? She's completely knocked out in the back seat too."

More mumbling, which I take as acquiescence. It's after three a.m. and we finally arrive at our picturesque little cabin at Yosemite. Four bedrooms, a wood-burning fireplace, and two thousand square feet of cozy goodness with no Wi-Fi. I can hardly contain my glee. The thought of hanging out with the people I love most and unplugging from the world brings me so much joy rivaling the rush of filing an audit on time *and* rewarding myself with luxury chocolate.

Steven grabs the key and drags Emily from the car. "Hey, watch the jacket, it's a limited edition," Ems mutters as the two of them stumble toward the cabin. I shake my head in amusement. Siblings, you got to love them. Liz and James should already be fast asleep since they were able to arrive earlier in the day.

I quickly run through the to-do list in my head, my mind clear and energized despite the long drive and the late hour. I guess having a highly demanding job that sometimes requires burning the midnight oil has its advantages. *Unload the car, bring in the luggage, get the groceries, load the groceries into the refrigerator and freezer, set the goodie bags in front of the bedroom doors to surprise them tomorrow.* I go through my mental checklist as I park the car under the wooden canopy serving as the garage.

I pull on my black beanie, zip up my shiny new black North Face jacket to my chin and slowly creep into the house, not wanting to disturb its sleeping occupants. Warm air assaults my senses, a welcoming change from the biting night chill up in the mountains. The cabin is equipped with a functioning heating system, which I'm very thankful for. I make a few rounds to unload the luggage and groceries.

The living room and kitchen are mostly dark, with only a faint glow emanating from the hallway sconce. From what I can make out, the living room is basic but cozy enough, with a large stone fireplace that's currently not lit, two leather sofas, a few throw pillows and blankets, a large wooden coffee table with what looks like snacks on top of it. A giant flatscreen hangs on the opposite side of the sofa, bringing the room into the twenty-first century. I rub my hands together in glee. *Harry Potter* marathons here we come!

Bringing the groceries in the kitchen, I check out cooking central, my haven when I actually have time to cook. Stainless steel appliances, a four-burner gas stove (awesome, gas is much better than electric for cooking), a rustic wooden island with metal barstools, and a set of dark cabinets. There'll be some good cooking to be done here this weekend. I quickly stash the groceries inside the refrigerator and check out the rest of the cabin.

Tiptoeing to the hallway, I cringe as my feet hit a creaking spot on the floor. Hearing no one stirring, I continue down to check the four bedrooms to see which one is still available. The original plan was for Emily and I to share a room, and James, Steven, and Liz each have their own rooms. The photos on the booking website were not very clear on the bedrooms, but hey, I'm not picky. This should work out.

Going to the first door, I quietly turn the doorknob. It doesn't budge. Locked. Okay, this one is occupied, most likely by Liz or James. The second room is the same. Trying again with the third room, I let out a sigh of relief when the doorknob turns. I quietly peek inside and see Emily sprawled in the middle of a twin-size bed, sleeping away. There's a pile of blankets and a human-shaped lump on the floor, snoring away. I assume this is Steven. I duck back out of the room and proceed to the fourth room.

I turn the doorknob. The door creaks open. Yes! The beginnings of exhaustion prickle in my body. I yawn softly, ready to crash onto a bed and fall into what I predict will be a deep slumber. I peek into the room and frown when I notice there's no bed in sight. Hold on a second. This is an office. Floor-to-ceiling bookshelves filled with musty volumes crowd the walls. A large desk and some armchairs decorate the room. Normally, the book lover in me would gasp at the pleasant surprise, but in this case, this means there are only three bedrooms and all of them are occupied. Crap. Where on earth am I going to sleep? Didn't the rental listing say there are four bedrooms? Did I misread or do I need to give a piece of my mind to the rental agency?

I trudge back toward the living room, resigning to the fact that from the looks of it, the leather sofa will have to do for tonight. We'll figure out the rest tomorrow.

Creak. Creak. Creeeeak.

I freeze in the hallway. What's that? I listen carefully, the previous cobwebs in my mind completely wiped away. Silence. I laugh nervously and mutter to myself, "Jess, you're going crazy from lack of sleep. Everything's okay, you're fine."

Creeeeak. Smash.

Glass shatters on the floor, followed by a faint *shit*. Shit, that's right. I'm not imagining things. There's someone awake in this house. It can't be the others because I just checked in on them, right?

I freeze. Crap, crap, crap. What am I going to do? Should I wake everyone up and cause a commotion? But what if the intruder has a gun? Isn't surprise the best plan of attack? My heart is stuck in my throat. Ugh. Why me? Accountants aren't made to handle these situations, damn it. I'm teetering on the edge of sanity and freaking out. *Calm down, Jess. Deep breaths. Maybe it's just someone in the house who has woken up and wants something from the kitchen.* Yes, that must be it.

I scan the area around me to see what I can use as a potential weapon. Spotting a fireplace poker next to a smaller fireplace in the library, I grip it tightly and creep toward the kitchen, taking slow, measured breaths. *Channel your inner superhero. Channel your inner badass.* It's in there...somewhere. A litany of curses floods my brain.

A tall, hulking shadow is rummaging through the cabinets. Okay, this is a very bad idea. I'm going to wake Steven up, or maybe James. Nope, not doing this. This is how the innocent coeds in *Criminal Minds* get killed in the first five minutes of the show. I back up slowly and turn around to run to the bedrooms.

Clang.

The fireplace poker hits the kitchen island and falls to the ground.

This is why accountants should be holed up in front of a computer and not be an extra in an action movie. I shriek and make a break for it, not caring about the noise I'm making. This accountant isn't staying around to channel her inner assassin.

Footsteps pound after me and before I round the island, a hand tugs my arm in a death grip and twists it behind my back. Another powerful arm spins me around, slams me face first against the refrigerator, and locks me in a choke hold. I claw and kick like a madwoman as I'm lifted into the air, my back plastered to a very warm body behind me.

"Let. Go," I wheeze loudly between struggling breaths. "Of. Me." Black dots begin to form in my vision. I'm not lasting long, the seconds feeling more like minutes to me. I claw with my free hand at the muscular forearm, my brain starved of oxygen. I'm going to die. I'm going to be the sad auditor who dies without meeting her one true love and experiencing the great sex they describe in romance novels.

Suddenly, the grip around my neck loosens and my feet hit

the ground. I gulp in mouthfuls of oxygen, my pulse thunders in my ears.

"Jess?" The warm baritone voice of the super soldier behind me questions in what sounds like horror.

My coughing fit slows down as I slowly turn around, my back against the refrigerator, and stare at my would-be murderer.

"James?"

My eyes adjust to the dark, making out the messy hair, sharp jawline, and the glint of intense eyes staring at me. His hands cage me in as I take in the rest of him. The very naked rest of him. His sculpted chest, abs that would make a swimsuit model jealous, and the deep V leading to his lowly slung boxer briefs. My face flushes, and I'm ever thankful for the darkness coating our surroundings.

"Fuck. Jess, you scared the shit out of me. Are you okay? What the fuck are you doing creeping around the cabin at night, wearing all black, and running away when I saw you? I totally thought you were an intruder!" His hands cradle my face as if checking for injuries. His chest heaves from the exertion moments ago.

I push him. It's like pushing a brick wall.

"I scared you? You scared the hell out of me with your ninja whatever skills! I thought I was going to meet my maker without experiencing life-altering sex." I clasp my hand over my mouth at my irrational outburst. Apparently, stress and oxygen deprivation completely eliminate my filters.

James stills, his chest brushing against mine with every breath we take. My skin prickles with awareness. His hand tilts my chin up as he stares at my lips. Even in the dark, I can make out his blown pupils. My breathing picks up and warmth courses through my veins down to my core as I realize how small I am against this massive masculine specimen in front of me.

His hand slides down my body, skimming over my curves, leaving goosebumps in its wake. I gasp as my pulse speeds up.

"James?"

He closes his eyes at my breathy whisper and lightly places his forehead to mine. Sandalwood mixes with strawberries, our combined scents mingling in harmony as if they belonged together all along.

Kiss me. The unbidden thought forces itself into my awareness.

I whimper, my body aching for something, something primal I've never felt before. I arch my body into his and he groans, his lips millimeters from mine. He grinds once on me, a thick hardness pressing against my stomach. I moan, wanting him to be closer but afraid of asking for it.

My eyes flutter close as the background chatter in my brain quiets down. His nose trails my cheeks, eliciting shivers in areas I don't even know can be so sensitive. I let out a breathy moan as my nipples prickle into hard buds. He catches my moan with a light brush of his lips, testing the waters, carefully wading into the deep end. I melt against him, and he pins my body down with his as he slowly nips at my lower lip before dipping his tongue out to test the seam. My body is on fire. This tame kiss is threatening to burn me alive and even my ex-boyfriend has never been able to elicit such sensations in me. I can't believe I'm kissing my best friend.

Shit. Best friend. James. What the fuck am I doing?

My eyes snap open and I freeze, suddenly terrified at this change in our friendship. The chaos resumes in my brain, flooding me with one negative scenario after another.

James stops, as if sensing my hesitation, and slams his fist into the refrigerator door in apparent frustration, jerking me awake from my ruminating thoughts. He releases me and steps back, his hands giving his tented boxer briefs one long stroke, his burning gaze never leaving mine as he backs up to lean against the island.

My lips dry at the sight of this Calvin Klein model, who apparently is my best friend, being turned on by me. Is that an eight pack? What kind of nerd is this guy? My tongue darts out to wet my parched lips.

He groans, his eyes fixating on the movement. "Don't do that, Jess," he rasps. "I'm hanging on by a thread." He turns around and faces the dark living room, his back muscles flex and bunch in the dim glow of the hallway light.

What. The. Heck. Just. Happened? I will my nerves to settle even though I'm burning hot. My panties are embarrassingly soaked through from the last few minutes of interaction.

Crickets chirp outside. Drops of water drip from the leaking faucet. Seconds pass as we both come down from the lust-filled adrenaline rush. James slowly turns around, looking a little more like my best friend and less like the alpha predator from a moment ago.

"You just got in?" he asks gruffly.

"Y-yes. There was a little more traffic than I expected. I already loaded the fridge with a bunch of goodies for this weekend. Ems and Steven are conked out in one of the bedrooms already. I checked the other rooms. Two of them were locked, which I assumed were yours and Liz's rooms. The last room was an office, so I was just getting ready to crash on the couch for the night. Didn't want to disturb you guys until the morning. I know you guys are tired and everything. Sorry for scaring you; I thought there was an intruder—" I ramble on. Apparently, the lack of sleep and the night's events have rendered me into an incoherent mess.

James pins me with a sharp stare. "And you thought it was a good idea to check things out when there was an intruder? What were you going to do? Hurt yourself with a..." He stares at the poker lying on the ground. "A fireplace poker?"

"I decided against it at the last minute and was running away—"

"You *never* should've ran toward danger. *Ever.* Don't do anything so fucking *stupid* again," his reprimands, his voice full of restrained anger.

I stiffen, not liking the direction of the conversation. "Hey, James Chapman. If *you* had bothered to turn on the *freakin'* light, none of this would've happened. Don't blame this on me!"

"If *anything* were to happen to you, I *won't be able to live.*" His eyes flash in the relative darkness and his hands shake against the island. "Do you understand me? Don't you *ever* put yourself in danger again!" He slams his hands on the island for emphasis.

Shocked into silence, I stare at him dumbfounded. Seconds pass as we stare at each other, our chests heaving from restrained emotions.

"Look, sorry for my outburst. You... You're just too important to me. That incident just freaked me out." James rubs his temples, deflating in an exhale.

"Let's just put this behind us. It was a one-off incident, but your concern is noted. No running into danger again. I think I learned that lesson today. Dude, what have you been doing these past ten years, learning to fight MMA?" I attempt a halfhearted joke, eager to dispel this weird tension between us.

He grins. "Boxing, jiu-jitsu, and swimming. Not bad for the little nerd from a long time ago, right?"

"I'll say." I smile back and mutter under my breath, "And you look nothing like the little nerd from back then either."

"What did you say?" he asks, the teasing glint in his eyes making me wonder if he heard the rest of my sentence.

"Nothing. Nothing at all." I clam up before I can embarrass myself further.

"So, you're going to sleep on the couch? That's not comfortable at all. Let me sleep there. You can take my room. I can't sleep well, anyway. I was just out here getting a glass of water, but accidentally dropped the glass in the sink."

"No way," I reply indignantly. "I'm like half your size. You won't fit on the couch. I'll be perfectly fine here for a night."

James shakes his head. "There's no way the gentleman in me will allow a lady to sleep on a couch while I take the bed."

We stare each other down. I narrow my eyes. He follows suit and ups the ante by crossing his arms, once again highlighting his strong musculature. Damn it, why am I noticing these things now?

"It appears we are at an impasse," I observe, which he replies with a curt nod.

A thought occurs in my mind. This is so cliché, but I don't see any way out of this late-night kitchen standoff.

"What if we share your room? Will that make you happy? That way we can all go back to sleep, seeing it's probably closer to four now," I blurt out, internally cringing at my forwardness. I squeeze my eyes shut, not wanting to look at him, especially after my behavior a few minutes ago.

"If you can handle it, I can handle it."

I see how it's going to be. He's provoking me on purpose. Game on. There's no way I'm folding.

"Okay, fine."

He cocks his head. A ghost of a smile appears on his face, as if I've played right into his hands.

"Okay, then."

He sweeps his hand out toward the hallway. "Ladies first. The open door is my room."

I stomp past him toward his room, his chuckles behind me infuriating me for some reason even though I was the one to suggest the one-bedroom solution.

His room is small but organized, his clothes neatly laid out on top of the dresser. I make note of the four-poster full-size bed in the middle of the room and the clean en-suite bathroom on the side. *This is nothing, Jess. You're just sleeping in the same bed with your best friend. You have done this before,* I grumble to myself. *Yeah, when you guys were in elementary school.* I curse myself. *Nope, I got this. I'm calm and poised. Graceful.* I scrunch my face as I realize I don't have my toiletries and pajamas.

I trudge past James, who is now standing inside the room staring at the floor and shaking his head, as if hiding his amusement.

"Dude, wear a shirt." I brush past him.

He bursts out in laughter. "What? Does this bother you?"

His cackling follows me into the hallway. I don't even bother answering him. I quickly retrieve my bag from the living room and bring it back to the bedroom, where he has thankfully donned an MIT T-shirt, which stretches against his muscles every time he moves. Better than nothing, I suppose. He sits on the bed, eyeing me in smugness, as if he knows what's going on in my mind.

I huff and lock the door behind me in the en-suite, disgruntled at the fact I'm suddenly viewing my best friend as...a man, someone who has sexual allure, something that has never crossed my mind before he came back to LA. I quickly brush my teeth and wash my face. Changing into my oversized sleep shirt, I stare at myself in the mirror. A bit of redness in my face, dark eye circles, the same old freckles. I look tired, but presentable. I pad back out into the bedroom and gingerly crawl to the vacant side of the bed.

He snickers and turns off the light. I pull the covers to my chin, my body tired but my mind fully awake and very much aware of the masculine body next to me, warming me even though our bodies aren't touching.

"Stop thinking, Jess. I can hear your mind whirring all the way over here. Go to sleep." His voice is soothing in the darkness.

I hear the rustling of the bedsheets as he turns to face away from me. I steady my breaths, my mind eventually catching up to the fatigue of my body. I murmur, "Good night, James."

He whispers something back I can't make out as darkness overtakes me into a dreamless sleep.

CHAPTER 18

James

I wake up multiple times in the night. Each time, I'm startled to find Jess lying next to me, something that has been in my wildest dreams for the longest time. Jess is a terrible bed partner, which amuses me as she's always so poised when she's awake. She constantly rolls around in bed, kicks off the comforter, then proceeds to shiver and steals *my* side of the blankets. Her arms and legs are flailed in odd positions, sometimes whacking me in the middle of the night.

And yet, I wouldn't trade my place for anywhere else in the world.

I look at the clock on the nightstand. Five a.m. Jess is currently curled around me, her head tucked under my shoulders as her arms wrap across my chest. I softly kiss her hair, careful not to wake her up.

This is where I should've been all along. Instead of wasting my time halfway across the world in a futile attempt to shove our relationship into the friend zone. It's like a toddler repeatedly trying to insert the square into the circle-shaped hole in the popular sorting toys.

How much time we have wasted.

Or perhaps, the scenic routes we take in life ultimately leads us to being with the right person at the right time.

• • •

Six Years Ago

I sit in my London flat, staring at the dark clouds outside my window. They weren't kidding when they say it rains a lot here. London is a beautiful city, especially during the summer when the sun makes an appearance and the weather is warm and pleasant. But when the weather rears its ugly head, the dreary rain feels relentless. The metro is a mess and I just want to hole up in my flat and hibernate until the rain stops.

I stare at the offer letter on my desk, rereading the words for the tenth time.

Dear Mr. Chapman,

Offer of Employment

Congratulations! We are pleased to offer you employment in the role of Senior Data Analyst at Wilmington and Ferris (referred to as "the Employer", "the Firm", or "we", in the rest of this letter). Your accomplishments at the London School of Economics make you an excellent fit at the Firm. This letter will summarise the main terms and the conditions of our offer.

Spinning my office chair in a circle, I lean on the headrest and close my eyes. I have a decision to make, one to most people will be a simple one. Wilmington and Ferris is the largest data analytics firm in the UK and getting a job here will open many doors for me no matter where in the world I go to later on. It should be a simple decision for me to take this job, a perfect fit after my graduate education at LSE. But somehow, something is holding me back. Taking a job in London feels very permanent and perhaps a big part of me still feels the pull of home in the States. My phone buzzes.

Claire: Thanks for dinner, James. Fancy going to the theatre with me next weekend? (Notice my usage of British words?)

Claire moved here for a post with King's College London. Our paths keep crossing since our days at MIT and despite how things ended with us before, we remained friends and depending on whether or not I stay in London, we may become more. Another incoming message comes through, this time from Jess.

Jess: Got some news for you! Can't wait to share it with you on our call later!

I smile at the text, warmth filling my veins. I've long resigned myself to my Pavlovian reaction to Jess. I'm just happy she's doing well. After all, it's all I've ever wanted for her.

After a quick shower, I quickly turn on my laptop and connect to the online video chat. Jess's smiling face comes onto the screen.

"Wow, just took a shower? Your hair is all crazy looking." She motions to my hair, which I'm sure is a big mess as I haven't combed it yet.

"You got me. I had dinner with Claire earlier and it was raining outside, so I wanted to clean myself up." I smooth my hair out as best as I can, trying to be inconspicuous.

Jess twiddles her fingers and wags her brows. "Claire, huh? Soooo how is she doing? Isn't it awfully convenient she moved halfway across the world and just *happens* to be in the same city as you?"

I snort. "Oh please, not everything is the next great American romance. She had a good opportunity, and she took it. She's doing well. I think she likes it here."

Jess fiddles with her red bracelet. A jolt of satisfaction rushes through me when I see her wearing the bracelet I gave her all those years ago. It's as if a piece of me is with her at all times. *Just like a piece of her remains with you always.* The lucky penny is still in its place in my wallet. Despite the penny not bringing any special luck to me, I still can't bring myself to part with it.

"So, have you given your offer some thought? A response is due back to them soon, right?"

"Yeah. They were good at granting me an extension for a few months since I was finishing up a project with LSE, but I don't think I can delay it any longer. Good offers like that don't come by easily."

Jess frowns, as if deep in thought. She always takes on other people's problems as if they were her own. "Selfishly, I want you to come back to the States. I haven't seen you in person in years. But you need to do what's best for you." She stares into my eyes, sincerity in her voice. "I want you to be happy, James. That's what I wish for."

It's uncanny how two people oceans apart can have the same wish at the same time.

"I know you do, Jess, and I love you for that," I reply softly. "I'll let you know what I decide."

I cough in an attempt to clear the lump in my throat. "So, tell me your good news."

She squeals, as if suddenly remembering the purpose of this call. "Yes! Well, you're looking at the newest audit senior associate! Mid-year promotion!"

"All right! Good job, Jess. What did I tell you? And you were all worried about your performance reviews last month because you got one 'meeting expectations' instead of 'exceeding expectations.' Congratulations. Looks like taking on those inventory counts during holidays finally paid off." I smile smugly at her.

"Hey! My job is a lot more than just counting inventory. There's some technical accounting guidance involved…"

"Spare me the details, please. No generally accepted accounting principles or audit standards talk or else I really will fall into a food coma and won't wake up for a long time," I tease. "So, did you think more about the audition opportunity you told me about last time?" Jess's college friend from the acapella group at ULA is trying to recruit her into auditioning for a role in her off-Broadway musical. I know singing was always her passion, even if she still refuses to take it seriously.

Jess's face darkens and she lets out a heavy sigh. "I told her I'm going to pass on this one. Work is busy and I simply have no time. Plus, I can't imagine getting up there and having to sing solo with all these people judging me. It just gives me the hives."

"But isn't this something you really love? Shouldn't you make time for something you are passionate about? What are you afraid of?"

She shrugs, her hands playing with the jade heart on her bracelet again. She is nervous. Jess has the worst tells in the world.

"I—I..." She takes another deep breath and continues, "I'm comfortable with my job. I do it well. It pays enough for now. Mother and Father are happy with my career choice. It's stable and has a visible career ladder. Why ruin a good thing on something that may be good in your imagination, but maybe when it becomes reality, might not be so great?"

"So, you rather stay in status quo than take a risk?" I push her, because deep down, I know she is not completely fulfilled with her job. I've seen it time and time again when she sang for me in the past, how her eyes would sparkle and light up with fire. The love she has for singing is something I've never seen on her face when she talks about her job.

"I'm just not ready yet. I feel in control in my job. I can keep my anxiety at bay and I like that. I don't want to change something that's working right now. I wish people would stop asking me that." I wish she could see what I see, someone who has so much love and life to give to those around her, someone who is worthy of receiving the same love and life from other aspects in her life.

"Okay, just checking." I smile in encouragement, not wanting to stress her more as I know she is constantly undergoing a lot of internal and external pressures. I wish I could be there to help shoulder some of her burdens and be a source of comfort for her. "I'm proud of you, Jess. I know you worked really hard for your promotion."

She smiles at me, her eyes softening. "I know, James. I know you're looking out for me. You really are the best friend a girl can ask for."

My heart clenches involuntarily. "I owe you a meal the next time I see you. So, anything else new with you?"

Jess tucks a strand of her lush locks behind her ear. She shyly says, "Ben is going to Chicago to work for a few years. He's asking me to go with him. I said yes and my firm has agreed to transfer me to the Chicago office."

I flinch, the sharp pain following a familiar dull ache in my heart. I bite my cheek and clench my jaw in an attempt to retain the neutral expression on my face.

"I see. Congratulations. That seems like a big step for you, Jess."

She beams, oblivious to my internal turmoil.

The call ends soon thereafter and I once again take out the penny from my wallet. I toss it in the air. *Heads, you go back to the States and tell her not to go. Tails, you move on for good.* I slam my hand on the table, covering the coin. An incoming text chimes from my phone.

> **Claire:** My treat, James. My treat at the theatre! You know you want to go. You are chuffed, right? This is ace?

I slowly relax my hand and look at the coin.

Tails.

I laugh humorlessly, shaking my head at the fates, yet completely unsurprised. After all, having Jess in my life as a friend is better than not having her at all. Perhaps this is the final sign I need to stay away from her and truly move on.

I type out a message and click send.

> **James:** Theatre sounds jolly good. We can celebrate some good news. I'm accepting the offer at Wilmington and Ferris.

• • •

What would've happened if I didn't take the offer back then? Would we have been together sooner or would she still be with Ben? I guess I'll never know. What matters is now, and she's sleeping soundly next to me, right where she has belonged all along.

"I love you, sweetheart. I've always loved you. I hope one day, you'll realize how much," I murmur softly to her.

Jess mumbles something unintelligible and burrows closer. She wraps one long, shapely leg around my torso as her hands skate down my abs. I groan as the blood rushes south.

This is going to be a long night.

snuggle closer to the source of warmth, relishing the heat and the feeling of security. This is the best dream ever. I've never felt so... safe, so protected. There is shuffling in the background and my furnace moves away.

"No. Don't go," I mumble.

The furnace stills. I wrap my legs around the warmth. *There, I got you. You can't go anywhere.* If I were a cat, I'd be purring right now. This is so comfortable. Sandalwood hits my senses, the familiar smell eliciting tingles throughout my body. The dream quickly changes flavors, becoming more sensual. I chase the tingles, my body softly grinding on the warmth, my hands trailing on this hot, hard pillow. This pillar of heat, with dips and ridges, moves with my hand. My hand grasps for purchase, finally setting on a long, velvety protrusion on the furnace. My hand curls around it automatically, like a reflex. The tingles blossom into shards of heat, prickling my nerve endings, as I settle into a rhythm, chasing the intensity. A deep sound rumbles in the background. More shifting. *Don't go.* I grip harder. A deep groan reverberates in the background. I shift closer—

A deep groan. Harsh breathing. Sandalwood.

My eyes flutter open, squinting at the morning light illuminating the room. A large body slowly comes into focus.

James.

His arm covers his eyes, his sturdy bicep flexes against his shirt, and his hand curls in a tight fist. He appears to be in pain, his teeth biting his bottom lip, his jaw locked tight. Worried, I crawl closer but realize...

I am already practically on top of him.

My legs are hooked around his waist. I look down in horror as I realize my hand is rubbing the very erect steel rod protruding from his boxer briefs. Oh God. He is *huge.*

I scramble back in horror, my hands recoiling as if I just touched a hot stove. *I was dry humping my best friend and copping a feel.* A red flush creeps up my body as I take in my aroused state. My sleep shirt is hiked up to my waist. My nipples poke through the soft material, begging to be touched. My panties are soaked through.

What should I do? Should I apologize? Is he awake? He looks like he's awake, but I still can't see his eyes because he has covered them with the gorgeous, strong bicep of his. What did I do? This is so inappropriate. Did I do irrevocable damage to our relationship? A thousand thoughts cross my mind, none of them good, as my pulse pounds in my ears, and my intrusive worrying ratches up to nuclear levels.

James's erratic breathing slows down, and he curls to his side, feigning sleep. I gingerly poke him. It's like poking a rock. He doesn't stir. Okay then. I doubt he's really asleep, but it appears he's giving me an out...and I'm *definitely* taking it, the coward that I am.

I scramble off the bed and softly tiptoe to the en-suite bathroom, grabbing a change in clothing along the way. I look back at his figure on the bed, as still as a statue, still "asleep." This man is dedicated to his acting. I have to give it to him. I softy close the door with a click and lean back against the wall, my thundering pulse finally slowing down as I recount the events this morning. We better figure out alternative sleeping arrangements today.

A cold shower and a blow-out later, I feel much more like myself. I don a white cotton button-down, a thick wool sweater, fleece-lined jeans, and turkey socks because it's Thanksgiving weekend after all. I tame my hair into loose curls, apply light makeup on my face, and, on a whim, spray a small amount of James's cologne on me, the fragrance smelling different on me than on him, yet equally comforting. I steel myself, take one calming breath, and open the door, poking my head out to survey the bedroom.

James reclines on a worn velvet armchair in the corner of the room, glasses perched on his nose in a sexy, scruffy way. One ankle is casually crossed over his knees and he's reading a book. He looks like a Tom Ford ad coming to life. James glances up and flashes me a stunning, bright smile. A burst of butterflies appears in my stomach.

"Morning, Jess. You woke up early today. Did you sleep well last night?"

I blink at his nonchalant attitude. Was he really asleep? He stares at me innocently as if waiting for me to respond.

"Y-yes. Sleep was great. Had an interesting dream this morning, but overall feel really rested. What about you?" I squint my eyes at him, trying to decipher any potentially hidden emotions in his gaze.

He shrugs, as if he has all the time in the world. "Great sleep. Can't complain." He slowly grins. "So...what was this interesting dream?" His eyes gleam, as if daring me to confess.

"Did I wake you up this morning?" I can't help myself. I'm going crazy in my mind remembering the events of last night and this morning, thinking I've somehow made things awkward in our decade-long friendship.

He blinks his eyes slowly, his gaze guileless and genuine. There's a reason I never win any poker games against him. "Nope. Did something happen?"

"Nope," I quickly respond. "Nope. Everything was fine. Glad you had good sleep." I feign a yawn. "I can use some coffee this morning."

James gets up from his armchair, his towering stature once again surprising me. How is he this tall now? He swipes a to-go cup

I did not notice before from the nightstand and ambles toward me. "I figured. Here you go. Pumpkin *flavored* latte with light whip."

I gleefully take the cup from him and inhale the seasonal special. "How did you manage this?"

He chuckles. "They have an espresso machine in the kitchen and I brought my own pumpkin syrup." James shakes his head. "I've never met anyone who drinks pumpkin spice latte without the spice. Cinnamon is what makes the drink."

I stick out my tongue. "Yuck. I hate cinnamon. I know, I should be arrested." I gulp down my drink, the caffeine fortifying my frayed nerves. "Let's go outside. I think I hear the others awake. I have some activities planned for today."

"Of course you do, Ms. Organizer."

"Whatever. You know you love me for it."

We walk over to the kitchen island where Emily, Liz, and Steven are all bright-eyed and bushy-tailed, laughing about some comment Emily made.

"Morning, guys. Slept in, didn't you?" Emily's lips split into a wide smile. She winks.

"Ugh, I don't need to hear this." Steven groans and Liz bursts into laughter.

Steven changes the subject. "Did you guys break something last night? I found a few small pieces of glass shards in the sink this morning."

Emily and Liz stare at each other in confusion. "Not us. Sound asleep. Dead to the world."

James stills and places his hand on my back. I look down on the ground, my face aflame as I recall his body upon mine last night. "Sorry, guys, I accidentally broke a cup." He clears his throat. "So, Jess, what are we doing today?"

I clap my hands, shaking myself out of the trip down memory lane. "Okay. Seeing as it's almost lunchtime, I'll make you guys a brunch of French toast and Denver omelets. Then, board games. Afterward, everyone gets some free time to rest, read books, relax, whatever. Dinner afterwards, old-fashion barbecuing in the large fire pit in the backyard. I even brought s'mores," I proudly announce, a perfect off-the-grid day with the best people in the world.

"Sounds good to me. Free food and a chill day. Perfect." Steven crosses his arms behind his head.

Emily throws a dish rag at him. "Dude, dish duty for you if Jess cooks." She looks at me. "I'll help you with brunch."

"Thanks. Okay, the rest of you guys get out of my way and do a nature walk or something. I'll see you back here in one hour."

Liz and Steven walk toward their rooms to grab their jackets. James lingers behind, his eyes questioning. "You sure you don't need more help, Jess?"

I shake my head. *Please get out of here.* I need space and the familiar routine of cooking to clear my thoughts and get my mindset back to the way it was when he was in London.

With a nod, he departs, leaving behind his special blend of spicy fragrance. I start whipping the eggs while Emily prepares the toast. She glances over at me. "Okay, everyone is gone. Spill."

"Spill what?" I keep my focus on the eggs, fighting a blush on my face.

"You know you have the worst poker face, sis. Something happened. I can feel it with my Spidey senses. James was tracking you with his eyes all morning. Why were you guys sleeping in the same room, anyway?"

"Because you and Steven so kindly claimed the last room with a bed, leaving your poor big sister out there hauling in luggage and groceries with nowhere to sleep." I start dicing the ham and green bell peppers, my hands settling into a familiar rhythm. "James happened to wake up in the middle of the night for a drink of water and told me he couldn't let me sleep on the couch. So, we decided to be adults about it and shared his room instead."

"Huh. That actually sounds...plausible," Emily replies, still sounding unconvinced.

"Yep. That was it. End of story. Nothing happened." Onions, I hate chopping onions. My eyes begin to prickle as I rapidly blink away the discomfort.

"Hold on, was he on the floor or were you guys in the bed together?"

"I invaded his room! I wasn't going to let him sleep on the floor. We just shared a bed... like we *used to do*."

She harrumphs. "In *elementary school*. When you were kids." Emily shakes her head, laying out the freshly toasted bread. "Aaand nothing happened?"

"We are adults. We can share a bed without anything happening." *Keep telling yourself that, Jess. Maybe if you repeat it one thousand times, it will actually be true.*

"Well, that's boring. I still think something is going on between you two. I can smell it in the air." She sniffs. Then she sniffs closer and jams her nose in my hair, then on my shoulder.

I push her away with the back of my spatula. "What are you doing? Are you a dog?"

"You smell different. You smell like...James. Yes, that's it. You smell like him!"

"Oh my gosh. I just used his cologne this morning. I wanted to see how it smells on me. Ugh. Get away from me." I groan, exasperated—and guilty—and start frying the omelet.

Emily steps back and I can feel her stare. "Jess, be careful. Maybe I'm being too sensitive, but I tell you, the guy has had a thing for you for the longest time. Don't hurt him. Don't hurt yourself. I really, really like him for you, but you guys have such a long friendship. Just be careful and make sure you think things through."

I stay silent, mulling over her words. James liking me for a long time? I snort, my initial reaction is to deny it but then I reflect back on what happened in the kitchen earlier. But we've been the strictest of platonic friends all these years. Heck, he has been my sounding board for guy problems. I mean, he even met Ben before we broke up. Sure, there's sexual tension now, but...it can't be, he couldn't have liked me for so long and I didn't notice a thing. Emily is wrong.

"Don't worry. I'm sure I'm better at worrying about things than you are. I know what I'm doing," I reply, resolute.

"Ooookay, sis," she replies, still sounding annoyingly skeptical.

The hour passes by swiftly and the rest of the group trail in from the great outdoors commenting on the gray skies and chilly weather. Everyone consumes the food with gusto, and I grin with satisfaction. There is nothing more fulfilling to a chef than seeing your creations being devoured.

Steven begrudgingly does the dishes then trudges to his room for a well-deserved nap as he's still a bit jetlagged from the East Coast hours. Liz and Emily huddle around the kitchen island, giggling, most likely discussing Emily's latest dating exploits. I think she has moved on from Antoine to another poor dude she met at a club. I envy her carefree nonchalance, her free spirit, her dive in first and ask later type of attitude.

I curl up on the sofa, wrapped up in a throw blanket, and stare at the snow-capped pine trees outside. Up here, I feel like I'm a world away from my anxieties and troubles, from the job that doesn't truly inspire me but I excel at, from my parents. Surrounded by the closest people in my life, I feel like I can finally breathe, the usual heaviness in my chest lightening. I crack open a novel and start reading.

James stokes the fire in the impressive fireplace, the logs crackling, bringing an additional layer of winter ambiance to the cabin. He settles himself at the foot of the sofa, with his own novel flipped open. His black-rimmed glasses once again perched on his nose, making him infuriatingly sexy. The sexy nerd, my kryptonite.

"What are you reading?" He senses my perusal but still stares at his novel, flipping through the pages quickly, showcasing his speed-reading capabilities.

"Romance novel...what else?" I whisper back. There's an intimacy existing between two people who read next to each other. A thread connecting us.

He flips another page. "Of course. I shouldn't have asked." He laughs softly. "Why are you so drawn to them?"

"Because of the happily ever after. The nervous Nancy in me likes to know no matter what the author throws at the main characters, they'll overcome all hardships and end up happy at the end. Even though that doesn't always happen in real life. But when I'm reading, I get to be those lucky main characters for a while, taking a journey toward my own happily ever after."

He glances up at me, his eyes a deep ocean blue this morning, with light flecks of gold dotting the irises. "Why do you think you won't get your happily ever after?" he inquires with a frown.

"It's not like I don't think I'll get it, it's more like I don't know. Life is full of unknowns and is often not within my control and I feel...scared, unbalanced. I feel like I'm living my life as carefully as I can, making the smartest and most logical of choices, but I still can't guarantee things will turn out fine. And that freaks me out." I shrug, resigned to my reality.

His gaze darkens with intensity, and he rubs the scruff on his chin as if contemplating my concerns. "What if taking risks and leaping into the unknown will put you on a better path to your happily ever after? What if staying safe is what's dragging you behind? What if the future already holds great things for you and all you need to do is to trust it?"

I hold his stare, the intensity thickening with each second. "Maybe. I...don't know. Perhaps I'm just messed up. I never feel grounded, and I'm always unsettled." I sigh humorlessly. "Maybe someday I'll figure this out. But in the meantime..." I tap my novel, my lips tipping up. "I have Lord Wickersham, Viscount Westford, and Lady Constance Collington to give me a taste of that happily ever after."

James's gaze warms to a mellow blue and he resumes reading.

'll give you your happily ever after, my love.

I sneak a glance at her. Jess's raven hair covers half of her face, but I can still see her lips tipping up in a small smile as she turns the page. Her pale skin flushes pink as she bites on her plump bottom lip.

"You're reading something naughty, aren't you?"

She slams her book closed and stares at me, her eyes wide as if she has been caught stealing. Her pink tongue darts out to sooth her previous bite. I groan as I take in her flushed appearance. What I'd give to put that expression on her face.

"No...w-what are you talking about?"

I get on my knees and lean toward her. Her mouth falls lax as she backs away until her head rests against the sofa.

"Your skin is beautifully red. Your breathing is shallow," I whisper in her ear, enjoying her shivers. "You were biting your bottom lip."

"Ugh, stop it. What I'm reading is none of your business." She huffs and pushes me away. I chuckle and sit back down on the floor. Unnerving her may be my favorite pastime now.

"Just saying, books never compare to reality." I open my book and resume reading. "Reality will be so much more...satisfying."

She throws a pillow at me. "Stop distracting me. Ugh, is this what you do with girls...like Claire? Is this the side of you I've been missing out on all these years?"

I still and keep my gaze on the pages in front of me. "No, definitely not. It was never like this with Claire or anyone else," I murmur.

• • •

Four Months Ago

"Hey, sorry for being late. A meeting ran long at work," I huff as I take off my suit jacket and drape it over the open seat at the table. Claire told me she wanted to talk today, and she has been waiting for me at the café a block away from my office. The café bustles with activity despite the late hour, people still eager for a steaming cup of joe to kickstart Friday night. I walk over to Claire to give her my usual kiss in greeting, but she places her hand on my chest, stopping me.

Claire looks up at me, her tawny eyes fill with an unidentified emotion. She appears...skittish? Dread settles in my gut as I stare at her somber face. I think I know what this conversation is going to be about, something I've suspected for months. She nervously twirls an amber lock of hair in her hand as she motions for me to sit down.

I take a deep breath, releasing it on a slow exhale, and I swallow the lump in my throat. I brace myself for whatever she is going to say. "Is this the conversation I think we'll have?" I ask softly.

She blinks and dips her head in acknowledgement. "James, you know I love you so much. You have such a great heart and are capable of such powerful love. But I don't think we're going to work out. I think we've given it our best shot this time around. We are at the right place, at the right time, looking for the same thing." She releases her hair and holds her cup of coffee in front of her with trembling hands.

I reach out and place my hands on top of hers, wanting to reassure her and let her know I understand. Her trembling calms, and she laughs mirthlessly. "Always the gentleman, even now, when I'm breaking up with you."

I give her a small squeeze and wait for her to continue, knowing I owe her at least that.

"I know you really gave it your best shot. I do see your effort and how you really try to give me all of your attention, all of your extra time outside of work, but I know I don't have all of your heart. I think I've known for some time now."

"Look, if I gave you the impression—" I begin, wanting to reassure her.

She stills me with a stern gaze I've come to know as her "I'm not finished" look. I sit back and motion for her to continue.

"You're a great guy, and I think I'm pretty awesome as well. I think we both deserve to be with someone who wholeheartedly loves us. While I think I can be that person for you, I know you're not that person for me. I don't know what's going on between you and Jess, but deep down, I think you and I both know I'm the third wheel in this strange love triangle." She stares at me, resolute in her opinion.

A dull pang reverberates in my chest, a sensation I've come to know as normal whenever I think about Jess. "There's nothing going on between Jess and me. You know we're just the best of friends. Nothing more. She's halfway across the world with her boyfriend and probably soon-to-be fiancé. I haven't done anything—"

Claire stops me, this time with her hand on top of mine. She gently uncurls my fingers that were unknowingly clenched in a fist. "I know you haven't done anything with her. I'm sure she probably doesn't know you feel this way about her either. I recognize you've stayed away and haven't even gone back to visit her these past few years and you've made every effort to be with me. But deep down in your heart, I think she has always occupied a very important space. Don't you owe it to yourself to give it a shot? To go after her? To leave no regrets?"

She shakes her head and stares into her coffee cup, recognizing the irony of this discussion. "I love you, James. I want you to be happy. Truly happy. What we have is good, but I think there's something better than 'good' out there. I haven't found it yet, but I think you have. You just need to do something about it, or at least try. You never know, and maybe what you're looking for is within reach, waiting for you to go after it." She pauses, taking a deep breath. "I think I also deserve to be with someone who wholeheartedly wants to be with me." Claire stares at me, tears swimming in her eyes as she lets go of my hand, the action symbolic of the end of our relationship.

I slowly sit back, rapidly blinking my eyes, surprised at the moisture gathered there. I rub my face with my hands, wondering how we got here. Claire stands and slowly gathers her belongings. This time, she walks to my side and pulls me up from the chair. She slides her hands around my waist and gives me a tight hug.

"Goodbye, James. Thank you for the memories and for your love. I know you gave it your best shot, so don't beat yourself up for it. I wish nothing but the best for you," she whispers.

I return her embrace with a light kiss in her hair, my head incapable of forming any words. Sometimes, words aren't needed.

We pull apart. She gives me a shaky smile, steels her shoulders, and walks out of the café, out of my life.

I collapse into the chair and stare into the night. People laughing on the streets, commuters hurrying to their next destination, double-decker buses stopping to take on more passengers, the world moving on as mine slows to a standstill. A moment of clarity, deep-seated calmness enters my body and mind.

Claire is right. Perhaps I need to risk it all, risk the most important relationship in my life, to give my soul an answer once and for all.

Resolve permeating my veins, I grab my jacket and stride out into the night, becoming part of the Friday night energy saturating the air. A new emotion floats to the surface.

Hope.

CHAPTER 21

Jess

Playing Monopoly with my siblings is brutal. They are the sorest losers on the planet. Liz and James don't help at all, with Liz egging the drama on and James being one of the most competitive alpha-holes on the planet, another quality of this new manly James I'm getting to know since he came back to LA.

"Six! Yes. Boardwalk, peoples. Here's the money for a hotel. You guys are going to go bankrupt when you land on the blue. Suckers." Emily claps gleefully as she builds yet another hotel on her blue empire.

"Whatever, with the speed you're spending the cash, you'll go bankrupt before any of us," Steven quips, rolling his dice. "Much like your real life." He sniggers.

Liz gives Steven a high five. "That's a burn. Come on, Ems, you aren't going to take that lying down, right?"

"Damn right I won't. Don't come crying to your big sis when you're strapped for cash, little bro. I'm going to kick your ass, just like the way I did when you were ten."

Steven rolls his eyes. "I'm an investment banker. I think I'll do just fine on the cash front. And how long are you going to hold that one over me? That was twelve years ago. I'm pretty sure if we have a rematch today, I'll be the winner." He puffs out his chest. "But since I'm a gentleman, I won't fight the ladies."

"Bring it on, little bro," Emily taunts. "There are many ways to defeat the egotistical adult male. Even though you may be taller than me now, I still know your Achilles heel, like the weak spot when you broke your tibia in seventh grade."

"Be quiet. I'm thinking guys." I wave my hands in the air as I scrutinize the board. "Should I get this property? If I do, then they'll need to pay more when they land on this...but if I don't, I'll have more cash, so I can buy the other one I want. But everyone has bought up most of the board already...ugh decisions, decisions..."

Sitting next to me, James starts shuddering, his shoulders shaking as he covers his face with his palms. Concerned, I look over. "Are you okay—hey! You're laughing at me." I give him a shove.

He shakes his head. "If your brain activity is indicative of a country's GDP, that country of yours will be the richest in the world."

"I take life seriously, James. Effort equals result." I motion to his body. "But I guess if someone looks like this, you don't need to try as hard to get what you want," I blurt. Belatedly realizing what I just implied, I slap my palm over my mouth. I'm sure my face is turning an shade of beet red.

He pins with me an unfathomable stare. "I look like what?" His eyes darken, as if daring me to clarify my statement.

My face is scorching hot, and I grab the glass of water on the coffee table and take a big gulp, the cool liquid doing nothing to bring down the flush.

"Oooo...what's going on over there? Sis, your face is bright red," Ems points out unhelpfully. I'm going to strangle her.

The room quiets as everyone pauses. I feel four pairs of eyes staring at me as mine remain glued to the game board.

"Absolutely nothing is going on. I'm just a bit warm from sitting by the fire," I reply nonchalantly. "Anyway, we need to talk about sleeping arrangements tonight. I'm thinking I can room with—"

"Oh! Ems and I are rooming together. She's giving me tips on the modern dating world," Liz exclaims, her eyes big and innocent.

Emily nods enthusiastically next to her. I don't buy it for an instant. These two are up to something.

"I guess you can have my room, sis. I mean, it's a twin, so I can't share the bed with you..." Steven offers, but Emily gives him a hard shove. "Ouch! What was that for!" He glares at her as she gives him a quelling look.

"Of course not. That won't work," Liz chimes in. "If you give her your room, then you'll need to share the bed with James, and both of you are well over six feet. It won't be comfortable, with two giant men huddled together in a small bed. That makes no sense."

"I can sleep on the couch or on the floor—" my helpful little brother begins. I make a note to treat him to a steak dinner before he heads back to New York.

Ems interrupts him, "That's ridiculous, *Steven*." She gives him another hard glare. "That couch is way too small for you to be comfortable. And the floor, don't get me started. I think there may be bugs down there. I think I got bitten this morning when I was sitting on the floor." She scratches the imaginary bug bite on her leg dramatically.

"But I didn't see anything—"

"Hush. You don't know anything, little bro. Listen to your sister for once."

Steven stares at the ceiling in exasperation. "Whatever. So what? I keep my room?"

Liz nods. "Yes. James, you don't mind sharing your room with Jess, right? I mean, you guys shared last night and you two looked relatively unscathed this morning."

James takes a sudden interest in the board pieces, as if the dice is carved from crystals. He shrugs. "I don't mind if you don't, Jess."

I flush, thinking about the events this morning. Damn my fair skin. "I'm fine with that," I reply meekly.

Liz claps her hands. "Okay! That's settled then." She looks suspiciously smug. "Why don't we put this game on hold? It's getting dark outside, so we should start our firepit barbecue."

Everyone gets up and heads to the kitchen to take platters of marinated meat, vegetables, and other dishes to the large backyard. James stays behind with me to tidy up the living room. Ever the accountant, I task myself with packing up the Monopoly game after taking a photo of the current setup and inventory each player's cash.

He picks up the trash and gives me a sideways glance. "You okay with sharing the room with me again? I don't want you to agree to something if you're uncomfortable. I'm more than happy to sleep on the floor or on the couch."

"That's silly. We already shared the room last night. What's one more night between friends?" I laugh nervously, twiddling the bracelet on my wrist. "It's not like anything happened anyway, right?" I sneak a glance at him, wondering if he really was asleep this morning.

He pauses in the midst of picking up empty bottles. He stares at the bottle in his hand. "Right," he grunts.

We hurry to join the rest of the folks outside. The backyard is pretty much an extension of the forest, with a stone firepit, a large shed, and a grass clearing that's currently covered in snow. Steven stokes the fire in the pit and begins grilling some chicken wings on skewers for the group. Liz happily plays mother hen and directs Emily on seating arrangements and instructing Steven on what to grill next.

"There you guys are! What took you guys so long?" Emily exclaims when she sees us.

"Someone has to clean up the mess you made in the living room," I retort.

"Hey! It wasn't all me. Steven here made his fair share of garbage with all the snacks he was consuming."

Steven looks up from the chicken wings. "Way to throw me under the bus, Ems."

I smirk. Emily and Steven bicker all the time, but I love them just the same. I look at Liz, who is putting paper plates on the stone ledge surrounding the fire pit. "So, Liz, how are your parents? They're traveling, right?"

She grins. "Yes, I'm so happy for them. They've worked so hard all their lives to support James and me. Now that we're independent, they've finally cashed in on some of their savings to travel the world. It's so awesome."

"I think they're somewhere in Spain right now. Barcelona or something. Then they're heading to Germany because they want to visit some of the famous Christmas markets," James adds, settling in the seat next to me.

"I want what they have. That's what I'm holding out for." Liz has the same faraway look whenever she brings up the epic romance of her parents. She is a romantic at heart and won't settle for anything less than the so-called "true love."

Emily sighs. "Look how well-adjusted Liz and James are, with their perfectly functional family. Parents met in high school, got married, had two kids, did the entire white picket fence thing, and are still hopelessly in love with each other." She snorts, no doubt thinking about our family. "And how dysfunctional we are."

"Hey, call yourself dysfunctional, don't pull me into it," Steven grumbles.

"Well, it's true! Jess here has the blinders on when it comes to men, I don't do relationships, and you, well, you don't date," she points out.

I frown. "What on earth are you talking about? I don't have blinders on. I like long-term relationships and I just got out of one." I take a piece of chicken from Steven and set it to on the ledge to wait for it to cool.

Liz bobs her head in agreement. "No offense, Jess. Now that you and Ben have finally broken up, I don't mind telling you, he wasn't good enough for you. And you stayed in the relationship for far too long. I honestly think maybe you did it out of comfort." She sneaks a glance at me as if debating whether or not she should continue. "And I think I agree with Ems's comment about blinders... You can be a bit, um...oblivious at times." She digs into her food, leaving me mystified by her baffling comment.

"Come on, guys, don't gang up on her." James's knee nudges mine. I shoot him a warm glance of appreciation. My trusty, loyal defender.

"Just because I don't bring any girls home doesn't mean I don't date." Steven allocates second servings to everyone. "And it's not like I have time these days. Investment banking hours are the worst. A bunch of guys are partying like there's no tomorrow and going through girls like clothing. I just prefer to spend my time learning the trades and the markets. I'm young. No need to think about settling down anytime soon."

Emily pats him on the shoulder. "For once, I agree with your priorities." She raises her beer bottle in a toast. "Here's to all of us getting what we want in life, whatever that is, since we all seem to have different opinions."

We clink our bottles together. "Hear, hear."

"This, I can finally agree with," I mutter under my breath, still a little peeved about the blinders comment.

James takes a sip of his beer and whispers to me, "I happen to admire your dedication to your relationships, Jess. Don't mind them."

Warmth spreads through my limbs, perhaps not necessarily from the alcohol alone. I smile internally. How lucky am I to be friends with someone who truly understands the real me beneath the façade.

• • •

A sudden breeze heralds a change in weather. Stars hide behind the layers of dark clouds littering the sky. Liz yawns and rubs her stomach. "Guys, I'm beat. The nature walk this morning and this food completely did me in. I'm going to head in and crash. Ems, what about you?"

Emily finishes her fourth bottle of beer. "Yep, right there with you. I think I'm going to make use of the clawfoot tub in our en-suite, then head off to dreamland. But before then, I need some advice on investments."

We all gape at her. That is the most random thing out of her mouth tonight. Liz snorts beside her.

"Since when do you invest, sis?" Steven stares at her incredulously.

"Since now. This means I need to consult with you, *Steven*. Enjoy it while you can."

I scoff at this sudden change in events. "Okaaay. I guess that means I'll stay here to make sure the fire goes out." Every year there are news of wildfires in California brought on by some idiot camping who forgot to make sure the hot embers are fully extinguished. I will not become a statistic. No, thank you.

"I'll stay with you, Jess." James's deep voice rumbles beside me.

The girls drag the very unwilling Steven back into the cabin, leaving James and me by the fire pit. The breeze picks up, stirring the flames. "Here, let me help you with that."

James rolls up his sleeve, picks up a shovel and starts scooping up the mud and snow sludge from the ground to dump on the fire. His biceps flex under his gray cable-knit sweater with each movement, drawing my eyes to his corded forearms, illuminated by the dimming glow of the fire. *To have all his strength focused on me... He can easily lift me up like a feather.* Wayward thoughts filter into my mind as memories of last night and this morning resurface. My face heats, and I can't even blame it on the warmth of the fire, which has now been reduced to dark-blue and orange embers.

"There. Let's wait fifteen minutes and if no fire sparks, I think we're good to go." James shovels the last heap of sludge in the fire-pit, extinguishing any remaining glow.

The wind picks up in speed and strength, the weather taking a turn for the worse. Flurries of snow start to fall, coating the ground in a fresh layer of white. I shiver. The wool sweater and shirt combo that felt right a few minutes ago is now a tad too thin for the inclement weather.

"Come over here." James beckons me over and tucks me against him.

"How are men so warm?" I huddle next to him, inhaling his sweet scent.

He laughs softly, the tremor felt throughout my body and suddenly, I'm not so cold anymore. "Bigger mass, more muscles, higher metabolism."

I snuggle closer to him, and he wraps his arm tighter around me. I feel so safe, so protected.

"So, aside from you being busy with work...are you seeing any-one these days?" My stomach churns when I think of him with an-other woman. No, it must be indigestion.

He stills. "No. There's no one else." I frown, perplexed at his phrasing. No one else aside from whom? "What about you?"

"I'm meeting a guy named Parker from *InstaConnect* next week. Just going to utilize those skills you taught me and try to get myself out there again."

James stays silent, his muscles tensing as if he wants to say something. "Right," he murmurs. "Let me know how that goes."

Silence ensues as the snowfall picks up in intensity. The white powder swirls in the air, covering the moonlight. I peer up at him and find him staring at the now dark firepit, his jaw locked, a mus-cle twitching in his face.

"I think there's a storm coming in. The firepit looks okay now. I'm going to stoke it a bit just to confirm, but I think we should be good. We should probably go inside before this turns into a legit blizzard." He stands abruptly and picks up the shovel to check on the ashes in the firepit.

I rub my hands together in a futile attempt to warm them. The breeze turns into a gale, the snow now covers the entire ground in a thick blanket of white. "All good? It's freezing! Let's head in," I cup my hands and call out to James.

He gives me an okay signal and hollers back, "You go inside. I'm right behind you." I can barely see him anymore as the snow whips up into a frenzy, turning the world around us into a winter nightmare.

Mother Nature demonstrates its temperamental self as snow coats my sweater, adding ten pounds of dead, soggy weight to the material. I hurry to the backyard door and turn the doorknob.

Locked.

I turn the knob again, shake it, push it, tug it. Still locked.

Shit.

"It's locked, James!"

"What?" He wipes the snow from his face, his cable-knit sweat-er not faring any better than mine, and wrenches at the doorknob.

It doesn't budge. Got to give it to the cabin owner for installing some really strong doorknobs.

"Crap, I left my phone inside," he mutters. "Do you have yours?"

I take out my phone from my pocket and press a few buttons. "The battery's dead. What are we going to do?"

Taking control of the situation, James calmly instructs, "Okay, you check the left side of the building. I'll check the right side. Let's see if the front door or any of the windows are open. Let's meet on the other side of the cabin."

I nod and proceed to check anything and everything a human being can squeeze through, only to find the cabin sealed tight. I try banging on the windows to see if I can create enough noise for the occupants to hear, but the strong, howling winds and the rustling of the trees are too loud, covering the sounds I make. We meet up on the other side of the cabin and huddle beneath the awning, a temporary haven from the vicious elements.

"No l-l-u-uck? I tried knocking on the doors and windo-ows, but no response." My teeth clatter as the coldness of the melting snow seeps through the material of my sweater.

"Same here. Crap." He takes in my shivering form. "We need to find some sort of shelter; we'll get hypothermia if we stay out here." He jogs in place, most likely to keep his body warm, as he scans around our surrounding area, which is a sea of white. Even the trees aren't visible.

"Oh my God, we're going to die." I start panicking. "I can't die yet. I still have so much to do. Shit, this is it." I hyperventilate as thoughts race through my mind and my heart threatens to give out.

James places both hands on my shoulders and leans down, his face mere inches from mine. "Jess."

I keep mumbling to myself, oblivious to anything but my thoughts.

"Jess!"

I stare at him, tears threatening to spill as panic overrides as my main emotion.

"I won't let you die. I swear on my life. We'll get through this."

A determined glint shines in his eyes, as if the thought of me dying is unbearable to him.

I nod and attempt to take one calming breath, the icy air chilling me down to the core.

He calmly instructs, "Let's go around again and see if there's anything else we missed. I think there's a shed in the backyard too. Let's see if we can get in there."

James grabs my hand and pulls me behind him, using his body to block most of the wind and snow as we make our way to the direction of the shed, checking the doors and windows along the way to no avail.

"Hey, Jess, I think I found the shed," he shouts into the gale, his back barely visible in the blizzard. I hold my hands out and hit solid wood. We skirt around the building, using our hands and what remains of our dim vision, and locate the door.

Please be unlocked. Please be opened. Please let us survive this, I pray, holding my breath as James turns the doorknob.

Click.

The faint sound has never sounded any sweeter.

"Yes," James mumbles as he pushes the door open and ushers me in the dark shed.

Flicking on the light switch, I gasp in surprise as dim, yellow lights illuminate the room. This "shed" is actually not a shed after all.

"The missing fourth bedroom!" I look around, noting another wooden four-poster bed identical to the ones in the main cabin. The furnishings are rustic and simple, with carpeted floors that have seen better days and a small bathroom. Consistent with the main cabin, there's a statement stone fireplace with logs in the hearth, ready to be used.

"Well, this isn't so bad. Looks like our luck hasn't run out—" I begin.

Buzz. Buzz. Pop.

The lights flicker for a few seconds, then the room is plunged into darkness.

"You were saying?" James's sardonic voice comes from right beside me.

I groan. Why did I have to open my mouth? I shiver, the chills slightly better now that I'm not outside in the wind.

"I'm going to start a fire in the fireplace." James walks over to the fireplace and gets to work. A few moments later, a warm fire burns brightly, filling the space with a soft, golden glow.

"You'll want to take off your layers to avoid hypothermia." He motions at the wet clothing plastered to my body. He slicks his wet hair back and warms himself by the roaring fire. "You can use the bathroom first."

I shudder as I head into the bathroom, hoping there are some towels in there. No such luck. I peel off my pants and sweater, wringing them dry in the shower before hanging them behind the door. I take off my soggy bra next, breathing a sigh of relief after unhooking the garment. This is probably how women in the nineteenth century felt when they took off their corsets. Thankfully, my shirt is oversized and hangs past my hips. The material is cotton and should dry relatively quickly. I wring out the moisture from my hair as best as I can and pad out to the main room.

My breath stutters as I walk toward the warmth emanating from the fireplace.

James has stripped off his clothes as well, his bare back facing me as he bends over to stoke the flames. Clad only in his boxer briefs, the scene is reminiscent of last night, except with the glow from the fire, I can see every dip and curve of his muscles, his strong buttocks and legs akin to the Greek sculptures at the Louvre. The warm light caresses his body, highlighting his masculine strength as his muscles flex with each movement. Unwittingly, I find myself moving toward him, stopping only a few paces away.

"Jess, I think the fire should be warm enou—" James turns around and freezes. His cerulean eyes darken in the firelight as he takes in my appearance. His hungry gaze roams over my body, stopping at my chest. His nostrils flare as he takes in a ragged breath. I glance down at myself and gasp. The white shirt, still damp from the elements, plasters to my breasts like second skin. My dark nipples harden under his gaze, saluting to attention, begging him to touch them.

Seconds pass, feeling like eternity as he catalogues every inch of my body. His chest heaves, but the rest of him stills. His muscles lock into place and the man turns into a predator, and I'm the prey. Thick tension hangs in the air and my breathing quickens, my breasts heavy, and tingles of arousal gather at my core.

"Jess," he rasps, his burning gaze pinning me in place as he steps closer until we are a hair's breadth apart. His chest grazes mine, skimming the sensitive nubs. I bite my lip to stifle my moan. James's hand brushes against mine as he waits for something, for anything. The world ceases to exist around us as I stare at his lips, his attractive mouth that has been taunting me for a kiss since last night. My tongue dips out and his eyes zero in on the movement, his pupils dilating.

My eyes flutter shut, my mind shutting down as I surrender to the primal needs of my body.

He groans in response, one hand reaching to cup the back of my neck, the other snaring me around my waist as he descends on me. Soft lips dance with mine, testing the waters as his tongue darts out to tease the seam of my lips. Heat courses through my body and I gasp, arching my head back as he takes advantage and plunges his tongue inside. Hot need awakens every inch of me. I let out a whimper. He responds by pulling me flush against his body. I can feel every inch of his flexing muscles molding to my curves.

"Oh God, Jess." He grunts as he ravages my mouth, not coming up for air. My body is on fire, wetness seeping through my cotton underwear as I hike one leg around his waist, my core struggling to line up with his steel shaft. He lets out a tortured groan as he grabs my ass and hauls me up against him. My legs wrap around his waist as he grinds against me, hitting my bundle of nerves. I moan loudly as he walks me back a few steps and lays me on the bed. His underwear-clad erection thrusts into my center. I claw at his back, desperate to be closer to him. Too many layers of clothes between us. I want them gone.

He groans as he thrusts against my core. I moan, my body arching up, and chase his movements with my hips in desperation. "More...oh my God, right there...more." I'm delirious with pleasure.

James reaches up to clasp my breasts through the thin cotton of the shirt, kneading the sensitive mounds. He pushes up my shirt, exposing my breasts to the cold air.

"You are perfection, Jess."

He flicks my nipple with his tongue as I arch my back, thrusting my heavy breasts at him.

"I've waited for so long..." He sucks the nipple in, and I moan loudly, the sound inflaming him further as he flicks the nub in a frenzy. I wrap my legs tighter around his hips, wishing the layers of clothing were not between us. He releases my nipple with a pop and moves on to the other breast. "Nothing compares to this." He lavishes his attention on the other nipple and snakes his other hand over my stomach, creating tingles in its wake. "Nothing," he rasps. "I could barely resist you this morning." I whimper, his words reaching my mind on a delay, and I belatedly realize what he just said.

His fingers slip under my underwear and delve into my folds. "You're so wet..." He groans, his breathing harsh against my ear as he teases the bud. "I'm going to burst." My train of thought scatters as pleasure and lust guide my hips against his fingers.

I arch into his touch as his thrusts become more erratic. The pleasure from his fingers combined with the hard thrusts against me inflames my senses.

"Just like that...oh God...please," I cry as his lips capture mine in another obliterating kiss.

"I'm trying to be a gentleman and not rush this, but damn if I don't satisfy you tonight." He thrusts harder while his fingers pluck at the hardening nub.

Pleasure builds through my body as I chase the aching pressure. My hands grasp his butt as James moves against me. He thrusts two fingers inside me and the sensations reach a crescendo as I shatter into a million pieces. He captures my cries with another drugging kiss as he softens his touch while I ride out my release. He bucks his hips against mine and releases a deep groan as he follows me into the abyss.

Boneless and satisfied, I curl myself onto my side as sleep threatens to overtake me. James brushes his hands over the hair plastered to my face and laughs softly as his breaths calm into a steady rhythm. He lightly drags off my sodden underwear and positions me farther onto the bed, covering me with the thick down comforter. He treads lightly to the bathroom to clean himself up and joins me back in bed, his arms curling against my waist as he tucks me against him. Still recovering from the most intense sexual experience of my life, I snuggle closer to him, my mind still incapable of forming coherent words.

"Go to sleep, beautiful," James whispers as my eyes slowly shut and I drift off to into a relaxing, deep sleep.

Sunlight streams in from the windows as I slowly awake from the most restorative sleep I've ever experienced. I shift on the bed, relishing the feeling of clean sheets against my legs. As cobwebs slowly clear from my mind, I notice the reassuring weight of a thick, muscular arm curled around my hips, long fingers drawing small circles on my upper thigh. Images from last night flood through my brain. Kisses. Muscles. Gasps. Thrusting. I still, my muscles lock with tension, as I realize the significance of last night.

I had the best almost-sex of my life with my best friend. Oh shit. Oh shit. Oh shit.

The anxiety and panic that took a brief hiatus arrives with full fanfare. What have I done? What's going to happen next? How can I look at James in the same way ever again? What if I jeopardize the most important friendship in my life? My mind races as I recall the words Ben said to me before he left. I'm not a good girlfriend. I can't even keep a guy who has been with me for over a decade. What if this changes James and me? What. Have. I. *Done?* I start hyperventilating as a million thoughts race through my mind, none of them good.

James turns me around as I clutch the sheets to my chest. I stare at his broad chest and his sculpted abs, my mind warring with my body, which very much wants to lick its way down those dips and valleys.

"Jess, look at me," a low, rough voice commands me.

I continue staring at this solid wall of male chest, unwilling to look up.

He tips my chin and brings my eyes to his. His beautiful sapphire-blue gaze stares at me with warmth. "Hey, hey. Where did you go there? You're worried, aren't you?" His voice, a sensual caress, elicits a fresh wave of need.

I nod, mesmerized by the familiar eyes and soothing voice as I clench the sheets tighter to stop myself from touching him. My mind riots with conflicting emotions, fear warring with want, anxiety sparring with giddiness, my body telling me yes, but my brain resounding with no.

"Nothing needs to change between us." He cups my cheeks, his hand instilling warmth to my chilled face. "We can take this slow, as slow as you want. I'll always be here."

"Last night, I-I think...we just got carried away. It was the adrenaline and a p-physical reaction between two adults." Fear and anxiety win out, parading in my mind in a victory lap.

James stills, his eyes piercing mine. "You think it was a mistake?"

The silence in the room is loud as I find myself unable to answer. *Yes? No? I don't know! Why is this so complicated now?* The warring factions in my head clamor to speak over each other.

Apparently, the silence is sufficient enough of an answer for him. James promptly withdraws his hands, leaving me feeling suddenly bereft at the cold.

"I see," he mutters as he clambers off the bed. I turn my head away from the brief flash of muscular ass as he wraps his waist with a blanket on the bed. He heads to the bathroom, his shoulders slumped in defeat.

"Actually..." He turns around, his fists clenching, his eyes burning with anger. "I *don't* see." He thumps his hand on the wall. "This is *not* a mistake, Jess, and I'll prove it to you. You and me, we were always, *always* destined for more and there's no chance in hell I'm letting you talk yourself out of this." He prowls closer to me as I sit up and stare at him, captivated by his impassionate speech. "Give me a chance to prove this to you. Give us a chance. You don't need to decide now, just don't close the door on the possibility," he whispers, his forehead touching mine.

My head dips in the barest of nods. I'm a fish out of water, a sailor charting the stormy seas without a compass or a map. I don't know what's up or down or what to do anymore. Chaos flutters within me, spreading its wings and making a home in my beating heart.

Seemingly satisfied with my reaction, he promptly turns around and strides to the bathroom, closing the door with a click, leaving me with my quiet thoughts echoing in the silent room.

We tidy ourselves to the best of our abilities. The atmosphere is charged with unspoken words and unspeakable emotions. I hurry to the door, eager to leave this tension-heavy room. James catches my hand as I pass him by, his fingers softly interlacing with mine. I pull to a stop as I look back at him and find him staring at my crimson bracelet, his thumb caressing the jade heart in a manner I'm very familiar with.

"Jess." He looks up, his eyes glittering with unspoken truths. "Whatever happens, you'll always have me. I just want you to know that."

My heart flips and skips a beat as I give him a halfhearted smile. He always knows just what to say. I squeeze him softly, acknowledging his sentiment. He gives me a sad smile in return and releases my hand.

We exit the shed-cabin to find Liz, Emily, and Steven walking around the premises, hollering for us.

"You guys locked us out last night!" James strides toward Liz, his steps heavy with anger. "There was a blizzard last night. We could have frozen to death!"

Liz spots us and hurries over. "Oh my gosh, I'm so sorry! We didn't realize we locked the door behind us until this morning. We were all tired and crashed last night after we went in."

"You guys found the mini cabin, right?" Emily chimes from behind her as Steven also joins the group.

"You knew about the shed?" I ask incredulously, since I didn't even know about it and I was the one who booked the accommodations.

"Yea, we saw it when we came outside to set up the campfire last night. It looks like there's a fourth bedroom after all," Steven comments with a nod.

James's frustration vibrates off of him and I lay a hand against his back. "It's okay. We survived, so all is good. It's not like you guys did it on purpose. Come on, let's get back inside and not let this ruin the last day of vacation." James's muscles slowly relax, and he takes in a deep breath.

"I'll make brunch. I think you guys want to do a *Harry Potter* marathon, right?" he says gruffly.

"Yes!" Emily and I exclaim as Steven rolls his eyes. The books were a source of comfort when we were moving around the country as kids.

Liz and Steven trail in after James as Emily sidles up next to me. "You guys okay? I sense a vibe."

"We're fine, just a bit traumatized from the events of last night," I reply, not wanting to lie to her but not ready to share the intimate experience with her yet. Before I figure out what I want to do, I want to keep this between James and me. My relationship with James is changing before my eyes and I'm helpless to stop it. Deep down, I don't know if I even want to stop it.

Emily glances at me with one crooked brow, seemingly unconvinced. "Okay. Whatever you say. I'm here if you ever want to talk." With that, she trots off to join the group, leaving me to my thoughts.

I pause and turn toward the forest, the trees glimmering against the sun, the fresh snow capping the greenery in a scene straight from a fairytale. Birds harmonize in a beautiful melody; squirrels springing across the soft snow, mouths full of tree nuts; the air is crisp and refreshing. Another day begins anew. Life continues, but I have a feeling my world has shifted on its axis.

Fuck.

I've gone too fast. I should have controlled myself better. But who could have resisted her last night, when she stood before me like a wet dream come alive, her shirt plastered to her body like a second skin. I'll never forget the way she looked when she came out of the bathroom. Her dark nipples puckered against the cold, saluting me in the firelight. The way she melted against me when I kissed her. Her gasps. Her tiny moans. How fucking responsive she is to me. The way her walls clamped against my fingers when she came.

If I were a lesser man, I would have taken her right there, intentions be damned. But I know she wasn't ready for that yet. She's only beginning to recognize me as a man, as someone she's attracted to beyond the boundaries of platonic relationships. If I go too fast, she'll panic and shut down.

Damn it.

"Bro, you're attacking the onion like it's your worst enemy," Liz comments as she creeps up next to me and leans against the counter.

"Don't just stand there, do something. Make yourself useful," I grumble, not in the mood for her observations again.

She whistles. "What happened last night? And don't bother giving me some BS answer. You guys were fine last night before we went in and now you look pissed, and she looks embarrassed."

I throw the onions into the pan and start to sauté the rest of the ingredients in a quick breakfast scramble.

Liz holds her hands up. "Before you rush to answer me, know that I only want the PG version. I told her the same thing when she asked you to be her 'dating coach,' I knew something was bound to happen at some point in time."

I ignore her and add some seasoning to the pan, cover it with a lid and let the contents simmer for a minute or so.

"Okay, don't rush to answer me all at once." Liz grabs some plates from the cabinet and sets them on the counter. Her tone softens, and she asks, "But seriously, are you guys okay?"

I sigh, not wanting to worry her. "Hypothetically speaking—"

"James, I think we are beyond the point of hypotheticals now."

"Fine. I think we're fine. I may have moved too fast with her and spooked her. Now I'm beating myself up for not being more careful." I turn off the stove, spin around, and stare at her. "There. Happy now?"

Liz's eyes turn sympathetic as she wraps me in her arms. Well, as much as she can since she is a full head shorter than me. "Don't despair yet. Jess sometimes can be slow on the uptake, but she isn't stupid. Whatever happened between the two of you last night, she wouldn't throw your relationship away just like that." She disentangles from me and stares into my eyes. "If you haven't noticed, she has already changed around you. It's obvious to all of us... Well, except maybe Steven, who hasn't been around either of you too much to notice the changes. Jess has always loved you all these years, even though she may have believed it to be pure friendship, but you were the one person she truly opened her heart to, and she's the most guarded person I know. That says something."

"Thanks, Liz. Don't worry about me. I didn't come all the way back over here to give up so easily."

Liz pats me on the shoulder and takes the plates to the dining table.

I chuckle softly at my dilemma. I've managed to do everything I wished I could do as a child. I bulked up, grew those last inches, received top grades, climbed my way to the top of the company ladder. I have everything little James wanted. And yet, Jess is still out of reach and if I can't convince her this time... I don't know how I'll be able to face the reality. Perhaps part of the reason I never told her about my feelings is to keep the kernel of hope alive. If after last night, she still insists everything is a mistake, then how will I ever convince her otherwise? I sometimes just want to shake her, to force her to see how good we are together.

You're already making progress, James. Slow and steady wins the race. Fuck, but last night...

Last night was the best night of my life.

Too late to turn back. If this is a head-on collision, I'm plowing full speed ahead.

glance at my watch. Five minutes past six. Crap, I'm already five minutes late. I quickly pack up my laptop and throw it into my work tote with a speed that'd make the Road Runner cry. I quickly jot out a message on the *InstaConnect* app.

Jess: Sorry, I promise I didn't flake on you. Got carried away with work. I'm on my way.

I'm meeting Parker, the architect, today at a coffee shop near my office. There's no way I'm braving the traffic to go anywhere at this hour. Thank goodness Parker's office is located a few blocks away in downtown LA, so we're able to pick a close, central location for our first date. After returning from Yosemite last week, I wanted to cancel the date, but Becca suggested I still attend. "Use it as a practice round," she said. And so, here I am, running as best as I can in three-inch heels, a purple sheath dress with a modest neckline, and a thick, white coat because the weather is below seventy and officially in the freezing-cold territory for me.

Opening the door of the coffee shop, I'm greeted with the relaxing jazz music completely at odds with my pounding heart. I scan the room, trying to locate anyone who resembles the man in the profile photos. Out of the corner of my eye, I spot a tall figure in a business suit stand from his seat in the back.

He waves tentatively, his smile unsure. "Jess?"

Brown hair, green eyes, dimples. Yes, this must be Parker. He actually resembles his photos, even better than his photos, if I'm being completely honest. Emily and Liz have warned me there are a fair share of men out there posting old photos of themselves and the reality often pales in comparison.

I walk quickly, but as gracefully as I can, to his table. *Treat this like a networking event, Jess. This is a potential client, nothing more.*

I tip my lips in a practiced smile and extend my hand. "Hi, Parker. I'm so sorry to keep you waiting."

He flashes a quick grin. "No problem. I just got here myself too. Want anything?"

"Sure. Why don't I go with you to the counter? I want to see what seasonal specials they have." Another tip from Emily and Liz—always get your own drink on the first date. You don't know if the guy is a serial killer or someone who'll ransom you for money after taking suggestive photos of you. I guess some things never change, whether it's the old-fashioned meeting a guy at a bar or online dating.

We quickly place our orders with the barista—salted caramel latte for me and a double shot espresso for him—and I reach into my bag to pull out my wallet, but he stops me.

"My treat. The gentleman in me never lets a lady pay on the first date."

My heart stutters as I remember what James told me on our practice date. *"Call me old-fashioned, but as a gentleman, I like to pay for dates, even if this is a fake one."* His words and seductive voice echo in my brain on repeat. He texted me earlier today, telling me he misses me and he hasn't given up changing my mind, but I haven't replied yet. I don't know how to respond when part of me wants to say the hell with it and take the next step to see where this takes us but the conservative auditor in me is giving me harsh warnings, saying I'll ruin the most important relationship I have. I quickly quash the thought and the subsequent guilt. *You're such a hypocrite, Jess. You already took the next step with him. Heck, you went all the way to third base with him last week!*

"Jess?" Parker's gravelly voice wakes me from my trip down memory lane. He looks at me in apparent concern.

"Sorry. It's been a long day. My brain still hasn't left work." I laugh awkwardly as he grabs our coffees, and we walk back to our table.

"No worries, happens to me a lot too." He winks at me as he sets our coffee down.

Settling down into our seats, I take a sip of the fortifying liquid, relishing the familiar creamy taste on my tongue. For the first time since I entered the coffee shop, I take a good look at the stranger before me. His brown hair reflects burnt gold in the warm lamplight. Small wrinkles around his eyes, indicating someone who likes to smile, a five o'clock shadow on his jaw, lending an air of ruggedness to an otherwise aristocratic face.

"So, I know we chatted a few times on the app, but tell me about yourself. Why are you on the app?" He sits back, his legs crossed, giving off an air of someone who is used to being in control.

I fiddle with my wrist. "I just got out of a long-term relationship and wanted to see what's out there." The words out of my mouth hit me with a sense of déjà vu as I remember the dinner I had with James. "What about you?"

Parker's emerald gaze dims as his polite smile falters. "My wife, or I guess my late wife, Abby..." He pauses and clears his throat as reaches for his coffee as if needing a moment to compose himself. "She passed away two years ago, and I guess I want to take a step forward in life, if that makes any sense." He forces a smile as his hands clutch his cup in a death grip.

I nod, my heart clenches in sympathy. He obviously loves his late wife and while I don't have anyone in my life to show me what life-altering love looks like, my guess is, it'll look something like this.

"I'm sorry for your loss."

"Thank you. It's something I don't wish on anyone." He chuckles halfheartedly. "Man, I suck at this, don't I?"

I laugh softly. "Don't you worry about it. This is my first date as well. I was with my ex for a decade, long before the dawn of online app dating. So, from my perspective, this is going just fine."

His eyes crinkle. "I guess luck is on my side, as my partner in crime is a novice as well." He winks again and his posture relaxes.

"So, you have a daughter? I think I saw her photo on your profile?"

"Yes, Lucy is four years old and a downright terror. She loves all things related to princesses and unicorns." He chuckles, his eyes full of warmth at the mention of his daughter. "You don't mind kids, right?"

I shake my head. "I love kids, always planned to have some myself. I'm the oldest of my siblings and none of them are married or have kids yet, so unfortunately, no little nieces or nephews for me to play with, but kids are so adorable."

He nods, satisfied with my answer. "So, you're an accountant...audit, tax, or corporate?"

"You already get a point for not automatically asking me if I can do your taxes." I grin. "I'm in audit. I like it. Things are relatively straightforward in a sense there are a certain set of regulations. Follow those rules and you're good to go."

"Like to have things under your control, huh?" he muses. My mind starts spinning in overdrive again. Did I give the wrong answer? Is that a compliment or a criticism? It sounds more like the latter. Maybe I should backtrack—

"I'm the same way. I can't live on the fly like some people," he agrees. My muscles relax marginally. See? There is nothing wrong with speaking your mind.

I shift the conversation back to him. "So, why did you decide to become an architect?"

"I enjoy designing homes for people."

My heart thumps with longing. *Home.* Something I've been chasing after and never quite feeling like it's within my reach, even though I've been in this city for so long and have no intention of leaving.

"Growing up, my family was poor and we would move a lot, from apartment to apartment, never quite settling down." Parker leans forward, his hands clasped in front of him. "I guess I always dreamed of having a nice home for myself. So, when it came to picking a major in college, it was easy. Now I get to build homes for a living and watch families move in. There's a lot of satisfaction in that."

Longing invades my senses, like a child staring at the window display of a candy store with only a quarter in her pocket. Will he be the one to help me find the elusive home I've been searching for so long?

The rest of the date passes by quickly as we learn some interesting factoids about each other. He in fact loves to read—science fiction is his jam. He thinks romance novels are cringe-inducing—the audacity—but he's open to me changing his mind. I tell him I hate cinnamon; he gives me a high five at that; apparently, we are a rare breed. Parker checks all my boxes: has a good profession, is mature, seems to have a sense of humor, and I find I don't have to be as on guard with my answers as I usually do with others. Yet somehow, the date feels more like two friends getting reacquainted after being apart for a long time. Something is missing, an elusive spark that exists between a man and a woman. *Much like the tension you felt this weekend with James, you idiot.* My inner critic gives me a proverbial slap across the head.

I glance at my watch. Eight p.m. I need to head home to eat something and finish working if I want to have any shot of going to bed before midnight. I put my cell phone in my purse and take out my keys. Parker's eyes shift to my hands as he picks up my intention.

"This has been fun." He stands and throws away the empty cups before walking to my side.

I smile genuinely; it really has been a pleasant meeting. "Thanks for the coffee."

He steps closer and gives me a light hug. Amber and bergamot permeate the air. "Thank you for going easy on this newbie," he whispers in my ear. I close my eyes and find myself pining for sandalwood and spice. He steps away and we walk outside. The streets have cleared up significantly, as most of the commuters have gone home.

"Let me walk you to your car."

"Sure." I park across the street at a public parking flat rate lot. Having a strapping, tall man next to me makes me feel safer now that the sidewalks have emptied out.

Upon reaching my sedan, he leans in and gives me a quick kiss on my cheek, stepping back before I have a chance to react.

"I'd like to call you again." He runs his hands over his lush hair. "Let's take it slow, if you don't mind. I'm rusty at this and can use a bit of a slow onboarding, and it's definitely not on you. You're everything a man is looking for." His right hand rubs his left ring finger, a phantom itch, I presume.

I know his statement may offend some people, but I find it oddly refreshing and release a breath I didn't realize I was holding. A sensation akin to relief floods my senses. "That sounds...perfect, actually. And yes, I'd love to do this again."

He cocks his head to the side and tips up his lips in a half smile, showcasing one of his dimples. He motions for me to get in the car. As I drive away, I look in the rearview mirror and see him staring down at his left hand and, if I'm a betting person, the missing ring on his finger.

I plop down on my sofa with a sigh, having finished reviewing my last file for work. I look at the clock. Eleven thirty p.m. on a Friday night. Clad in a long-sleeve cotton nightshirt, I'm ready for my favorite pastime, reading my stack of novels before bed. I pad to my kitchen, pour myself a glass of rose, and grab a small plate to portion out some of the special chocolates from James I'm storing in the refrigerator. If I take the entire box with me, I'll inadvertently finish them all in one sitting, and my waistline won't thank me.

Settling in my high-thread-count sheets with pillows fluffed up just right, I sigh in contentment. A beep from my phone indicates an incoming email. I forgot to shut off the notifications, darn it. If I don't do that, I'll be forever haunted by the constant pinging from incoming messages and will be completely glued to my phone the rest of the night as my control-freak tendencies won't let me leave a message unread. The preview on the screen catches my attention: "Partner Panel Information." Unable to resist the headline, I pull open the email on my phone.

Dear Jess,

The partner group has discussed the candidates we are putting up for panel interviews this year. As you know, the economy is tough these days, and the firm is going through a restructuring. Therefore, we had to make the hard decision to eliminate certain panel positions. While we recognize the hard work and contributions you have made for the firm, we believe it will be better for you to go through panel next year instead so you have more time to demonstrate your commitment to the firm. I understand this may come as a disappointment, but this in no way undermines our appreciation of your quality of work and work ethics. Let me know if you have any questions.

Best regards,

Dick

My ribs grow tighter, restricting my airflow as a heaviness settles in my body. My hands are clammy as I drop the phone on the bed, my previous good mood gone. That slimy bastard! Telling me this over an email on Friday night because he's too much of a wuss to tell me in person, or at the very least, over a phone call. I've worked so hard to be in the running this year, pulling late hours most weeks, painting myself as the bad guy on engagements to make sure we meet our deadlines. I didn't even have time to spend with my now ex-boyfriend. I've poured most of my energy into my work for this opportunity, only to have it canceled via a measly email.

Blood pounds in my ears as disappointment bleeds into rage. *Calm down, Jess. This is not a no, it's a not yet.* My hands shake as I grip the wineglass and swallow the contents in one gulp, the light burn of the alcohol not even registering. I stomp to the kitchen to take the entire bottle and drag a big gulp directly from the source. I pace around the living room, my emotions in a riot, as I mutter a litany of curses under my breath while chugging the wine as if it's water.

I stare at my reflection in the window. Twenty-eight, supposedly at the prime of my life, alone on a Friday night, dumped by my long-term boyfriend, apparently not good enough at work, in the process of messing up my relationship with my best friend, an anxious mess who can't get anything right. Tears pool in my eyes as the rollercoaster of emotions makes a hard stop at sadness.

. . .

"Do you know why the rose is called the r-rose?" I hiccup as I slump over the sofa, staring at my ceiling.

"Jess?" My favorite baritone voice in the whole wide world sounds concerned, but that may just be wishful thinking. "What?"

"Rose, the flower, like the wine. The wine is so pretty...pink, such a cute color," I slur as I put my phone on speaker.

"Are you okay? Where are you?" Rustling comes through the phone as if James is gathering something on his end.

"Don't worry. I'm a-at hoooome." Another hiccup. Where was I? Oh yes. Rose. "Anyway, the rose... Aphrodite named the flower in honor of Eros, her son. She rearranged one letter of his name." More hiccups. "A-a-and he gave the flower to Harp-o-c-crates, who's the god of silence... It was a bribe to hide the gods' weaknesses. So that's why the flower is a symbol of secrets, silence, and love. At least, that's what a website told me."

"How much did you have to drink? What happened?" More rustling and the sound of keys.

"I didn't know the flo-ower represents secrets and silence... I always thought it means love," I mumble, my head groggy. "Why is love so hard? Why must there always be secrets and silence? Why can't people just say what they think instead of k-eeeeping it inside?" I turn the wine bottle upside down. Oops, I must have drunk all of it. "Maybe it's because love is one of the few emotions that c-can kill...you know, heaaart-break...and people are scared or worried a-and that's why there's a-all these sec-rets a-and unspoken words when it co-omes to love." I'm a budding philosopher when drunk, apparently.

"I'll be there in ten. Don't go anywhere," the deep voice commands, sending shivers over my body, which seems to be the norm with this new and improved grown-up James.

I drift in and out of a light sleep, my body warm but uncomfortable.

The doorknob rattles as the door is pushed open.

"You didn't lock the door?" James's thunderous voice echoes in my brain, causing a flash of pain.

I stumble off the sofa and stagger toward a blurry figure clad in jeans and a Henley. The fuzzy form seems to be splitting into multiple clones. What's better than one James? Three Jameses? My mind warms, thinking what three Jameses could do to me in bed. My face flushes as I relive yet again that one night in Yosemite. With Ben, I was unable to relax in bed, always worried if I was too quiet, too loud, if my body was attractive enough for him, if he felt good. James turned my noisy mind off that night and all that was left were the sensations, the *oh my God I want a repeat perfor-mance* sensations.

"James," I slur, tripping over my feet and stumbling into him. He wraps his sturdy arms around me as I take in a greedy breath of my favorite sandalwood and spice. I push him against the closed door and climb him like a bear. I nuzzle my nose against his neck, searching for the source of the scent.

"Oh God, you're killing me," he groans as he grips my ass, the hard edge from his voice replaced by a deep smokiness.

I latch my lips onto the small area of skin where the neck meets the ears and gently suck as if I can swallow the smell of man and sex. I moan, rubbing my soft body against his hard muscles as my nipples bead into sharp points.

He quickly turns us around, pins me against the door, and slams his mouth on mine, swallowing my whimper. He grinds against me and his tongue twirls with mine in the second most in-tense sexual experience of my life. He grunts as I dig my nails into his neck, scoring his tender skin with marks.

"J-aames, take me, please." I gasp as we come up for air.

His blown pupils stare at my hazy ones and he abruptly releas-es his hold on me, and I slide down the door in a puddle.

James turns his back against me, his hand gripping his hair as he chants softly, something resembling "she's drunk." His clenched fist pounds the wall as he struggles to regain control of his body.

I stare at the gladiator before me, my warrior, the person who has been with me through thick and thin, together in spirit even when we are physically far apart. My mind quiets as the flurry of thoughts is quashed by my rioting pulse.

His shoulders rise and fall with each labored breath, the thin material of his Henley shirt doing little to disguise the ropes of muscles hidden beneath. He slowly turns around and picks me up from the floor and carries me bridal style to the couch.

"What happened, sweetheart?"

I sit on his lap as he tucks me under his chin. My nerves thrumming as he cuddles me against the sofa.

"I met up with Parker and he's nice and all that..." I begin, not wanting to call it a date. Somehow, I feel like I'm betraying James if I'm going on a date, even though we aren't a couple, despite his intentions.

James freezes at the mention of Parker. Then, as if remembering our conversation in Yosemite, *whatever happens, you'll always have me*, he softens. He plays with a lock of hair and murmurs, "And?"

"The D-dickhead sent me an email saying I'm out for the partnership consideration. They didn't even give me a chance to go through the panel inter-r-views," I stutter, my tongue still feeling thick and foreign. "They di-idn't even have the gu-uts to tell me in person!"

James massages my scalp and I whimper at the sensation. "Shhhh...they don't know what they're missing," he consoles me as he continues his ministrations.

"And the holiday gala is next week and I have to face these two-timing bastards with a smile on my face. And I don't even have anyone to go with..."

"I'll go with you." He lightly rubs my temples.

"I tried so hard..." My eyes feel heavy as my senses dull. "Why don't people like me? Why am I never good enough?" My heart feels like lead and the temporary feelings of euphoria from the wine fade as sadness creeps in again. A stray tear slips down my cheek.

James brushes the tear with his thumb and hugs me closer to him. "You're more than enough, Jess. I wish you could see what I see. Anyone who thinks otherwise does not deserve your tears."

His words rumble through the haze as I close my eyes and surrender to the darkness pulling me in.

The next day, I wake up with a splitting headache. I groan as I turn away from the sunlight penetrating in from the curtains. I pat the empty space next to me. James? He must have carried me into the bedroom after I passed out last night. My skin prickles with embarrassment. *I made out with him again! And I told him about Parker. Is he upset at me? I mean, he knew I had an appointment to meet Parker after Thanksgiving, and I didn't promise him anything last weekend. What on earth is going on? How did I go from over a decade of platonic friendship to...this?* I pull the covers over my head, not wanting to face the day.

After hiding under the covers for a full five minutes, the maximum time I allow myself to wallow this morning, I slowly crawl out of bed. Is he still here?

"James?" I call out but am only met with silence.

I notice a glass of water, two extra-strength ibuprofen on my nightstand, along with a note:

I have to go to the office this morning. A large project is going on and requires some weekend hours. There's breakfast on the counter and a pumpkin latte sans cinnamon. Take the meds and rehydrate.

Love,

James

P.S. You are very much loved.

P.P.S. No, I'm not mad you told me about Parker. I want to strangle him, but that's neither here nor there.

P.P.P.S. And also no, this doesn't mean I'm giving up on convincing you about us. I'm always right. You'll see.

I clasp the note to my heart and the day ahead suddenly seems...better.

"**A**re you sure about this dress?" I feel the silky fabric in my hands and step back to stare at the gown Emily picked out for me for the gala tonight.

"Yes, sis, trust me, the dress is very flattering on you. Screw those old farty partners. This is your I am a phoenix rising from the ashes redemption dress." Emily's voice rings loud and clear on the speakerphone.

The dress is really beautiful but a little more revealing than what I usually prefer. It's a ruby-red silk dress with two thin spaghetti straps on each shoulder, a plunging neckline showing a hint of cleavage but not to the point where it's obscene, and a fitted silhouette flaring to a full A-line skirt with a thigh-high slit. The red definitely brings out the Christmas spirit and, as Emily says, will draw every eye to me, which honestly makes me a bit uncomfortable. *I don't know why I let her talk me into things.*

"I don't know..." Yes, I'm chickening out last minute. "I can always wear the green sheath dress I wore to your birthday lunch last year."

Emily groans. "No, no, no. That was a casual lunch, not a formal black-tie affair. Trust me, Jess, I makeover people for a living. Even though technically the outfits are chosen by the wardrobe department, I've seen enough makeovers from work to know what's best for you."

"Fine." I take a deep breath. I can do this. Besides, I won't be alone tonight; I have James. My heart flips at the thought of him, another seemingly normal response to James 2.0. "Crap, I don't have much time. I need to get ready!"

"Love you! Video chat after you're done getting ready and remember to add Liz too. She wants to see the final look as well."

I roll my eyes, but my chest warms at the thought of these two ladies. I'm so glad we're meeting up more often now. Nothing can replace the bonds of female friendship (and with Ems, sisterhood).

I run to the bathroom, quickly shower, and shave everywhere, leaving my skin silky smooth. I dry my hair and put it up in hot rollers while I apply makeup. Since the dress is the center of attention, I keep my makeup light with a simple cat eye, dark mascara, and my favorite red lipstick to match the hue of the dress. I take out the hot rollers and add a few more curls to my hair with a curling iron, then brush out my hair in loose waves that fall to my waist. Pinning up one side of my hair in a small diamond barrette, my final look is done.

I slip on the dress, and it clings to every inch of my body until the skirt flares at my hips. Damn it, it totally shows the bra and panty lines. I toss my strapless bra and lace panties on the bed and opt for thin nipple pasties and a thong. I walk to the full-length mirror and take in my reflection. The confident woman in the mirror is at odds with the rioting emotions inside me. I feel naked without all my layers. My hand clasps the bracelet on my wrist, appreciating the familiar texture as I take calming breaths... Longer exhales than inhales, repeat, and repeat again. Feeling a bit more in control, I start a video chat with Emily and Liz.

"Okay, what's the verdict?" I hold out my camera so the ladies can see the full look.

Liz's eyes are as round as dinner plates as she blinks at the camera, seemingly speechless. Emily wags her brows in approval. "You are smokin', sis. This is the best comeback from rejection I've *ever* seen."

"W-wow, Jess, you look beautiful!" Liz gushes, having recovered her voice. She chuckles. "Man, you're going to kill James. He's literally going to *die*. If you don't resuscitate him when he has a cardiac arrest, I'll kill you."

I blush at their effusive compliments. "Aww, thank you, girls. I'm dreading the gala, but at least I look good while I'm navigating the shark-infested waters. If I'm going to die by embarrassment from being a loser, at least I'm going to die gorgeously."

"Aww hush, none of the negative self-talk. They don't know what they're missing!" Liz waves her fists in the air, her expression remarkably similar to her brother.

The doorbell rings.

"Hey, James is here. I need to go. Love you guys."

"Knock 'em dead!" Emily gives me a wink.

"Remember, if you kill my brother, I'll kill you." Liz's cackling laughter fills the room as I shake my head and disconnect from the call.

I put on my strappy nude heels, grab my clutch, and open the door.

James leans on the wall opposite my door, his brows furrowing as he types furiously on his phone with one hand and holds a bouquet of deep-red roses in the other.

Nothing can prepare me for the sight of James in a tuxedo. The perfectly tailored suit clings to his muscles, his dress shoes shine in the dim light, and his hair is artfully arranged in an effortlessly sexy style. He looks like the other James of the 007 variety. My mouth waters as I take in this perfect male specimen in front of me.

"James?" I whisper, suddenly finding myself breathless with butterflies in my stomach.

James looks up and freezes. His fingers pause on his phone as he stares wordlessly at me, his eyes darkening with each second as the air grows thick between us.

Seconds feel like minutes as he immobilizes me with his heated gaze.

"You're breathtaking," he rasps, his voice taking on a gravelly undertone. "You're in red again, just like Homecoming."

I close the door behind me with a click and lean against it, my back relishing the coolness of the wood against my flaming skin. He remembers what I wore back then.

He slowly straightens from his position and prowls toward me, determination in his fiery gaze. I flatten my back against the sturdy door and tilt my head up at him, our breaths mingling in the inches between us.

James slowly dips his head down as I close my eyes, helpless to this sizzling attraction, like a prey ensnared in a black widow's web, knowing the inevitable, yet powerless to resist the lure.

His lips caress my ear as he whispers, "Part of me doesn't want to let you go outside looking like this…" His tongue darts out in a brief lick of the lobe, eliciting another full-body shudder, the pasties doing nothing to hide my response to him. "But part of me wants to show you off to the world on my arm, so everyone knows you're mine." He softly nips me and soothes the sharp sting with a suck. "You don't know it yet, but you…are…*mine*." He punctuates each word with a gentle kiss as he steps back.

My brain malfunctions and I stare at him, my chest rising and falling rapidly as my pulse races in my ears. Wetness gathers at the thin scrap of material between my legs as I drown in his molten eyes.

"These are for you, but not even the most beautiful of roses can compare to you in this dress." He hands me the bouquet of flowers and I hold on to the bundle for dear life.

"Thank you," I murmur as I bury my nose in the petals, doing anything I can to avoid staring at him.

"Come on, let's head out." He intertwines his fingers with mine and leads me to his car, a beautiful sedan with the softest leather interior.

The car ride is quiet as I try to sort out my confusing emotions. Ever since James came back, I feel like the relationship I depend on all these years is changing rapidly, like a rollercoaster barreling down the next curve with its occupants split between feeling terror or exhilaration. *Or perhaps both.*

Perhaps that's the trick with technology, a phone call, a text message, or a video chat can trick you into believing something when the reality of the situation is something else altogether. Perhaps the changes have been there all along, but I've been oblivious, blinded by the distance between us and my memories of the little boy who left for Boston all those years ago. Now, I'm having a difficult time reconciling the past with the present and am intimidated by what this means for our future.

"A penny for your thoughts?" James clasps my hand with his as he takes the carpool lane on the 110 Freeway toward downtown.

I don't even know where to begin. If this were the past, I would have verbally vomited all my thoughts and feelings to him. But now, in this relationship purgatory, I've no idea how to explain the dizzying thoughts to him, to this man who's no longer the boy I remember, but perhaps someone who has become more. *See, you aren't even officially dating him, and your friendship is changing. You're starting to do what Ben said you did when he broke up with you. You're going to mess this up and you'll lose James forever,* my inner critic warns me as my hands become clammy at the thought of losing him.

"Jess?"

"O-oh, sorry, just thinking about how to face Dick and the others tonight. It's really embarrassing, as all the partners know I got crossed off the list for the panel interviews," I fib, redirecting my thoughts to another worry of mine. I tug my hands from his and fiddle with my bracelet instead, the motion comforting.

"You know, you have nothing to be ashamed of or to be embarrassed about. You didn't do anything wrong."

"But I failed, and you know me, I hate failing. Ugh, what will my parents say? Before, even though they were unhappy with me being unmarried, at least I was moving up the ranks in my career. Now, I'm not only single, but also not in the running for partnership."

He looks at me and squeezes my hand. "If this were Emily or Steven, what would you tell them?"

"Screw everyone else and live for yourself. If you have tried your best, then you have nothing to be ashamed of." That's what my therapist used to tell me.

James chuckles at my quick answer. I shove his arm playfully. "Fine, you got me. I don't practice what I preach."

"Don't we all... Got to flex those muscles, Kingsley," he teases, his eyes twinkling in the dim lights on the freeway. "Sometimes you grow out of your most uncomfortable experiences, and this time, you don't have to go at it alone. I'm by your side every step of the way."

"I'm happy for Becca though, I truly am. She totally deserves the chance to pave the way for the rest of us. She has worked her ass off for this opportunity. I really hope she gets it."

"And this is another example of who you are as a person, and that's much more important than any job title or accolades your parents give you."

My breathing calms as our conversation treads familiar waters. My best friend is back and for a moment I don't need to think about changes.

"So, how are your parents? Are they back from their trip yet?"

"They just got back two days ago. Mom said she has had enough traveling to last her for the next five years. But I think they had a great time. Mom said they bought a lot of souvenirs for us, and you're included too."

I laugh. I can imagine Mrs. Chapman saying that. When I was younger, I used to wish she were my mom instead, and I would immediately feel guilty whenever the thought crossed my mind.

"I need to make a trip out to Boston to see them. It's been too long. The last time I saw them was when they came to visit Liz five years ago. I've been collecting postage stamps I want to add to her collection." I usually pay attention to the postcards or holiday cards I get in the mail and cut out unique stamps for her. Then, I give them to Liz to give to her when she goes back to visit, but for the last few years, they have been piling up in a box on my bookshelf.

"She'll be so happy, I'm sure." He smiles, clearly thinking about his parents.

Time passes by quickly as James successfully distracts me from my nerves about the gala, and frankly, the direction of my life in general. Before I know it, he is pulling up to the valet line at the new five-star hotel that's popular with the Hollywood elite these days. My firm decided to join the hip crowd in an effort to prove accounting is not boring and host our annual gala here.

"Ready?" James gives me a wink as he pulls me out of the car. "Just imagine everyone naked and balding."

I burst out laughing. "Oh my gosh, I so didn't need to have that image in my head."

He wiggles his brows, the silly expression completely at odds with his debonair look. "It worked, didn't it? You're laughing."

I bite my cheek to keep from smiling, my heart a bit lighter. Maybe this night won't be so bad after all.

The firm rented the fiftieth floor for the annual holiday gala. There is one large ballroom decorated in a winter wonderland theme. A large, white dance floor is surrounded by circular tables lit up by centerpieces of mini trees sprayed with artificial snow and decorated with Christmas ornaments and icicle lights. Candles surround the centerpieces, creating the effect of glowing tabletops. Regular chairs are swapped with clear acrylic chairs that reflect the blue backlight under the tablecloths. The walls of the ballroom are lit up in blue and white and massive faux-snow-dusted Christmas trees add a finishing touch to the room.

"Wow, they really went all out." I breathe in as I take in my surroundings.

James wraps his hand around my waist, the heat of his palms transferring through the thin silk to my skin. He surveys the room as if familiarizing himself with the folks I spend most of my daytime hours with.

I recognize both clients and colleagues mingling in corners and by the open bar. A friendly, familiar face approaches me.

"Jess!" Becca squeals as she walks over with Craig. She gives James a not-so-subtle once-over. "So...this is the 'best friend' right?" She lifts a brow at the friend comment. "Hi, I'm Becca."

"Something like that." James laughs softly and extends his free hand to Becca. "I'm James. Nice to meet you. I've heard a lot of good things about you."

Becca shakes his hand enthusiastically. "Oh, so have I. Lots of great things, right, Jess?" *I'm going to kill her after this.* She points to Craig. "And this is my boyfriend, Craig. He's in the tax department. I'm in audit, just like Jess. I'm essentially her partner in crime."

"Which means I shouldn't ask you if you can do my taxes but instead talk about quarterly and annual filings," he recites sardonically.

Becca clasps a hand over her heart. "Oh, a guy after my own heart." Craig smirks beside her, no doubt used to her antics. She quirks her brows at me and mouths, "He is such a keeper."

"Incoming," James whispers to me, staring to the right of us. "Let me guess, the Dickhead?"

I stiffen as I turn my head to the right. Sure enough, Dick is strolling toward us with a jolly smile on his face. That sleazy prick. James rubs his fingers along my waist, temporarily distracting me from the incoming turd.

I paste on the fakest smile I can muster. "Dick."

"Jessica, auditor extraordinaire. It's so good to see you here tonight." Dick flashes his teeth at me. "No hard feelings, right? Of course not, you're always so professional and polite." He laughs at his own monologue. I can feel James's chill emanating from next to me. Dick clears his throat and stares at James. "No Ben this year? And who's this?" I really, really want to punch him right now. He extends his hand to James. "Richard Prescott, but people call me Dick, not that I am one. I'm one of the senior partners here." He chuckles again at his own joke. No doubt he has already had more than one drink tonight.

"James Chapman, Chief Director of Data Science at Brighton Capital."

James's blunt answer surprises me. He's never one to flaunt his position or the company he works at. James returns Dick's handshake and steps back. "I was just telling Jess how fed up we are with our audit firm, even though they're supposedly one of the best firms in the world. But they give us a good deal on their fee. We won't ever consider leaving them unless we get a good partner." He smiles at me. "Someone like Jess. I think we can consider switching if our partner is as brilliant and hardworking as Jess."

Dick laughs awkwardly and quickly recovers. "Jess has a bright future here. We have nothing but good things to say about her." He pulls out a business card from his wallet. "In the meantime, if you ever want to discuss your options, feel free to call me."

James smiles politely and pockets the card. "I'll let Jess know if we have any questions. There may be a request for proposals in the works."

It's very unfair how as a high-ranking female in the business world, our word is often questioned and our worth is measured by others' opinions of us, especially other males. Case in point, Dick is now staring at me with renewed interest in his eyes.

"Of course. Jess, see you in the office next week. I'm sure we have a lot to discuss regarding your future here." With that, he walks away, no doubt to terrorize someone else.

"The dickhead," Becca mutters as soon as Dick is out of earshot. She looks at me, her eyes sympathetic. "Sorry, Jess, I know you worked hard for the panels this year. It must be disappointing."

Oddly, at this current moment, I don't feel so bad. Perhaps seeing Dick being politely put into place by James has elevated my mood. I give Becca a hug. "It's okay. Now you're going to do it for all of us. You so deserve it, and you'll rock the panels. I'm rooting for you from the sidelines."

Becca gives me a teary smile. "Sisterhood solidarity, my friend." She tugs Craig's arm. "Come on, honey, I want to find our seats and rest my legs." I give her a wink as they walk away.

"That was subtle, James." I nudge him in the side.

"You've no idea how much effort it took on my end to keep myself from strangling him." His fingers move in circles on my exposed back, sending renewed flutters through me. "Come on, let's find our seats. At least we're getting a nice meal out of them tonight." He laces his hands with mine and leads us toward our table.

The dinner is surprisingly delicious for hotel fare. The Dungeness crab cakes are perfectly seared and fall apart in your mouth.

The fresh lobster with herbs and lemon garlic butter is a welcomed distraction from the otherwise monotonous droning of our office managing partner welcoming everyone to the gala. We are seated at a table with the other senior managers and their spouses. Everyone does their best not to mention the elephant in the room that is me not getting into panels this year. Even though I only found out last week, within one week, the power of the gossip grapevine has spread the news to everyone else at the firm. I internally cringe at some of the sympathetic stares from my colleagues. *Reframe, Jess, they don't think you're stupid, they just feel sorry for you because, well, it's embarrassing to be in your position. Okay, there are no upsides to this.* I wish they didn't put me up to panel only to take it away from me at the last minute. Embarrassment washes over me.

Just then, the DJ plays the first song of the evening and couples make their way to the dance floor. The first bars of "Can't Help Falling in Love" by the King, Elvis Presley, plays through the ballroom speakers. The hairs on my arms stand up as I remember my first Homecoming where James and I danced to this very same song.

I clutch James's arm playfully. "James! They're playing our song. Remember, Homecoming?" I admire the beautiful couples twirling around the dance floor in their evening attire. "Let's dance."

Silence greets me. Frowning, I glance over at him, freezing at his expression. James is looking down, pensively staring at my hand on his arm as if having an internal debate. I give him a squeeze and he slowly looks up, his eyes burning with an unidentified emotion as he catalogues my features. He breathes in shakily, as if making a decision, and stands up, bringing my hand to his soft lips.

Placing the gentlest of kisses on the back of my hand, he holds his gaze to mine and whispers, "Jess, will you do me the honor of this dance?"

The moment slows and I nod wordlessly, following him to the dance floor, taken aback by the sudden intensity emanating from him. He wraps one hand on my back and clutches the other between us, his grip tight and warm. We wordlessly sway to the music as I look into his sapphire eyes, searching for an answer to a question I don't have. He swings me out into the gentlest of dips as the voice of the King croons on about unrequited love. James gently tugs me back against his chest. He dips his forehead against mine as I close my eyes. The world falls away in his embrace. My mind quiets and nothing exists other than this man holding me as if I'm the most precious thing in the world. Our breaths dance between us as he tightens his hold on me, our scents mingling as if they belonged together all along.

"Jess," he whispers, his deep voice reverberating to my soul. "I promised myself I'd never—"

Never what? Applause sounds on the dance floor, waking us up from the daze as I realize the last bars of the song have finished playing and couples are heading back to their tables. A new ballad plays, "The Joker and the Queen" by Ed Sheeran and Taylor Swift. I stare at him, waiting for him to finish his statement, but his eyes sharpen to something behind me.

I turn around and find a familiar man with golden-brown hair and emerald eyes striding toward us, flashing his dimples in a wide smile.

"Parker? I didn't know you were coming."

"Jess, I didn't know you work at this firm. My firm is one of your clients. I'm the sacrificial lamb who got sent here to represent tonight." He chuckles, oblivious to the tension radiating from the man behind me. He stares at me with warmth in his eyes. "You look stunning tonight, Jess."

I blush. "Thank you."

Parker finally tears his gaze from mine and looks at the man behind me. His expression briefly falters at what he sees, but he recovers quickly. He takes control of the situation, extending his hand toward James. "I'm Parker Wellington. Nice to meet you."

I step back as I take in the appearance of the two men. James is a slight smidge taller than Parker. His posture is stiff as he shakes Parker's hand in a firm grip.

"James Chapman. Likewise."

The infamous broody Chapman is making a reappearance.

Seconds pass by that feel like eternity as the men stare at each other, passing silent messages through their eyes. Parker finally steps back and releases James's hand. He winces imperceptibly and flexes his hand. He turns to me, affection in his eyes.

"Jess, may I have this dance?"

I look at James, but his gaze shutters, his eyes unreadable. I glance at Parker's outstretched hand and place my hand in his. *There's no reason I can't have a friendly dance with him. Let's not keep him waiting in the middle of the dance floor.* Parker swings me into position as we move around the dance floor in sync.

"You're an excellent dancer," I compliment as my eyes dart behind him to search for James.

Parker laughs, his gravelly voice drawing my eyes back to him. "Thank you. I actually took ballroom dancing lessons when I was in college."

"What? Seriously?"

His eyes crinkle at my surprise. "I know, shocking right? I'm quite flexible." He winks at the innuendo and my face flushes.

Parker pulls me closer and whispers in my ear, "So, who is James, and why does he look like he's about to murder me on the spot?"

I find James's hulking figure at our table, his scorching eyes locking on to mine, his hands clenching into fists.

"He's..." What is he? What are we now? "My best friend," I reply, uncertainty lacing my voice.

"Riiight, and I'm the pope," he replies sardonically. "Doesn't matter. I'm not the type to be intimidated by competition." He pauses, most likely staring at James. "Let's give him something to look at."

"What?" I gasp as Parker spins me in a series of dips and twirls and I shriek as he expertly maneuvers me into a few positions I'm not even sure I'm capable of. I laugh as he twirls me close again. I lightly punch the solid wall of muscles of his chest and exclaim, "Warn the girl the next time, okay?" I chuckle and add, "But you're smooth. I'll give you that."

He gives me a wink as the song ends. He takes a step back and bows, and I fight the urge to curtsy back like a scene from the regency romances I read. Parker places a soft kiss on the back of my hand. "Thank you for the fun dance, Jess."

"Likewise, Parker." I smile at him and back away. "I need to make a stop at the restroom. I'll see you around later." He nods and walks back to his table.

Not finding James anywhere, I quickly head to the restroom and relieve myself. I inspect my reflection in the mirror. My face flushes pink from exertion. I fix my hair, reapply my lipstick, and head back out into the foyer.

James materializes from the shadows, his face tense and muscles taut. He strides up with determination and takes my hand, pulling me behind him.

"James? What's going on? What's the matter?" I struggle to keep up in my dress as I follow him.

He leads me to a small, dark room next to the ballroom. The door shuts with a click, and darkness surrounds us, the room only illuminated by the moonlight and the glittering lights from the surrounding buildings in the business district. He walks to the floor-to-ceiling windows and stares at the gleaming skyline below, his posture straight as he clenches and unclenches his right hand. He radiates intensity from his tall frame.

"James?" I quietly walk up behind him, unsure of the source of his sudden change in mood. "Is everything okay?"

He laughs mirthlessly, his shoulders shaking from a mysterious tension.

"No..." He rasps between chuckles as he places both fists on the window, his head dipping down to the glass. "No, I'm *not* okay, *Jess.*"

I stand there awkwardly, a thousand scenarios running through my mind. Is he upset I danced with Parker? Is he upset I haven't said yes to his proposition? Is something else going on?

He drops his fists by his sides as he slowly turns to face me. The pale moonlight illuminates his sharp jawline, prominent nose, and smoldering eyes, a profile that's one hundred percent masculine. His eyes burn with an inferno as he stares at me. The air thickens between us, thrumming with intensity and before I realize what I'm doing, I find myself backing away.

"I promised myself all those years ago I wouldn't dance with you again unless..." He prowls toward me, loosening his bowtie as if he is having trouble breathing.

"Unless what? You're not making sense." My back hits the wall as I stare at him, feeling much like a prey to his predator. My pulse flutters and my mind screams for me to flee.

"Unless you felt differently about me," he whispers as he steps in front of me, the muscle in his jaw ticking.

James lifts his hand and brushes the hair that has fallen over my face in my hasty retreat. He clasps my hand and brings it to his chest. I can feel his heart racing, mirroring mine. I stare up at him, suddenly breathless with anxiety or anticipation, my mind fogging up.

"It hurts, Jess," he grates out, his eyes shining with unshed tears. He thumps my hand against his chest.

"It." *Thump*. "Hurts." *Thump*.

My eyes tear up at his anguish, even though I'm unsure what he's currently referring to.

"It hurts for me to see you with him." He clutches my hand tighter against him. "With anyone else but me."

I gasp, my heart beating out of my chest at the passion in his voice. Desperate to escape his searing gaze, I shake off my hand and step aside. I can't breathe. I can't think. I walk toward the door, afraid to look back, afraid to walk out. I grasp my bracelet as blood rushes to my ears.

"Why are you willing to give him a chance, but not me?" His low voice stops me in my tracks.

I clench the jade heart tightly. "B-because it's safer, because I h-have less to lose with him."

"What if you have more to gain with us?" His voice echoes in the silent room. *What if he's right? What if I stand to gain more than I lose if I take the leap?* My heart urges me to turn around and leap into the unknown. *What if you mess this up and you lose him too?* My brain pulls me back. My chest clenches in pain at the possibility of losing James forever, the agony of not having him in my life. *I can't risk it. I don't know if I can risk it.* Fear and anxiety take root in my thoughts, the familiar weight settling in my chest.

"James, you've always been my best friend. I-I don't know what happened between us these last few months. Maybe we're both looking for a rebound because we both just got out of long-term relationships and this is all a temporary infatuation, a fluke, but I think of you only as a friend—" *You're such a liar, Jess.*

Footsteps thunder behind me, reverberating in the small room. James grabs my arm and spins me around. He clasps the back of my neck in a swift motion and snares my lips in a drugging kiss.

"J-James." I gasp in surprise as he plunders my mouth, one hand cupping the back of my head and the other wraps around my waist, tugging me flush against him. My mind blanks as I lose myself in his kiss. He ravages my lower lip, nipping the plumpness and soothing the pain with another sensual lick of his tongue.

"Does this feel like *infatuation*?" he rasps, his voice taking on a rough edge as he moves his lips down to my throat, trailing kisses in the sensitive region, inflaming my senses.

I whimper, my nipples beading against his chest as he backs me toward the windows. He kisses my clavicles, his hands sliding the thin straps of my dress down my shoulders as I grasp his hair, my skin on fire from his attentions. He nips me on the upper swells of my breasts, sending a jolt of wetness between my legs. I moan, clawing at his hair, desperate to hold on to anything as he awakens every nerve in my body.

"Does this feel like a *fluke*?" He parrots my words back to me. He tugs the other straps off my shoulders as the silk slides off my skin, baring my breasts to him. James groans at the sight of my heavy swells, my chest heaving as I take in shallow breaths.

"Answer me." His deep command sends more wetness between my thighs.

He removes the pasties and thumbs my nipples to hard points. I moan, arching into his caress.

James pauses, as if waiting for my answer. "Answer me."

I mewl, my arousal seeping through my thong, my body desperate for his, my pulse wild. "N-no."

"Good girl."

He resumes his ministrations, gently kneading the globes then leaning down to suck one of my nipples into his mouth, each swipe and swirl of his tongue sending me spiraling toward madness. He moves on to the other side as his hands trail up my legs through the thigh-high slit of my dress and grasp my buttocks.

He kneels to the ground and sets one leg on his shoulder as he groans at the sight of the soaked thong. I flatten my hands on the cool window, desperate for release, aching all over.

"Oh God." I moan loudly as he pulls the thong to the side, his tongue dancing with my folds, laving attention to the bud. My leg threatens to give out at the onslaught of pleasure. "Oh God, James."

Climbing up my body, he pulls my head in for another punishing kiss. My hands move down his torso as I unbutton his shirt, desperate to feel his skin against mine. I draw my hands down the ridges of his flexing muscles and he growls into my mouth, his lips savage against mine. He brings my hands to his trousers, where I feel the hard ridge of him thrusting with every stroke of my hand.

"If you keep doing that, I'm not going to last much longer," he groans as he arches into my hand.

I claw at his trousers, releasing him from the confines of his boxer briefs. James grunts as skin touches skin, and my hands curl around his length. He releases his hands from my face as he takes out a foil packet from his wallet, rips open the package with his mouth, and slips the condom on his turgid cock.

He pulls back for a brief moment, his searing eyes searching mine for a blessing, a gentleman to the very end.

I wrap my legs around his waist in affirmation. He grips my buttocks and impales me on him in one swift stroke. I moan, the pleasure mixes with the pain in the most erotic feeling I've ever experienced in my life.

He groans as he moves, each thrust slamming my back against the window.

"Jess..." He breathes out.

"I've imagined this so many times..." He breathes in.

"So many places, so many ways..." He grunts with exertion as he moves faster against me.

"Everything pales to reality."

I tilt my head back on the glass, staring at the familiar cerulean eyes now filled with hunger and desperation, as my lips part from the exquisite torture that is pleasure bordering on pain. The room fades away as every sense is attuned to my body against his, our bodies moving in sync, our hearts beating as one.

This is more than sex. This is a communion of souls.

The pleasure builds with the rising tension, my eyes unable to tear away from his searing gaze, so full of passion and love. Sounds of skin slapping against skin fill the room as we chase the madness.

"James," I gasp as the pleasure sharpens to the point of no return. Words threaten to spill out of me.

He groans. "I know." His hips piston against mine, his thrusts erratic. Liquid heat gathers between my legs as he pounds into me. He arches his hips, his cock hitting a deep spot within and my mouth falls open, my legs trembling against him.

"I-I'm going to come." I arch my back and moan.

I burst into flames as I fall into the abyss, my cries echoing in the room. He captures my mouth with his as he shudders against me, his release following mine as my legs shake around his waist.

My body limp, my mind in a fog, I hang on to him as his kisses turn slow and tender. James slowly sets me down and holds on to me until my wobbly legs find purchase on the ground. He takes out his pocket square and cleans me up, dragging another moan out of me when he wipes over the sensitized nerves. He slides my thong into place, his hands worshipping my legs along the way. We stare at each other, at a loss for words, as he cleans himself and buckles his pants.

My mind slowly climbs out of the pleasure haze as the realization of what we did sinks in. *I just had sex with James in public. The room is not even locked! Anyone could have walked in. What was I thinking? What are we going to do now? Do you even know what you want, Jess? Oh crap.* My pulse kicks into high gear as I take in short bursts of oxygen, the panic rolling through my system in waves.

"Jess. Jess." I focus on my breathing, longer exhales than inhales. *Slow the nervous system down, Jess.* "Jess, look at me!" A deep voice penetrates my panic.

My eyes flutter open as James cradles my face tenderly in his palms. "Don't think. Breathe." He places his forehead against mine, his voice soothing as he slides his hands down my arms and interlaces both of his hands with mine. "Breathe in five counts. Breathe out eight counts. Let's do that again." The warmth of his hands feeds life back into my cold ones. We breathe together, moving as one, and my pulse slowly calms as the black dots fade away from my vision.

"Do me a favor," he whispers as he looks down at me, tenderness in his eyes. "Don't think. Give me this weekend. Let's just pretend you've decided to give us a chance. Just three days, Jess. You can do three days."

Three days, short-term. I can do three days. That's not permanent, that's not long term. We've already crossed that last line, three more days won't hurt, right? The anxiety in me abates at the short-term goal.

"If by the end of these three days you still don't see why we're good together, not as friends, but as lovers, as partners, then I'll let you go." His voice cracks at the last few words, his eyes pleading with me.

"And if that happens, you won't leave me? You'll still be my best friend? Nothing will change?" I whisper back, my muscles tight with apprehension.

James closes his eyes, his brows furrowed in concentration, a muscle twitching in his jaw. After a moment of silence that can be one second or one minute as the concept of time no longer applies here, he slowly opens his eyes, his gaze filling with renewed determination.

"Yes. We'll go back to what we were before, as if nothing has changed."

I let out a deep breath. "Okay."

He slowly exhales at my answer, his grip on my hands softens. He stares at our interlinked hands and chuckles softly, his head shaking as if he just realized he's the punchline to a joke only he understands. I stare at him in confusion, not comprehending his response. He slowly lifts his head and breaks into a dazzling smile as his chuckling turns to laughter. James's eyes, now a shade lighter, fill with joy. He cradles my face and brushes a light kiss over my lips. "Thank you, Jess. Thank you."

His eyes twinkling, he steps back, tugging up my straps of my dress and I jolt in surprise, realizing I was half-naked until this point. Lately, my brain has turned into mush around this man. He clasps my hand in his and leads me out of the dark room.

"Let's say our goodbyes, shall we? If I only have three days to prove to you how good we are together, I'm not wasting any time with Dickhead and Co.," he whispers as we step back into the brightly lit foyer, mirth in his voice.

I grin, giddiness filling me as we stroll back to the ballroom, our bodies and hearts in sync.

Her hips automatically arch in the air, chasing the myriad of sensations I inflict on her as she hovers between sleep and wakefulness. I caress her slick folds and skim her swollen clit. Jess moans loudly, her lust-filled sounds making my cock hard. I've lost count how many rounds we've had tonight. I'm insatiable for her. It's like everything I've been holding back is unleashed. Her eyes snap open, adjusting to the darkness that is illuminated only by a sliver of moonlight. My sleeping beauty is finally awake.

I dip two fingers inside her entrance, and she gasps at the pleasurable intrusion. Trailing kisses down her body, I spread open her thighs and suck on the juices seeping from her folds. She tastes like strawberries, just like her scent. I can never get enough. She grinds on my face as I lave the nub with my tongue, following by a gentle suction, my fingers thrusting in rhythm.

Her hips arch up and she whimpers, "James…"

"Awake, sweetheart?" I murmur as I continue to feast on her under the covers. "I know you love your sleep, but I can't help it… you're so responsive to me." I groan as I lick the essence seeping out of her body. "I can do this all night, every night."

Jess reaches under the covers in a desperate effort to grab any part of me as she thrashes on the bed, her body undulating in an erotic rhythm.

"James," she begs, her loud moaning so sexy, I may be able to come from just hearing her pleasurable sounds. "I need you." My cock has never been so hard, ever.

"Uh huh." My voice is muffled as I suck on her clit, releasing it with an audible pop. I give my cock a quick stroke as I climb up her body, kissing to every inch of her exposed skin.

I brace myself above her, my turgid length rests against her fluttering stomach as she gyrates against me, rubbing against the hard ridge of my cock.

"Say it. What do you want?" I grunt, barely holding onto my sanity.

She groans, her hips chasing mine as I hold myself still above her. The pulse in my neck jumps as I stare into her eyes, her pupils dilated, overtaking those beautiful hazel hues.

"You have to say it or else I won't move, sweetheart," I whisper against her ear, punctuating the sentence with a nip in the lobe.

"I need you." She thrashes on the bed, appearing to be desperate for me, desperate for my cock. Fuck, I knew we would be good together, but this exceeds my wildest imagination.

"To what?" I reward her with a slow grind of my cock against her clit. She cries out in pleasure as she attempts to roll her hips to chase the sensations. I pin her legs down to stop her motions, waiting for her answer.

"To fuck me," she whispers, the curse word from her innocent mouth sending a jolt of pleasure down south.

"My horny sweetheart needs my cock in her pussy? Say it again," I command, as precum leaks from the tip of my erection.

"Fuck me, James," she screams, clawing my back, her breasts heaving in the moonlight.

I swallow her scream with a groan and thrust into her, binding us together in mind and soul. We move in tandem, dancing to the ancient rhythm. I push, she pulls. I parry, she blocks. Our bodies are in sync as our breaths mingle. I pick up the speed, hammering into her deeply as I relish in her tight, warm grip on my cock. She screams loudly as her muscles tense up and her eyes roll back. I thrust harder upon hearing the lurid sounds of our lovemaking, the skin slapping against skin, the wetness of each thrust into her soaked core. The pressure builds and our breathing grows ragged. Her molten stare collides with mine as we lock our fingers and leap into the flames of madness together.

Minutes or hours pass by as time ceases to exist. She snuggles next to me, lethargic in the best way. My mind is a blank slate, with nothing but intense love coursing through my veins. She buries her nose into my neck as I take in a whiff of her hair, relishing in the familiar scent of strawberries and cream. Aside from the obvious closeness that's shared between a man and a woman after they make love, there's an additional layer of intimacy when you can identify all the specific notes of what makes a person smell distinct. With Jess, there are additional depths to her scent, a twinge of lavender, a dash of citrus, mixed with her uniquely feminine aroma, a cocktail blend tailored for me.

"Are you asleep?" I murmur, burying my face in her hair.

"No," she mumbles back, her ears against my chest. *Hear my heart, the heart that beats solely for you since the day we met.*

I press a soft kiss on the top of her head. "I love you, Jess."

Her fingers still on my chest as she freezes at my words. Disappointment floods my body as my chests tightens briefly in pain. *Give her time. We've just crossed so many lines it must be difficult for her to adjust to this new "us."*

I smooth my hand down my back and pull her close. "You don't have to say it back. I know it's too soon for you... But I just want to be honest with myself for once and let you know."

"Thank you."

"Go to sleep, sweetheart."

She drifts off to sleep with a smile on her face. *Please let this be enough to convince her. How can you walk away from this?*

• • •

Saturday passes by in a blur of lovemaking on every single surface of my apartment: on the kitchen countertop, against the window—I don't give a fuck if anyone saw us—on the sofa, in the shower, on the floor. It's as if we're making up for lost time. I've learned things about my best friend I never thought I'd know, the way she turns to putty when I dominate her in bed, the drugging pleasure of her kisses, the way her eyes flare when I whisper dirty things in her ears.

After the latest round of extreme exercise consisting of me twisting her lithe body in all the ways I imagine being described in a kama sutra book, she plops face down on my bed, appearing boneless, breathless, speechless.

I head into the bathroom to clean myself up and return back to the bedroom, chuckling at her state when I see her lying on top of my blankets in the same position I left her in. She opens one eye, squints at me, and flushes red as she takes in my nakedness.

"Did I tire you out, sweetheart?" I murmur as I tug her into a sitting position and slip one of my MIT t-shirts on her.

"Mmmrrrrgrrr..." she garbles, her head against my chest.

I bark out in laughter. "What?"

"You crazy, insane, certifiable sex addict." She attempts a one-eye glare at me as I prop her up against the pillows. God, she's so adorable.

"Better than your books, right?" I wink at her. "Oh, Your Grace, I'm going to swoon!" I fall dramatically on the bed.

Jess tosses a pillow at me, hitting me in the face as I resurface from the blankets. She pumps her hands in the air in victory.

I pull on a pair of shorts and settle on the bed, pulling her next to me, my hands rubbing circles on her back. Touching her is second nature now: swatting her butt when she passes by to go to the bathroom, a kiss on top of her head when she made us coffee this morning, my hands on her thighs now as I turn on the television.

"I never asked you before... Why did you come back to LA? Your parents are in Boston still. Is it really because of the job?"

My fingers now circle her thighs. "That's one of the reasons. Not the main one." I turn to her and look her in the eye as awareness settles in her gaze.

"Me?" She appears surprised, as if shocked I'd move halfway across the world for her. *That's only the tip of the iceberg. I'm willing to do anything to have you by my side. Absolutely anything.*

I press a kiss on her forehead. "Yes, you, sweetheart. We've spent too many years apart and yet during all this time, my heart has been tethered to yours." I nudge her, my heart bursting with happiness as I finally get to say the words I've been holding inside me for so long. "Even though you don't know it."

"I never knew…" She trails off, as if unable to fathom how I've been pining for her from afar.

"I know you didn't. I don't blame you and you shouldn't blame yourself either. Frankly, I think I've been trying to ignore it as long as I can as well. Too much is at stake."

She nods vehemently. She's probably terrified at the change in our relationship. Knowing her, she's most likely thinking of a million ways this can go south. Only time will be able to prove to her I'm not going anywhere.

"What made you decide to come back?"

"I don't want to live with any regrets." She stares at me as she contemplates my response. We are two sides of the same coin, my action against her inaction, my optimism against her pessimism, my bravery against her cautiousness, my yang to her yin. Together, we're in balance. We're whole.

Wordlessly, she sidles closer to me and presses a soft kiss on my shoulders. Hope flutters within me. *She's not retreating. She's still here.*

I flip through the channels on the TV and she squeals in delight when *Harry Potter and the Goblet of Fire* shows on the screen.

"*Harry Potter* again? Didn't we just watch this in Yosemite?"

"Hush… We only saw the first and second one. You were busy cooking and cleaning, so you missed most of it, anyway." She rubs her hands together in glee. "This one is where it starts to get dark."

I snort. "You watch this at least once a year. Is it even surprising to you anymore?"

"It's a religion and it's comforting. Don't say anything otherwise if you want to stay on my good side, Chapman." I smile inwardly, not shocked at her answer. She always hated surprises.

I mime zipping up my lips and blink innocently at her.

"You know, I was going to say maybe you should be upgraded to Gryffindor for your bravery in moving back to LA for me, and your loyalty." She takes a sip of water from the cup on the nightstand. "But now I think you should stay in Slytherin." She reminds me of our conversation all these years ago when we were kids. "You're definitely a devious one."

"And you like me for it." I smirk.

Her stomach growls and she scowls at me. "Feed me, Chapman. I'm starving. You did this to me."

"Oh yeah? I seem to recall you were the one to initiate the last round...with this gorgeous mouth of yours..."

She bites her lips at the reminder. "Any more sass and you aren't getting any later."

I tilt her face up and caress her lips with mine, chasing her moans as she melts against me, and our kiss quickly deepens as my cock salutes to attention, ready for yet another round. I break off our kiss reluctantly and she whimpers in frustration, her breathing shallow.

"We'll see about that." I bite my cheek to keep from laughing at her disappointed face. I pick up the phone and scroll through my contacts. "Italian?"

"Yes. You know me too well."

"If it's up to me, every day I'll feed you anything that'll put that expression on your face."

"The good stuff is always so bad for you." She groans and pats her nonexistent pooch on her waistline.

"More for me to love. I love every inch of you."

She blushes prettily as I place our order with the restaurant for delivery.

"As much as I love staying in with you and convincing you with my sexual prowess, do you want to do something tomorrow? We can go to the modern art exhibit you were talking about last time."

She perks up. "You'll go with me to MOMA? I've been wanting to go for the longest time, but no one around me seems to be interested."

"I'll endure it and enjoy it because of that face, but you are watching the MMA fight with me tomorrow night." I lace my fingers with hers, my thumb pausing on her bracelet. "Why do you wear this all the time?" I murmur, staring at the gift I gave her all those years ago.

"It gives me comfort when I'm stressed or anxious. I think it gives me strength, perhaps borrowing from your belief in me...that maybe if you believe in me that much, I can do the same. Not sure if I'm making any sense."

"It does. I like it on you. It's like a piece of me is with you always."

She smiles, as if liking the idea of having part of me with her wherever she goes. "Fine, you sweet talker, I'll give you a special deal. I'll watch *two* of those MMA fights with you tomorrow night. But FYI, I have lunch with the girls tomorrow. We planned this a while ago before...this." She looks so happy—I'll do anything to keep that smile on her face.

"It's okay. By the end of this weekend, you'll see that we can be lovers and friends and we'll have all the time in the world."

She sighs contently as she rests her head on my shoulders. For the first time in my life, the void in my heart is filled and I'm content. If I die now, I'll be a happy man. I hope this happiness stays for good.

CHAPTER 29

Jess

"**S**pill, what's putting that glow on your face? Or better yet, *who* is putting that glow on your face?" Emily gives me a sly grin in the way of a greeting.

"Oooo, you are right, Ems, she's totally blushing, and not her normal flush. This is an 'I got it good and I'm still getting it good' type of look." Liz claps her hands together in excitement.

I bite my lip to keep from smiling and my face heats up; damn fair skin. Today, we're meeting at a small Greek restaurant in Pasadena, where Liz lives. I sit down and drink a sip of ice water, hoping it will calm my burning skin. The sun shining through the atrium windows does little to conceal my embarrassment. The little café is not packed yet, most likely because it opened a few weeks ago and people haven't caught on to this little gem. If the early reviews are any indication, this place will be packed in a month or two when social media gets a hold of it.

"What are you guys talking about?" I play innocent, but knowing myself, probably doing a horrible job at it.

"Come on. You might as well give it up. It's pointless." Emily sits back, smug. "Who is it? Parker or James?"

Liz groans and hides her face in her hands. "Remember the ground rules! If it's James, I don't want to hear about it. Okay, amend that. I want to know what happened, but not the juicy details." She shudders. "Definitely not the juicy details."

I stare at the menu intently, not wanting to look them in the eye. "James."

"Yeeessss! I *knew* it! Omigosh, was it good? It has to be good, right? I mean, look at your face. I've never seen you so relaxed. Tell me *all* the details."

Liz plugs her ears with her fingers. "Nope, nope, nope...absolutely *no* details. I don't want the image in my brain." She takes in my flushed face. "Or images..." she mutters.

"Hush, you just keep your ears shut." Emily scoots her chair closer to mine. "So, how was it?"

"Ugh, Ems, you're relentless. It was great, okay? The best I ever had. You happy?"

More shrieking. "He looks like one of those guys with a lot of pent-up energy. A secret alpha. Is that the case?"

Liz shuts her eyes and hums something like "Old MacDonald Had a Farm" under her breath.

"This is the last thing I'm going to say on the matter. Yes, he definitely is dominant in the bedroom. And I'm not telling you anything else."

Emily pouts and retreats back to her original spot at the table. Liz opens one eye and unplugs one ear. "You guys done? Not going to say anything that'll traumatize me for life?"

"Yes, we're definitely done on the subject."

"Spoilsport." Emily scowls, looking ten years younger than her actual age. Her expression sobers up, and she asks, "So, are you guys together now then?"

"We're not together, together in that sense yet... He's asking me for this weekend and tomorrow to give it a test run. I'm trying my best not to think too much right now. It's very difficult."

"For what it's worth, I know I told you to be careful before because you guys have such a long history, but I've never seen you so happy before and that's what we all really want for you, for someone to put that smile on your face."

I grin, the sparks of hope burning brighter. "I know, I feel happy. I don't know how to describe this feeling, but I've never felt so light before, like I'm not weighed down by much and my mind is calming down for once in my life."

"Yep. Orgasms will do that to you. Especially good orgasms," Emily quips.

"Aack! I thought we were done with that subject!" Liz exclaims, grimacing.

I laugh at Liz's dramatic expression. A thought flitters through my mind, perhaps the only thought humming in the background since James and I began this weekend test trial. "I just hope this is not a mistake. I mean, we both just got out of long-term relationships, and you know, rebound relationships aren't exactly known for their success rates."

"For what it's worth," Liz begins, her eyes earnest, "I don't think this is a rebound for him. I think this has been a long time coming for him. He's had a thing for you forever, Jess."

I shake my head. "No, that can't be. I never picked up on anything and he dated around. I mean, he also had Claire." I can't be that oblivious, can I?

"Well, you aren't exactly known for having the best 'gut' feelings." Emily, ever so unhelpful, offers her opinion.

"I'm not going to think about it. We agreed to try this out this weekend, then I'll think about it tomorrow and we'll decide what we want to do going forward."

"So, what about Parker? You guys had a good date, right? I think I saw some photos posted on Becca's Instagram of you and Parker dancing at the gala? Didn't you go with James?" Emily asks.

The waiter comes by and takes our orders. I got the Horiatiki salad, a classic Greek salad with juicy tomatoes, fresh cucumbers, tangy olives, topped with a generous helping of feta cheese. My digestive system needs a lighter fare after the heavy Italian meal from the night before. The other ladies order kebabs and salads as well.

"Yes, he was there because his firm is a client of ours. I was actually pretty surprised myself—" I stop. A tall figure by the entrance is heading toward our table. "Parker?"

Liz sips her iced tea. "Yes, we're talking about Parker. You were saying?"

"Jess? I thought that was you. What are the chances of seeing you here? I'm beginning to think you're stalking me." Parker walks up to the table, a teasing glint in his eyes, and flashes those gorgeous dimples at me.

I laugh, shaking my head at this series of weird coincidences. "I swear, this is just another coincidence. You know, I can also say *you* are stalking *me* since you went to *my* firm's gala, and I got *here* first."

He guffaws, his gravelly voice warm and full of humor.

Emily patiently waits for an introduction as she stares at us with interest.

"This is my sister, Emily. Emily, this is Parker, a...friend."

"Nice to meet you, Emily." Parker extends his hand and Emily clasps it in an enthusiastic handshake. She never does anything in half measures.

"Likewise. I've heard so much about you."

"All good things, I hope." Another charming grin.

"Of course." Emily winks.

Liz twists her chair around. "Hi! And I'm Liz, Jess's *friend* in every sense of the word." The cheeky girl. She'll get a ribbing from me later. Liz glances up at Parker, her eyes dancing in mirth. She extends her hand toward him.

Parker looks away from Emily. "Liz, nice to meet—"

His expression freezes as he clasps Liz's hand in his, his emerald eyes darkening in something akin to shock as unidentified emotions flash in his gaze. A muscle twitches in his cheek as he swallows, his Adam's apple bobbing up and down his strong neck.

Liz's mischievous smile falters and she glances at me, confusion on her face. She winces as Parker squeezes her hand tighter. "Ouch. You have a strong grip there."

Parker snaps out of his trance and drops Liz's hands as if he has touched molten lava. He tugs at his collar as a dark flush creeps up his neck.

"Sorry about that," he replies, clearly flustered.

He drags his hands through his thick golden-brown hair, his eyes darting away but quickly returning to Liz. He shifts his body as if uncomfortable and looks at me in apology.

"It's great seeing you, Jess. I'm sure we'll talk soon." Parker's eyes flicker to Liz again, intense emotions brimming in his gaze, then he promptly turns away and strides out of the restaurant.

"What. Was. That?" Emily asks, echoing my sentiments.

"I don't know," Liz's whispers, rubbing circles in her chest, as if assuaging a phantom pain. She stares at the door where Parker made his dramatic exit.

"Do you guys know each other?" I ask, curious at this turn of events.

Liz faces us, bewilderment in her eyes. "No, I definitely would remember a face like that. That was...bizarre."

• • •

"This piece is acrylic on canvas and represents the modern dichotomy of the rich and the poor in first world countries," I read the plaque next to the artwork.

James wraps his arm around me and stares intently at the canvas before us, a frown marring his beautiful face. "I don't know. I think this piece is made by Liz's kindergarteners," he murmurs.

I look around the quiet room and hush him. "Not so loud, Chapman." I turn my head around to look at the artwork from another angle. It's a white canvas with black acrylic paint splashed on top of it in a haphazard pattern and a red soda can affixed to the corner. "I mean, I guess if you turn your head ninety degrees, the black paint kind of resembles a dirty river...with litter, like the can of cola!"

"So, you need to look at this piece of work in some sort of bend over backward yoga pose?" He doesn't appear convinced.

"I'm trying to find the hidden meaning!" I turn my body to the side so my head is almost next to my waist. I'm sure I look ridiculous.

"Come to think of it, I think this artist is a genius. Maybe this... Gabriel Perez wants you to look at his art in a downward dog pose." James snickers. "I mean, I know I'll suddenly find the art much more interesting if you do that." He whistles slowly, his eyes glued to my ass.

"I never knew you were such a horn-dog. How did I ever miss that?"

"Oh trust me, I've never changed. I just didn't think it was appropriate to let you know, you know, best friends and all." He grabs my left butt cheek in a soft squeeze, and I swat his hand away. "Trust me, you've starred in all sorts of depraved fantasies, and you just never knew about them."

My face flushes as I pull myself into an upright position and we walk to the next piece. "Oooh this one supposedly represents the innocence of childhood. Wow, the museum purchased this one for three million dollars." The artwork is a 3D installation comprised of sequins in various sizes scattered on the floor and paper pom-poms coated with glitter slime dangling from the ceiling.

"If childhood equals someone throwing up a rainbow of glitter and random crap..." His tone is snarky as he fights a grin. "Actually...that does make sense. Kids eating random things and throwing up later. Sounds very on par. I think I get this one."

I bite my cheek to keep from laughing out loud. "Why did you even come?"

He tugs me flush to his chest and tilts my chin up, his eyes warm. "Because I know you love this stuff. And this makes you happy, so even though I think modern art is the most ridiculous thing ever and is probably made by a bunch of kindergarteners in disguise, I'm happy because you have that smile on your face."

I tug his head down and give him a chaste kiss, which he quickly turns dirty with his talented tongue. Breathing hard, I break away. "We are in public, James."

"Screw everyone."

"I can see the headlines already. 'Brighton Capital Chief Data Analyst and Big 8 Senior Manager Arrested for Public Indecency'." I give my best Audrey Kingsley's "I'm not impressed with you" look.

"Fine, you may have a point." He looks at my glare and chuckles. "Is this your disapproving look? Because if it is, you need to work on it a bit. You just look so adorable." He bends down and whispers in my ear, "And it turns me on."

"Ugh. You're insufferable."

"And you love me for it."

I ignore him as we continue through the museum. After the brunch with the girls this morning, I went back to James's place where he insisted driving us to the Museum of Modern Art. We have spent the last two hours wandering the halls of the famous museum. This is the best weekend I've ever had in a long time. Despite the disappointing news of the partnership panels, I don't think I've ever felt lighter. The near-constant tightness in my shoulders and chest have not made an appearance yet. I may have only had one mini anxiety attack when I was thinking about the decision I have to make tomorrow, but I'm able to distract myself with breathing exercises.

"Dinner out or dinner in?" he murmurs into my hair.

"I want to say dinner in. Does this make me too much of a boring homebody?" I've been told by many people I'm not fun because I always prefer staying in as opposed to going out. Sometimes, I fake enthusiasm and drag myself to go out with friends so I don't disappoint them.

"I love homebodies. Give me peace and quiet in the comforts of home any day of the week. I'll cook for you tonight."

"You cook? Since when?"

He smiles smugly. "Since college. Jess, must I remind you that you haven't really been with me since over a decade ago? I'm not the nerdy kid who buries himself under books and games anymore. I actually have survival skills."

I roll my eyes. Oh, I definitely know he is not a kid anymore. Glimpses of his six-pack abs and solid pecs flash through my mind. My skin heats up at the memory.

James's eyes darken. "Should we go home? I'd give anything to know what you were thinking about just now."

Feeling naughty, I tiptoe and place my mouth next to his ear. "I was thinking…" I lightly nip his earlobe and his grip tightens around me, his fingers digging into my waist. "I'd love to explore those survival skills of yours…in a deep and thorough way."

He groans and a vein pulses on his forehead. "Okay, that's it. Exhibit's over. We're going."

I laugh as he drags me out of the museum and unceremoniously pushes me into his car. The sun is warm and the breeze feels hopeful as we head home. This is quite possibly the best weekend ever. For once in my life, I only exist in the present and am not ruminating over the past or worried about the future.

CHAPTER 30

Jess

The light melodies of birds chirping filter through the windows as I slowly come to my senses from the best sleep I've ever had in recent memory. I feel completely refreshed, with a bone-deep sense of peace. The salty ocean breeze fills the room and I bury myself deeper into the comforter, relishing the silky sheets against my bare skin. A heavy arm is slung across my waist. *James.*

I smile, my body warming with the memories of last night. After proceeding to show me all the ways he worships my body when we got home from the museum, James whipped up the most tantalizing platter of paella paired with a white wine for dinner. Apparently, he picked up the recipe when he was in Europe. James, half-naked in the kitchen cooking food, unlocked a different level of fantasy for me. As promised, I watched two MMA fights with him where I proceeded to pepper him with many questions about the fighters, the rules and regulations—I'm an auditor after all—ultimately culminating into a half-drunk fest where I tossed a pillow at the TV when the referee made a call I didn't agree with.

Chuckling softly at the events of last night, I burrow closer to the pillar of heat at my back. James's arm tightens around me, his scent of sandalwood and spice surrounding me like another blanket. I slowly turn around to look at him. I catalogue the features I used to take for granted but have come to love: the strong shoulders I can lean on, the muscular arms wrapping me up in the warmest embrace whenever I need it, the strong jawline, peppered with an overnight's amount of growth, the sharp nose, the softly tousled dark hair.

Somehow, over the last few months, this man beside me, who used to be the best friend a girl could have, has become the romantic partner I've always wished for. My heart pumps with joy, but there is a curl of unease gathering in my chest. What if I mess this up? The stakes are so high. If this does not work out, I'm not only losing my lover, I'm also losing my best friend, the person who has been with me through thick and thin, my constant, for all these years.

A jolt of panic flares inside me as I quash it down with a few deep breaths. *Don't think about it, Jess. Focus on the present. Today is the third day. You still have time to make a decision and James said he won't blame you either way. You still have time. Ugh. Control your damn anxiety, Jess.* My body slowly relaxes as I pretend I'm an ostrich, burying my head in the sand at the sight of impending doom. Having experienced this side of James, I don't know how I can ever walk away, if I even wanted to walk away.

I trail my fingers along his stubble as I reach up and kiss his parted lips, conveying the emotions I can't say in words through my lips to his. His eyes, deep blue this morning, slowly flutter open as he registers my kiss, his lips automatically tangling with mine. His arms curl tighter around me as our legs intertwine, our bodies melding together where one does not know where one begins and the other ends.

Pushing him flat on his back, I straddle him, the comforter slipping to my waist. The cold air prickles my nipples into hard buds, my breasts swollen under his heavy-lidded gaze. I bring my hands up to my nipples, plucking at the nubs begging for his touch. His pupils dilate as his breathing turns ragged. I slowly gyrate my hips against his erection, my wetness coating him. James grasps my hips, moving me against him, his fingers digging into the tender skin of my thighs.

I keep my eyes on him as my mouth parts on a moan. His hips move faster, rubbing against me in precisely the right way. I bring one of his hands to my mouth and I make love to his fingers, swirling my tongue against his digits. His gaze flares as he bucks harder against me. I pull out a foil packet from the nightstand and roll a condom on his thick cock, his body shuddering at near release.

Wordlessly, I slowly take him inside me, inch by inch, as we both hold our breaths at the connection. He groans as he bottoms out, his gaze pinning mine. I bring his hands up to my breasts as I move against him, chasing the fulfillment only he can provide. The bed squeaks as we move together. He stares up at me, his fingers flicking my nipples as I close my eyes to the sensations gathering below. The pleasure builds, beautiful and bittersweet. I whimper at the friction.

With one swift motion, he flips me onto my back, his body still connected to mine in every way that matters. James pins my hands above my head and slowly interlaces his fingers with mine as he thrusts against me. His groans meld with my own as sounds of our lovemaking fill the room. I stare at him as wetness gathers in my eyes, my heart feeling so loved and scared at the same time. A stray tear slides down my cheek and he kisses me, our lips and tongues saying words that aren't invented yet, our bodies leaving pieces of each other behind with each glide.

He draws back and stares into my eyes as his thrusting becomes more erratic and the pleasure builds to a pinnacle. A loud moan escapes from me, my mouth falling open as I teeter on the precipice.

"I love you, James," I whisper as I fall into oblivion, my eyes closing at the soul-shaking intensity.

He captures my lips in a drugging kiss as he shudders against me, his fingers gripping mine, our bodies becoming one in both spirit and form.

"I love you so much, Jess. So, so much," James rasps against my lips as we come down from the highest of highs, our souls plummeting back to earth, forever changed.

After what feels like an eternity, he rolls off the bed to clean up in the bathroom and returns with a warm towel to gently attend to my needs. He crawls back into bed and pulls me to him as we listen to the morning quietness in the room with nothing but the squawking of seagulls and chirping of birds to keep us company.

"I know you called in sick today and I originally had the entire day off, but an emergency came up at work with one of the foreign markets, so I need to spend a few hours in the office this morning," he whispers as I snuggle closer to him, not wanting to break our connection. "I'll be back after lunch and we can spend the rest of the day together..." He trails off as we both realize today is the third day and I owe him an answer.

I nod. "I'll be here waiting for you." Tension releases from his body as he lets out a breath at my response.

Giving me a lingering kiss, he swings off the bed and proceeds to get ready for work. I pull the covers over my head and cocoon myself in the warm darkness, surrounded by his scent intermixing with mine as I drift off into a dreamless sleep.

• • •

My phone ringing jolts me awake from the best morning nap I've ever had...ever. My hands blindly reach for my phone on James's nightstand.

"Hello?" I mumble, not bothering to check who is calling.

"Jess?" Sniffles come through on the other line, effectively clearing the remaining haze from my mind.

I glance at the caller ID. *Becca.* "Becca? Are you okay?" I sit upright on the bed, fully alert and ready to be the best friend I can ever be for her.

"Did I wake you up? I'm so sorry. Why don't you go back to sleep?" More sobbing ensues.

"Oh my gosh, don't mind me. I'm just sleeping in. Honey, what's going on? Are you okay?" Ugh, bad question, she's obviously not okay. Idiot. I slap my hand on my forehead.

"Craig broke up with me. He's moving to the East Coast. He... doesn't want me anymore."

"What? I thought you guys were doing better!" My heart drops at the news. Becca has regained her sparkle the last few months as she and Craig seemed to be on the up and up again. They have been together for so long and good friends for even longer, to suddenly lose all that must be heart wrenching. How do you even move on when the person who knows you the best, who has been through everything with you, voluntarily leaves you? My pulse speeds up as I can't help but empathize with her plight.

Becca blows her nose and replies, "I thought so too. But apparently, he has been putting up a front. He told me because we were together for so long, whether it was as friends or as partners, he thought he owed it to me to try falling back in love with me. He said we grew apart and he wants something new."

"Oh honey, I'm so sorry."

"He said he was sick of my work hours, which is ironic considering he's in tax and their hours are terrible too! But apparently, it's okay for him to pursue his career, but it's a no-no for me to dedicate most of my time to my work."

"What bullshit. That's some stupid double standards right there." I grip my phone tightly, anger roiling inside me.

Becca adds, "He also said the habits he used to find endearing have grown to really annoy him now that we spend so much time with each other."

"What habits? What is he talking about? I'm sure he is not a paragon of perfection either."

She whispers, "You know, I always think I'm not good enough. I'm really good at faking it until I make it, but I have a lot of self-doubt sometimes, so I'll always ask him if I'm handling this conversation correctly or addressing this problem appropriately. I guess when we weren't dating, he thought it was cute I was trying so hard, but now we've been together for so long, he is resenting me for all these questions. He's tired of being my sounding board and listening to my negativity."

"But you're the most positive and badass person I know!" I gasp, shocked at her revelation. Becca always comes off strong and in control at work. Heck, she always gives me advice on how to handle myself when I have problems.

Becca sniffles as her voice sounds watery again. "I'm better at giving other people advice than taking it myself," she murmurs. "I didn't know I was annoying him so much. I never knew."

My heart is beating against my ribcage as my anxiety reawakens after hibernation in the last few days. If Becca, my strong, warmhearted friend, and colleague-in-arms, can't make it work with Craig, one of the nicest guys I know, what are the odds for me and James?

"He also told me he's annoyed at some of my smaller habits too. I'm not exactly the cleanest person. I mean, I'm not dirty, but I leave my clothes on the furniture, and dishes may remain in my sink for a day or two before I get to them, stuff like that. Little stuff!"

I clench my hands. "I'm sure he leaves the toilet seat up and you're annoyed about that too."

"Exactly!" Her frustration overpowers her sadness at the current moment. "This is minor stuff, right?"

I hum in agreement as she whimpers, her distraught manner bleeding through the line.

"Oh honey. My heart hurts for you." I clutch my chest to soothe the heaviness gathering there.

"Jess, I don't know who else to call. Aside from you, Craig, and work, I don't think I have much going on in my life."

"My dear, you can call me anytime. I wish I could do more to take away some of your pain. Why don't I drop by later with some ice cream and food?"

"I'm traveling tonight for a job, but thanks for the support. I just need to tell someone who'll understand." Her weeping pauses as she struggles to calm her breathing. "I wish...Jess. I wish we never started," she whispers. "If we never started, I'd still have my best friend. What hurts me more than losing this relationship is losing my soulmate. I feel like I gambled my entire hand and lost everything."

My heart pounds in my ears as her words sink in. *I feel like I gambled my entire hand and lost everything. No, no, no, other people's situations aren't equal to yours, Jess. You and James are different, and he's not Craig.* But are we really that different? If Becca, the girl who appears to have it all, who appears to have everything together, loses so terribly, what chances do I have with James?

"I'm here to listen and you can call me anytime," I reply, not knowing what else to say because I know there's nothing I can say that'll take away her heartbreak.

"Thanks, Jess for listening. Sorry for disturbing your day. I have an incoming call from my manager. I need to go." She clears her throat and hangs up.

The silence in the apartment, once comforting and relaxing, is now too quiet and oppressing. A million thoughts rush through my mind as fear hits me head-on. My breathing comes in short bursts as my chest feels like an anvil is placed on top of it. I grab my bracelet. *Deep breaths, Jess, Becca is not you,* I repeat, but my pulse refuses to settle down as the kernel of doubt grows into a monster, overpowering my insides.

I throw back the curtains and open the window, desperate to get some fresh air in as I suffocate from the negativity consuming my thoughts. My body is telling me to flee this invisible war raging inside me. Dark clouds gather outside, the chill biting in an unusual deviation of the usual sunny Los Angeles weather. *A harbinger of doom, Jess, even the skies are sending you a sign.*

My phone rings again and dread coils in my stomach. I take a look at the caller ID this time. *Mother.* My finger hover over the decline button, but I know if I don't pick up, I'll regret it later when she'll no doubt berate me for ignoring her calls.

"Mother, this is not a good time—"

"Jessica, why am I hearing from Cheryl you seem to be dating James Chapman? Her daughter is a client at your firm and said she saw you two looking very cozy together at the gala."

"I—" I don't know what to tell her, because I don't even know what to tell myself.

"You what? What are you thinking, Jessica? James has done well for himself, I'll give him that, but he's not of the pedigree you should be looking for. His family has no connections, is staunchly in the middle class. You should be dating the people I suggested last time."

Thunder rumbles on the horizon as lightning flashes across the sky mere seconds later. It appears we are near the eye of the storm.

"Why would you even mess up your friendship, Jessica? What are you even thinking? Why would you date someone unsuitable for you and gamble your friendship away? He knows you too well and he knows all your faults. One day, he'll wake up and regret this and tell himself there are better women out there for him. Wake up, Jessica!" Mother's words pierce the last vestiges of my defenses. Families always know where the weakest kinks of your armor are located.

"Mother, sorry, I just can't do this right now. You can nag me later."

I disconnect the call and sink to the carpet, burying my head between my knees as fear mixes with panic in a combustible cocktail. My chest hurts as I struggle to breathe. I can't lose James. I can't do this. What was I thinking? I close my eyes as silent tears roll down my cheek, as devastation joins my despair. Breathing in deeply, exhaling fully, I slowly calm myself down as the path forward illuminates clearly.

I know what I should do.

CHAPTER 31

Jess

I sit on the couch, my knees bouncing up and down in a nervous tic as the lump in my throat grows with each passing moment. My bag is packed and by the door. A big part of me wants to take the coward's way out, to leave a note behind and to escape before James comes home. The urge to run away is so strong I have to grip the cushions to keep myself from bolting. Unable to sit still any longer, I scamper to the windows and stare out onto the street below. The rain comes down in a deluge and the streets empty as Californians stay indoors in this unusual weather. I see a few seagulls on the lawn, walking toward the shelter of some bushes, a sign this storm is not a passing fancy but may be here to stay for a while. The skies darken as storm clouds invade the normally sunny skies, very fitting for my mood.

"Be strong, Jess. You need to do this, to save your relationship with James before this goes south," I mutter to myself as I wring my hands, dreading the inevitable conversation. "For the greater good... You want him in your life, right?" The words do little to settle the tempest inside.

A key rattles at the door. *He's home.* I take a full breath to steel myself and I turn to face the opening door.

"Hey, sweetheart, I'm home. Sorry, the mess at work took longer than expected, but we still have the afternoon ahead of us. What do you want to—" James's smile falls off his face as he stares at my bag at the door.

Wordlessly, he looks up at me, his piercing gaze searching mine as his hands curl around the small bouquet of roses he brought back home.

For me.

Tears gather in my eyes as I bite down on my lower lip, unable to form words. Comprehension dawns in his eyes and the flowers slide out of his grip, scattering on the floor, the red petals marring the plush turquoise carpet like a crime scene.

"You're leaving."

His voice thickens as a muscle ticks in his jaw. We both know this is more than me leaving his home for mine.

This is my answer.

He slowly strides toward me, his steps heavy and full of intention. A flash of lightning illuminates the room, briefly lighting up the harsh features on his face.

I nod, still unable to find any words that can make this better for both of us.

"Why?"

"J-James, I think it's better if we remain friends. It's s-safer that way." My lips tremble as I force the necessary words to sever the intimate link we have formed the last three days.

"What the fuck are you talking about?"

"I-I can't lose you, James, and I will if we're together. One day you'll wake up and you'll be sick of me, sick of my anxiety, sick of my insecurities, sick of my panic attacks. But if we stay friends, we'll be like how we always were, before these three days, and we'll always be in each other's lives."

"What kind of sick logic is this?" he roars, the vein in his forehead pulses as he pins me with his stormy eyes.

The room suddenly feels claustrophobic.

I can't breathe.

I back away, needing space from his disappointment, his anger. "It's not all in my head, James, I got a wake-up call today.

Becca just called me to tell me she and Craig broke up." I look up at him, pleading for him to understand. "She lost her boyfriend and her best friend because he got sick of her. They have been best friends for such a long time and now she doesn't have him in her life anymore."

"What the *fuck* does that have to do with us?" James shouts as he runs his hands through his hair, tugging the strands in frustration. He paces the living room and a sense of déjà vu washes over me as I remember Ben doing the same a few months ago.

"It's a sign! It's a warning for us, can't you see that?"

"Screw Becca and Craig, screw these so-called signs. I've always been patient with you and your worries, but this...this is taking it way out of proportion."

"See? You're already getting sick of me! Can't you see this is the best thing for us if we want to remain in each other's lives?"

An invisible hand claws at my throat. I need air. I need to get out. Nausea roils in my stomach, threatening to make my breakfast reappear. I shakily retrieve my keys and phone from the kitchen counter and get my bag.

James stands still as a statue as his eyes trail my movements, his frame shuddering from anger. "So that's it, huh? I don't even get a say?"

"I'm s-sorry. You'll see in time this decision is the right one."

I throw open the door and dart outside as I gulp in the cold air in ragged gasps. The pouring rain drenches me, but I don't feel the wetness, the coldness. I just feel numb as I stumble toward my parked car down the street, my vision blurry from the rain or the tears or a combination of both. Wet, pounding footsteps sound behind me as a warm hand grips my wrist, twisting me around.

The phone clatters on the cement as an incoming call flashes on my screen.

Parker.

James bends down to retrieve my phone. He stares at the caller ID, his hands tightening against mine. Rain slushes down his features as he slowly looks up at me, his eyes a reflection of pain.

"Is it because of him?" he whispers as he hands the phone back to me, his hands shaking.

"No, James. It has nothing to do with him. I meant every word I said just now. I love you too much to lose you."

"You won't lose me! I love you, Jess, with every atom in my body, every particle of my soul, every breath I take. Don't you see? You'll never lose me," he rasps, his voice thick with emotion, his ocean-blue eyes burning with unshed tears. He grips my hand tightly in his, his large hands warming my cold ones. He gives, I take. I need to stop this cycle.

I attempt to tug my hand loose, but he holds on tighter as if he's clinging on to the last lifeline before plummeting over a cliff.

"It was a beautiful dream, James. That's what it was. But we always wake up from our dreams." Tears stream down my face, indistinguishable from the tears from the sky. "I want to walk away before we get shattered when this dream turns out to be what it was all along...a beautiful illusion." I try wrenching my hand free, to no avail.

"No, I don't buy that at all. Your judgment is clouded. You're speaking out of fear and anxiety." He clasps his other hand over mine. "What if you and I are the end goal? What if we live happily ever after like those books you read? Why can't you take a chance on us?"

James slicks his wet hair back away from his face. He keeps his tormented gaze on mine, oblivious to the harsh elements, the roar of thunder overhead, the flash of bright lightning.

"I can't gamble it all, James. I won't survive if I lose you in the end." I struggle to unlink our hands as he pulls me flush against him, his wet clothes plaster to his body like second skin, but neither of us feels the cold.

"Please, Jess. Please don't do this," he whispers, a last desperate plea of a dying man, his final wish. His hands cradle my head as I close my eyes, unable to stop myself from leaning into his embrace.

"You promised me, James. You said I can decide, and you'd respect it. This is my decision," I reply, plunging the knife into our hearts, severing our connection, the proverbial shove over the cliff.

The wind howls around us as the world stills.

Raindrops on cement.

Ragged breaths.

My dying heart.

James drops his hands, his body slumping in defeat as he stares at me, anguish overriding his features.

His haunted eyes. Something I'll never forget.

He retrieves his wallet from his pocket and pulls out something small. James places the object in my hands and gently wraps my fingers around it.

"Maybe this will bring you better luck than it did me," he replies, his voice choked up. He slowly stumbles back.

One step.

Two steps.

He continues to back away from me, the widening distance feeling wrong. I grip the object in my hand, the smooth edges cutting into my skin.

Pain. I deserve it.

I turn around and flee into the shelter of my car. The engine sputters to life and I drive away, looking into the rearview mirror. James stands there, as still as a statue, as water pelts his body. Tears pour down my face as his figure becomes smaller and smaller. I slowly unclench my palm to look at the object he gave me.

A shiny penny with my birth year. *My lucky penny. He kept it with him all these years.*

If this is the right thing to do, why does it feel so wrong?

CHAPTER 32

James

If I ever thought I knew what heartbreak was, I was grossly misled. Nothing I had ever experienced in the past compares to the agony I'm in right now. I haven't moved from my couch since Jess left yesterday. I called in sick at work. The sun shines brightly from the windows, the birds sing a beautiful melody from the outside, the storm from yesterday seemingly forgotten, but I'm dead inside.

I gambled away all my chips at the table. I went all in.

And I lost.

My phone buzzes somewhere in the pile of takeout containers on the coffee table. Swiping some of the trash to the floor, I locate the offending gadget.

Liz: I just heard! I can't believe it. I was so sure you guys would get together for good this time. Do you want to chat or do you want to be left alone?

I turn my phone off and stare at the ceiling. I know I promised to respect Jess's decision but having experienced heaven and suddenly plummeting into the depths of hell is too much for me to handle. I guess deep down inside, I was hoping once she had those few days of bliss, she would know, and she would be able to fight her inner monsters and come out alive...with me.

An errant tear slides down my face as the memories of the last few days assault me. Fuck. I can't do this. I can't be here, so close to her, and not have her.

Whoever said love conquers all is a piece of shit.

I need to get away, to clear my head, to figure out how I'm going to move on...or if I can ever move on.

Sometimes, words are just unnecessary.

It's strange how three short days can change the course of your life. *I'm just going back to the way things were. This will be fine. It will work out for the best.* Despite my constant internal reassurance, the gaping hole in my heart does not appear to be mending. It has been one week since I left James and we haven't contacted each other since. I'm giving him space to distance himself again and giving myself the same grace. Those three days were a dream, a wonderful, beautiful dream and I'll have these memories to keep with me whenever loneliness knocks on my door in the middle of the night.

> **Emily:** We need to meet up. I don't care if you don't want to see anyone. We are coming over today if you don't meet us! Liz and I are already on the way!

Another text from our group chat comes in. Emily and Liz have been calling and pinging me daily this past week, but I've been refusing callers. It seems like I can't delay them any longer.

> **Jess:** Fine, no need to drive over. I'm still very much alive and I appreciate your concerns. Meet up at the café a block over from my place?

It's time I drag myself out of my messy apartment and get some fresh air and sunlight.

The sun shines brightly, the skies nary a cloud in sight. Typical LA weather. Life continues, back to normal.

The storm clouds within me never left.

I drag myself into the café, finding Liz and Emily sitting at a table with three cups in front of them.

"Here I am. Alive and well."

"You look like shit, sis. This is worse than I thought."

I stare at my outfit and belatedly realize I'm still wearing my ragged ULA sweatpants and a large MIT sweatshirt from James. Yes, I've been living in the sweatshirt I nabbed from his apartment last week. The scent of sandalwood and spice is fading each day, even though my world is at a standstill. My hair is in a messy bun, and I don't have an ounce of makeup on me. I'm sure my raccoon eyes look horrific as sleep continues to elude me.

"I hate to agree with Ems, but I don't think I've ever seen you look so un-put-together. You look like you are at death's door. Have you been eating and sleeping?" Liz asks, her voice soft as if she is speaking to one of her kindergarteners.

I bury my face in my hands, my soul weary. "Not feeling much of an appetite these days and insomnia has been kicking my ass."

I don't tell her I've been having anxiety attacks almost daily, usually in the middle of the night. My mind will race as my pulse pumps, and I'm frozen by fear with no obvious reasons. The insomnia feeds my anxiety and panic in a sick cycle. The irony of it all is, as much as I like to be in control of my life, sleep is like the rebellious teenager who does the complete opposite of what you want her to do even though you've tried your best to raise her well.

"If you feel so sad, why don't you get back together with him?" Emily asks as she pushes a cup into my icy hands.

"I'll just ruin things. He'll get sick of my issues sooner rather than later. Being best friends works for us, has been working well for us since the beginning. Safer to stick with that." My words sound hollow to my ears and I brush away the nagging doubt in my head.

"Jess." Emily clasps her hands in mine, forcing me to look up. "I know we're very different. I'm blunt and act without thinking while you're pretty much the opposite. I won't pretend I understand what having anxiety is like, but have you considered this is just your distorted thoughts talking to you? You're letting your life be ruled by a thousand what-ifs and not of the what if I win the lottery type but the what if I get sick and die variety. You'll give up so many opportunities for joy if you're always afraid of something."

I gulp down the hot drink, which can be coffee or hot tea, but my taste buds are taking a hiatus. Tears prickle in my eyes as shame washes over me. I know she's right, but I can't help what I'm feeling. I've worked so hard to appear calm and collected, but it appears my best efforts are still not enough. My life is still crumbling and I'm helpless to stop it.

"How's he doing?" I murmur, staring at the cup in my hands.

Silence follows my question. A pregnant pause. I snort, why do people say pregnant pause? From what I've seen, pregnancy is no joke and definitely anything but a pause. Tears drip onto the table as I chuckle at my own joke. I'm sure I look deranged right now.

"Jess, I won't sugarcoat this for you because you need to know. He's a mess. I've never seen him like this before. He wasn't even like this when Claire broke up with him and they were together for a long time. He called in sick this past week and has been working from home but he isn't eating, sleeping—he's short-fused. His apartment looks like a hurricane went through it. I mean, he looks a lot like...you."

My gut wrenches at the image of James being in so much pain and the culprit of such agony is me. What seemed to be a sound idea suddenly seems more and more like a mistake.

"We aren't going to be what we were before, are we? I already screwed it up by being with him these three days, didn't I?" I look up at the blurry images of the girls and wipe my eyes with a tissue Liz holds out to me.

"Honey, you can't just put the genie back in the bottle with the type of love you guys have. If you weren't my good friend, I'd be so pissed off right now for what you're putting my brother through. But I know you, your heart is in the right place. You're letting your mind and emotions drive what's an obvious choice to all of us."

Emily places her hand over mine in comfort. "You can't always apply other people's problems to yourself. If we all did that, we'd go crazy given how many tragedies are in the world. What Becca went through with Craig is very sad and while I don't know her very well, I can imagine how hard she must be taking her breakup. But you guys aren't them. If you both care about each other this much and both continue to spend the energy to nurture your relationship, I don't see why you can't have the happy ending you wish for." She laughs nervously. "Of course, I'm not exactly the paragon of stable relationships, but I'm pretty good at examining problems and finding a solution."

"What if this is just a rebound for both of us and we're leaping into this too impulsively?" I whisper, voicing one of the million worries I have in my arsenal.

Liz's eyebrows rise comically. "You are kidding me, right? I don't know about you, but this has been *years* in the making for him. If you're searching for excuses to hold you back, you'll find them, and I can't stop you from believing them." Her tone softens. "Only you can dig deep and figure out what's right for you and whether or not you're willing to overcome the obstacles or perceived problems to make the right choice for you."

I nod, understanding where they're both coming from. I look up at their faces, both of them frowning in concern, and say, "Thank you for being here. I know this is probably stupid from your point of view. I just feel so paralyzed and it seems like no matter what I do, the answer is wrong and I'll always be worried. But regardless of what happens, I appreciate you both a lot."

Emily and Liz stand up from their chairs and gather me in a group hug as I shake from the torrent of emotions coursing through me. *I'm loved*, I repeat to myself. *I'm loved*. Maybe someday I'll feel worthy of this love.

• • •

Three days after the intervention from the girls, I throw myself back into my work. Maybe if I bury myself with work, an environment I'm comfortable with, I can forget about everything else. It works sometimes, but it's only temporary. As soon as I get off a conference call or whenever I finish reviewing a file, my thoughts will stray back to James. Sleep is still sporadic, and when I do final-ly fall asleep, my dreams are filled with him. It appears my body's yearning for him has not abated.

Jess: James, I miss you.

I start typing a text as I enter the café down the street for more caffeine to get me through the evening of work ahead. I stare at the text as I get in line and hastily delete the message. *You're the culprit. How dare you contact your victim.*

Jess: I still care for you as my best friend.

Another draft. I delete this one a few seconds later. Pouring salt on the wound?

I wish I could just hear his voice again and see if he has for-given me. Maybe if we get back to our normal communication, this pain will finally start fading. Maybe I'm a selfish coward, hoping this will all blow over and someday I'll feel the way I used to feel about him. *But is that what you really want? No one has ever demonstrated true love and acceptance to you like he has shown you in those three days.* I shove the thought away and glance at the time on my phone. Eight p.m. Maybe I shouldn't get the coffee. I haven't really slept this past week and a half and my anxiety is at an all-time high. I shouldn't pour fuel onto the fire.

Still staring at my phone, I turn around to leave the line and bump into another patron. My delayed reflexes are unhelpful and the phone slides out of my hands and clatters onto the floor. The stranger and I reach for the phone at the same time, our hands colliding.

"I'm so sorry," I apologize profusely as I look up.

"It's okay, no worries," a chirpy voice replies.

Beautiful red hair, dulcet tones, slender frame. This woman looks familiar, but my mind can't place her.

I stand up and put my phone in my purse and give her a half-hearted smile. Recognition dawns in her eyes.

"Are you...Jess?"

"Yes, I am... So sorry, I should know you, shouldn't I? You look really familiar."

The stranger smiles, her expression warm and immediately likeable. "We haven't officially met, but I've seen you in video chats and photos before. I'm Claire." She extends her hand.

Claire. James's Claire. My mouth dries as I stare at this gorgeous woman who James has loved before me.

"Are you guys buying anything or not?" a high school student asks us from the line, jolting me awake.

"Gosh, sorry, please go ahead." We wave him forward as we move to the side.

"Claire, I thought you looked familiar." I scan around the room, searching for something or nothing at the same time. "Aren't you in London? How are you here in LA?"

She smiles at my baffled expression and beckons me to follow her. "Hold that thought. Let me order something first. Do you want anything?" I shake my head as she orders a tea. She laughs, noting my bewildered appearance. "Can you believe me? I'm ordering tea at a coffee shop. I used to be addicted to coffee, but it seems like the Brits have rubbed off on me. Now I can't go a day without tea." She grabs her tea from the counter and walks to an empty table and motions for me to sit down.

"I'm in town for a conference. Actually, I'm on my way to see him, to catch up and see how things are going." Claire glances at me, her eyes shrewd. "You know, I've always wanted to meet you... to see the actual person who has James so mesmerized."

"What are you talking about?"

She takes a sip of her drink and stares at me. "He's a great guy and I've nothing but good wishes for him. You really are a lucky woman and I hope you know that."

I stare at her, motionless, my tongue in knots.

"So, are you guys together now?" she asks, her eyes shining with warmth. It's really hard to not like her.

I tuck a strand of hair behind my ears, suddenly feeling self-conscious. "No...we aren't. I mean, we were for a few days, but decided it was a bad idea."

"Oh? Forgive me for being bold, but it must have come from you, right?"

"Huh?" This is the strangest conversation I've had in a long time.

"The James I know wouldn't give up after a few days. Especially when it comes to you."

I frown, feeling defensive from the opinions of my former lover or best friend's former lover; ugh how convoluted. She doesn't even know what happened the last few days and she's offering her thoughts? "Look, with all due respect, you don't know me or what happened to us. It was an informed decision to part ways. We both just got out of long-term relationships." I glance up at her. "Not in the best position to jump into a new one."

Claire nods as if she's listening to a friend vent. In another world, we would be good friends. She seems to be confident, warm, fun...everything I'm not.

"I know you think this is weird, so let me tell you where I'm coming from. James and I gave it our best shot. I know he did because he's that type of man. But you can't change who you love and for the longest time, I think we were both trying to ignore the fact someone has always occupied his heart. And I didn't want to share his heart with anyone. I'm selfish that way, if you can call it that. But I think I'm awesome and I deserve more than what he can give me." She winks and continues, "And I really want him to be happy. So, if you're under the impression you guys are a rebound...man, then you're so far off the mark, I don't even know what to say. The man has been in love with you forever. I don't think he's capable of falling out of love with you."

Pain spears me in the chest as I feel the invisible hand wrapping around my neck, cutting off my oxygen supply. My breaths come in rapid gasps as I grab my bracelet in a tight clasp. I can't breathe. Dots dance in my vision as pain throbs in my head.

"Are you okay? You look really pale," Claire asks, concerned.

I shake my head as she disappears from view, reappearing a moment later with a cup of warm water.

"Take a sip." She pats my back, rubbing it in soothing strokes. "Take a deep breath. Inhale slowly...there, there, just like that. Exhale slowly. Good. Now repeat that." I slowly come down from my panic as oxygen floods my system.

"I have a sister who has general anxiety and panic attacks. I can recognize an attack when I see one. She's doing well ever since she got help and meds, thankfully." She answers the question in my eyes.

I wipe down the sweat on my forehead with a napkin and gulp down some water, relishing the liquid in my parched throat. "Thank you for helping me there."

"You're welcome. I didn't mean to intrude, really. I just want James to be happy. He deserves that and I guess I sense you don't know the depth of his emotions, or maybe other things are cluttering your feelings. Whatever it is, I hope you get your issues sorted out and things work out for you guys."

Claire stands and motions for me to keep sitting. "Stay, catch your breath. I got to get going, but I wish you well."

I muster up a shaky smile. "Likewise." I take a deep breath, steeling myself. "Thank you for your candidness. You're a better woman than I am. I probably wouldn't be able to do the same if I were in your shoes."

She cocks her head to the side and smirks. "I guess I'm pretty great, aren't I? Take care, Jess." Claire strides out of the café, and I sit there, staring into the night, pondering her words, my pulse calming but still frantic.

The quiet chatter in the café slowly fades to near silence. The clanging of utensils from the kitchen as the staff prepares for closing wakes me from my daze as I realize I've sat there for almost two hours. I keep replaying the last few months in my mind. How did I mess things up so spectacularly? How is it sometimes when you want to run away from something, you end up running smack into it? I get up from my table and inadvertently knock over my purse to the ground, the contents scattering on the floor.

Groaning, I crouch down and begin gathering the contents back into my bag. A familiar glint of copper snares my attention. My lucky penny, the one James has kept with him all these years until now. Tears prickle my eyes as I stare at the token, a million regrets flashing by.

They say, if it looks like a duck, quacks like a duck, then it probably is a duck. If everyone around me is telling me I'm making a mistake, am I just letting my anxiety and worries get the best out of me?

I'm not well.

Despite my best efforts to be "normal," to reject the idea I have a mental illness, the mess I have created will indicate otherwise. It's time to face the music. After all, is there such a thing as "normal?" My carefully crafted life is falling apart and the harder I try to fix it, the more I'm crushing the soul out of it.

I need help.

And perhaps, seeking help is the bravest thing of all.

I take out my phone, scrolling through my contacts and type out a message.

Jess: Hi Marybeth. This is Jess Kingsley. It has been a long time and I hope you are doing well. If you are still accepting patients, I'll like to make an appointment with you. My anxiety has been rearing its ugly head and...I need help.

My fingers hover above the send button, my mind flashing back to Mother's words about how anxiety is a disease of the privileged and the weak and I'm useless for needing help to manage my emotions. *No. It's time I do something for myself.* I take a deep breath, close my eyes, and hit send.

CHAPTER 34

Jess

"No! No, no, no, no, no!" I jolt awake, sweat soaking through my night shirt as I reel from a nightmare I don't remember. My body is bone dead tired, my head pounds, most likely a tension headache from running on fumes for so long. My eyes feel like sandpaper as I blink, attempting to focus on the soft light coming through the drapes. I grab my phone, squinting at the screen. One text message and one voicemail. It's eight thirty a.m. Shit. I'm so late for work. I scramble off the bed and dig through the pile of clothes on the floor to find something remotely presentable.

"Hey, Siri, read my message."

"Marybeth Connors sent a message. Jess, it's nice to hear from you. I'm glad you reached out to me. I'll email you with some availability for a session and we can go from there. Hang in there."

I grab a dress that appears to be semi-decent and perform a sniff test. Dress still smells decent. Oh, how Mother would cringe if she saw me now. I laugh halfheartedly at myself, at this situation I seemingly created. I'm so tired mentally and physically. I have Siri play the voice message on my phone. *Please don't be the Dickhead. I just can't deal with him today or this week or any time in the near future.*

A familiar baritone voice sounds through the phone. "Jess..." James pauses, taking a deep breath. Tears gather in my eyes as my heart clenches. I miss him so, so much. "I can't do this anymore. I just...can't. I'm leaving, back to Boston. Don't bother coming over or trying to stop me from leaving. I don't regret us...or whatever we were. Thanks for being you, Jess. I wish you the best. Goodbye."

My heart drops to the floor, the silence deafening. No, no, no, no, no. What have I done? I clasp my chest as another panic attack hits. I don't have time for this. I gasp for air as the attack peaks. I curl myself into a fetal position as I force air into my lungs. I need to get to James.

I stand up, wobbly, as I throw on a pair of sweatpants, sneakers, and a coat over my sleep shirt. I grab my phone and keys and run out the door. I dial his number as I start the ignition. Voicemail. Blood rushing in my ears, I slam on the gas pedal and gun it toward his place. There is a cliché saying, "You don't know what you have until it's gone." The old me would say that's just silly. This is why you have contingency plans to prevent these bad outcomes. Now, I belatedly realize, despite all my worries, my ruminating thoughts on how to prevent all types of disasters and outcomes, I am the cliché.

Tears stream down my face as I climb out of my car, keys still in the ignition, and I ring the doorbell.

"James!" I pound on the door.

"James, it's me, Jess! Please don't go! Please open up!" I sob as I desperately pound on the door again.

No response.

A neighbor opens her window. "Hey, there's no use in breaking down the door. You're looking for James? I saw him leave around half an hour ago...with a bunch of bags too. He told me to keep an eye out on his place for him."

No. No. No.

I wipe my runny nose with the sleeve of my coat, no doubt looking halfway to deranged.

"T-Thank you!" I race back into my car and speed down Pacific Coast Highway toward Los Angeles International Airport.

"Crap...crap crap crap!" I mutter to myself, sweat beading on my forehead, my heart racing a mile a minute.

Please let me make it in time.

I'm stuck on PCH in the infamous Los Angeles traffic. I grumble under my breath, praying to any higher power to miraculously part the cars in front of me, like Moses with the Red Sea, so I can find parking at LAX.

I redial James's number for the thirtieth time on the Bluetooth in the car.

"Hi, you have reached James Chapman. I'm currently unavailable to pick up your call. Please leave a message after the beep and I'll return your call as soon as possible." Hearing James's gravelly, deep voice through my speakers sends another shard of pain in my chest.

"James, please don't go. I beg you. Please don't go. We need to talk. I have so much to say. I'm so sorry I hurt you. I'm a coward. Please don't go. I'm on my way." I frantically dictate to the answering service.

I press redial again. Persistence has gotten me far in places, right?

"The mailbox of the recipient is now full."

"Argh!" I scream, surely looking like a madwoman to the cars next to me in the ant crawl toward the Departures fork of the road.

Five counts in, eight counts out.

I attempt my breathing exercises. Marybeth says breathing out for longer than breathing in will help calm my nervous system and stop anxiety in its tracks. I try to focus on my breathing.

Nope. Not happening.

My heart clenches and my breathing becomes erratic as I come to face the reality James may leave me...forever. He has been my one constant by my side all of these years. Everyone aside from family has forgotten about me or left me during my childhood. A childhood consisting of moving from place to place like a nomad. Everyone has disappeared.

Except James.

And now, I may lose him too.

I play with the jade beaded red-string bracelet on my right hand, the familiar coolness of the stone doing little to soothe my fried nerves. Traffic finally starts moving again and I stare at the fifty-car lineup to the parking structure and decide against getting into the line, and instead swerve to park against the red curb of the nearest terminal.

"Hey, ma'am, you can't park here!" a parking enforcement officer yells as I dash out of the car toward the entrance.

"I'm sorry, I know, but the love of my life is getting on the plane right now and I need to stop him. Go ahead, ticket me. Again, I'm so, so sorry!" Yep, I'm a rule breaker right now. Will wonders ever cease? I slam the car door shut and take off running through the terminal, weaving through families, business folks, and vacationers.

I beeline straight for the Sigma Airlines counter, as James has frequent flyer miles there. Hundreds of eyes glower at me as I cut the line and run straight to the agent with an opening.

"Miss, you need to get in line." Her face is stern as she admonishes me.

"I'm so sorry!" I say loudly enough for the first few grumbling passengers in the line to hear me. "Please help me. The man I love is leaving me. I need to know if his flight has left yet. Please help me. I never *ever* do this, but if I don't do this he'll leave, and my heart will be empty and I won't know what to do." Tears pool in my eyes as I pander to her inner romantic, not caring I'm making a fool of myself.

"This is my grand gesture; I can't let him go without telling him how I feel. Please help me," I sob.

"Lady, just help her out. She seems desperate enough." The elderly man next in line took pity on me and I shoot him a grateful glance.

The agent's eyes soften, taking in my disheveled appearance and flushed face. "Well, I'll make an exception. What is his name and flight?"

"James Chapman. I don't know his flight number, but he is going to Boston this morning."

She glances around and lowers her voice. "You didn't hear this from me since I can't share any details about passengers, but I can tell you there's a flight going to Boston this morning. SM5936 is boarding right now and will depart in twenty minutes. I can't confirm nor deny whether he's on the flight."

"Thank you." My heart pounds so loudly I swear the whole terminal can hear it. I spin around and set off toward the nearest security check, desperate for a sight of the dark-brown tousled hair that always looks like it needs more combing and the broad-shouldered man who always walks with a purpose.

"You go get him, girl!" a teenage girl with pink hair and goth makeup yells at me from behind the elderly man. Apparently, my grand gesture has gotten through to her hormone-laden emo self.

"Thanks!" I yell, feeling the heat on my cheeks from exertion or embarrassment or both as I take in the numerous pairs of eyes tracking my movement light a spotlight.

"Incoming! So sorry! Excuse me!" I push against a young woman moving at the speed of a sloth and feel the weight of her disapproval like daggers at my back. I round a row of empty check-in counters as I beeline toward the security checkpoint.

I spot a familiar tuft of brown hair ahead and my heart skips a beat. I take in the rest of the imposing figure forty feet ahead of me, the full six feet one inches, wearing his favorite army-green jacket paired with dark-wash jeans. He hands his ticket and ID to the TSA agent.

"James!" I scream as I hurry toward him. "James!"

He stops, seemingly aware someone is searching for him. I hold my breath and wave my hands in the air. He scans his surroundings, not seeing me, and adjusts the backpack on his shoulders. My heart sinks as James walks farther away.

"Miss, please step back from the ropes. If you have a ticket, please get in line, or else quiet down or I'll have someone escort you off the premises," the TSA agent in front of the line barks at me, his hand on a walkie talkie.

I barely spare him a glance. I cup my hands to my face and yell, "James! James Chapman! I love you. Don't leave!"

"Miss! This is your last warning."

I stare at his diminishing figure as the distance between us widens, my thundering heart threatening to give out. I use my right sleeve to wipe the tears now free falling down my face. He didn't hear me.

My sobs break through the ruckus at the bustling airport. The TSA agent is taken aback, unsure what to do. "Look, miss, this isn't the time or place for this. I'm sorry for whatever you're going through, but you can't be here."

James is now a tiny dot in my vision and he rounds a corner, disappearing from my sight.

He is gone.

I collapse on the floor, black dots clouding my vision, my breathing erratic. My body gives out as fatigue slams into me, and I surrender to the darkness.

"Keep me posted on the side effects, okay? If we need to, we can move up our next appointment." Dr. Sandra Cheng looks at me, her brown gaze reassuring behind her dark-rimmed sunglasses.

"Can I ask you a question?"

"Sure, Jess. Ask away."

I take a deep breath. "Why me? Did I bring this on myself?"

"What do you mean?" She furrows her brows, trying to understand my question.

"I mean, did I cause myself to 'get' this condition?"

Dr. Cheng smiles at me, finally understanding my question. She shakes her head and answers softly, but resolutely, "Jess, you didn't do anything to cause this. I can tell you, based on all my years in practice, there's no such thing as 'normal.' Everyone has anxiety and, like everything in psychology, all these traits and conditions are on a spectrum. For someone like yourself, you're already genetically predisposed to being more susceptible to the more extreme end of the spectrum, that's all. Some people have severe nut allergies, and some people have anxiety to the point it interferes with their everyday life."

She stares pointedly at me. "Just like you don't blame someone for having a nut allergy, you shouldn't blame yourself for having anxiety. You just make lifestyle adjustments and treat it like any other medical condition. And we all have something in our lives we're grappling with. Now *that's* normal."

"Thank you, Dr. Cheng." I brush my hair from my face as I tug the MIT sweater over my sport leggings and stand up.

I walk out of my psychiatrist's office, my heart lighter. It has been two weeks since James left. I woke up in the hospital, surrounded by my family and Liz, after I fainted at the airport. James, the most considerate man I know, sent me a text when he landed in Boston in response to the voice message I left for him.

> **James:** I don't want you to worry, Jess. I...got your message and I need time to think, to be away from this. Please give me some space. I'll be in touch.

Mother, in classic fashion, berated me for not taking care of myself, for making her worry, for looking like a sloth, and for causing an embarrassing scene at the airport. Father, gruff as always, pulled my mother aside and reminded her this was not the time or place. Despite their nagging, they were concerned about my wellbeing and underlying issues which landed me in the hospital. I begged Liz not to let James know about my hospital stay. I didn't want James to feel guilty when everything started because of me.

The doctors at the hospital said I fainted because of a combination of prolonged lack of sleep, not eating enough, and urged me to see a psychiatrist for help with my anxiety and panic attacks. With Marybeth's help, she introduced me to Dr. Cheng, who she coordinated care with in a combination of medicine and talk therapy to help me better deal with my anxiety in healthier ways and to set better boundaries with my parents. I spent Christmas and New Year's Day at home, taking some time for myself to regroup and rest. The girls would sometimes stop by to hang out or keep me company, but for the most part, things were quiet, which I very much needed.

I type a message on my phone to the girls.

> **Jess:** Just wrapped up with Dr. Cheng. On my way to Green Food Kitchen, see you soon.

I'm meeting with Liz and Emily for a quick Friday lunch at my favorite healthy food restaurant on Colorado Blvd. in Pasadena.

The sun shines brightly and the skies are clear with nary a cloud in sight as I park and walk over to the restaurant, passing by shoppers and other restaurant patrons sauntering down the busy street during lunch hour. Teenagers walk out of stores, giggling at their purchases, parents hurrying after their kids as they sprint toward ice cream shops. Why are so many people out and about on a Friday, I wonder to myself. Ah yes, winter break.

The girls are sitting at a table under a large umbrella sipping iced teas when I walk up to them. Emily looks radiant in a tan power suit with a magenta silk blouse and Liz appears relaxed in a striped maxi dress and boots. The weather is a balmy seventy degrees, which is warmer than expected in January and many people are taking advantage of the comfortable weather by sitting outside.

"Jess!" Liz exclaims when she sees me and wraps me in a tight embrace.

Emily gives me a once-over and grins. "I never thought I'd see the day when I dress better than my sister."

I glance at my casual outfit, feeling self-conscious, but quickly shove the negative thoughts out of the way. Old habits die hard, but I'm trying to change, to be truer to myself, starting with the clothes I wear. "I'm working from home today. This is comfortable. I like it."

"I love it, sis. You look so much more approachable these days. What's more important is for you to be comfortable with what you wear, whether it's designer wear or sweats." Emily waves the waiter over and we quickly place our orders.

"So, how are things going with your therapist and the doctor?" Liz inquires.

"Things are going well. I should've gone back to see Marybeth a long time ago, but somehow, I just thought if I can grit through this, I can do it by myself, and I don't need help. But she's helping me realize I'm just wired differently, like how diabetics have issues with their insulin levels. I happen to have issues with some of my biochemistry, neurotransmitters and all. With the help of the meds Dr. Cheng prescribed for me, I can improve some deficits and learn some skills to combat the negative thoughts."

Liz nods. "That makes sense. Are you feeling better with the meds? I know you were against them in the beginning."

"They say it can take a few weeks to start working, but I think my body is pretty sensitive to medicine, so I'm already starting to feel calmer, fewer panic attacks and ruminating thoughts...a little more hopeful about the future. I think in the beginning, I was just buying into the stigma that taking the medicine means I'm weak, but I really should frame it another way. Do we give grief to diabetics when they take insulin? No, we don't. Do we look at people differently when they take ibuprofen for a headache? No, we don't. So, why am I giving myself such a hard time for taking a small pill that helps my situation?"

The salads arrive quickly and Emily digs in. "I'm so proud of you for doing this, Jess," she says with her mouth half-full. She takes a sip of water and continues, "No matter how things work out, this is healthier for you. Have you told our parents?"

"Father is, you know...Father. He really doesn't say much other than the 'take care of yourself, Jess.' Mother, well, she threw a fit at the hospital when the doctors suggested I get psychiatric help. She kept saying how I don't have mental issues and how this will look horrible if it gets out." I shrug. "I'm working with Marybeth to set some boundaries with her. I can love her, be a good daughter, and need to distance myself from her simultaneously. Doesn't have to be exclusionary. What she doesn't know won't kill her."

Deep down, I felt a calming sense of relief when I decided I needed the help to work on myself. I need to feel better about myself and to learn to cope with my worries before I reach back out to James. He deserves better. He deserves someone who can love him despite her fears, someone who won't shirk and flee at the first sign of discomfort.

"Enough about me. How are you guys doing?"

"Last day of winter break! I don't know whether to be sad or happy. I miss the kiddos a lot, but the last two weeks have been amazing. The peace and quiet is such a welcomed break from all the usual ruckus. I was even able to get some planning done for the upcoming quarter." Liz leans back, sighing contently.

"Too bad you didn't come out with us for New Year's, sis. We had a blast at Universal Studios!"

"I'm sure you guys did. I needed some quiet time this year, to think about some things and to just catch up on sleep. I feel like a new person after a good eight hours of shut-eye."

I finish my salad, my stomach satiated but not overly full. I peer up at Liz and say softly, "How's he doing?"

Liz pauses for a minute, as if debating how much to reveal to me. "He's doing better. My parents said he's eating again and has been going out to meet up with some old friends. He has been working remotely over there."

"Has he mentioned me?"

Seconds pass, the silence speaking volumes.

"I'm sure he has thought about you... You're quite unforgettable." Liz chuckles nervously. "Don't think too much of it, dearie. I have faith things will work out the way they should."

My appetite wanes as I take a deep breath. My old self would probably ruminate over all the negative reasons James has been MIA, but I'm trying to change now. *Don't assume what other people are thinking,* Marybeth's voice echoes in my head. *Don't catastrophize. Things are rarely as bad as they seem.*

Whether it's the medicine or the therapy, I do find it easier to calm down now after the initial wave of negative thoughts, and for that, I'm grateful. I wet my lips and muster a half grin. "I hope so too."

"Are you planning to go get him?" Emily squints at me, her hand blocking the sun in her face.

I shake my head. "He asked for space, so I'm giving that to him and using this time to work on myself. If he doesn't reach out to me in a few weeks, I'll go out there. I owe it to him and to us to try."

"Go, sis, we are rooting for you!"

"Thanks." I smile at them both. "There is one more loose end I need to take care of."

"Hey, Jess, sorry for being late." Parker's eyes, the lush green color of the rainforest in the sunlight, crinkle at the corners. He sits down on the couch in front of me at the café of our first date.

"No worries. Sorry for being MIA the last few weeks. I was dealing with some things."

"Don't sweat it. How are you doing? Everything's okay, I hope?" He frowns, concern brimming in his gaze.

I smile. He really will be a wonderful partner to a lucky woman, but that woman isn't me. "Things will be okay eventually, or at least I hope so."

"Good, you look refreshed, by the way. I like this look on you." I'm in my latest favorite casual outfit, a regular pair of boot-leg jeans paired with a simple turtleneck.

"Oh, it's noth—" I catch myself. "Thank you." My lips tip up in a grin. "How are you doing?"

"Good, can't complain. The firm has been busy; working on a design for a homeless shelter, which is something I'm passionate about. The kiddo is on winter break right now, so she has been keeping me on my toes." He chuckles, no doubt thinking about his daughter.

"Do you have help with her while you work?"

"Yeah, we have a nanny and my mom is also visiting, so she has been a godsend. She and Lucy are tied at the hip right now. It'll be interesting once she leaves, and it's just us two again."

"Aww, you'll get through this. I haven't seen you as a parent yet, but if you're anything like the person I've come to know, you'll do just fine."

He shakes his head and swallows, then lets out a heavy breath. "Thanks, it helps to hear that." He clasps his hands in front of him and focus on me, his gaze sharpening. "So, let me guess, I'm here for the 'it's not you it's me speech?'"

I twist my bracelet nervously. I'm not a big fan of confrontation, but as part of this self-improvement journey I'm on, I'm making my best attempt at it. "How did you know?"

"My intuition is usually pretty spot on. I had a feeling something was holding you back this entire time. I'm even going to venture a guess." He pauses, his piercing gaze peering into mine. "Is it...James?"

I laugh softly. Apparently, this is an obvious observation to everyone except for myself. "Yes, and I don't want to lead you on."

"Thank you for your honesty. I appreciate it. I like you, Jess, and thank you for being my first experiment partner for this modern dating thing." He chuckles, shaking his head as if laughing at his gaffes. "It has given me some thought... Maybe I need a little more time as well. So, are you two together now? You guys looked great at the gala."

"No...I mean, we were for a little bit, but I messed it up. I got a bad case of cold feet." Something about Parker makes me feel comfortable in confiding in him. Perhaps it's the reassuring presence of his.

"You know, I hope you don't mind some unsolicited advice. If you find real love, don't let it go. We don't always get all the time we want with the people we love. Don't waste any of it." Parker gazes faraway, his expression solemn. Slivers of pain mingle with gratefulness within me. Pain for Parker's loss and gratefulness that despite my misstep, I still have a chance to be with James.

"Thank you for your advice." I place my hand over his and give him a brief squeeze. "I'll take it to heart."

His mouth twists into a half smile as he lets go of my hand. "I hope we can stay friends, Jess. You're easy to talk to."

"Likewise."

Parker rubs his hands together. "So, as a first step to our friendship, let me help you get your man."

I cackle, clapping my hands at this sudden change in subject, the sound feeling foreign to my ears as I realize how long it has been since I sincerely let my guard down and laughed without reserve. "I'm all ears. I really, really messed this up and I don't know how to fix it."

"Well, I'm here to help troubleshoot and problem solve. Tell me what happened."

I lean forward and proceed to tell him the highlights of my friendship with James and what transpired between us the last few months. Lunch is definitely on me this time. Sometimes, fate puts the right people in your life at the right time, even if they end up serving a completely different role than originally intended. We just need to keep our hearts and minds open.

CHAPTER 36

James

"Thanks for calling. I'm fine. Did Emily put you up to this?" I sit on a stool at the local college bar by MIT and watch the TV on the wall. It's pretty early in the evening on a Thursday and the ruckus hasn't started yet.

"She may have mentioned it," Steven utters as the clacking of the keyboard sounds in the background. He's a workaholic in the making. "But seriously, gastropub by a college campus? You're not in school anymore, why would you eat there? So many delicious restaurants in Boston. I can recommend you some, if you like."

I polish off a slice of greasy pizza. "I just want to revisit my old haunts and think a little bit. But seriously, I'm alive and well. You can report back and call off the cavalry."

"This is why I don't do love. Too messy with little rewards."

"You're such a jaded, old soul, you know that? You're in your early twenties and supposed to be partying it up and having a rosy outlook on life. What happened to you?"

The keyboard sounds stop. "Hey, we're talking about you, not me. I just want to make sure you're doing okay. And it seems like you are fine. The girls miss you—make sure to call them every so often."

The girls. *Does this include Jess?*

I shove the thought away. It doesn't matter anymore. It's been one month since I left LA and while the pain is still there, at least I can breathe here. I took a few weeks off work and am working remotely now.

"I will. Thanks for checking in. Means a lot." I bite my tongue before asking, "How is she?"

A few seconds pass by as Steven contemplates how to answer me. "She's working on herself. There are things she's dealing with… but she misses you."

I miss her too.

I don't think I can ever give up Jess. Time and time again have taught me that's an impossible task. I just need to figure out how I can face her again. How I can handle being next to her and not kiss her, not touch her, not hold her in my arms. Until I have the answer, I can't go back to LA yet.

"I'm glad she's taking care of herself. Don't tell her I asked about her…I'm not ready to face her yet."

"Of course. I understand. Let me know if you need anything. It's a short flight from NYC."

I smile sadly and disconnect the call. "Check please." I flag down the bartender.

Despite everything that has transpired the last few months, somehow, deep in my gut, I don't think this is the end of our story. I was so close to victory this time I could actually taste it. While I don't know what the future holds for us, whether it's just friendship or something more, I know this is only a temporary setback, and someday, a path will yield itself to me.

I just hope that someday is soon.

"Mother, you sprung this on me last minute. What can't wait until our next dinner?" I slip out of my heels in my parents' large foyer and shut the door behind me. "I don't understand why you can't tell me over the phone. I have a meeting in the office in the afternoon, so I can only eat a quick lunch with you."

I walk toward the dining room, following the sounds of quiet conversation and...laughter? I slow to a stop as I take in the scene before me. My mother, looking perfect as always, nary a hair out of place, tossing her head back and laughing. My father briefly glances up from his phone, shakes his head, and resumes swiping on the screen. A stranger also sits at the table. Blond hair carefully coiffed in a hairstyle reeking of money.

I clear my throat and mother glances up. "Jess, you got here just in time for lunch. I was just laughing at something Charles said. He's such a great storyteller." She beams at me.

"Mother, what is this? You said you needed me here for something important. I had to move some meetings around to be here."

She gives me a quelling look as Charles stands. "I see we ambushed you. I'm Charles Vaughn. Our parents know each other from their days at Yale. I'm here for a business trip and my parents insisted I pay my respects to the Kingsleys." He extends his right hand toward me, his Rolex glinting in the light.

This is a setup.

I grit my teeth as I take a deep breath. *This isn't Charles's fault.* I take his hand and reply, "Nice to meet you. I'm Jess."

"The Vaughns are major stakeholders in the Bank of Columbia. You two should talk. You both work in finance." My mother smiles at the thought of adding a Vaughn to our family tree.

I take another breath and roll my shoulders.

No.

I refuse.

"Charles, I'm sure you are a wonderful and accomplished person, but let's cut the pretense here. This is a setup for the both of us. I don't know if they forced you to come to this meal, and if you were, I'm truly sorry. But in case you're here willingly, hoping to meet a special someone, I need to be honest with you and tell you I'm unavailable." My voice shakes toward the end as I clasp one hand on top of the other, steadying myself.

"Jessica Kingsley. This is appalling behavior. We didn't raise you this way." Audrey Kingsley is noticeably red and shaking with anger. She grits her teeth and turns to Father. "Say something!"

Father sighs and puts down his phone. "Audrey, look, we can't really force this—"

Mother cuts him off and swivels her head to Charles. "I'm so sorry for my daughter and my husband. Please don't listen to her. She is single and very much unattached—"

"I'll speak for myself. Charles, yes, I'm currently single, but my heart is with someone else, someone I've hurt deeply and will do everything in my power to get back. I'm so sorry you came all the way out here for nothing."

Charles purses his lips in an expression looking an awful like amusement. He chuckles and shakes his head. "Don't worry about it. I have to say, this is the first time I got rejected before drinks and appetizers. Takes you down a peg for sure." He sobers up and continues, "Point taken. I appreciate your honesty."

He turns to my parents. "Thanks for the hospitality, Mr. and Mrs. Kingsley. I believe you may have something to discuss with

Jess, so I'll take my leave now." He gives us a nod as he picks up his jacket and leaves the room.

Once he is out of earshot, my mother unleashes her fury. "Jessica Kingsley! That was the most embarrassing, despicable behavior I've *ever* seen from you. Charles is the perfect partner for you, even better than Ben."

"I love James and I'll always love him." I grip my bracelet tightly as my heart threatens to give out.

"He's not suitable for you and our family. He's fine as a friend, but how will being with him elevate our status? What will he bring to the family?"

"Mother, I've tried... *God knows* I've *tried* so hard to be a good, obedient daughter. I've followed the path *you* laid out for me without complaints. I know in *your* mind, you believe you're doing the right thing, but I'm here to tell you, *I. Am. Done.* I can't be the perfect daughter anymore. I can't ignore my desires or pretend everything is fine when it isn't. I can't live my life for you. Mother, I love you, but if I have to choose between you or me, I choose myself."

She stares at me, speechless at my outburst. Father gives me a quick nod as he puts his hand on Mother's shaking shoulder.

"I'd love for us to continue to have a relationship because you're my family, but if you don't respect me as an adult capable of making choices for myself, I'll need to distance myself from you and I really, really don't want to do that. So *please*, don't force my hand."

My hands tremble as I pick up my purse. "I'll leave you both to it. Let's not say things we'll regret." I swallow the lump in my throat and turn around, leaving my astonished parents behind me to contemplate my words.

Once I step outside the house, I clasp my hand to my heart, still feeling the rush of adrenaline. Guilt eats at me, but I shove it away. Someone needs to break the cycle.

I smile, the heaviness in my chest lifting as I take a breath that's truly mine.

The chatter stops as I enter the conference room. I sigh inwardly and attempt a joke. "Seriously, guys? I won't bite." I chuckle at myself. Being a comedian is definitely not in my genes.

My team stares at me wide-eyed and bursts out laughing. "Crap. We thought you heard the tail end of our conversation about Dick."

I peek behind me to make sure the door has closed properly. "What did the Dickhead do this time?"

"Oh my gosh, you call him that too? I always thought you were friends with him or something and we didn't want to offend you," Carly, the senior associate on my new engagement, chimes in.

I roll my eyes. "Please, who's really friends with him?" I sit down and cross my legs. "Let me share a secret with you, to make it up the ranks, you need to learn to mingle, small talk, put a smile on your face in tough situations, but it doesn't mean you need to roll over and do everything they say. Trust me, I'm still learning the same lesson. Some of you guys are probably better at it than I am."

The team nods at my statement. "How do you find the balance?" a first-year associate asks from the end of the table.

"I don't know, to be honest. It's different for each situation, but I think it's important to communicate. I think there's a way to be polite, to offer alternatives, but also to air out any concerns you have. If you keep things inside or let the fear of getting into trouble rule you, other people can't help you." I shrug and let out a sigh. "Trust me, that's also something I'm working on." I grin. "So, after this heart to heart, will you guys finally tell me what the Dickhead did this time?"

Gary, the manager, replies, "He just asked Mandy to prepare and mail out over two hundred confirmations tonight and she actually has an early Valentine's Day slash anniversary dinner with her boyfriend to go to in two hours. Apparently, his engagement team is traveling, and he offered to find someone to take care of this mess while they are in flight."

"Huh, why am I not surprised." I look at Mandy, the first-year associate in question. "Where's your dinner?"

"Santa Monica."

We all groan collectively. The traffic from downtown to Santa Monica will take every minute of the two hours. I look at the clock. Five p.m. My flight to Boston is at midnight. I still have some time before I need to go home and pack.

"Do the rest of you guys have time to stay a little later today?" The team looks at each other and nods. "Let's borrow the motto from the Marines, 'Leave no man behind.' Mandy, why don't you leave now, and we'll take care of the confirmations."

"Seriously?" Her eyes appear hopeful as her hands start packing up her things.

"Totally." I wink at her. "Enjoy your dinner."

Mandy thanks everyone profusely and rushes out of the room.

I clap my hands. "All right, team, there's three of us here. If we split this into three piles, we should be done within half an hour."

Gary and Carly grab the stack of papers and envelopes and split them into three piles as we get to work. Carly nudges me and whispers, "That's pretty cool of you. Mandy was so miserable just now."

I smile back at her, feeling for once in my life part of the team.

• • •

"He won't think I'm intruding in his space, right? I mean, he asked me to give him some space and aside from the occasional text to confirm he's still alive and well, I haven't really bothered him." I sit in the backseat of an Uber on my way to the airport.

Liz tsks on the other end of the phone call. "Jess, originally you were going to give him one month before you head out there... Now it's already two months. I love my brother and all, but I think it's high time he gets his ass back here. So no, you're not intruding on his space at all."

I tug at my bracelet; old habits are hard to break after all. My palms grow damp as I think about tomorrow. My heart thunders inside my chest. *Deep breaths, Jess. Don't catastrophize. You don't know what's going to happen yet. Things may work out for the better...and even if they don't, you'll be able to handle it.* The combination of therapy and medicine in the last two months has greatly helped with my anxiety and panic issues. The flare-ups are less common and when they happen, I have more tools to deal with them than before. I'm working on myself and becoming someone who deserves James's love.

"Jess?"

"Oh, sorry, zoned out there for a second. Thanks for the encouragement."

"That's what I'm here for. I already gave my parents a heads-up for them to 'disappear' in the morning. They are telling him they're meeting with friends for breakfast. You have the address, right?"

"Yes I do, gosh, what would I do without you guys?"

"Well, lucky for you, you won't need to find out." I can imagine the beaming smile she has on her face. Liz radiates positivity and warmth. I seriously don't know why she is still single.

I take a deep breath and exhale loudly. "Okay, we're approaching the airport. Got to go. I'll keep you posted. Wish me luck!"

"Good luck! You got this, Jess. I have complete faith in you." Like brother, like sister. I smile and hang up.

One advantage of going to LAX late at night is there is absolutely no traffic on the road until you get into the airport, where cars congregate in the snail crawl for the international terminal as most of the long-haul flights are red-eyes. Lucky for me, I don't need to go to the international terminal tonight, so I ask the Uber driver to drop me off at one of the closer terminals.

"Uh, hey, I couldn't help but overhear your phone call..." Bob, the Uber driver, smiles sheepishly at me. "But uh, good luck. Go get him! I'm a sucker for happy endings." Bob has a buzz cut, scruff on his face, and is built like a wrestler. This goes to show you can't judge a book or a person by its cover. Who would have thought he was so sweet?

I grab my overnight bag from the seat next to me and step out of the car. "Thank you. I'll need all the luck I can get." I grin and close the door.

Steeling myself, I walk inside, my head high and shoulders straight as the errant pulse flutters inside me. *Excitement, not stress*, I whisper to myself. Dr. Cheng says the physiological signs for the two emotions are similar.

My phone chimes with two messages.

Emily: Keep me posted, sis! Rooting for you here! XOXO.

She then sends me a gif of a fairy sprinkling magic dust.

Steven: Everything will be fine. Mark my words. That guy can't quit you.

I roll my eyes at his attempt at reassurance.

Jess: And how do you know that, dear brother?

Steven: Dude's intuition. I have eyes and I'm a man. I know things.

I smirk, imagining his sardonic tone.

"Hello, how may I help you?" I pocket my phone and smile at the agent at the Sigma Airlines counter. My eyes widen. This woman looks familiar. I peer at her name tag. *Debbie*. She squints her eyes at me as recognition dawns on us.

"The grand gesture girl!" Debbie exclaims, her lips tipping up in a wide smile.

I blush, thinking back to my haggard appearance two months ago. At least I look a little more presentable right now with my cable-knit sweater and jeans. "I can't believe you remember me," I mumble, my hand touching my warm face.

"It's not every day I get a movie worthy grand gesture scene. You made my day. We all talked about you afterward and were wondering if you ended up getting your man."

I smile sheepishly. "I missed him by a hair that day. But I'm going for my grand, grand gesture today."

Debbie places her hands on her chest. "Whoever he is, he's one lucky man. I wish you all the best. So, let's see what I can do to help you out. Can I have your ID and flight number?"

"Thank you." I hand her my driver's license and flight confirmation.

She types rapidly on the keyboard. "Any check-in luggage?"

"Nope." More clicking of fingernails against keys sound in the air. I tap my fingers on the counter.

Debbie glances up and leans forward. "I upgraded you. There's a first-class seat open. Get some rest before your grand, grand gesture. The food and alcohol are much better in first-class. Liquid courage, you know." She winks and steps back, handing me my boarding pass and driver's license. "Good luck! Sending you all the good vibes."

I thank her and clutch my boarding pass in a tight grip. Just as I entered the waiting area by the gate, my phone rings. *The Dick-head.* "Hi, Dick, I'm about to board a plane. How can I help you?"

"Jess! Thanks for picking up. I know you are technically on vacation now, but I need you to help me with the acquisition memo and consultation for the client. I sent it to your email. Can you look at it and get back to me in the next day or two?"

I purse my lips as I refrain from telling him how I really feel. There's only so much emotional outburst I can handle in one day without completely blowing the rest of my life up.

"Dick, isn't the consultation due the week after next?"

"Well, yes, but I'll be in Dallas for a conference most of next week, so I need to review it before I go."

I feel like I'm really working on my deep breathing a lot these days. Taking another deep breath to steady my nerves, I respond, "Dick, I can't move my vacation and I won't be able to look at it in the next four days. I'll be back on Monday and will log on early in the morning to get it done and have it in your inbox by noon. Hopefully, that'll give you enough time to review before you leave for your conference."

Silence follows my response. *Respectful and setting boundaries at the same time. I achieved that, right? Did I mess it up?*

Dick exhales. "That should work timing wise. You know this is an important client, so I'm sure you'll take care of it."

I let out a breath I was holding. "You know I always get things done. I have it handled."

"Good. Well...I don't want to take up too much of your time. Have a good vacation."

"Thanks." I turn off my phone with my sweaty hands.

I tremble as I slowly sit down and wipe my hands on my pants. *Five counts in. Eight counts out.*

You did a good job today. First with Mother, then with Dick. Why are you shaking so much? Why can't you get a grip? Oh God, I'm going to see James now. What if he doesn't want to see me? What if he can't forgive me?

The thing about generalized anxiety is it never truly goes away. Therapy and medication make things more manageable, but it always lurks around the corner, sneaking in to attack when you least expect it.

The familiar and oddly reassuring chaos of negative thoughts swirl inside. It's the familiar path; the foreign path is learning to say no and be true to myself. I continue my deep breathing and utilize the skills I've been practicing with Marybeth. *Don't catastrophize. When has the worst-case scenario ever come to fruition for you before? What if he forgives you? What, you'll just walk away without trying? You are in charge of your own destiny. You can break the cycle.*

"Miss? Last call for Boston. Will you be boarding the flight?"

I peer up at the gate attendant who is pointing to the now-empty gate. My immediate impulse is to turn back, to live in denial. *No. I can do this. And if the worst case happens, I'm strong enough to survive it.*

"Here goes nothing," I whisper.

Gathering my hair to the side, I pick up my overnight bag from the floor and stride to the gate, walking toward the unknown.

This time, I don't have a Plan B.

Shivering in the cold, I rub my hands together as I walk up the steps of a beautiful brownstone on Beacon Hill. A thin layer of snow coats the bare branches of the trees surrounding the steps to the front door, the whiteness of the snow contrasting with the black door and the warm amber hues of the building. The air is crisp and the clear skies are dotted with fluffy clouds with morning sunlight peeking through and highlighting the glinting fresh snow on the ground. Boston is a veritable winter wonderland, but this is coming from a visitor who welcomes the occasional change in scenery from the year-round warm weather. I'm sure the locals will say so otherwise.

I brush out the loose waves in my hair and straighten my down jacket over James's MIT sweater. I set my overnight bag on the top step as I pull out the papers I prepared last night from my tote. My flight arrived early morning Pacific time, and I hailed a taxi to take me straight to James's family home. I was able to catch a few hours of sleep on the flight. The first-class furnishings and drinks were unparalleled (thank you, Debbie). Nervousness hums through my body as adrenaline courses through my veins.

I draw in a deep breath of chilly air and ring the doorbell.

Birds chirp in the background as I wait, tapping my boots on the floor.

The door slowly swings open as warm air wafts to my face, bringing notes of sandalwood and musk. The towering man at the entryway freezes.

James's right hand grips the doorway. His piercing eyes, the color of the deep ocean this morning, glitter with emotions as he stares at me. His hair is a tad longer than I remembered and is artfully tousled. A day's worth of scruff accompanies the strong jawline. His chest heaves as he takes a shaky breath, highlighting the muscles stretching under his thin, navy-blue sweater. His left hand hooks into the pocket of his gray sweatpants, his fingers clenching against the soft material. Seeing James standing before me, within arm's reach, sends a pang of longing in my chest.

We stare at each other as time slows to a crawl.

This man.

My heart.

My whole.

Wordlessly, I stare into his impassioned eyes as tears gather in mine, my lips wobbling. I clear my throat and sing the first few verses of our song, "Can't Help Falling in Love." I curl my hands into tight fists as my singing draws the attention of neighbors and passersby. I feel the weight of their stares, hear their murmuring, see their pointing fingers. My voice breaks as I sing louder so everyone will know I'm crazily, madly, in love with the man before me.

Blinking the tears away, I continue the song as I hold up the small stack of papers à la the movie, *Love Actually*.

"James, the last two months have been the longest two months of my life." I flip the page.

"I'm so sorry for being a coward, for not being the brave woman you deserve."

The world falls away as blood rushes in my ears. My hands shake. The papers crackle from my tight grip.

"I love you so, so much and I miss your smile, your smell, your laughter."

James's glistening eyes darken with intensity as he stares at the paper. A wide array of undecipherable emotions shines in his eyes. His left hand curls into a tight fist, his knuckles white.

"I miss you, James. You're my best friend, my soulmate, my end all be all."

I swipe an errant tear from my cheek and wet my lips. I flip to the final page. The last verse of the song draws to a conclusion and silence surrounds us.

"Will you forgive me and give us another chance?"

My heart thuds so loudly in my chest, I'm sure he can hear it. I slowly lower the page and stare at him, my heart in my eyes.

He blinks rapidly, his sapphire gaze holding unshed tears as his face flushes pink with emotions.

"Are you sure?" he whispers, "because I can't go through this again."

"I'm sure. It's the one thing I'm most sure of in my life."

He steps forward, barefoot and all, and pulls me into his arms.

"Jess," he whispers into my hair, his voice hoarse. He tightens his arms around me as if he's afraid I'm a figment of his imagination. The papers flutter onto the ground, scattering over the steps. Applause breaks out around us as the neighbors return to their normal activities.

Tears trickle down my face as I shake in his arms, finally releasing the underlying tension from these past few months. "I'm so sorry for hurting you, James. I don't deserve you, but I'm trying. You see, I'm finally getting help for my anxiety, not only for you, but also for myself. This is it... I'm showing my entire hand. I can't promise you I won't regress and be anxious or scared every now and then, but I'll keep trying."

"That's all I'm asking for, for you to keep trying. I'll be with you every step of the way." His voice is husky as he catches his breath. I tremble in his arms, overcome with emotions.

Relief. Joy. Fear. Love. Happiness.

He hushes me as he smooths his hands over my back, rubbing reassuring circles. I bury my face in his muscular chest, inhaling his sweet scent.

I whisper, "I've been looking for it all wrong. I've found my home a long time ago. With you. You're my home."

James cradles my face and tips my chin up. I can see gold flecks shining in his smoldering eyes. He gently wipes the tears from my face as he slides his hands behind my neck, his fingers tangling with my hair.

"I love you, Jess. I always have and I always will."

His head dips low and his lips catch mine in a soul-searching kiss. My hands slide up his chest, his muscles flexing under his sweater, and I wrap my arms around him. My body tingles with awareness and I gasp as he swipes his tongue at the seam of my lips. Taking advantage of my parted mouth, his tongue slips inside and tangles with mine as I wrap my legs around his waist.

Groaning, he squeezes my butt and hoists me up so we align in all the ways that matter. We kiss as if the fate of the world depends on it, as if this is the first kiss, the last kiss, and everything in between. Liquid heat rushes through my veins, igniting my senses. I claw at him, wanting to get closer so one can't tell where I begin and where he ends. His grunts answer my moans as we tangle in a deep embrace.

I need him now and always.

The sound of the horn from a passing car reminds us we're still standing out in the open. The rest of the world comes into focus as he releases my mouth, tugging on my swollen bottom lip before he rests his forehead on mine, our breaths ragged.

I slip an object into his hands and curl his fingers around it.

James opens up his palm. "Your penny."

"And a quarter...I hunted down a special one with your birth year and fashioned both of them into a keychain."

He stares at the keychain and smiles. "I love it."

"Together forever. This penny *is* lucky. It led me to you. Even if our journey took longer than either of us anticipated."

I wrap my arms around his tall frame. He tucks me against him and tightens his grip around me. I can finally breathe for the first time in the last few months. I am where I have belonged all along.

James carries me across the threshold and sets me down to the ground as he retrieves my overnight bag and the fallen papers. I survey the cozy home, the walls full of photos of Liz and James throughout the years, a well-worn brown leather sofa with throw blankets and statement cushions decorating it, a brick, wood-burning fireplace with a fire burning in the hearth.

Shaking his head, he walks up to me and links his fingers with mine, his warm hands transferring heat to my cold ones. "I'm thinking, if I said no, what would you have done?" His eyes twinkle with amusement.

I give him a light shove. "Hey! Don't joke about that. I was about to have an aneurism at the door just now." I reach into my tote and pull out a small envelope to hand to him. "But...I did come up with a backup plan."

"What's that?"

"My failproof plan. I even consulted Parker on this."

"Parker, huh? So, you guys are friends now?" He glances up, skepticism in his gaze, as he tears open the envelope.

"Yes we are, just look at it."

His eyes widen as he peers at the contents inside. "Shit, this is a grand gesture, huh?"

"Gloat while you still can. I love how you didn't make any comments about me flying almost three thousand miles to see you, but you're impressed with the tickets."

"I don't think any sane man will say no to center court, courtside seats to a Lakers playoff game."

I step in front of him, my hands sliding under his sweater as my fingers trace each slab of muscle. He shudders, his eyes growing dark as his mouth parts. I tiptoe up to him and whisper against his ear, "So, those tickets are yours if you come back home." I seal the promise with a quick swipe of my tongue against his earlobe.

His hands release the tickets as he grabs my hips in a tight grip. "Oh yeah?" he rasps, his voice guttural. "And you?" He grinds his hips against me, his cock standing at attention.

I moan as wetness gathers between my thighs. "I'm yours too."

"Well, you're presenting me with a deal I can't refuse." He hoists me up against him as I climb him like a tree and fuse my mouth with his. Tongues dueling, our mouths make love with each other as we pour unsaid emotions through the passion of our kiss. James carries me upstairs as I move my way down his neck, sucking the tender skin there and soothing my suction with a soft lick, just the way he likes it. James grunts as he wraps a hand around my locks and tugs, forcing my face to tip up.

Embers of lust burn in his eyes as he says, "Any more of that and I'll take you on the staircase."

A gush of wetness seeps through my panties as I envision us tangled on the stairs, making love in wild abandon.

"Don't make promises you can't keep." I whimper and bite my lip.

He growls as he throws me over his shoulder. "If we weren't in my parents' house, I'd throw you down and demonstrate how I want you so much I can't even wait to get to the bedroom." He gives my butt a quick slap, the stinging pain soothed by his soft caress afterward. "And this is for making me the most fucking miserable guy on the planet for the last few months. Heck, for years."

James carries me into the first room on the right of the stairs and tosses me on a queen-size bed. His eyes gleam with dark intentions as he shuts the door and prowls slowly toward me like a predator cornering his prey. Instincts drive my motions as I crawl backward on the bed, stopping when I hit the oak headboard.

He takes off his sweater with one arm, and steps out of his sweats and underwear and slowly advances toward me. Wetness coats my mouth as I stare at his body, muscles flexing in the morning light, the V line of his abdomen leading to his throbbing cock beckoning me to touch it, to taste it, to impale myself on it. James climbs on the bed, his eyes pinning mine, and he pushes me down onto the pillows.

Holding himself over me, his biceps flexing, we gaze at each other, so close I can count the individual flecks of gold in his eyes.

"This is it for us, Jess. No going back," he murmurs, his lips less than an inch away from mine.

I stare into his eyes, drowning myself in those dark pools of blue and answer the only way I can. "No going back. I'm yours forever," I whisper.

Groaning, he slams his mouth on mine as he tears off my clothing in record speed. My nipples prickle into hard nubs as he grips my left breast in one hand, flicking and pulling the tip as I moan, arching my back. I'm so glad Liz arranged for her parents to go out for breakfast or else I'm sure I'd wake up the entire house. James sucks the whole nub into his mouth, his tongue twirling at the tip as I whimper and pull at his hair. He moves onto the other side, and I thrash on the bed, needing release, needing him, needing an end to this torture.

I tug a thick lock of his hair and he hisses. James climbs back up as he nips my neck in punishment. I buckle against him, grinding my heat against his hardness, earning me a litany of curse words from his mouth. I slide my hands between us as I curl my hand around him, smoothing the wetness at the tip to the rest of the shaft.

He grunts as he pulls my hands above my head, pinning them into place as he grabs a condom from the dresser and slips it on. Our chests heaving, the room silent except for our heavy breathing. We stare at each other, his pupils blown, my eyes glazed, and he slams his mouth against mine as he thrusts to the hilt in one motion. I scream from the pleasure, the fullness, the rightness of it all.

Our teeth nip at each other, our tongues tangle together, our mouths dueling a battle where both of us are neither the victors nor losers. He hammers inside me, his movements forceful. Sounds of skin slapping against skin and the headboard bumping against the wall fill the room. Grunts mingle with moans, whimpers blending in with sighs, as we chase the building tension.

I close my eyes as the friction builds, my heart beating rapidly, blood rushing in my ears. He tilts his hips in a different way, hitting a deep spot within me and I scream my release, my throbbing muscles grasping his cock as he tightens against me. He lets out a deep groan as he shudders against me.

"Mine," he rasps as his hips move in erratic motions. "Fucking mine."

"Yours," I echo, my limbs shaking from the pleasure.

His long fingers interlace with mine as we ride out our orgasms, our kisses softening to gentle suctions and teasing licks.

James braces himself against me, his breathing ragged. He stares into my eyes as his bottom half stills against mine. "I love you, Jess. I love you so, so much."

Tears prickle my eyes as I'm overcome with emotions. What have I ever done to deserve this unwavering love? I give him the only answer I have to give.

"I love you, James. I think I always have." I slide one hand across his stubble, slowly cupping his cheek as he leans into my caress. "Thank you for loving me."

Moisture gathers in his eyes as he smiles at me with joy, his gaze full of love and tenderness.

I return a wobbly smile, my heart filling to the brim with happiness.

I'm finally home.

Sometimes, the best things in life are the same things you fear losing the most. I can't let fear and anxiety rule my life. I may trip and fall, get scrapes and bruises, but I'll stand up again and prevail.

James

One Year Later

"**N**ervous, man? Not going to pull a runaway groom, right?" Parker clasps a hand on my shoulder as we stand in front of the altar, dressed to the nines. Steven stands next to him, tugging at the lapels of his tuxedo.

"Fuck off, dude." I unclench my fingers and roll my shoulders, releasing the tight tension there as I paste a polite smile on my face. Nerves gather in my stomach as I stare at the pews filled with friends, family, and colleagues who have gathered here to celebrate Jess and I. Becca walks in with her date, giving me a thumbs up as she takes her seat next to their colleagues. I nod my head in acknowledgement as I continue to scan the crowd.

Parker smirks, highlighting his annoying dimples on his face. Due to his instrumental role in helping plan Jess's grand gesture last year, I gave him the role of best man for our wedding.

I've been regretting the decision ever since.

"Just saying, marriage is for a lifetime. Speak now or forever hold your peace. I mean, Jess and I had pretty good chemistry, you know? If you have any doubts, I don't mind stepping in."

I roll my eyes. Why am I putting up with him? "Someday, Parker, someday I'll return the favor on your own special day, just you wait and see."

Ironically, despite my initial hatred toward him, once it became clear he and Jess are just friends and how he was actually rooting for us the entire time, I warmed up to him. Then later, we found out we had similar interests in sports, reading, and other random hobbies and, unfortunately, he has stuck to me like glue ever since.

He bursts out in laughter, earning us a few curious gazes from my parents and Mrs. Kingsley, who are sitting in the front row. Mrs. Kingsley gives me an arched look of minor disapproval. I give her a quick smile of reassurance. Despite our differences, the Kingsleys have come to accept come hell or high water, I'm marrying Jess, whether they like it or not.

Parker chuckles. "Oh God, you're wound up so tightly, I can't resist. You know I'm kidding, Chapman."

"Good thing you're actually a pretty cool person to hang with normally, or else you can consider yourself uninvited to my wedding and reception."

"Not very nice to uninvite the guy who helped get you guys together."

"That's literally the only thing keeping me from escorting you out myself right now," I retort. I bite the inside of my cheek to keep from smiling.

"Kids, kids, behave yourselves. I never thought I had to referee the two of you at your wedding, James. And I thought I'm supposedly the baby of this trio." Steven's sardonic tone adds to the camaraderie in our little group.

Parker cracks up and wipes a fake tear from his eyes. He gives Steven a high five as the two of them snigger at my apparent wedding nerves.

"Seriously though, I'm very happy for you two. You guys have what it takes. Life is full of ups and downs, and I'm glad you guys found each other." Parker's gravelly voice turns solemn. "Take care of each other. Life is too short to waste."

I look at him as he stares into space, his mouth flattening into a firm line. I reach out and squeeze his shoulder. "Thanks, man. I'll definitely cherish every moment with her," I say under my breath as wetness prickles my eyes, the thought of life without Jess unbearable. I don't know how Parker is still standing right now after losing his wife.

"Can't wait to see Lucy as the flower girl."

Parker's eyes warm at my mention of his daughter, who is absolutely ecstatic with her role in the wedding. Copying Jess, she refuses to show me her flower girl dress until the actual ceremony. That five-year-old is the cutest little person I've ever met. Warmth fills my chest, chasing away the earlier tension, as I imagine having a little mini me or mini-Jess in the future.

"She was so excited last night; she could barely sleep. She loves you guys. She practiced the song Jess taught her all day long. She can't wait to perform it at your reception." Parker chuckles, no doubt thinking of his little angel.

"Can't wait to hear her." I smile, thinking of the "rehearsals" Jess had with Lucy for this song Lucy wants to sing to us as her wedding gift. Jess has started teaching singing and music class to little kids on the side, something to fill her creative soul but also allows her to stay on the sidelines away from the spotlight.

Steven hushes us. "Stand up straight and tall. Game on, guys." The Kingsleys training in manners and bearing filters all the way to the youngest sibling.

I smile as the wedding coordinator asks everyone to be seated and the beginning chords of Pachelbel's *Canon in D* fills the church. The sturdy double doors open as Lucy walks in with Oliver, my colleague's seven-year-old boy. Lucy has a rose crown on her dirty-blonde curls and she is wearing a puffy white dress—which Liz tells me is made of tulle—befitting a princess. She beams, her little dimples flashing, as she carefully throws rose petals in the air. I glance at Parker, who is smiling like a proud father, giving her two thumbs up as she finishes her march down the aisle.

Liz walks in, her golden hair twisted in an elaborate updo. Her one-shoulder lavender bridesmaid dress flatters her complexion. She holds a small bouquet of red roses, wedding flowers Jess insisted on, due to the undying love the roses represent. Liz gives me a warm smile, a vote of confidence, as she heads toward us. Her smile freezes briefly as she glances over at the groomsmen. I glance at Parker out of the corner of my eyes. He stiffens up, his eyes trailing Liz with an unfathomable gaze. The brief intensity in his expression disappears as quickly as it appears, his gaze softening as he looks away. Liz snaps out of her trance and continues walking, stopping to stand on the other side of the aisle.

Emily strides in, confidence in her bearing, as she winks at us. She stares at me and slowly mouths, "Treat her well or else." I swallow my chuckles as I look at my feet. Ever the firecracker, the life of the party.

Finally, as the bridesmaid and maid of honor settle in their positions on the other side of the aisle, the final chords of the music linger in the air. I take in a deep breath and wet my lips, anticipation flooding my body as my heart pounds in my chest.

Jess steps in, a cathedral veil hiding her face. Pausing at the stream of sunlight shining in from the skylight on the high ceiling of the church, she looks like an angel descending upon mankind, so breathtaking and ethereal I forget to breathe.

The wedding march beings as she slowly glides down the aisle, her father at her side. She smiles at me through her thin veil and I struggle to rein in my emotions. I mouth, "I love you" as she walks toward me, holding an enormous bouquet of red roses. The people in the room fade away as I stare at this goddess gliding toward me. Tears gather in my eyes as emotions clog in my throat. I can't believe she loves me.

I step to the center of the aisle as her father places her hand on my outstretched arm. "Take care of her, son." He gives me a stern look, very befitting of Mr. Kingsley, and steps to the front row.

I lift the veil and stare at my bride. Jess's hair is pinned up in an elaborate hairstyle, her makeup light, showcasing the freckles I worship and highlighting the lush lips painted in red. Her eyes glimmer with love as she holds my gaze. My pulse flutters quickly as I take her hand, which is enclosed in the most intricate lace gloves. I place a soft kiss on the back of her hand, a symbol of my undying love and devotion, before we turn around and face the priest.

"Dearly beloved, we have gathered here today to join this man and this woman in holy matrimony..."

Jess glances over at me, love overflowing in her beautiful hazel eyes, as I return her gaze with a worshipping stare of my own. Images of the brave little girl coming to the rescue of a helpless little boy flash before my eyes. Love overwhelms me. In the words of the fairy tales Jess loves to read, "And they live happily ever after." While I wish life were straightforward, I know we'll have our ups and downs, but with her next to me, we'll come out the other side stronger than ever.

Always.

. . .

Thank you for reading THE SWEETEST AGONY. Hope you've enjoyed Jess and James's story as much as I did writing it. Please consider leaving a review on the retailer website and Goodreads. Your reviews will really help this author out and will allow for more readers to find this book.

Do you know Liz and Parker are going to star in the next book, THE COLDEST PASSION? Their story is filled with angst, steam, all types of swoon, and features a tortured, dirty-talking hero. Don't miss it. Order it here: https://geni.us/thecoldestpassion

Want to spend more time with Jess and James and find out happens when James's parents come back home after their pre-arranged breakfast one year ago? Also, why did James stay in Boston for two months? Sign up for my newsletter to get this bonus scene, new release alerts, exclusive bonus material, and more: https://dl.bookfunnel.com/gzzvnntvzo

Join my Facebook group, Victoria Lum's Luminaries (https://www.facebook.com/groups/576423100572205) for sneak peaks, exclusive giveaways, and to chat about all things book-related! You can also find me on Tiktok @victorialumauthor (https://www.tiktok.com/@victorialumauthor), Instagram @authorvictorialum, and other sites at this link https://linktr.ee/authorvictorialum.

ACKNOWLEDGMENTS

They say it takes a village to raise a kid. Well, it definitely takes a village to write a book. It feels very surreal writing my very first acknowledgements section and I'm moved beyond words. I have so many people to thank and it's very hard to know where to start. Many thanks to (and not in any order of importance):

My family: Without you all, this book won't be possible. Thank you for your patience, your support, and all the extra help around the house while I type and type away as Jess and James take over all of my free time. To my husband, thank you for cheering me on and being my first reader. To my children, I hope someday, when you're older, you'll pursue your dreams just like your mommy is doing now.

My editors: Becca Mysoor, Grace Bradley, and Amy Briggs, thank you for being so kind and patient with this new author. Your insight and wisdom are very much welcomed and treasured. I look forward to working with you on more stories in the future.

Proofreader and Formatter: Thank you to Virginia Tesi Carey and Elaine York of Allusion Publishing for your help in fixing and preparing the book for the finish line.

My PAs: The awesome Stevie Schneider and Nikki Johnson, thank you for helping manage and direct the forces. Thank you for all the late night chats, phone calls, and all the advice you give. I can't get this done without you ladies.

Cover designer: LK Farlow of Y'All That Graphic, how are you so talented? Being a successful author and an awesome cover designer? Such an inspiration. Thank you for your keen eye on all the details, from the fonts to the colors to of course the cover model selection. I love the cover and can't wait to work with you on the covers for the rest of the series.

Beta readers: Malia, Jenn, Jess, and Fiona, I don't know how many times I've re-read your notes on my first draft. Thank you for your constructive comments and feedback. Your encouragement has kept me going as I'm rewriting and revising the book. Also, thank you for being such great cheerleaders for me on social media. It really means a lot to me.

Fellow authors: As a new author coming from a non-publishing background, I've been fortunate to meet fellow authors who are so giving with their advice and encouragement. Brit Benson, thank you for keeping me sane in so many ways. Stacy Reid, Annika Martin, Carian Cole, Breanna Lynn, AK Koonce, and of course LK Farlow, thank you for all your guidance and positive energy when this newbie author was floundering at times. Thank you to the other authors who have given me guidance as well. I truly appreciate you ladies—you all have a heart of gold.

PR Firms: Thank you to Greys Promo, Wildfire Marketing, and Give Me Books for your promotional efforts and helping me get the word out.

My Fellow Readers: I can't be an author without your support. Thank you for reading James and Jess's book. I hope you loved them as much as I do and I can't wait to share more stories with you in the future. To anyone who, like Jess, ever feels less than, for whatever reason, know that you're worth it, and you deserve your happily ever after.

With love,
Victoria

ABOUT THE AUTHOR

Victoria is a lover of all things romance, including movies, books, and television shows. A hopeless romantic since childhood, she is always dreaming up stories and happily ever afters. Caramel lattes are her fuel in the morning and she can usually be found reading anything she can get her hands on. She lives with her family and a beautiful Siberian husky in sunny California.

Keep in touch!
Sign up for her newsletter below:
Newsletter
https://dashboard.mailerlite.com/
forms/289149/81041142820374109/share

Follow Victoria on social media:
Tiktok
@victorialumauthor
Instagram
www.instagram.com/authorvictorialum
Facebook Group
www.facebook.com/groups/576423100572205